I0654333

SandStarr Publications
A division of SandStarr Entertainment
2500 Sheridan Rd., PMB 402
Zion, IL 60099
www.sandstarrpublications.com

This is a work of fiction. Names, characters, places, and events either are the product of the author's imagination or are used fictitiously.

BloodLust: The Beginning
ISBN 10: 0-9826-6970-4
ISBN 13: 978-0-982-66970-9

A battle will soon be waged...

Vampires are growing restless. They no longer want to hide who they are and they no longer want to play nicely with humans. The most twisted vampire of them all proposes a plan of increasing the vampire population. He wants his people to claim what he feels is rightfully theirs: the world.

But first they have to go through him...

Fifteen years ago, he hung up his sword and turned his back on his own kind. Filled with self-hate, he grieves for a humanity that he hasn't possessed for nearly five hundred years. His mourning is brought to an abrupt halt when he hears what the vampires are up to. He'll stop them from taking over the world if it's the last thing he does.

And he's not alone...

The Native American reservation that she lived on was brutally attacked and her family was slain by evil incarnates. She vowed to have vengeance and ever since, she has fought and killed every vampire that she has come into contact with. She's never made an exception...that is, until now. When she realizes that the man who saved her life fifteen years ago is a vampire.

"The fire died down and darkness wrapped around them. Jordana raised a hand with all of her fingers spread and instantaneously, the fire was rejuvenated. 'And then there was light,' she said softly."

Front cover by Beth Gualda and Dori Hartley
Back cover by Dori Hartley

BloodLust: The Beginning

STARR SANDERS

For my mother and my father...
Thanks for all that you've done for me.
For my brother and sisters, who are the coolest siblings
that a writer could have.
This one is for my family.

BloodLust:
The Beginning

PROLOGUE

1462

The ambush had come close to being a failure. Most of the men in his army littered the land surrounding the Turks' camp. He, himself, had barely survived. His armor was battered and beneath the armor, his body was badly bruised. He slumped over his horse with his hands loosely gripping the reins. The horse seemed to know where it was heading on its own.

A harsh and unforgiving sun was breaking over the Carpathian Mountains as the horse neared a towering castle. The dark-bodied beast galloped, only stopping once it reached a gate where two knights stood post.

One of the knights approached the horse cautiously. The rider's face was hidden beneath a mass of dark, curly hair. The knight brushed some of the man's hair back and gasped. He turned and called to his comrade.

The gates swung open and the two men escorted the unconscious rider through. They led the horse to the front entrance of the castle and left the dark-haired man in the care of the servants.

The servants bustled about the castle, gossiping to each other in Romanian.

"Lord Vlad has been harmed."

"What of the rest of his men?"

"Is he the only one who survived?"

"We cannot tell him about our lady, not until he has recovered."

The household of servants catered to the dark-haired man known as Lord Vlad. They lay him upon a pallet and swathed him in warm, fluffy bed garments. It took him several days to come to consciousness and when he did

1

slowly open his eyes, he took in his surroundings. The large room was familiar to him; he was home.

By some sweet miracle, the horse he'd been riding had brought him to his castle. *It wasn't a miracle,* he thought to himself, getting to his feet and rubbing the sleep from his eyes. *It was the Lord's doing. He knew that I was fighting on His behalf and spared my life.*

He left his room and padded down the cold, stone hall in bare feet. The light from a setting sun poured in through every window of the castle. He was home now to enjoy the company of his wife and his child.

Usually there were servants milling about throughout the day. As he passed by rooms and walked down the stairs to the main floor, however, he spotted not one servant. The castle was encompassed in an unfamiliar silence.

He started to wonder whether or not he was really home. Perhaps he had been harmed during the surprise attack on the Turks. It was possible that he was simply dreaming or hallucinating to distract himself from feeling an unthinkable amount of pain.

Or perhaps the Turks launched an attack on your castle and killed everyone in it, he thought to himself as he stepped into the mess hall.

There were two of his servants whispering in the dining hall. When they saw him, the color left their faces. Both of their backs went ramrod straight and they addressed him with respect.

One of his brows arched in question, but instead of inquiring about their odd behavior, he asked in his native tongue, "How long have I been ill?"

"You have been in and out of consciousness for four days, sire," one of his servants responded after being nudged by the other.

"What of my lady? What of my child?" Lord Vlad demanded.

The two servants exchanged nervous glances.

"Well?" Vlad barked. "Where are they? Why is it so quiet here?"

The servant who had first responded to him took a deep breath. "Sire, your son is in good health," the young blonde man began, "but I'm sorry to say that tragedy struck while you were gone."

Vlad ran a trembling hand through his hair. "I want to see my lady," he said in a stony voice. His heartbeat pounded frantically beneath his chest. He knew that something was wrong and he knew what was wrong before he was told.

"I'm afraid that is impossible, sire," the other servant said quietly, bowing her head.

"Impossible?" Vlad snapped. "I know no such word."

"While you were gone, the Turks sent an arrow through one of the windows," the second servant hurried to explain. "There was a note attached to it announcing your death. Our lady was overcome with grief and despair."

The young lord shook his head. "No," he whispered weakly. He felt his knees buckling.

"We are so sorry to have to tell you this," one of the servants said, but Lord Vlad was no longer listening to them.

He could no longer hear them. His own pulse was beating loudly in his ears as he fell to his knees. The servants were telling him that his wife had killed herself because she thought him to be dead, but they couldn't be right. They had to be mistaken. The love of his life wouldn't be taken from him, not when he was fighting a battle on God's behalf, defending the name of Christianity.

God had made sure that he'd returned home safely. The horse couldn't possibly have remembered the way back to the castle; a horse was just a beast. It wasn't able to construct productive thought. The fact that he had returned home safely was proof of God's kindness.

Being so kind, God surely would not smite him in the same breath and take all that he held dear.

"I don't understand," he muttered aloud, pounding his fists at the hard, stone floor. "I've been fighting for You. I left my family for You. Everything I've done, everything that I am, is all because of *You*. How could You do this to me? Why? Why would You do this to someone who loves

3

You so dearly? Who worships You with every breath that he breathes?" Vlad rammed his fists into the floor until they were bloodied.

His servants fled the room, fearing that their sire had lost his mind.

"How could You take my dear Elizabetha from me? How could You allow her to take her own life, knowing that I was still alive and well? I don't understand. I don't...I just don't understand." He lifted his bloody hands and stared at them. "I no longer worship You. I no longer love You. I *hate* You.

"Do You hear me?" He jumped to his feet and shouted towards the ceiling. "I hate You! I no longer do Your bidding and I no longer fight Your wars. You can fight them Yourself. You have taken from me and I shall have my vengeance."

A loud commotion assailed his ears and he whirled around to face a large group of servants. One of the women held Vlad's son close at her breast.

"My Lord, the Turks are coming."

"The Turks?" Vlad repeated dumbly.

"There are many of them and they are coming fast."

"They are coming because I'm supposed to be fighting His war," the young lord said, his voice drained of emotion. "First He takes my father away from me. Now, He has taken my wife, my lady."

"Sire, we must take leave of the castle," one of the servants said calmly.

Vlad couldn't think straight. Memories of his wife danced before his eyes. "I want to see her. I want to hold her."

Seeing that their sire was going to be of no help to them, the servants shouted orders at each other. Pack up the horses and round everyone up, posthaste! No one was to leave through the front gates; everyone was to use the secret passageway that had been constructed to provide escape from attacks such as this one.

There weren't enough horses for all of the servants.

Some of the servants had to leave the castle on foot. Through the passageway and into the woods everyone traveled, trying to be as stealthy as possible as to not alert the Turks of their whereabouts.

After a day of travel, Vlad announced that they would stop and make camp so that the horses and servants who were walking could rest. While everyone else rested their feet and sought nourishment, he held his baby son.

In his son's face, he saw his wife. He thought that he would find solace in his son's innocent gaze, but he only felt more saddened. This little boy, this heir, was the last piece of his wife that he had. "No one will take you away from me," Vlad promised his baby son. "Not even God Himself will take you away from me."

He slept with his son close to him, but was aroused by loud shouts. He sat up and rubbed the sleep out of his eyes.

The Turks had found them and were attacking his servants. Vlad grabbed his son and scrambled to his feet. He wasted no time in mounting the nearest horse, holding his son close to him. He kicked the horse's sides even as spears sailed in the air towards him.

His son, jostled awake by the bouncing horse, started wailing. He couldn't take the appropriate measures to soothe his son. There were two Turks catching up to him on their horses, shouting in their native tongue. They shouted at his back, probably pledging to seize him and kill him.

Tree branches slapped at his face, but still he rode. The harsh, bitter winds of Romania sucked the moisture out of his skin, and still he rode. The horse started to slow down and Vlad glanced over his shoulder.

The two Turks were gaining on him with their cumbersome weapons raised in the air.

His horse wasn't going to make it. The Turks were going to get him. They were going to catch up to him and slit his throat. He had attempted to ambush them with his army and they had responded in kind, tenfold, with an attack of their own.

Something was slipping from his grasp and he didn't

realize what it was until he heard the sound of something rolling on the ground. Vlad blinked his eyes and stared down at his hands. His hands were empty. He shot a desperate, disbelieving glance over his shoulder. A small bundle was rolling out of the way of the advancing Turks and into some foliage. His son...he'd dropped his son.

"Not even God Himself will take you away from me," Vlad had promised his son the night before. It hadn't taken God long to prove him wrong.

He stared over his shoulder. He could turn back and attempt to retrieve his son, but then the Turks would be on him. There were two of them and one of him. There would be no escaping them. He made a vow to himself that he would go back and search for his son, but he wasn't sure that he could get to his son before someone else did.

Years ago, he'd lost his father. His heart had grown cold. Earlier today, he found out that his wife had committed suicide, granting herself eternal damnation for taking her own life. That information had broken his cold heart. And now, on top of both of those tragedies was the loss of his son by his own folly.

His hatred for life grew. His hatred was a plague, a disease that completely consumed him. Life was too fragile. It was too easily taken away. It shouldn't be so. People shouldn't have to lose the ones that they love. They shouldn't have to worry about losing their *own* lives.

Vlad brought the horse to a halt and turned the beast around to face the Turks pursuing him. "You want me?" he shouted at the Turks in Romanian, not even sure whether or not they could understand him. "You want me? Come get me."

The Turks slowed their horses and hesitated, glancing at each other in confusion at the man's actions. Their hesitation only lasted a few moments. They charged at him with their weapons aimed in his direction.

Vlad jumped down from his horse and faced them with a steely look in his eyes.

One of the Turks still charged him, aiming his spear at

Vlad's forehead.

Vlad reached out and, by grabbing the spear, he yanked the man off of his horse. Rage consumed him...it was coursing through his veins. He readily welcomed evil into the broken shards of his heart.

When he was finished impaling the two Turks, he made a vow that he would live the rest of his life in the name of vengeance. After his natural life was over, and after he was blessed with death, he would rise again and continue to carry out the sentence he'd granted to the rest of the world. His accomplishments, his failures, and his losses would all be marked in history books. He would later be known as Vlad the Impaler, or even more haunting yet, *Dracula*. It would be forgotten that this man once had a heart, an incredibly *pure* heart. The tragedies in his life would be overlooked; all that would be remembered were the brutal murders he committed and the thirst that he acquired for human blood. Later, he would be characterized as a monster. In all truth, after the loss of his father, his wife, and his son, that is what he became.

I've never known my parents. I don't know where I come from. All that is certain of my early history is that the only mother I have ever known, Dinah, spotted an abandoned bundle in the forests of Romania. She was a teenager traveling with a band of gypsies at the time.

I grew up knowing that I was different from the children that I saw in the towns we traveled through. They were the prim and proper sons and daughters of society. One day, they would be old enough to marry. Then, they would bear children of their own. Even at a young age, I knew that a fate similar to this would not befall me.

When I was six years old, I began having nightmares. The same nightmare would come to me almost as soon as I closed my eyes. In this horrid dream, a stalker would follow me and pounce on me when I least expected it. He would harshly whisper cruel, prophetic words into my ear. I would always wake up, drenched with sweat and inflicted with an intense fear that I couldn't even fully understand at that age.

I continued to travel with the gypsies. When we came across England, I was enthralled and entranced. I snuck away from the gypsy camp and witnessed my first joust. Armored knights mounted on strong, able horses bore long, dull-pointed lances.

I wished to be a knight. I was sure that nothing was more honorable than being a warrior fighting for some important cause. Knights possessed an exaggerated amount of respect that I, myself, was unfamiliar with. The townspeople of England and France viewed gypsy folk as filthy heathens. I saw my own "mother," Dinah, tolerate a great amount of verbal abuse.

I saw the shame in Dinah's eyes when we walked the streets of the town. She would walk with her head bowed. I hated seeing that look come into her eyes, because she was the kindest woman I'd ever met. When my own biological family left me to rot there on the ground in that forest, she came to my rescue. She delivered me from certain death. She didn't deserve to feel shame. She didn't deserve anything except everlasting happiness.

When we sang and danced into the long hours of the night in our camp, it seemed that she was happy. Her enchanting smile would light up the forest more so than the campfire.

Her happiness did not last as long as it should have. She soon perished, afflicted with a disease that I knew not the name of. The other gypsies assured me that I was a part of their family and that they would care for me always, but I was filled with so much grief. I couldn't bear the thought of living without Dinah.

At twelve years old, I wandered away from the gypsy camp never to return. I walked the streets of England and was drawn to a blacksmith's shop. It was there that I met Edgar, a local townsperson who taught me the craft of forging swords and other metal wares.

Forging a sword that a knight would soon wield was the closest to being a warrior that I thought I would ever get. Of course that didn't prove to be true, but at the time I felt great pride whenever I created a worthy weapon with my own bare hands. I was instilled with a sense of purpose and there was no other feeling like that.

Shortly after my apprenticeship was over, Edgar fell ill. He told me that he wanted me to carry on the work he had started in his shop. I didn't feel confident enough with that task. I had talked little with the patrons who entered the shop. Whenever I had opened my mouth, they'd remarked on how "funny" my accent was. Whenever I told someone what my name was, they responded with, "Well, what a strange name that is."

I didn't want to be forced into dealing with the patrons on a daily basis; I preferred working in the back room, out of plain sight of the customers. However, Edgar was ill and taking over his shop was the least that I could do for the kindness he'd expressed to me.

I quickly became well-known for my workmanship. The swords that I fashioned were unique and one-of-a-kind. I was patient with my craft, and in turn, everything that I created was a treasure.

Not long after I fell in love with my work, I fell in love with a woman. Her name was Bridgette of Lancaster, and my eyes first beheld her when she was shopping in the marketplace, escorted by one of her servants.

She was the most exceptional woman that I had ever set my eyes upon. Wispy tendrils of flaxen gold kissed the tops of her shoulders and curled down her back. Her eyes were the color of emeralds and she always had them lowered in the most coquettish of ways.

Alas, she was betrothed to another. I entertained fantasies about this woman, but I knew that I didn't have a snowball's chance in hell of gaining her love. Betrothals were the end all and be all in those times. A lot of thought and planning went into whom a duke, duchess, king, queen, and even some commoners, would allow their daughter to wed.

After having given up all hope of winning over Bridgette, I met another woman. In truth, that might have been when my life truly began.

She was as beautiful as the Mona Lisa and as graceful as a lioness. The sounds of the tavern muted. It was as if she and I were the only ones in the place. Her dress swished as she walked towards me with her eyes locked on mine. I felt heat in her gaze, heat and longing.

Her hair was the deepest shade of red that I'd ever seen, piled on top of her head save a few curled ringlets framing her face. Her skin was milk-white, pale and creamy perfection. She was tall for a woman and enticingly voluptuous, with a bosom mounting over the plunging neckline of her lavender gown's bodice.

She looked too privileged to be in a tavern after sundown, but she definitely didn't look too innocent. Her eyes were as lavender as the gown she wore and had a cold, calculating look in them. Ice and fire mingled in her eyes; they mingled and then proceeded to dance.

She approached me with a rare confidence and claimed the stool beside mine. "I'll have what he's having," she told the man behind the bar counter.

I smiled into my glass of ale. There's nothing as humorous as a woman who thinks that she can handle liquor but can't. I watched as the bartender graciously filled a mug with strong, amber-colored liquid.

The woman accepted the mug gratefully and lifted it to her lips. She tossed the liquor back and swallowed it in two gulps. "Another, please," she said to the bartender.

Some of the other patrons were staring our way at this point, looking towards the woman who was taking in her liquor a bit too quickly. No doubt, some of them were considering taking advantage of her as soon as she stepped outside of the tavern.

I don't know why I felt protective of her. After all, I didn't even know her. For some reason, though, I felt the *need to protect her. So I started a conversation with her. Soon, we were laughing uncontrollably. We laughed and talked until a shrieking bell tolled.*

It was the curfew bell, a bell that alerted townspeople that shops and taverns were closing. I escorted the lady out of the tavern. She held on fast to my arm and leaned into me, but she wasn't the least bit intoxicated.

She curled her fingers into the inky black hair at the nape of my neck. "You do not look like anyone I have seen around here before," she said softly. "What is your name?"

"Iancu."

"Yahn-what?"

"Ee-yahn-koo. Iancu."

"That sounds foreign."

"I am not originally from here."

That information seemed to fascinate her. She tilted her head back so that she could peer up at me.

"What is your name?" I returned jovially as we walked. I wasn't overly concerned that I was spending time with a woman out in the open without a chaperone. If she could overlook this small bit of indecency, then so could I.

"Jordana." She twirled a strand of her shimmering, red hair around a slender index finger. "Before I walked up to you, I noticed that you looked troubled. I hope I am not delving into private matters, but I was wondering why you looked so melancholy."

I shook my head dismissively, narrowing my eyes as I gazed at the well-worn path that stretched ahead of us. An ivory crescent moon shone high in a star-studded sky. I'd always favored the night over daylight hours.

She was watching my face attentively. "I know it has to do with a lady."

I arched a glance at her. I'd never talked to a woman about another woman before. "I was not in the highest of spirits earlier, but you have helped that."

"You have dodged the question," she pointed out. "You did so quite skillfully, I might add."

"I would rather not talk about it, if you do not mind."

11

"I do not mean to pry," she said softly. With those words, she stopped walking. "But what if I told you that all of your troubles could come to an end?"

I stopped walking as she had. The soft clatter of a horse's hooves sounded in the distance. "I would not believe that for a second," I said after some thought.

"I know more about you than you do about yourself," she told me.

I folded my arms across my chest. "Fine," I allowed, playing along with her game. "Tell me about...me."

She circled around me, looking me up and down, sizing me up. Her dark cape fluttered and billowed around her; the wind caressed her hair and ruined the style she'd molded it into only hours before. She made no move to readjust her hair or cape; she was focused solely on me. Her eyes searched mine and then pulled back from my gaze without warning. She said after a few minutes, still circling around me like a vulture did its prey, "The reason you were miserable earlier-the reason you still are miserable-is because the object of your affections does not know that you are alive."

I flinched as if I'd been slapped.

She flipped over one of my hands and stroked my open palm. "You are a craftsman," she somehow observed, sliding delicate fingers over the unblemished skin on my palm. "You forge necessary utilities, and yet you take great care with them. You care for them as if they are your children."

I yanked my hand from hers, my eyes wide with disbelief. "How did you know that?" I demanded.

"I know things," she said simply.

"A witch?" I croaked.

"No," she replied, smiling softly.

The sound of clattering hooves sounded nearer, but I found that I couldn't take my eyes off of Jordana. "What are you?" I whispered.

She closed the distance between us in one dramatic step and snaked an arm around my neck. She whispered roughly into my ear, "I am the answer to all of your prayers. All you have to do is trust me. All you have to do is close your eyes. Then, nothing in the world can stop you from having everything that you desire, including the woman."

She had to be a witch. There was no way that she could know everything she knew. There was the slightest chance that she could be a gypsy fortune-teller, but I highly doubted it.

She was no gypsy. The grace that she possessed when she moved her body was otherworldly. She didn't walk so much as she slithered. The hem of her dress brushed the ground, but I noticed that not a smudge of dirt touched the dress. I wouldn't have said that she was a gypsy, but she could have definitely been a witch.

She laughed abruptly and shook her head. She pressed the length of her body against mine. "Allow me to show you all that I can do for you," she said, brushing my shoulder-length hair off of my neck.

A moment later, her lips were on my lips. Kissing her was addictive; whenever she pulled away, I felt as if she'd taken my very breath from me. I held her tightly to me. I couldn't get enough of her. I think that at one point, I wanted to swallow her whole. We were kissing and panting, a moment away from rolling around right there on the filthy ground in the town square.

Her lips moved from my mouth to my cheek and from my cheek to my earlobe. Then I felt her teeth gently tugging at the spot of skin just beneath my ear. She nicked me with her teeth, gently at first. She whispered dirty things into my ear that a lady wouldn't dare utter. Her hands moved to my waist and started to tug at my trousers.

Never before had I met a woman this aggressive. It was beginning to frighten me. All of a sudden, I didn't want to be touching her. I didn't want to be near her. Both of my hands closed over her hands.

She pulled back and saw the hesitancy in my eyes. A flash of disappointment crossed her beautiful face, but the expression was gone as quickly as it had appeared.

"I do not want to do this," I whispered, squeezing her hands with mine.

She turned her back to me and pulled her cowl over the top of her head.

"I do not wish to taint your spirits," I said quickly.

She hugged her arms around her torso and ducked her head. I couldn't be sure, but I think I saw her shoulders shake. She seemed to be sobbing.

I rolled my eyes heavenward and cleared my throat. *"I will escort you home. The hour grows late."* I slid an arm across her shoulders.

She raised her face to look up at me, and it was not the face of Jordana that stared at me, but the face of Bridgette.

My breath caught in my throat. I didn't trust my eyes; I couldn't trust my eyes. The woman standing before me wasn't Bridgette. I knew that, and yet...my hand stretched out and brushed wavy strands of gold from her cheeks.

Her eyes were lowered coyly. It wasn't Bridgette, and yet...it was. Her sweet, flowery scent teased my nostrils. Her shy, gentle smile beamed at me with the brightness of a thousand suns. *"Iancu,"* she breathed, cupping my face in both of her hands.

I closed my eyes and closed a hand over her right wrist. As much as I knew it wasn't Bridgette, I allowed myself to believe that it was. In my mind, I was slowly bending to kiss the lips of Bridgette. My arms were snaking around the waist of Bridgette. I was lowering onto the grass with my lady, the love of my life.

"I have always wanted you," she said softly and even her voice had changed. *"I have wanted to tell you all this time how I feel about you, but I could not."*

"I understand," I said, my voice choked with emotion.

The grass around us bent at the heat of our passion. Our kisses were frenzied and our lovemaking was anything but gentle. Her nails dug into my shoulders and her ankles locked behind my back.

I barely felt the sharp incisors piercing my throat; the ecstasy rocking my body was that intense. My blood stained *her teeth and dripped onto the pristine white collar of my shirt. I began to feel dizzy; I could barely keep my eyes open. When the sensation of her teeth on my flesh finally registered to me, it felt wondrous. She pressed her wrist to my lips and without being told, I pierced her skin with my teeth and drank from her.*

A world of color exploded behind my eyes as her rich, dark blood coated my throat. I was hungry for her body, hungry for her blood, hungry to have every bit of her inside of me. I didn't have an understanding of my feelings and emotions at the time. I don't have an understanding of those feelings to this day. All I knew was that I wanted to sink my nails into her skin and carve my name into it. I wanted to peel her open and climb inside of her. All of the actions that I pictured inside of my head were barbaric and carnal.

I pressed urgent kisses to her brow, her cheeks, and her mouth. I pawed at the bodice of her gown and howled at the crescent moon. At that moment, I couldn't have cared less if all of the neighborhood residents exited their houses to see what all of the commotion was about. I had my woman beneath me, and that was all that mattered.

When the last of the tremors shook from my body, I stretched out on the grass beside her. Her fingers were intertwined with mine and mine with hers. Our eyes met, but the blonde hair changed colors before my tired eyes. The roots of her hair darkened to a glossy, dark red. The color spread from root to tip of each strand of hair on her head. The emerald green eyes turned violet and her complexion paled.

I hadn't made love to Bridgette at all, of course. I'd made love to Jordana...a stranger, a woman I'd barely known. The scent I'd recognized, the voice I'd heard, and the woman that had seemed so familiar...all of that had been a ruse.

"It is called glamour," Jordana said, sitting up and adjusting her gown. "Soon, you will have the ability to do it as easily as I did."

"I do not understand."

"You are not the man you were twenty minutes ago," she informed me, rising to her feet. *"I have enabled you with the power to obtain your every whim, your every desire."*

"I still do not understand."

"You soon will," she assured me.

Before I knew what was happening, I was introduced to a different type of life. My humanity was snatched from me as if it were a ripe berry, plump for the picking. It was devoured and nothing was left but an empty shell. All of the information that I had gathered previous to this particular night meant nothing, because as of that night, I was changed.

I was no longer a mere human man. I was so much more than that. I was at that point a breed of vampire, sired by Jordana. My strength was magnified at least tenfold. I was able to fool the naked eye with glamour, an ability that leads one or many to see what is not truly there. At times, I had the ability to be invisible to the naked eye. I could travel nearly at the speed of sound. I had heightened senses and the power to read minds. I could manipulate the energy around me and move objects without physically touching them.

I loved hearing the tales that she told me about her people. She was a natural vampire; that meant she'd been born as a vampire. No one had stolen her humanity; she never had humanity to begin with.

She explained that vampires were rumored to be the undead, trapped between the world of the living and the world of the dead. *"I don't like to think of us as being the undead,"* she said to me one night beneath a starlit sky. *"Our bodies operate much like the bodies of humans. We just need human blood in order for our bodies to function. Our hearts don't beat consistently unless we provoke it. We don't have a pulse steadily thumping at our throats. That is why we need to feed so often; the blood in our systems isn't circulated quickly enough to sustain us for long. But we cry, we sweat, we require sustenance in order to survive, and although we are often referred to as being immortal, we can die."*

She told me about the different vampire clans who made up the majority of the population. There were too many clans to keep up with, but the five largest clans were: the Arati, the Toltecs, the Kavir, the Vikara, and the Tudhani.

The Arati, she told me, was a clan that possessed a very animalistic nature. They were avid hunters and known for their inability to remain in one place for a long period of time. Hooligans, street thugs, and assassins made up the majority of this nomadic clan. It wasn't uncommon for a vampire from another clan to hire an Arati as a contract killer.

Toltecs were another matter. Most vampires in this clan were high class executives, lawyers, and scholars. "As vampires they have a thirst for blood," she told me with a serious look in her eyes, "but as Toltecs they have a thirst for knowledge, success, and power."

From what she told me, the most intriguing of the clans was the clan called Kavir. The Kavir clan was made up of humans whose minds couldn't handle the transformation. Because of this fault, the Kavir had to roam throughout the ages as raging lunatics and psychotics. A small consolation for the members of this clan was the fact that even though they were often incoherent and delusional, the majority of them were gifted with psychic abilities. While their behavior was bizarre and unpredictable, their wealth of insight was something to be admired by the other clans.

The Vikara, much like the Kavir, was a clan made up of humans whose bodies couldn't handle the transformation. The difference between the two clans was that while the minds of the Kavir were warped for all eternity, the minds of the Vikara were very sharp. The vampiric transformation disfigured the bodies of the Vikara-not their minds-and because of this, they were recluses who kept to themselves, mostly in sewers and other underground facilities. "They may be solitary," Jordana told me of the aesthetically-challenged clan, "but they have a remarkable knack for stumbling upon information. No one knows how they do it, but for the right price, they'll tell you what you want to know."

Last but not least, there were the Tudhani, a clan made up of artists in every form: writers, singers, dancers, painters, sculptors, musicians, and actors. The Tudhani clan was a clan consisting of some of the most beautiful people known to walk the face of the earth. They were beautiful vampires surrounded by anything and everything beautiful, for the two most important things to them were beauty and art.

"Each clan has a leader," she told me, "and once in awhile the clan leaders will convene and discuss important topics. Each clan leader is given a region to reign over, and each dwells within that region. Often, they choose to dwell in the largest city within the region, because the largest cities boast the most in entertainment and...potential.

"I'm not a clan leader," she went on, "but one day I do hope to be the clan leader of the Tudhani."

When she told me her stories, she made the world of immortals sound appealing. She had not outlined for me any of the side effects, so to speak, that I would have to endure.

The lust for blood disgusted me. I resisted it, and yet it grabbed a hold of me and forced me to partake in the disgraceful, shameful acts that I performed in order to achieve satisfactory nourishment.

It didn't take long for me to revolt against what I was. It didn't take long for shame to set in. I wondered if this was what my mother, Dinah, felt whenever she walked the streets of England. Did she feel shame to the same intensity that I did? Did it rule her every action when she was around the self-righteous townspeople?

Early on, I made a vow that I would not cause unnecessary harm to humans. I swore to protect the affairs of the innocent. Jordana was more than a little displeased, but what she thought mattered little to me.

In the days of my childhood I would watch the knights competing in jousts, and I would pray for the day when I would be an honorable warrior. That wish was granted to me the day that I vowed to protect the innocent.

In Edgar's shop, I forged a sword for myself. It took months for me to make; it was the most complicated sword that I'd ever had to create. The flat of the sword was a hard, special kind of wood that I'd obtained from the gypsy camp that raised me. The wood was protected and enforced with an assortment of gypsy spells. The blade of the sword, I made with steel. Amazingly, it is a sword that I still possess to this day.

Vampires have evolved over time. A lot of the weaknesses that we used to have no longer ail us. After centuries of having to avoid harsh and unforgiving sunlight, some of the oldest vampires (that would include Jordana and myself) are able to tolerate sun exposure without bursting into flame. Granted, we can only tolerate exposure for only minutes at a time, but Jordana and her beau, Aryk, are searching for a way to grant full immunity from the sunlight to our kind. Once immunity is gained, the world will most likely be bathed in blood.

I already know what you're thinking. You're thinking, If vampires existed, someone would know about it. To some extent, you would be correct. There are humans who do or did know about us. For the most part, they have cooperated with us and kept our secret. The few who have attempted to inform the world of our existence were looked upon with skepticism and doubt.

Humans never stay a threat for long, you see. Because they die. They cease to exist, while we are cursed to roam the earth for hundreds and thousands of years.

In any case, those of you who are reading my words would be surprised at just how much you don't know about your world, or even the person who is sitting beside you at this very moment.

Forget what you've watched on television, seen in movies, or read in books. Forget what you've heard through the rumor mills. Vampires exist and the majority of them *aren't cheerful, slap-happy characters. Evil is running amuck on Earth.*

How could we have flown beneath the radar of the public for this long? The answer to this question eludes me. However, if Aryk's flashy, classically-brutal actions persist, we will not be a well-kept secret for long.

CHAPTER ONE

1985

Darkness consumed Standing Rock Reservation and invaded every corner visible to the naked eye. The Native American community consisted of roadside crafts shops, modest houses, and decrepit, abandoned warehouses.

The sun had long since set over the South Dakota horizon and no children were playing on the sidewalks. The streets were devoid of traffic. The neighborhood seemed to be holding its breath.

Through the neighborhood they crept, sinister evil incarnates. Many of them were dressed like typical teenage hoodlums and several of them were dressed in dark suits. It was every creature for itself as they dispersed and scattered, slithering into houses through cracked windows and manipulating the locks on house doors.

A grim moon was one of two witnesses to the bloody massacre that ensued on that warm, autumn night. The other witness was crouched beside a giant oak in the front yard of one of the neighborhood houses. This second witness was dressed completely in black; the darkness of night was his ally.

A gentle breeze whispered over the reservation, causing the lapels of his cloak to flutter about his calves as he rose to a standing position. Narrow, frosty blue eyes gauged the situation at hand.

He rushed towards the front door of the white, one-story house at superhuman speed and gripped the brass door handle. With little effort, he influenced the locks on the door and shoved it open.

A picturesque scene greeted him upon his entry. A middle-aged woman and her three children sat on the couch and she was reading a story to them.

At the sound of the door clicking closed behind him, all four faces lifted. The mother stood up from the couch, appraising the stranger with wary eyes. In a calm voice, she issued an order to her children in Lakota, the native language spoken by most of the Sioux residents of Standing Rock Reservation.

The cloaked man with waist-length, dark hair gestured for her not to panic. "I'm not here to harm you," he told her, and felt guilty for having to probe her mind. She was thinking of making a run for it, but he crossed the room in a couple of short steps. "I don't have time to explain everything right now, because there are other families that I have to get to. But something is happening, and you have to get your kids out of the house right now."

The brown-skinned woman with straight, black hair nervously nibbled at her fingertips. Her doe brown eyes were wide and frightened. She didn't know what to make of him. It didn't take long for her to make a decision, however. She nodded her head silently and followed the curt orders he gave her.

Pack up some clothes for her children as quickly as possible, pack some food and other necessities, and make her way to the community college down the street. He'd made sure to unlock all of the back doors. "Don't turn on any of the lights once you're in the building and make sure to tell everyone who joins you not to turn on any of the lights." He saw the fear in her eyes and comfortingly squeezed both of her hands. "Everything is going to be all right. Don't worry."

While he strode out of the front door, the woman and her children scurried out the back. He moved about the neighborhood, warning families of the impending danger that was drawing near.

Standing on the rickety porch of the last house on the block, he stretched a hand out to grab the doorknob. Before he could touch it, the door was yanked open and a young girl who couldn't be any older than ten years old peered out at him. Her dark brown hair was pulled back in one long, thick braid and her hazel, almond-shaped eyes managed to convey both wisdom and innocence. She didn't speak. She stared up at him for several moments with an expressionless face.

The cloaked man returned the frank perusal, momentarily stunned by her startling beauty.

Wordlessly, she stepped aside and allowed him inside. She led him into the living room, where her grandfather had lulled himself to sleep in an old, battered rocking chair. "Pa," she called out, walking over to him and tugging on the sleeve of his flannel button-down shirt. "Pa."

The dark-haired stranger took in his surroundings. The living room was cramped and cluttered with a stained flower-print couch, a couple of mismatched armchairs, and a large throw rug that looked as if it had been literally *thrown* on the floor.

A couple of paintings graced the walls. In one of the paintings there were lean, muscular Native American men mounted on strong horses. Determination had been etched in the faces of these men. Some of them had bows and arrows in their hands and others had long spears. Facing them were English settlers, also mounted on horses with bulky muskets in their hands.

In the other painting there was a woman wearing an animal skin headdress. The colors that had been used to draw her were extraordinary. Her complexion was rich and brown, and her dark eyes blazed from beneath the brim of the headdress. The words beneath the image of the woman read, "Buffalo Woman."

The old man's eyes came open and he looked around. His scraggly gray hair was pulled back and secured with a rubber band. A cane leaned against his rocking chair and his eyes had a consistent blankness that led the stranger to believe that the man was blind.

"Pa," the girl said again. "There's a man here. He has something to tell us."

The old man fumbled around for his cane and shakily rose to his feet.

The younger man approached him and settled both hands onto the older man's shoulders. "I have to get you and your granddaughter out of the house." He glanced down at the young girl. "Can you lead me to the back door?"

A loud crashing noise sounded from the rear of the house. The cloaked man's eyes narrowed. He looked towards the front door, then towards the long hallway that must lead to the kitchen. He could smell them circling the house; this must be one of the last houses left on their agenda.

The little girl's eyes widened. She glanced up at her grandfather and took his hand in hers. "Mama and Papa," she whispered. "And Randy."

The stranger ushered the girl and her grandfather into a closet located near the front door and proceeded down the hallway with his left hand beneath the right lapel of his coat where his sword was sheathed.

A warm yellow light flooded the living room and hallway, but beyond the hallway there weren't any lights turned on. That wasn't a problem for him because he had excellent night vision...so excellent that it didn't take long for him to spot the still, dark figure hunkered down near the kitchen table.

He whipped his left hand from the inside of his cloak. The jeweled hilt of the sword reflected the light filtering in from the hallway. His booted feet thundered over the tiled floor.

The still shape jumped to life with arms outstretched. In its human life, it had been a teenager with thick, red hair and constellations of freckles across his cheeks. The freckles were already starting to fade and a face that had already been pale was becoming even paler. Ripped jeans were baggy around his thin legs and the old, stained t-shirt he wore looked too big for his bird chest. Thick, red goo dribbled down his chin. He'd already fed tonight and he was looking for more innocents to tear apart.

The kid tilted his head with an eerie, elastic grin on his rubbery lips. "I know who you are," he taunted, hopping from one foot to the other. "You're Iancu. You're one of us, but you hunt us, right?"

The cloaked man with the strange-looking sword didn't respond.

The kid stumbled backwards until he was flat against the kitchen wall near the window. "Yeah, yeah, you're him," the kid said. "I've heard about you. You've got that weird-looking sword, the one that is a hybrid between a sword and a stake. The flat of the sword is wooden, right? And the blade is steel? I heard you've killed a lot of people with that thing."

Iancu raised the sword and held it to the teenager's throat.

"You don't have to do this," the kid whined, starting to look afraid. "I don't have anything against you or your cause, man. I just...got hungry, that's all."

"You've already fed and yet you're in here, terrorizing this family," Iancu accused through clenched teeth.

The kid stammered, but couldn't get a sentence out.

Iancu nicked the kid's throat with the sword. "I need to know why this place is being attacked."

"I told you," the redhead punk insisted. "We got hungry."

Iancu remembered seeing the suit-clad men who were accompanying the hooligans. Something more than a late night snack run was going down. He leaned into the kid, making sure to hold his sword steady. "Something's going on," he said in a low, menacing voice. "I *know* that something is going on. You can continue to play the dummy, or you can fess up. Either way, I'm going to kill you. The next words out of your mouth are just going to determine how slowly you'll die."

The kid glanced left, then right, then left again, as if waiting for someone to come to his rescue. His voice shook when he spoke and he refused to look Iancu in the eyes. "The girl," he said finally.

"What girl?"

"The girl who lives in this house. They want her."

"Why do they want her?"

"I don't know!" the kid exclaimed with a slight shrug of his shoulders. "All I know is that these big shots told us that we can invade this place and take our fill. The girl, though... the girl is to be left untouched."

Iancu arched a look over his shoulder. The hallway was empty and the house was silent, but he knew that the girl and her grandfather were hiding in the closet. He wanted to return to them as soon as possible and get them out of the house. "You don't know what they want with the girl?"

"I don't, I swear I don't."

Iancu didn't hesitate in decapitating the kid. When he had first started hunting his own kind, he had felt guilty for killing them. He had hated killing the ones who'd been children or teenagers before the change. As he killed the redhead street punk, though, he felt nothing. He felt no remorse at all.

The head topped with wavy red hair dropped to the floor and collapsed in a pile of dust. His body followed suit, wavering for a moment on its feet until it could no longer stand on its own.

Iancu turned and stormed down the hall. He reached the closet door and whisked it open. To his relief, the young girl and her grandfather were huddled on the floor, holding each other. "We have to go," he said.

Iancu barely had to say a word. The young girl led them to the back door and out of the house, making sure to tiptoe as quietly as she could. She held on fast to her grandfather's hand and once in awhile looked to Iancu for direction.

He couldn't take his eyes off of her. For some reason, the clan leaders wanted their hands on this little mystery of a girl. What was so special about her that she'd managed to grab the attention of the clan leaders? Did she have psychic abilities? From the smell of her, she was human, but there was something different about her. He didn't know exactly how she was different from other humans, but the way she moved as she led her grandfather off of the property and the way she'd opened the door before he'd had a chance to manipulate the locks...

Something is definitely going on here, he thought to himself as he followed the girl and her elder. He hadn't yet sheathed his sword because he had a feeling that he'd have to use it again.

The old man walked or, rather, limped with the assistance of a gnarled cane with white paint chipping off of it. He shuffled after the young girl, exhibiting an exemplary display of trust in the youth. She probably took care of him more than he took care of her; that would, at least, explain the level of maturity that she'd achieved.

"What's your name?" she asked him as she trudged through the grassy field located behind her family's house.

It took moments for the question to register to him. He snapped out of his thoughts and replied, "Iancu."

"Yahn-koo?"

He managed a smile. "Close enough."

"My name's Charlie Strong Wolf," she introduced, "and this is my grandpa, Jim."

He almost laughed outright. It seemed fitting that she had a name uncommon for most females, seeing as everything else about her was unusual. "Your name fits you," was all he said in response.

She beamed at him. "After all of the bad guys leave, are we going to go back for Mama, Papa, and Randy?"

He'd smelled the death in the house before leaving. They'd left no life behind, and that meant that her mother, father, and sibling were no longer breathing. He didn't know what to tell her. He didn't want to lie to her, mostly because he didn't like to lie, but also because he sensed that she would know he was lying. She seemed *that* intuitive. He cleared his throat and looked at some point over her head. "After everything settles down, we'll see."

One of her brows arched. "What does that mean?"

Jim, her grandfather, gave her head a reassuring pat. "It means what he said, Char. Let's wait for everything to settle down."

Screams for help pierced the night. They were difficult to ignore, but Iancu had to for the time being. Young Charlie was what the clan leaders were looking for. He had to make sure that they didn't find her. Only God knew what they would do with her once they had her.

"I don't want to wait," the young girl was saying stubbornly. "I want to see Mama. And Papa. And Randy." She had stopped walking and was beginning to pout.

He wasn't used to dealing with children. Children were as foreign to him as the sunlight was these days. He started to reach out to her. He didn't know why; he felt that maybe his touch would comfort her or soothe his own nerves.

She moved backwards until she was out of his reach. Her eyes never wavered from his face. "No," she said slowly, speaking so low that he could barely hear her. She looked at him for a long moment before shifting her gaze to her grandfather. "I want to see Mama."

Iancu knelt to the ground. "We have to keep moving. If we don't, then the bad people are going to find us."

"I don't care."

"Charlie-"

"Don't call me Charlie!" she screamed. "You don't know me. Where's Mama? Where's Randy? What's happening? Why didn't they come outside with us? Did you see them?"

He shook his head. "No," he said, and that much was truth. He didn't have to see them to know that they were no longer of this earth.

"But you know," she whispered with her eyes narrowed into slits.

"Charlie-" he said again, sounding more helpless.

She turned and fled.

This is not happening, he thought. He glanced at the grandfather, who was staring into some blank vacuum of space.

"You have to go after her," the old man told him. "You have to go after her and make sure she's all right."

Iancu looked around. He could smell the scent of tainted blood; the scent was growing stronger with every minute that passed. If he left the blind old man's side now, chances were that the man wouldn't survive.

"It's all right," the man assured him. "I'll be all right. Just take care of little Charlie for me. She's special."

Iancu grabbed the older man's hand and shook it briefly. "I'll come back for you."

"Just make sure little Charlie is all right," Jim repeated.

Iancu inserted his sword into its sheath and took off in the direction of Jim's house. The lapels of his cloak slapped against his legs as he ran. He didn't tire easily and hadn't broken a sweat by the time he reached the back door, which had been left open.

He entered the house with all of his senses on alert. "Charlie!" he shouted. He wasn't familiar with the house's layout, but the smell of blood directed him.

The hallway was lined with doors and he opened a door that was on his right. The room that he looked into probably served as the house's master bedroom. The walls were smeared with blood. The king-sized bed's blood-stained sheets had been carelessly tossed to the floor. What remained of Charlie's parents lay side by side on the bed. They'd been gutted and emptied out. Whoever had fed from them hadn't only taken their blood, but many of their organs as well.

I should have smelled the blood sooner, he thought to himself. He didn't take one step into the room. One look told him that the girl wasn't in it, and that left the room directly across the hall from this one.

He pushed open the door and was panged to see Charlie hugging her older brother's corpse. He couldn't bring himself to step inside of this room, either. He extended a hand to her. "Charlie, we have to get out of here."

She didn't acknowledge him. She remained the way she was, sitting on the edge of her brother's narrow bed, hugging his bloodied body to her chest. "I'm staying here," she said determinedly. "I'm staying with my family."

"Charlie, if we don't leave now, we're going to end up *like* your family," he told her. The scent of blood teased his nostrils. His eyes illuminated, glowing an iridescent, sparkling blue. His face contorted and he gripped the doorjamb to keep himself from falling to his knees.

As much as he tried to deny what he was, he was a vampire. He could fight the thirst with all of his might, but in the end, it would always win.

He considered leaving the girl there. He figured that whoever wanted her would probably get her eventually. She didn't want to leave her butchered family, so she might as well stay with her family and end up like them. The hunger was weakening him, and if he didn't get out of that house in a matter of minutes, he was going to shove her little body aside and feast on the leftovers that she was holding in her arms. "Charlie," he gasped, leaning heavily against the doorjamb. "I had to leave your grandfather in order to come here and get you. If we don't leave right now, he's going to be killed."

She rocked back and forth with her brother's body in her arms, but something in her clicked and she blinked her eyes. "Grandpa?"

"He's out there all by himself and he can't see," he went on, seeing that he'd struck a chord with her. "We have to get back to him."

In all honesty, her grandfather was probably already dead, but at that point in time he would have said whatever he needed to say to get the two of them out of that house. She slowly nodded her head. "We have to get Grandpa," she agreed, and detached herself from her brother. She stood on her feet and moved to join Iancu.

The sheets rustled. In the quiet room, it might as well have been the sound of thunder striking. Iancu stiffened and grabbed for Charlie. His movements were too slow.

Her older brother, Randy, sat up and said, "Char?"

She whirled around with her eyes wide. "Randy!"

"Oh, for God's sake," Iancu muttered. He briskly strode into the room, unsheathing his sword. He raised the heavy weapon and brought it down with cruel efficiency.

The boy exploded into a cloud of dust and his younger sister lost her mind. She ran from the room, screaming her head off.

Cursing himself under his breath, he followed her out of the room. "Charlie!" he yelled, stalking into the living room. He stopped in his tracks once he was behind the couch. The undead was in the house. He could feel it.

His hand reflexively tightened its grip on the sword. He knew better than to call out the young girl's name now. Someone had her and someone had his hand over her mouth. She couldn't respond to his calls. She couldn't say anything, not right now.

He moved in a slow circle around the room, taking slow, quiet steps. He was being watched and whoever was watching him was attempting to probe at his mind. *Whoever it is, it's not a new vampire,* he realized with a start. *Whoever it is has some years on him.*

"I'll be all right. Just take care of little Charlie for me. She's special." The grandfather's words echoed in his mind and a wave of guilt washed over him. He wouldn't be able to get to the old man in time to save his life, and the way things were looking now, he might not be able to save the young girl, either.

"I know you're here," he said in a low voice. "You might as well show yourself."

"What fun would that be?" came the response. A six-foot tall man with spiky, bleached blonde hair and a bad case of acne appeared in the middle of the room. He'd been cloaking himself and Charlie, an ability that made the user invisible. The fact that Iancu couldn't spot him said that the vampire holding onto Charlie by her hair was at least a couple hundred years old.

"What do you want with the girl?"

"This girl right here is very special," the bleached blonde said, looking down at Charlie.

"She's just a kid," Iancu insisted.

The blonde vampire clucked his tongue. "That didn't even sound convincing, my man," he said. "Come on! I mean, you're legendary, right? You're Iancu, defender of good, extinguisher of evil and all that jazz, right? Tell me that you can do better than that."

Iancu threateningly lifted his sword and pointed the tip of it in the blonde's direction.

"What are you going to do?" the other man teased. "Are you going to cut me with your little butter knife, there? What...you haven't heard of guns?"

"Let the girl go, or I swear to God..."

"You swear, do you?" Aryk threw his head back and laughed. "You swear to *God*? Are you serious?"

Iancu took a step towards the man several inches shorter than he.

"You can swear to God all you like, Iancu. You know why?" Aryk tapped his right ear. "Because He's not listening. Oh, no. He turned a deaf ear onto us a long time ago, because we're despicable. We're not worthy of His love. I shouldn't have to tell you this. You should have all of this memorized."

"Let the girl go."

"I *can't*." Aryk smoothed a hand over the girl's hair and grinned perversely. "She's the slayer."

Iancu's eyes snapped down to Charlie as realization dawned on him. No wonder her grandfather had wanted him to go after her instead of staying with him. No wonder she seemed mature and intuitive for her age, and no wonder the clan leaders wanted her. They wanted her because she was the slayer, the one human designated to kill them. If they killed her outright, another human would be deemed slayer and pick up where she left off. So instead of killing her, they would imprison her and torture her for the rest of her years.

The thought of that little girl going through any such torment sickened him. He couldn't allow it to happen.

"Ah, I see," Aryk said. "You didn't know that she was the slayer, did you? Then again, of course you wouldn't.

You've turned your back on our world. You've denounced us and waged war upon us. In a sense, you're a slayer yourself."

"I can't let you take her," Iancu said.

"You have no choice," Aryk pointed out. "There's nothing you can do to stop me. You refuse to use your powers in battle and all you have for a weapon is that dinky little sword. You have no chance of beating me. Making an attempt would be begging me to take your life."

Charlie had long since given up on struggling. A somber resignation had taken over the features of her face. Her eyes were downcast. She couldn't meet Iancu's eyes. She was probably feeling guilty for having brought them both back here.

"To underestimate me would be a grave mistake."

"You think so?" Aryk bent his fingers in a beckoning gesture. "Then show me what you've got, Iancu. Show me why you're such a big legend amongst our people."

Iancu rushed at the blonde vampire. Aryk shoved Charlie out of the way and braved the blow. The spiky-haired blonde was pushed to the floor and still he laughed at the dark-haired man on top of him.

A sharp cracking sound reached Iancu's ears, but he didn't dare acknowledge the sound. Any distractions would cost him his life. He felt a tap on his shoulder. Without glancing behind him, he asked, "What?"

Something heavy and pointed was pressed into his left hand. He knew what it was without looking.

Sensing impending harm, Aryk writhed from beneath Iancu and rolled away. He rose to full height and dusted off his dark dress pants. "You didn't think that it was going to be that easy, did you?"

Not knowing exactly what his next move would be, Iancu raised the broken rocking chair leg in the air.

There was a gentle nudging at the corners of his mind and he heard Charlie's voice inside his head. *No, don't throw it. He's going to catch it and use it on you.*

His eyes widened and he turned, staring at her in shock. He felt a hard shove at his back and found his face pressed against the wood floor. *How is it that this child slayer is able to communicate with me telepathically? I'm more than five hundred years old.*

Aryk pressed a heavy boot into his back. "Made you look," he said after a dry chuckle. "I've got to tell you...I'm very disappointed about the way our encounter is going down.

"When I was first turned, I heard so many stories about you. There are so many legends, so many fables going around about you. I know that at least half of them are false, but I still wanted to believe in you, you know?" He paused. "It's kind of like meeting Clark Kent and being told he's Superman. Is that it, ole' buddy? Are you just having a Clark Kent moment?"

The grip that he had on the chair leg loosened. He felt it being pried from his fingers. A moment later, he could hear Aryk's sharp intake of breath. The faintest scent of tainted blood touched his nostrils. His eyes began to illuminate. He fought against the transformation attempting to take place.

The foot that Aryk had placed in the middle of his back was removed. A loud, resounding thud echoed throughout the house as the blonde vampire collapsed to the floor.

Iancu jumped up and brought his sword up with him, ready to wreak havoc. He looked down and saw the chair leg protruding from the blonde's back.

Charlie stood in the middle of the living room floor breathing heavily and looking up at Iancu. The innocence that he'd seen in her eyes just half an hour ago had vanished. Located in the place of that innocence was wisdom too vast for someone her age.

2000

"That movie was ridiculous!" a twenty year old college student named Steve McGrady exclaimed as he and his girlfriend exited the movie theater. "I can't *believe* I paid ten dollars to see that!"

"We should have waited for it to come out on video," his girlfriend Patricia Wilson agreed, tucking strands of auburn hair behind her ears. She leaned slightly into her boyfriend as the two of them walked towards the parking lot where his dark blue Ford Explorer was parked.

He slipped an arm around her waist. "It's a shame, really," he went on. "I love vampire movies just like every other horror movie fanatic, but it seems like no one is coming out with original material anymore."

Patricia rolled her eyes and didn't respond. When her boyfriend started on a tangent, it usually took him a significant amount of time to calm down. It was a habit of his that she'd grown accustomed to. Most of her ex-boyfriends were men of few words, so when she'd first met Steve, the fact that he liked to talk had been refreshing. Nowadays, though, whenever he opened his mouth, she had to fight back the urge to plug her ears with her fingers.

"The movie was unbelievable from the get-go, really," he continued as he unlocked the passenger door to his car. He opened the door and gestured for his girlfriend to hop in. Then, he walked around the car and unlocked the driver side door. "That movie wanted me to believe that after all of this time, humans didn't know that vampires existed? I mean, come on. With all of the technological advances that we've discovered, I'm sure that someone would have found out about the existence of vampires."

"Well, you never know," his girlfriend said as she buckled in her seatbelt. "Anything is possible."

"Anything except *that*," he muttered and started the car. "If vampires really existed, we would know about it."

"If vampires looked like us, it would be kind of hard to tell the difference."

"It wouldn't be that hard." He pulled the car out of the parking lot. Then, he rolled his car window down and savored the warm air blowing in from the Pacific Ocean. "The stereotypical vampires are usually really pale. They never eat normal food. They don't come out in daylight and...hell, I don't know. If they really existed, we would probably be able to tell the difference."

She didn't feel like arguing about it, so she let the subject drop. They settled into a comfortable silence. She leaned forward and turned on the radio.

"...And on WROK, we give you less talk and more rock," the radio deejay was announcing. "In the next hour of uninterrupted music, we're giving you a little bit of Nine Inch Nails, a little bit of Papa Roach, some 311, and old school Ozzy Osbourne."

Steve's car headed out of Los Angeles towards the neighboring suburbs. The bright lights of the city diminished until they were nothing but a glimpse in the rearview mirror mounted on the inside of the windshield.

While he drove with his left hand, his right hand drifted over the console to Patricia's bare thigh. He tugged playfully on the hem of her miniskirt. "Did you have fun tonight?"

"I did," she answered, swatting his hand away from her.

"I've never done that in a movie theater before," he confessed.

She turned to look out of the passenger side window. "I've never done that in a movie theater either," she admitted quietly.

He lifted a hand and lovingly caressed her hair. "You look so good tonight that I'm tempted to pull the car over so we can finish what we started."

That idea should have repulsed her, but it didn't. His words sent a small shiver running up and down her spine and excited her. Determined not to show him just how excited she was, she casually flipped her hair over one shoulder and quipped, "What makes you think that I would let you do that?"

He glanced in the rearview mirror. His car was the only one on the road. No other cars were behind him or in front of him. "I don't know, but I'm seriously considering pulling the car over."

She giggled and twisted around to peer out of the back window. "You are so bad," she said with an exaggerated roll of her eyes.

He rounded a sharp curve. The road straightened and the headlights of his car washed over a lone figure walking in the middle of the street.

Her eyes widened and her mouth dropped open. "Steve, stop the car!" she screamed.

He dropped his speed and swerved into the lane designated for oncoming traffic, but not soon enough. The fender of the car struck the man and sent him flying into the air. The car teetered on its left front wheel and left rear wheel for several seconds, then righted itself and dropped down onto all four wheels. Steve worked the steering wheel and the brakes, bringing the car around in a full circle. The headlights of the car cast two barrels of light over the road and the fallen body.

"Oh my God," he muttered.

Patricia unbuckled her seatbelt and jumped out of the car. "Steve, what did you do?" she demanded, covering her mouth with both hands.

"There was no way to avoid it," he insisted. "I couldn't pull over to the side of the road because this road has no shoulder. We're lucky we didn't go off the cliff!"

She shook her head. "We have to call an ambulance. You have your cell phone with you, don't you?"

"I'm already on it," he called back to her. He grabbed his cell phone from its stand on the dashboard and punched in the numbers 9-1-1. "Yeah, um, this is an emergency," he told the operator who answered.

"What is the nature of your emergency?" the female operator asked him in a calm voice.

"A-a man was w-walking," he stammered, climbing out of his car. "My car hit him and now he's on the ground. I don't know if he's alive."

"Have you tried taking the man's pulse?"

He shook his head and realized that the operator couldn't see him. "Um, no," he answered.

"I need you to try to find a pulse," the operator told him.

Easy for you to say, he thought, throwing a desperate glance over to his girlfriend.

She looked at him over the top of the car. "What is it?"

"They need us to see if the guy has a pulse," he informed her.

"They want us to go over to him?" she shrieked.

"We've got to do it," he said. "We hit the guy."

"*We* didn't do anything," she corrected him flatly. "*You* hit him with your car."

Cursing under his breath, he walked towards the still figure lying in the middle of the road. He could hear the ocean crashing onto the rocks below the edge of the cliff. The sound of crashing waves did little to soothe his nerves.

The operator waited patiently as he advanced on the collapsed pedestrian.

Steve reached the man, who was wearing a long, dark trench coat, a dark shirt, dark slacks, and a pair of dark dress shoes. The man was dressed extravagantly and yet had been walking the streets this late at night. It didn't add up and still, Steve knelt down and pressed two fingers to the man's neck. "I'm not getting a pulse," he said into the phone. His voice was shaking and he couldn't control it. He was nervous and he didn't know why.

"What about a heartbeat?" the operator asked. "Check for a heartbeat."

Wincing, Steve lowered his right hand from the man's throat to his chest. He waited for a few moments, but there was no subtle thump beneath the man's chest. "I don't have a heartbeat either," he said into the phone, "but the guy isn't bruised or bleeding or anything."

The operator hesitated. "All right," she said. "I'm going to send a unit out there. Can I have your name?"

"Steve...Steve McGrady," he replied.

"And where are you?"

He quickly told the operator where the accident had occurred and where the body was located. "Should I move him out of the street so no one else hits him?"

A loud beep sounded in his ear. He pulled the phone away from his ear and stared at it. The battery had died. "Great," he muttered, getting to his feet. He glanced over his shoulder at his girlfriend, who still cowered near the car. "An ambulance should be here soon."

"Is the guy alive?" she asked him timidly.

"I don't think so," he told her. "He has no pulse and no heartbeat."

"This kind of reminds me of a scene from the movie we saw tonight," she said nervously, wrapping her arms around her torso. "Wait."

He arched a brow at her. "What?"

"I think I just saw his leg twitch."

He looked down at the man stretched out on the ground. "What are you talking about?"

"It just twitched again," she called to him. "Did you see that?"

He *had* seen it.

The man on the ground bolted upward in a sitting position, rubbing the back of his neck. "Ouch," he grumbled and struggled to his feet. "I forgot how much it hurts to be hit by a car."

Steve turned on his heel and ran towards his car. "Get in the car!" he shouted to Patricia, who was staring dumbly at the dark-haired stranger.

She blinked her eyes and did as she was told. Seconds later, Steve joined her in the car and slammed the driver side door shut. He didn't hesitate before locking all of the car doors.

The man who'd been lying on the ground ran towards them at an incredibly fast speed. Once he got close to the car, he leapt into the air and landed on the hood of the car. His mouth stretched into a grin as he peered at them through the windshield.

"What's going on?" Patricia asked in a frightened voice. "Is this some kind of joke or something? I don't understand."

"Neither do I," Steve muttered. "Buckle in."

"What are you going to do?"

"Just buckle in!" he yelled, putting the car into Reverse.

She drew her seatbelt across her chest, secured it, and closed her eyes.

He pressed his foot on the gas pedal, twisting around to look through the back window. The car lurched backwards and, due to his maneuvering of the steering wheel, made a one hundred eighty degree spin.

The man was still on the hood of the car, staring in at them with a hungry look in his cold eyes. The lapels of his coat flapped in the air around him.

Steve changed gears and stomped on the gas pedal. The car shot forward, moving at thirty miles per hour...forty miles per hour...fifty miles per hour...

The man kneeling on the hood of the car rose to his full height and rode the car as he would a surfboard.

"He's crazy," Steve whispered.

The car was moving at sixty miles per hour...seventy miles per hour...eighty miles per hour...

Steve didn't even glance at his girlfriend as he warned, "Hold on tight." The car stopped accelerating as he switched his foot from the gas pedal to the brake pedal. The car's tires shrieked in protest of the abrupt halting of the vehicle.

The man drew an arm back and shot it forward, sending his fist through the windshield. He grabbed Steve by the throat and squeezed.

Patricia took control of the wheel as the car slowed down.

Steve waved his hands around, his eyes bulging out of their sockets. "Patty-" he gasped, reaching for her.

The car slowed down to a stop. The man on the hood of the car released Steve and jumped down from the car. He walked around to the driver side door and yanked it open.

The young college boy slumped back in his seat, lightly touching his bruised throat. The corners of his eyes were damp with tears.

As the dark-haired man yanked the blonde boy out of the driver side seat, Patricia jumped out of the car. She walked around to the front of the car. She moved through the two bright beams of light shining from above the car's bumper.

The dark-haired man stared at her for a long moment before saying, "Dinnertime."

Patricia knelt down and looked her boyfriend in the eyes. She clucked her tongue in mock sympathy. "You were so certain that vampires couldn't exist without humans knowing," she said to him while brushing his hair out of his eyes. "You regretted paying ten dollars to see that movie because it wasn't plausible to you."

Steve shook his head and closed his eyes. "No," he croaked.

"Yes," she said, yanking him off of the ground by his hair. She waited until he opened eyes. Her own eyes shined with an unnatural brilliance. "Is the movie a bit more plausible to you now?"

He didn't have to answer the question. The sound of crunching metal disturbed the passing silence. He glanced up to see another cloaked figure crouching on the roof of his car. *This can't be happening,* he thought. *I fell asleep in the movie theater. All of this is a dream...or a nightmare. It's not really happening.*

The cloaked figure descended from the roof of the car and landed on steady feet. A gentle breeze caused the hem of the person's cloak to flutter.

Patricia stood slowly, standing at the dark-haired man's side. "What is this?"

The dark-haired man grinned wolfishly. "It is dessert," he replied, charging at the shrouded character.

The cloaked one hardly moved. A subtle movement of the arm and a flick of the wrist sent a sharp stake directly into the dark-haired man's chest and through his heart. All was still and all was quiet. The man stared in bewilderment at his attacker.

His attacker looked back at him with sparkling hazel eyes. The attacker's face was conveniently masked by the darkness that the hood provided; the eyes were the only features of the face that could be seen in the moonlight.

The dark-haired man struggled to get the stake out of his chest and collapsed on his back. He was reduced to nothing but a pile of dark powder.

The dust clouded and limited Patricia's vision, but she sensed movement directly in front of her. She threw a misguided punch into thin air.

As she threw the punch, her legs were pulled from beneath her. She screamed as a blunt object pierced through her chest. Her eyes flashed from brown to a bright red. Red tears dropped from her eyelids and her incisors lengthened into fangs. Her body was rocked with a jolting spasm. Her back arched once, then twice, as her life was extinguished. She exploded into a thick cloud of dust. The clothes of both vampires lay neatly on the ground, so neatly that they could have easily been a department store's window display.

The cloaked avenger knelt and emptied the pockets of the dead vampires, flipping both wallets open to find wads of crisp dollar bills.

Steve got to his feet, breathing heavily. When the dust settled, he stood staring at his rescuer. "I...I don't know how to thank you," he started in a shaky voice.

His knight in shining armor rose to her feet and swept the hood of the cloak back to reveal an abundance of shining dark brown hair. It was a woman who had come to his rescue, a Native American princess with long, dark hair, bronzed brown skin, and wide set hazel eyes. She swept the lapels of the cloak aside and withdrew a syringe as she walked towards him. She roughly grabbed his right arm.

He felt a tiny prick as the syringe was inserted directly into one of his veins. He didn't even think to fight her off, since she'd risked her life to save his. As she assisted him in the passenger seat of his car, however, he started to wonder who she was. He started to wonder if she was even one of the good guys. He started to wonder a lot of things as his thoughts tumbled around in his mind the way clothes tumbled inside of a clothes dryer. The events of that night became blurry and melted away altogether. He was barely aware of the fact that he was sitting in the passenger seat of his own car while a stranger drove him to the nearest gas station.

He drifted into an undisturbed slumber and awoke hours later when the sun was high in the sky. It took him awhile to realize that he was sitting in his car and that his car happened to be parked at a gas station. Had he slept here all night? He couldn't remember.

Quiet chatter filled the large boardroom overlooking the Pacific Ocean. Clan leaders were seated along the large conference table and their assistants sat beside them, dutifully taking notes. Two of the four walls were lined with wide expanses of glass windows.

Alexei Lishnevsky, standing at one of those windows, peered down upon the city of angels with one hand stroking his angular jaw. He was tall with glossy, jet-black hair and pale green eyes. At two hundred thirty-seven years old, he was the clan leader of the Toltecs. He'd flown into Los Angeles from Chicago, Illinois, early that morning.

He glanced over his shoulder at the leaders conversing at the table. Fiero Giovanni sat near the head of the table, his head ducked low as he spoke with his assistant in a hushed voice. His incisors gleamed whenever the conference room lights hit them, because unlike the Kivar, the Tudhani, the Arati, and the Toltecs, the Vikara were unable to retract their fangs. His cheeks were sunken in, his pale complexion had a blue-green tint, and his eyes were a nondescript gray color. Whenever he spoke he had the tendency to run a hand across his bald head; whether or not it was a nervous gesture, Alexei wasn't sure.

Seated across the table from Fiero was Jason Edwards, who preferred to be called "Chase." The nickname was accurate enough, since the Arati leader was often difficult to keep track of. At fifty-six, he was the youngest clan member in the room. No one else in his clan challenged him for the position because the Arati were known for being rugged individualists who didn't care for politics or responsibility. He'd killed the previous Arati clan leader in a bar brawl a decade ago and had served as the clan's leader ever since. He sat with his arms folded across his chest. He hadn't bothered to dress accordingly; instead of a suit, he wore a dirty t-shirt and a worn pair of ripped jeans. His shaggy blonde hair was unruly and beard stubble bristled through the flesh of his jaw. Ruddy, brown eyes stared blandly at nothing in particular. A pair of expensive sunglasses perched on top of his head. Several times he glanced at his watch, most likely wondering what was keeping Jordana and Aryk.

Chase's assistant sat beside him, appearing to be just as bored and disinterested. She repeatedly tapped the end of her pen on the gleaming glass conference table.

Beside Chase's assistant there was an empty chair; that was Alexei's seat. Beside the empty seat, Isabel (or Bella, as he called her) was seated. She was his assistant, but she was so much more than that. She was his assistant, his advisor, his confidante...his lover. Tall and leggy with dark brown skin, deep brown eyes, and full lips, she had been his companion for half a century and counting. She didn't judge him for his lack of corporate ethics. She didn't judge him for his many perversions. She was there for him whenever he needed her, and had been for more than fifty years now.

As wonderful and supportive as she was, though, there was one setback: she had Tudhani blood flowing through her veins. Vampires from different clans were discouraged from forging romantic or sexual relationships with each other. They didn't want a mixing of clans. They wanted each clan to remain true and pure. While this was understandable to Alexei, he didn't give a damn what was encouraged or discouraged. Old traditions would not keep him away from the woman that he most enjoyed.

The conference room door opened. Jordana and Aryk entered the room, nodding a greeting at each person present. A third person trailed in behind them. She had spunky, plum purple hair pulled back into a severe ponytail. The way her features were molded gave her an exotic look. She was most likely of Middle Eastern descent. She had an athletic build and didn't have many curves in the breast or hip area. Her name was Jade. Alexei had met her once or twice; she was the head of security at Jordana's estate. She crossed the room and stood in the back corner, silent and unreadable.

Not making an effort to conceal his interest, Chase perked up in his seat and watched her every move.

Alexei glanced at Jordana and Aryk as he made his way to his chair.

Although Aryk was decked out in an expensive suit and standing in an extravagantly-furnished conference room, he still didn't look a day over twenty-five years old. His hair was bleached and spiked, his round eyes were the color of pure amber, and there were so many holes pierced into his face that it was a wonder the blood coursing through his body didn't leak out. A nervous tic worked his right eye. It wasn't a habit of his own; it was probably a habit of one of his victims that he temporarily had to tolerate.

Jordana, always regal and lavishly dressed, had her red hair pinned back in a neat chignon. She'd applied heavy eyeliner and eye shadow over her violet eyes. Her statuesque figure was packed tight into a gown the color of green olives.

There were two chairs at the head of the table. She claimed one and Aryk claimed the other.

"I am glad that you all were able to make it today," she greeted.

The greeting was returned.

"Aryk is my advisor, and he is the one who has summoned you here today," she continued. "He will now address you all."

Aryk gave her a curt nod before turning to face everyone seated at the table. "I'm not one for small talk, so I'll get right to the point. Early in the week I was informed that someone out there is killing our kind." He tilted his chair as far back as it would let him. Then, he linked his hands behind his head and propped his booted feet on the table. He sat that way for several minutes and basked in complete silence until one of the suited men at the table cleared his throat. "When I heard this news, the first thought that came to my mind was that it must be Iancu. He's such a relentless little warrior that I figured that he must have gotten back in the saddle. If someone is out there killing us, I thought that Iancu surely must be hunting us down and exterminating us. You see, I was almost fooled.

"But then I was reminded of a foiled attack that went down fifteen years ago. I had been assigned a mission of retrieving the new slayer. Due to factors beyond my control, that mission was unsuccessful and we were unable to capture her. To this day she has eluded us, and something in my *gut* tells me that she's the one who is hunting so many of us down."

With arched brows, Alexei turned his gaze down upon Bella's notes. Her neat script flowed from one line of the page to the next as she outlined what Aryk had just told them.

"If the slayer is still out there," Fiero said, "then our first priority should be to find her and subdue her."

"You're right," Aryk agreed. "That *is* our first priority. No one is to, under any circumstances, kill her or taint her, though. I want her to be alive and clean when she's brought here."

Chase was barely able to smother a wry chuckle with the back of his hand. *Who is this douche bag and since when has he been calling the shots?* he wondered. Aryk wasn't a clan leader and the only power that he could boast of was the fact that he had Jordana on a short leash.

"With that aside, I got to thinking after I heard that news. I got to thinking about our history and traditions. Traditionally, our kind has stayed in the shadows, blending in with humans and interacting with them when we know what they truly are to us. They're nothing but a meek herd of sheep and yet we are civil to them and treat them as our equals. I was just wondering...why is that?

"We are superior to humans in every way that counts, so why is it that we cower in the darkness? Why is it that we abide by *their* rules and follow *their* customs? Why can't we just be ourselves and live our lives the way we see fit?" His eyes scanned down the length of the conference room table.

"Are you serious?" Fiero asked him. "In the past, we have posed as humans and hidden our identities in order to maintain peace. If humans found out what we are, a lot of us would end up on lab tables being poked and prodded."

"Is that the only reason, Fiero?" Aryk demanded.

Fiero's expression turned stony at the blonde vampire's tone. "Humans outnumber us," he continued, gesturing with his hands as he spoke. "In the event that a war broke out, the humans would probably obliterate us."

Aryk hoisted a slender eyebrow in question. "So let's change that."

"*Change* that?" Alexei repeated.

"If our lack of population is our biggest weakness, then why not change it? We could easily double our population. Is that the only thing holding us back? Is there anything else?"

Chase and Fiero restlessly shifted in their seats.

Alexei was slowly shaking his head in disbelief. "You are seriously entertaining the thought of doubling our population?"

"That would be ludicrous," Fiero spat. "It would be more difficult to hide what we are. Each generation gets more and more detached from our traditions and practices. They are more and more difficult to restrain from shouting to the world that they are vampires. We can't possibly control a population that large."

"You aren't looking at the big picture," Aryk insisted, lowering his feet from the table.

"It is *you* who aren't looking at the big picture, man," Chase muttered. "We can barely keep our existence a secret as it is. If you throw in another five hundred thousand vampires into the mix, it's just going to create chaos."

Instead of continuing to address Aryk, Alexei turned to Jordana. "Is this what we were summoned for?"

"Aryk has some very refreshing ideas and a very unique point of view," she responded. "And he brings to attention some very valid points."

"He is speaking as if *he* is the clan leader of the Tudhani," Alexei said. "He is a subordinate. The only purpose for non-clan leaders being in attendance here is to take notes for their respective clan leaders. He has no place to speak to us as if he is on our level. It is quite remarkable, actually, that you allow him to speak so freely."

Jordana's jaw squared and while there was a gentle smile on her face, the mirth didn't quite reach her eyes. She leaned forward with her arms folded atop the conference table. "Would you not allow your beautiful assistant to speak freely if she so desired?"

Whipped or not, she still knew how to hit him where it hurt. He leaned back in his chair with the challenging look still in his eyes. "I don't support his cause," he said finally. "This coast, however, is your region, Jordana. If you support his cause, then you can do whatever you like. I refuse to enforce this ridiculousness in the Midwest."

"I feel the same way," Fiero announced.

"So do I," Chase concurred.

"I assume this meeting is over?" Alexei asked, signaling to Bella.

The assistants didn't wait for an affirmation before collectively shutting their briefcases.

"That is all for now," Jordana said in a quiet voice. "Feel free to stay in Los Angeles and enjoy all that it has to offer. You're even welcome to stay here, at my mansion, if you like." She stood from the table and escorted the clan leaders and their assistants out of the room.

For the first time since the meeting started, Jade moved from her corner and made as if to leave the room.

Aryk caught her by the elbow and deliberately drank in the scent of her. His ego had been badly bruised and he could use an ego booster about now. "If there's even the slightest chance of Iancu or the slayer hunting us down, I want our perimeter to be protected."

Several years ago, he and Jordana had entrusted her with being their head of security, mostly because the feisty girl wasn't even quite half a century yet and already seemed to have mastered a lot of her vampiric abilities. In addition to supernatural abilities, she possessed a vast knowledge of the martial arts.

On more than one occasion, Aryk had attempted to hit on her or flirt with her, but she always turned him down. He couldn't face the fact that the girl was way out of his league.

She tilted a sly smile at him, only looking at him out of the corner of her eye. As she reached up to stroke his jaw, a dragon tattoo peeked out from beneath the sleeve of her leather jacket.

He slid an arm around her tiny waist and pulled her against him. "Talk of putting humans in their place has made me extremely horny," he breathed into her ear.

She laughed and pushed away from him, giving his cheek a final pat. "If you're feeling horny, then you should summon Jordana," she advised, turning and disappearing out of the room.

Harsh sunlight blurred Alexei's vision as he exited the double doors of Jordana's mansion. He shaded a hand over his eyes, barely noticing that Bella was leading him forward by the elbow.

Their limousine pulled into the circular driveway and came to a halt at the end of the short walkway. Bella opened the back door to the limousine and all but shoved Alexei inside.

He collapsed onto the backseat and tilted his head back. "The sun still gets to me," he croaked, drawing an arm across his forehead. He didn't hesitate in peeling his suit jacket off and ripping open his white, button-down shirt. His skin was sizzling. "Rumor has it that Jordana can withstand sunlight for an hour without beginning to feel any sort of physical effect."

"It's just a rumor," Bella reasoned as she sat across from him with her back to the lowered limousine partition. "You haven't seen this for yourself."

"Still." He wrapped his arms around his torso. "Roll down a window. I'm burning."

After giving the limousine driver orders to drop them off at their hotel, she did as Alexei asked. Then she sat back and watched him.

"Even you seem to be unaffected by the sunlight," he said after a moment's thought.

"It takes a few minutes to affect me," she told him. "Then I start to feel nauseous and my head starts reeling."

"I don't know why I came out to Los Angeles," he mumbled in an agitated voice. "I prefer Chicago. Six months out of the year, the sun is covered by clouds."

"You came out to Los Angeles because you were under the impression that there were pertinent issues that needed to be talked about," she said flatly. "And instead, Jordana's boy toy just spouted his radical ideas."

He shook his head as the effects of the sunlight began to wear off. The surface of his skin cooled and he was able to think clearly. "Out of all of the clan leaders, Jordana is easily the cruelest and the most feared. It was unnerving to see her so quiet and reserved. I've never known her to be that way."

"And you don't agree with anything Aryk had to say?" Bella questioned with a raised brow.

Alexei shrugged his shoulders. "I agree with the fact that it should be our first priority to capture the slayer," he said. "If she is out there exterminating us, then *she* deserves to be exterminated. I *don't*, however, believe that we should go around populating the world with vampires so that we can wage war upon humans."

"When are you expecting to return to Chicago?" she questioned, deciding to change the subject.

"I'm not in a rush to return just yet. I think we should stay here for a couple of days."

She nodded her head and glanced away from him. Her dark hair spilled down her neck and behind her shoulders. His eyes trailed down to the turquoise dress suit that hugged her slender waist and toned thighs. She caught him staring at her and gave him a flirtatious smile.

He pushed himself off of the backseat and kneeled at her feet. "You might want to raise that partition," he told her as he parted her knees and slid between them.

"You didn't know she was the slayer, did you? Of course you wouldn't. You've turned your back on our world."

"I can't let you take her."

"You have no choice. There's nothing you can do to stop me."

Iancu stood before her, most of his body concealed by the large cloak that he wore. He held his sword at his side, protecting her and speaking on her behalf. After she'd staked Aryk in the back, Iancu had stretched an arm out to her and waited for her to grab it. Then, he had led the way towards the back door and they left the house.

That was the last time she'd seen that house. She had glanced back at it as she half-ran, half-stumbled behind the tall stranger with the tumbling mass of dark hair and chilling blue eyes.

Charlie sat on the couch in the main room of her cabin, dressed in a t-shirt and jeans with her hair piled on top of her head. *Back then, I didn't know what kind of monsters I was dealing with,* she thought, *but now I do. And I have vowed to kill each and every vampire that I come into contact with.*

Her grandfather's gnarled cane rested on the couch beside her. After escaping the house, she and Iancu returned to where he'd left her grandfather. The old man had been brutally dismembered and plucked apart, but Iancu had lifted the cane in his hands and given it to her. It was the only possession she owned from those days on Standing Rock Reservation.

There was a cracking noise outside of the cabin's window. In seconds, she was at the window with a shotgun in her hands. The noise had probably been made by one of the critters inhabiting the forest, but she wasn't the type of woman to take chances.

She inched towards the cabin's front door. She nudged the door open with the shotgun and stepped outside. Her eyes narrowed as she took in the surrounding wooded area. A dim moon was the only source of light available to her. She crept around her property warily. She stopped walking when she reached the window to the main room of the cabin. She sensed that a strong presence had been standing here only a couple of minutes ago. She knelt and touched the broken tree branch she'd carefully placed on the ground several weeks before. Her suspicions were confirmed. Someone had been spying on her.

Many slayers before her kept vampire allies in order to keep tabs on their world, but she didn't befriend them. She killed them. There was always the possibility that her allies would become her enemy. Snitches were called "snitches" for a reason. They would sell any information to the highest bidder and she couldn't risk having the address of her residence or any other personal information about her known to the general vampire public.

This method had its pros and cons. Vampires were in the dark about her. They didn't know who she was and they didn't know that she was hunting them. She was sure that they knew she existed because of the attempted abduction that went down fifteen years ago, but they didn't know where to start looking for her. That was a good thing. Because she never paused to talk to a vampire before killing him though, she was in the dark about a lot of their abilities. The majority of the vampires she came across were relatively young and limited in their abilities. She didn't know what she would do if she came across a vampire with a significant amount of power. She was also in the dark about any possible plans that could be in the works. If she knew more about them, she would be able to fight them off even more effectively. She would be able to customize some of her weapons in order to take advantage of their weaknesses.

Then there was the fact that she was out of touch with the Council. After that night on Standing Rock Reservation, she was sent from foster home to foster home. Her grandfather had known that she was special, but the foster families didn't know anything about her. Most of them didn't *care* to know anything about her, either. There was a council of slayers and their guardians, a worldwide council that offered support, vital information, and strategy in the fight against otherworldly creatures such as vampires, werewolves, and demons.

The Council was extremely secretive and as such, she didn't know the first thing about contacting them. The only reason she was even aware that they existed was because her grandfather, Jim, told her stories about them. He most likely had been in contact with the Council over the years. Even if she *had* the means to contact them, she wasn't sure that she would. She had grown used to working alone.

It irked her that someone had been trespassing on her property. The energy that the lurker had left behind suggested that he or she wasn't human and this information surprised her. How was it possible that a vampire knew where she lived? Had he lured her out, waited in the shadows as she fought off some of his vampire buddies, and followed her home? She didn't spend too much time wondering who had been watching her. She returned to the front door of the cabin and entered the main room. There was no time to waste. She had to suit up and get ready for the night's hunt.

She'd vowed to terminate every vampire that she'd come into contact with and she was making good on that vow. Last night's hunt had proved successful. She'd saved a young man from being turned into a late night snack. She'd managed to defeat two vampires without any major or minor injuries-not so much as a scratch. The only consequence that she'd had to pay was the nightmare that had afflicted her when she'd fallen into bed shortly after sunrise.

She was plagued and haunted by nightmares about those she had slain. She remembered the face of each and every vampire that she'd killed. She didn't feel guilt for taking their lives. She doubted that the vampire who took her grandfather's life had felt any form of guilt for his or her actions.

I don't feel guilty, but I am haunted, she thought now as she disrobed and walked about the cabin as naked as the day she was born. She wouldn't bathe or shower until after the hunt. Instead, she walked into what served as her bedroom and rifled through her closet. She had two closets. One closet contained her hunting attire. The second closet was where she kept her street clothes.

She liked the look of jeans, but she found that when it came to hunting, it was best to go for comfort before aesthetics. She reminded herself this as she tugged on a pair of skin-tight black pants. She pulled a tight, black tank top down over her torso and stepped into a pair of black combat boots.

She strapped a double holster around her chest and buckled another holster around her waist so that two pistols were placed at her back. A knife sheath wrapped around the inside of her thigh housed a sharp dagger carved out of wood. When she carried stakes with her, as she did tonight, she typically jammed them in the inside pockets of her ankle-length trench coat. She could only carry four of them at a time, because they were heavy and weighed her down. For this reason, she kept a bag of stakes in her car at all times.

She stood before her bedroom mirror as she shoved her arms into the sleeves of her coat. Her nostrils flared slightly as she envisioned hunting a vampire down, tackling him to the ground, and staking him in the heart. She was more than ready for tonight's hunt.

"I should not be doing this." Bridgette tilted her head to the side as her neck was ambushed by kisses. *"This cannot be happening. I am to be married, and soon."*

He caressed her honey blonde hair and allowed his fingers to rest on the creamy skin of her shoulder. In all fairness, she was right. There was no way that her parents would accept him into their family. After all, he was a lowly blacksmith. He couldn't offer her a majestic castle or land as far as her eyes could see. All he could offer her was his love and undivided adoration.

She pulled away from him and giggled, swatting away his wandering hands. "You are insatiable, do you know that?"

"You love it," he taunted her, and rolled onto his back. He stared up at a sky empty of clouds. They often frolicked in the meadow behind his shop, certain that no one would find them there. She would talk to him about the pressures of being a baron's daughter and he would talk to her about the pressures of being a lowly craftsman.

She would stroke his face lovingly and tell him, "If only I could be with you. I would gladly throw away my title for just that. To be your wife for always."

She would speak those words with such conviction that he never doubted her. He would echo the same sentiment to her, knowing that there was no way for them to be together.

"And then she found out that you were a monster."

The voice in his head was familiar and yet he wasn't sure where he had heard it before. All the same, he sat up straight in bed and ran a hand through his dark, waist-length hair. The sheets he'd had pulled up to his shoulders were now bunched at his stomach. His bare chest glistened with a fine sheen of sweat.

He was plagued by nightmares reminding him of his past and haunted by voices and faces that he didn't recognize. An image of Bridgette was etched into his memory. He would never forget the way she looked or the way she smelled. It had been hundreds of years since he had last seen her, and still he remembered how sweet her hair had smelled and how lovely her melodic voice had sounded.

He had never met another woman like her and was certain that he never *would* meet another woman like her. He had lost her because of what he was, and because of that, he refused to accept what he was.

He used to hunt down his own kind and kill them. He was frustrated with the fact that innocent people were dying because of the lust that his people had for blood. For hundreds of years he fought for the sake of good, but nothing seemed to change. In those couple hundred years, he grew weary of fighting. He changed a lot about his life after that night on Standing Rock Reservation.

He studied business management and acquired several companies. Instead of living life as his brethren did, sleeping by day and hunting at night, he lived as most humans did. He worked during the day and slept at night. It was easy for him to work during daylight hours because most of his work was done from his modest, two-bedroom apartment. He usually didn't have to step one foot out into the sunlight to achieve his day's work.

He didn't have much of a social life, but over the years he had discovered that having a thriving social life only complicated matters in the long run. He was a vampire and as such, having friends meant having to watch friends grow old and die. Having friends meant having to explain why he never aged. Having friends meant having to fulfill certain obligations. All of that meant making his life more difficult than it had to be.

If at one time or another he longed for a companion, he was certain that he could reach out to one of his kind, but he never saw that happening. He detested what he was and he detested all of the other nightwalkers that fed on the blood of innocents. If he were face-to-face with another one of his kind, chances were that he would kill on sight rather than slap the man a high-five and invite him out for drinks.

There were only five hundred thousand vampires in the world (give or take), and for that Iancu was thankful. He hadn't encountered a fellow vampire in ten years and hopefully wouldn't bump into one for several more decades to come.

He knew vampires when he came across them. He could either smell the pure blood on their breath or the tainted blood pumping through their veins.

He stood at the glass balcony doors in the living room, staring out into the infinite, dark night. Even at this late hour, people were milling about below and unbeknownst to them, monsters awaited in the shadows for the moment when they were most vulnerable. Ignorance truly was bliss.

He turned his back to the glass balcony doors and was greeted with a somber, sparsely-furnished living room. The only decoration that the room boasted was a pair of crossed swords mounted on the wall. The Spartan look was a motif for the entire apartment. He had several apartments and a couple of houses spread across the United States and Europe. All of them were furnished minimally. He didn't crave material things unless they were a necessity.

His life was dreary and he knew it. Day in and day out he worked, keeping mostly to himself, mostly to his empty apartment. He never felt happy and rarely laughed or smiled. He was lonely and he knew it, but it was a fact that he struggled to ignore.

When he walked the streets at night, women would attempt to strike up a conversation, but he couldn't bring himself to actually take one to his bed. The last time he *had* taken a woman to his bed was more than a century ago. The only reason he'd taken her to bed was because she'd vaguely resembled Bridgette. Instead of calling the name of the woman lying beneath him, he'd shouted Bridgette's name in the throes of passion. Insulted, the woman underneath him had shoved him off of her and stormed out of his chambers.

His body ached for the touch of a woman and yet he threw himself into his work to the point of obsession. He worked off his frustrations in the gym located in the courtyard of his apartment complex. Late at night if he couldn't sleep, he would sit on a lawn chair on his balcony and strum the strings of one of his guitars while the wind combed through his hair.

Seconds passed, minutes elapsed, and hours went by, forming themselves into the pattern of a day. Days would go by, and weeks, pulling together to become months. Iancu's life grew to be a monotonous routine, one day after another, working in the daylight hours and crooning to the tune of his own music at night.

He'd been walking the streets the previous night and had witnessed the attack on the college boy near the Los Angeles city limits. Hidden in the shadows of night, he'd watched as the cloaked woman had fallen from the sky as it were and onto the idling Ford Explorer. She'd taken the Arati vampires down without so much as a thought and drove off in the victim's car, no doubt taking the traumatized boy to safety.

As recently as fifteen years ago, he had been that warrior, vowing to save the innocents of the world from immortals. The task proved to be a more difficult one than he had at first thought. He grew cynical. Good didn't always prevail over evil, and he was one man-or one immortal, rather-fighting the good fight. How much good could one immortal accomplish? What good would it do for him to kill one immortal if hundreds more were being made in that exact moment?

He couldn't explain the feeling that coursed through him when he saw the female warrior battling the two vampires, though. Something in him awakened and he longed to be the one driving the stake into their dead hearts. He followed her to a gas station, watched her leave the car, and followed her to her place of residence half an hour away.

He'd watched her enter the secluded cabin and had peered through the windows at her. She'd showered, put on a robe, and padded to the main room of the cabin where she settled onto the couch with a book in her hand.

She was a beautiful woman with glossy dark hair and she had skin the color of caramel. After watching her for an hour, he returned home to his empty apartment.

Earlier tonight, he'd visited her cabin again. He'd followed her as she hunted down several vampires and ended their sinful lives. When it was close to sunrise, she headed back to her cabin where she dropped into bed, still wearing her bloody hunting attire. Ever since, he'd been thinking about his life and whether or not he was truly living the way he wanted to. He was sure that the woman he'd been spying on was human, and she was risking her life to save others. He was a vampire, equipped with many abilities that he could use to his advantage, and yet he threw himself into his work. He was being selfish, really.

He paced the length of the living room and moved over to the fireplace. He was six-foot-three, but still had to stand on tip-toe to dismount the crossed swords from the wall. He leaned one sword against the wall and wrapped his left hand around the jeweled handle of the other sword.

The heavy steel felt good in his hands. He gripped the sword's handle in both hands and wielded the massive blade to and fro. Even though he hadn't handled the weapon in a long time, he hadn't forgotten how to use it.

Clad only in a pair of pajama pants, he turned this way and that with the sword in his hands. He sliced through the air with the weapon, unaware that a smile had carved its way onto his face. This was what his life was missing. This was what he needed on some level.

Try as he might, he couldn't deny what he was. The more he tried to live his life as a human, the clearer it was to him that he *wasn't* a human being. He was an immortal. As much as he wished that he could change that, he couldn't. He never would be a human again. The least that he could do was to make sure that no one else's humanity was stolen from them.

With a sigh, he mounted both of the swords on the wall above the fireplace where they belonged. A polished black guitar leaned against the wall near the balcony doors. He picked it up, pulled the sliding glass door open, and stepped out onto the balcony. He closed the door at his back. Then, he lowered into a forest green lounge chair. He temporarily laid the guitar across his lap so that he could secure his hair into a long, thick ponytail that draped down his back before recapturing the instrument in his arms. He closed his eyes and tilted his head back as he strummed the strings of the acoustic instrument.

In all his centuries of living, if he were asked what one thing he couldn't live without, his response would probably be *music*. Music was therapy for him. It soothed him to his very core. It was the one thing that could enrage, seduce, intrigue, and empower people of all races, religions, nationalities, genders, and age groups.

As his fingers gently plucked the strings of the guitar, memories sparked, illuminated, and died before his eyes.

"Vampires are condemned for all of eternity," Jordana had told him once while staring across a fire at him. "That is why we don't die of old age. That is why we have no reflections, no souls. We're refused true happiness. We're refused admittance through heaven's pearly gates. God's back is turned to us for all time.

"And still, some of my kind continues to remain true to Him. Still, they pray to Him, as if He is listening. He is not listening, because of what our lords have done in the past. In most of the tales in the Bible, God is forgiving, but we have yet to experience His forgiveness." Her voice turned bitter and the cold look in her eyes grew frostier.

The fire died down and darkness wrapped around them. She raised a hand with all of her fingers spread and instantaneously, the fire was rejuvenated. "And then there was light," she said softly, drawing her knees up to her chest and resting her chin between them. She proceeded to tell him about a prophecy that was sacred to her people. She closed her eyes and recited these words:

"The One who brings light
Shall turn dark
And against her and her maker
Two militias will stand,
One army formed for the sake of good
And the other formed for the sake of malevolence...
Greed.
Humans and immortals alike will fall
At the hands of the Light Bringer."

She stopped there and met his gaze over the flickering flames.

"What does it mean?" he asked her.

"I don't know," she admitted, shrugging. "No one does, really. It has been analyzed time and time again, and still no one knows exactly what it means. It was written by the hand of Lord Vlad, so it is held sacred and dear to my people. It is thought that these words predict what will happen in the future. We'd probably have a better idea of what it means if the parchment that it was written on wasn't torn."

He nodded in thought, not really knowing what to say.

"Each person interprets the prophecy differently. Personally, I think that some time in the future, there is going to be a devastating war that will kill both man and vampire. It will be the cliché battle between good and evil, of course." She tossed her lustrous hair over one shoulder and resettled her chin between her knees. "The torn half of the prophecy probably holds the result of that battle...it probably tells us who wins."

The day after they'd had that talk, she disappeared. It would be a couple hundred more years before he saw her again. He returned to blacksmithing and romancing Bridgette.

He didn't have the heart to bite her, and he had many opportunities to. It would be more than he could ever hope for, to have her by his side for all of eternity. At the same time, though, he didn't want to bestow upon her the same *curse he'd been handed. It would have been wise for him to sever all ties with her, but he found himself incapable of distancing himself from her. He continued to sneak off with her, continued to have secret meetings with her, until one night in particular.*

Several months after his transformation, he held the hunger at bay for many nights. He was sickened at the thought of drinking blood. The thirst caught up to him, though, and he ravaged the commoner nearest him.

Bridgette dropped by without a chaperone; she'd intended on giving him a surprise visit. It was she who received a surprise that night. She entered his shop and was greeted with the sight of him kneeling on the floor beside the corpse of one of her neighbors.

Iancu's eyes snapped open. Instead of seeing the vast skyline of Los Angeles, though, he saw the expression that had taken over Bridgette's face.

"I-I wanted to surprise you," she said with her hands flying up to cover her mouth. She backed out of the shop.

Iancu jumped to his feet. "This is not what it appears to be," he insisted.

She turned on her heel and made as if to run from him, but he moved with superhuman speed and clamped strong fingers around her upper arm. "Unhand me!" she yelled.

"You must let me explain."

"I must do nothing," she told him in a livid tone he'd never heard her use.

His grip around her arm tightened.

"I won't let you walk away from me," Iancu whispered aloud now, as he played his guitar.

"You have no choice but to let me walk away from you." Even after seeing him beside a bloodied body, she was brave enough to stand up to him and determined to get away from him.

His blue eyes turned icy and started to glow. "You are why I became this."

"What?"

"You are why I am what I am," Iancu said softly with the California breeze caressing strands of his dark hair that had escaped his ponytail. His grip on the guitar in his lap tightened. Red tears gathered at the corners of his eyes and escaped to the hills of his cheeks.

"You are blaming me for the bloodbath in there?" She struggled to free herself from his grasp and shrieked, "Unhand me!"

"I loved you so much...I wanted to be with you forever."

"I am to marry another."

"You are to marry me and only me."

"Did you drink too much ale? You are not sounding quite right."

He pulled her against him and forced her hands behind her back.

Her eyes widened when she saw his luminous cerulean blue eyes.

He saw the look in her eyes and it broke his heart. He abruptly released her and dropped to his knees. She didn't hesitate; she turned and fled.

His chest heaved as he pressed his hands flat against the dirty ground. "Don't run away from me," he whispered in a hushed voice. He spat on the ground and rose to his full height, staring hard in the direction she had run.

He now rose to his feet and stared out over the balcony. The guitar dangled at his side, but the weight of it didn't register to him. "Don't run away from me!" he shouted out into the night, tilting his head back and baying at the moon. The guitar dropped out of his grasp and thudded on the concrete.

He could still smell her; he could still sense her heartbeat. She was still running, but hadn't gotten far. He took off after her, through the town and into the forest. Bare branches slashed and tore at his arms. He didn't feel the pain from the various welts. The only pain that he felt was under his skin, beneath his chest, where the broken shards of his heart remained.

He pumped his arms as he ran, avoiding thick foliage. He was a hunter now. Hunting was what he did. She could have had a week-long advantage over him and he would still find her, still catch up to her.

"I did catch up to her," he said now, gripping the balcony rail so tightly that his palms bled. "I caught up to her and I drank from her. I drank so much that I killed her."

He saw himself bring her down in the forest.

She pushed against him and screamed for mercy. When she realized that he wasn't going to back down, she'd started reciting prayers.

"Lord, help me." He ran his hands over his hair and turned his back on the city lights.

He considered himself a warrior, a protector of all that was good, but he was by no means a saint or an angel. He'd committed many sins over the course of his life. Even though he knew that his people were said to be overlooked by the Creator, he still sought redemption for all of the wrong he'd done.

A loud knock sounded on the door to his apartment, bringing him back to the present. He bent at the waist, retrieved his guitar, and stepped into his apartment. After closing the sliding balcony door, he laid the guitar on the living room couch and answered the door.

Neil Gieryng breezed past him, dressed in a lilac-colored dress shirt, khakis, and dress shoes. "We've got a problem."

It had been more than ten years since Iancu had seen Neil, so it took a moment for him to wipe the stunned look from his face.

Neil turned and saw his friend's expression of shock. "Oh...hi, by the way. Long time no see."

"I haven't seen you in-"

"Ten years, give or take, I know." His light brown hair was cut short and shaped with the assistance of hair gel. He'd been twenty-seven when he was turned Toltec half a century ago. He'd had a tough time accepting what he had become. It was a difficult time that Iancu had helped him through and for that, he would forever be grateful.

They'd been friends in the past, but when Iancu had turned his back on his kind, he'd turned his back on them all. He hadn't been selective, hadn't taken time to sort through the vampires that he could tolerate and the vampires that he couldn't.

"I know you've gone into seclusion and all of that," Neil went on, "but we've got a major problem on our hands."

"We?" Iancu closed the door to his apartment and joined his old friend in the living room.

"Aryk is tired of us having to hide our identity."

"*This* sounds promising," Iancu muttered. He sat on the couch beside his guitar while his friend remained standing.

"He has issued orders for all of the clans in the area to feast like kings over the next few months. He has told them to feast well, but to kill no one."

"I don't understand."

Neil sighed and took a seat in the armchair. He rested his elbows on the tops of his knees. "He's trying to increase our population."

A muscle in Iancu's jaw twitched. "Come again?"

"You've grown slow in the past decade."

"Why is he trying to increase the population?"

"I don't have full details yet, but word is that he wants to increase the population so that he can declare war against humans and force them into submission."

Iancu's brows shot up. "Is he serious?"

"As serious as cancer, Iancu. Look." Neil made a steeple with his fingers and closed his eyes for a couple of seconds. "I know that you don't want to be associated with us. I know you've got this whole self-hating, tragic hero thing going on, but you've got to get back into the game. I don't know exactly what's going on, but whatever it is, it's not good."

"I don't hunt anymore." Iancu lifted his battered guitar onto his lap and played a few chords.

Neil sat back in his chair. His hazel eyes assessed his old friend with concern. "I know that, but if you don't get back in the game, then humans will become the minority. Once that happens, Aryk will go national and from that point, he'd be able to take over the world."

"There are a lot of other great vampire hunters," Iancu mumbled tiredly. "I'm not the only one."

"You're the oldest one, and you're the only one that *I* would trust...especially with a matter as sensitive as this."

The two men sized each other up without speaking. Neil shook his head slowly and chuckled to himself. "I should have known that you wouldn't come through."

"I don't have time for this, Neil."

"Look around you, man. All you *have* is time. Ten *years*, man. Ten years and I hear nothing from you. You don't come around and you change addresses so often that no one can keep up with you..." Neil threw his hands up in the air in exasperation. "We were friends, or at least, I thought we were. You dropped off the face of the earth without warning."

"I don't have to explain my actions," Iancu said softly, strumming the strings of his guitar.

Neil stood on his feet and brushed off his pants. "I'm wasting my time here."

"That is something that we can agree on."`

Uttering a sound of disgust, Neil escorted himself out of the apartment, making sure to slam the door behind him.

Iancu continued playing his instrument, shutting his eyes to the world.

"Come on! I mean, you're legendary, right? You're Iancu, defender of good, extinguisher of evil and all that jazz, right? Tell me that you can do better than that.

"What are you going to do? Are you going to cut me with your little butter knife, there? What...you haven't heard of guns?

"You can swear to God all you like, Iancu. You know why? Because He's not listening. Oh, no. He's turned a deaf ear onto us, because we're despicable. We're not worthy of His love."

Iancu opened his eyes and blinked rapidly. He was no longer a part of that world. He lived as a human now. He lived an ordinary life and worked with ordinary people.

"You have no choice. There's nothing you can do to stop me."

The fingers of his left hand trembled on the guitar strings as he recalled Aryk's taunting remarks. He licked his lips and tried to shake the words out of his head.

"You don't use your powers and all you have for a weapon is that dinky little sword."

"Fuck you," he whispered to the empty living room. Every muscle in his body tensed and his back went rigid. Anger flashed in his eyes and they began to shimmer with the shine of a brand new coin.

"You have no chance at beating me. Making an attempt would be begging me to take your life."

"We'll see about that," Iancu said, standing and furiously slamming his guitar into the nearest wall. His eyes illuminated and his fangs lowered. It was time to hunt.

CHAPTER FOUR

The rankness of sewage no longer affected Fiero Giovanni. He was accustomed to living in locations that were less than ideal. His boots splashed through the shallow, filthy water. He trudged until he found his brethren, fellow Vikara, clustered in one of the sewer mains chattering excessively with their eyes glittering.

His own gray eyes shimmered until they were a radiant silver color. He hovered out of the circle for several moments, shamelessly eavesdropping on their conversation. It wasn't an act of rudeness; it was only the way of his kind.

There were two things that the Vikara were known for: their appearance and their tendency to stumble upon crucial information that was often sold to those that were willing to pay the highest price for it.

His subjects were currently talking about nothing other than trivial matters, so he stepped forward and cleared his throat.

A crowd of bald heads swiveled around in his direction. There was nothing on his person to suggest that he wasn't just another one of them, a newly transformed Vikara who'd intruded on their conversation. This much was apparent by the way that they openly stared at him, a couple of them with scowls on their faces.

A ghost of a smile twisted Fiero's lips as he walked forward. He didn't walk so much as he glided over the ground.

Their mouths dropped open as they realized that he was an elder. Only elders had the ability to move with so much grace and ease.

"I am Fiero," he announced once the sea of faces parted to allow him within their circle. "I come from New York City, where I rule as the leader of our clan.

"I have recently attended a conference with fellow clan leaders and I come with news of that conference."

The only sounds that were audible when he wasn't speaking were the sounds of moving water and idling rodents. The glimmering eyes of his audience stood out against the dark, dank sewer.

"I am sure you all know Jordana well, for she is the clan leader who rules over this region. She and her lover were the ones that summoned the conference, and they spoke of dastardly plans to increase our population.

"They intend to eventually wage war on humans so that we no longer have to live in hiding."

An explosion of babbling ensued and Fiero allowed them to rant for a short period of time. A wave of excitement rushed over all of them at the possibility of no longer having to reside in isolated filth.

Fiero sighed and clapped his hands to regain their attention. "I know that it sounds promising," he began, "but Jordana and her lover don't have our best interests in mind. They are on an endless quest for power and won't stop until the world is theirs. We cannot allow them to use us as pawns and then discard us when we are no longer needed. I came here to talk to you all to relay this information to you.

"You are all my subjects, yes, because I am the leader of the Vikara, but you are also my brethren. I do not wish to see harm come to any of you. I fear that if you do join sides with Jordana and Aryk, grave circumstances will befall you."

The chatter became much more subdued as they considered his words.

Fiero blended into the crowd and moved amongst them, coming to stop before a female Vikara. Her gender was lost in her appearance because she had no hair and a concave chest, but he pressed a hand to the top of her head and closed his eyes in concentration. A whisper of a smile touched his mouth. "Your name is Sarah," he said in a hushed voice.

"You were turned eleven years ago. You left behind a son and a daughter and you haven't seen them since you were turned." His eyes fluttered open and he searched her bland, nondescript eyes. "You do not return to them because you fear how they will react to your appearance."

She bowed her head to hide her tears and the shame that accompanied them.

He swept her into an embrace, his hand gliding over the surface of the back of her head. His hand moved as if it were stroking a long, lustrous mane of hair. He pulled back from her and settled his hands onto both of her shoulders. "We are marked as the least attractive of the clans, it's true. That is something that I cannot change. However, your spirit is beautiful and within it shines a light much brighter than your eyes are shining now.

"You were a good mother and a good person. You still are both, to suffer the pain that you're suffering. You want to go to them, your children. You want to visit them and play with them and let them know that you're all right, but instead you suffer in isolation. It takes a woman of great strength and character to commit to something like that." With those last words, he moved away from her.

He came to stand before a tall brute of a vampire with a horribly disfigured face. His nose looked like a misshapen lump of clay and there were deep gashes in the flesh of his swollen lips. Fiero clamped a hand around the juggernaut's forearm. "You're still going through the transformation," the clan leader said knowingly. "You were attacked last night in your backyard. You heard strange noises and thought that it was the neighbor's dog. And you went to investigate." He stopped here and smiled.

"Tsk, tsk, tsk, John," he reprimanded. "You know not to investigate strange sounds, don't you?"

The brute's shoulders lifted defensively as he ducked his chin to his chest.

Fiero gave the man a pat on the shoulder. "If you didn't know then, you *do* know now." He moved towards the center of the circle and raised his hands into the air. "I hope the information that I've given you tonight was helpful and I do hope that you will all continue to do your best to maintain the traditions that were set up in order to protect the well-being of our species. If anyone has questions, now is the time to ask them. I won't be in town for long."

At least twenty hands were thrown into the air. One of those hands belonged to a tall, lanky vampire with spiky blonde hair and an array of holes pierced into his face. With sparkling amber eyes, he approached the center of the circle. He came to stand before Fiero with a smug grin on his face.

Fiero's mouth set into a grim line. "What business do you have here, Aryk?"

The blonde vampire sniffed haughtily, glancing over his shoulder at the many pairs of silver eyes focused in his direction. "If we could have a moment alone, I would be happy to answer that question."

The Vikara didn't have to be told. They dispersed at once, not bothering to mask their excitement as they chattered to each other.

Aryk sniffed the air. His nose wrinkled in disgust. "This is where you guys *live*?"

"We make do with what we have," Fiero responded.

"And you're never angry over the fact that you have to live in these dumps?" Aryk asked, turning his back to Fiero so that he could inspect his surroundings. The only calming effect was the consistent sound of running water. There weren't many sources of light in the place and it reeked of garbage and decay. He couldn't imagine for the life of him living in such a hellhole.

"I have made peace with what I've had to endure." Fiero gestured around him.

The blonde vampire shook his head in pity. "I feel sorry for you guys, I really do. Not only do you have to walk throughout the rest of your lives as ugly, grotesquely disfigured creatures, but you have to subject yourself to a depressing lifestyle such as this. It's just not fair."

"*Life* isn't fair," Fiero said, losing his patience with his guest. "I know why we 'subject' ourselves to this 'lifestyle,' but what has brought you down here?"

Aryk shrugged. "I just wanted to check out your digs for myself," he answered, turning to face the Vikara clan leader. "I must admit that I'm surprised you didn't support me at the meeting earlier. I thought that if any of the clan leaders were to agree with me, it would be you. After all, my plan would allow for the Vikara to live on the surface, among their other brethren, out of the darkness and into the light. They would be able to live a life in which they aren't judged for their appearance. As their leader, don't you want that for them?"

"Of *course* I'd like for them to have that kind of life," Fiero said fiercely through clenched teeth. "We have waited and are still waiting for the day when we can walk the surface and live just as everyone else does."

"Then why aren't you on my side?" Aryk demanded, spreading his arms out in frustration. "If that is truly what you want for the members of your clan, then why did you speak out against me at the meeting?"

"I'm not on your side because your plan is flawed. There is no logic to it at all and in the end, it won't benefit the Vikara. It won't benefit any of our clans. Your plan will end up *harming* us all."

Aryk shoved his hands into the pockets of his slacks to keep from strangling the clan leader. "My plan is foolproof," he insisted.

"*Foolish*, is what it is," Fiero spat, smoothing a hand over his shiny, bald head. "If we gained in numbers as excessively as you're proposing, then the clans will be more difficult to control. We hardly have a handle on them now."

"Well, I think that you should rethink your position." Aryk took a step forward and closed the distance between the two of them.

Fiero suspiciously narrowed his eyes but he didn't take a step backward. "You will never have my support, Aryk, not with a plan this reckless."

"You sure about that?" the other vampire questioned, his eyes glinting dangerously.

Fiero held his ground. "I'm positive."

"I'm very sorry to hear that," Aryk said softy. Shadows danced across his face as his eyes began to glow. He closed his eyes for the briefest moment and waved his hand in front of the clan leader's face.

Fiero's legs were paralyzed and he couldn't move. He didn't know why this shocked him. Aryk was sired by Jordana and Jordana was the oldest vampire known to their kind. In addition to that, Aryk was older than he was. Most likely in the event of his sire's death, Aryk would become the new Tudhani clan leader...which was a thought that frightened Fiero down to the marrow of his bones. Any clan with Aryk as their leader was doomed.

As the blonde vampire stood before Fiero with his eyes closed, his form began to change. His hair darkened and his cheekbones became more prominent. With his eyes still closed, he tilted his head back and ripped his expensive, silk button-down shirt from his chest. Muscles rippled beneath the surface of his skin.

Horror gripped Fiero. Still, he forced himself to watch the grisly transformation from gangly, pierced punk to suave, distinguished gentleman with a well-sculptured face boasting Italian influence.

Once the metamorphosis was complete, Fiero was granted the capability of movement. He didn't waste time in circling around Aryk now that he was released from the hold that the other vampire had on him. He wanted to reach out and touch the other vampire but he didn't dare. He was looking at his own face, the face that he'd had before he was bitten by a Vikara clan leader who had claimed him as his personal slave. He was staring into a face that he hadn't seen in hundreds of years.

"Don't you miss it?" Aryk asked in what used to be Fiero's voice.

Fiero brought a hand up to touch his throat and lips. He couldn't deal with the memories of his past life, his human life. He forced those memories into a dark, secluded corner of his mind that he never took the time to nurture. The memories that he locked away often resurfaced as delusions and nightmares.

As a clan leader, he had to be a pillar of strength. The members of his clan were appalled to find out that they would look like disfigured monsters for the rest of their years. Many of them committed suicide, deliberately baking themselves beneath the rays of the sun after finding out what they were. He would be lying if he said that he'd never thought about committing suicide. He'd considered ending his life more than once. He told his clan members that each day was a little bit easier, that they were better off alive. He told them a lot of bullshit that he didn't necessarily believe, a bunch of hogwash that they all forced themselves to believe because they had been human once. As humans, they'd learned about the power of hope and faith.

His hope had died a long time ago and his faith was no longer existent. He used to believe that he had a purpose in this world, but he no longer had any sense of guidance. He no longer felt that he had a predestined fate, other than that of being the leader of the Vikara.

Aryk had asked him whether or not he got angry. Of *course* he got angry. The only blessing in being a Vikara was the fact that he had no reflection he had to stare at on a daily basis. Others were cursed to see what he looked like, but he didn't have to look at himself at all. He told others that he'd adjusted to what he had transformed into, but that was a lie. There was no getting used to being a Vikara. There was no adjusting to having to live in dirty, filthy sewers where rodents frolicked. He *hated* his life. He hated having no one to share his life with. He hated not being able to walk the streets without fearing that a human would see him and shit his or her pants.

Seeing Aryk wearing his human face brought to surface a sadness that he had tried painstakingly hard to conceal.

Aryk brandished his new face, running slender fingers over the smooth planes of his cheeks. "You used to be quite a looker, eh, Fiero?" He stood behind the trembling Vikara leader and whispered, "Don't you miss having this face? You used to be *so* beautiful. I don't have to have a mirror to know how beautiful you were. I can feel it, just running my hands over my cheeks, my nose, and my jaw. How could you *not* miss looking like this?"

Blood tears glistened in Fiero's eyes.

"You want to live on the surface," Aryk continued. "You want to be able to walk amongst humans and other vampires without feeling self-conscious.

"We all feel self-conscious in one way or another. You, for your hideous appearance of course, and me...I feel as if everyone looks at me and sees nothing but Jordana's overzealous lover." He chuckled and drew a hand across his mouth, shrugging his shoulders. "When people look at me, they don't see a powerful vampire. They see Jordana's *boyfriend*, Jordana's *lover*, Jordana's...*pet*."

Fiero blinked his eyes rapidly to keep the tears from falling. He wasn't even listening to Aryk's rant anymore. He was fighting hard to keep from getting on his own soapbox and shouting to the world how much he hated his life.

"I'll admit," Aryk said slowly as he allowed for the dark hair to brighten back to his trademark blonde locks, "when I first came here I was intent on killing you.

"You made me look like a fool back at that meeting and I wanted retribution for that. I wanted to...I don't know, behead you or impale you. Something colorful like that." He paused and tilted his head to the side. "However, I feel that I would be doing you a favor if I did that."

Fiero didn't respond.

"Yes, I'd be granting you a favor if I killed you because unless I'm wrong, there are many days and nights that you wish you had the balls to kill yourself. You feign this bravado but I see right through it, brother. You're not *at peace* with what you are. You *hate* what you are, and come on-who wouldn't?" Aryk moved backwards into the shadows at a rapid speed, but his voice still echoed through the depths of the dark sewers. "Once you see how successful my plan will be, you will regret the fact that you weren't a part of it."

The moment that he was sure Aryk was gone, Fiero dropped to his knees and let the tears come.

Iancu crouched on the rooftop of an apartment building with his chin cupped in his hand as he watched the scene below unfold.

The hooded female warrior he'd observed the night before was battling three new vampires, landing well-executed kicks and punches when she didn't have the opportunity to send a stake through one of their chests.

The thoughts and voices of people in the vicinity trailed through his head. A resident of the apartment beneath him wondered if he'd gained a couple of pounds in the past few weeks while his teenage daughter was writing in her diary about the night she lost her virginity. Hundreds of jumbled words circled around his head until he blocked them out and focused on the situation at hand.

She hadn't killed one vampire yet, but she was still holding her own. He didn't want to jump into her fight unnecessarily. If she needed his assistance, then he would jump to action, but if she took care of these punks herself, then he would remain in the shadows.

She was resourceful and efficient in battle. She wasted no moves. By the look of her motions, she'd had self-defense classes and a great deal of martial arts training. She was lethal and incredibly entertaining to watch.

He watched as she extended both arms outward. In each hand, she held a sharply-pointed stake. Each stake hit their target, and the opponents who'd been flanking her sides evaporated into the night air.

The third vampire darted away, clearly intimidated by her. He had made the fatal mistake of underestimating her and for that, he would most likely pay dearly.

They fought for several minutes and neither one had an advantage over the other. Without meaning to, Iancu tapped into her thoughts.

If I could just get him flat on his back, I could do him in, she was thinking as she dodged a punch. *Oh, this kill would be divine.*

The contents of her thoughts made him cringe. He didn't know why; he shared her opinion of vampires. They should be killed and done away with. Perhaps it was the cold manner in which she'd thought the words or perhaps it was the chilling, determined look on her face.

The vampire got her in a headlock and held on tight. She clawed at the beast's arms, but he didn't react to the sensation of her nails digging into his flesh. He laughed maniacally and dragged her around the empty alley, lifting her into his arms and raising her over his head as he might a trophy.

That's my cue, Iancu thought, and jumped onto the apartment building's ledge. He spread his arms wide and leapt off the ledge. Air rushed at him from below.

He landed on booted feet just as the vampire tossed the warrior's body towards a dented, rusty green dumpster. He had the nerve to throw his head back and chuckle at his victory.

Iancu tapped him lightly on the shoulder.

The strawberry-blonde haired newbie turned, still chuckling. "Wow, dude," he exclaimed, and whooped with an even more intense laughter. "Someone should have called you and told you that the eighties were over." He was bold enough to lift a couple strands of Iancu's hair.

Iancu stood before him with an unreadable expression on his face.

"I mean...I've got this stylist," the kid rambled on. "He works wonders with a pair of scissors. You look like you haven't cut your hair in ages, man. Your hair takes me back to the days when I listened to Motley Crüe. Did you ever listen to them? Motley Crüe? And what's with the getup?"

Iancu's hand slipped beneath his long coat. When his hand emerged, it was gripping the hilt of his sword. Before the kid could say another word, he beheaded him. The kid's blood dribbled down the length of the sword he still held in the air. He waited patiently for the kid to turn to dust. Then, he proceeded to use the dead vampire's shirt to wipe the blade of his sword clean.

Applause sounded at his back as he sheathed his sword.

Without glancing over his shoulder, he knew that the cloaked and hooded warrior was clapping her hands at him.

"That was my kill," she told him. "You stole my kill."

"I'll interpret that as, 'Thank you for saving my life,'" he responded coolly.

"You didn't save my life," she spat, circling around to face him. "I would have gotten back up and taken care of him myself..." Her last words died in her mouth.

He hoisted an eyebrow at her in askance.

"You're him," she breathed softly.

He tried to peer beyond the darkness that her hood provided, but doing so was impossible.

"I can't believe it. You haven't aged a day. You look exactly as I remembered."

He turned as if to leave, but she reached out and grabbed his wrist. He arched a frosty look at her. "Release me and never grab me like that again."

"I'm sorry," she apologized quickly, and as she did so, she swept the hood back to reveal her face.

He recognized her immediately.

"What's your name? My name's Charlie Strong Wolf and this is my grandpa, Jim." She'd been so young, only ten years old.

"Just take care of little Charlie for me," her grandfather had told him minutes before his demise. *"She's special."*

She stood before him with strands of sun-streaked hair blowing across her face. The expression on her face darkened. He tried to read her thoughts, but found that he couldn't. She withdrew something from her cloak, stared at it for awhile, and caressed the smoothness of it. It was a stake.

She looked up at him again, but this time her eyes weren't welcoming or warm with recognition. "You haven't aged a day," she repeated in a soft voice.

He returned her gaze and awaited her next actions.

"Why haven't you aged in fifteen years?" she asked him outright.

"You already know the answer to that question," he told her.

She nodded her head, still stroking the smooth piece of wood. "That I do."

"So are you going to try to kill me now?" He couldn't keep the grin from appearing on his face.

"It's nice to know that you take me seriously."

"It's not that I don't," he said. "I saw your work last night. You were quick and effective. You were excellent, really. It was very entertaining to watch the way you handled those two."

Her eyes narrowed into slits. "You were there?"

"I stumbled upon the situation and waited to make sure you could handle yourself."

"And you saw that I could."

"I did."

"The night that you..." She stopped herself, thought about the words that she wanted to say, and made another attempt at getting the sentence out. "The first night we met, things were pretty intense. You were gone so fast that I never got a chance to thank you."

"I knew that you were grateful."

She tilted her head to the side. "I still have nightmares about that night. I still...think about it."

"So do I."

"I kind of thought that you would take me with you," she confessed, her voice growing quieter with each word she spoke. "I mean, since I had no family and all, I thought that you would take care of me from that point on. I never even considered that I'd be going to a foster home."

He was shocked at her words, but the shock didn't show through his facial expression. "I didn't know the first thing about raising kids," he said in his own defense. "There was no way that I could raise a kid, knowing..."

She searched his eyes even after his sentence trailed off. "Knowing what you are?" she finished for him.

He blinked rapidly a couple of times and turned his head. "They were what killed your family. I knew that I was the last person who should take care of you. Once you found out what I was..." He cleared his throat. "You were probably better off at the foster home than you would have been with me."

She looked down at the cracked alley street beneath her feet, stared at the bit of dust mingling with dirty puddles of water. "You just killed one of your own," she mused thoughtfully. "And back on that night...you protected me and kept me safe from them. Why?"

"They unnecessarily kill innocent people and I don't stand for that," he replied simply, turning his back to her.

She stared at his back and sighed heavily, storing the stake inside of her coat pocket. "There was so much that I wondered about you after you left."

There was so much that I wondered about you *after I left,* he thought, but didn't trust himself to face her again. "I'm glad that everything turned out all right for you."

"Turned out all right for me?" she echoed dryly. "Fighting is my life. I don't have friends, I don't have a real job, and I never date. If I weren't fighting a particular cause, then my life would be pathetic."

He arched a glance over his shoulder. "Why do you keep doing it?" he asked her.

A look shone in her eyes, a similar look to the one he himself would get whenever he thought of the way Jordana had lured him away from his humanity. "They killed my family," she said in a low voice. "They killed my brother, my mother, my father, my grandfather, and a lot of other families suffered great losses that night. I can't explain the feeling that I get every time I send a stake through their hearts."

She didn't have to describe that feeling to him; he felt it every time he drove his sword through the flesh of a vampire.

"I see the years have been kind to *you*," she said, changing the subject.

"Not exactly."

"You...you look good," she said, lowering her eyes and wrapping her arms around her torso. "And you still know how to use that sword."

He didn't want to stand around and converse with her. When he stared at her, he was staring into the face of his past and that was something that he wasn't ready to do. He made a show of looking at his watch. "I would love to stay here and talk more with you," he started.

"You don't have to lie to me," she said. "If you want to leave, then leave."

He walked away from her. For some reason, he couldn't get away quickly enough.

CHAPTER FIVE

Early Saturday evening, Iancu pulled his dark sedan into the driveway of a one-story house painted sky blue. He stopped the engine and stepped out of the car, looking up and down the streets of the neighborhood.

Children were bicycling on the sidewalk and rolling down the street on cheap, plastic roller skates. He would give anything to lead a life this simple, but that sort of life didn't seem to be in the cards for him.

He hastily made his way up the short walkway to the front door. He rapped his knuckles on the door and waited, glancing over his shoulder at the remaining slivers of light emanating from the sun.

The door was opened and Neil stood there, wiping his hands on a damp dishcloth. He didn't bother to hide his surprise. "You're the last person I expected to show up on my front porch."

"I've had some time to think about what we discussed the other day," Iancu said. "An issue this big isn't something that I can easily ignore."

Neil nodded his head slowly, squinting his eyes. He stepped aside so that his old friend could enter. "That's the Iancu that I know," he said, clapping the taller man on the back and closing the front door. He quickly moved to lead the way to the living room, where an attractive blonde in her late-twenties sat in an armchair reading a romance novel. "Uh, honey, this is one of my old friends from college. Iancu, Marilyn. Marilyn, Iancu."

Iancu shook the woman's hand. She stood and forced him into an embrace. His body went stiff in her arms, but she didn't seem to notice. "It's...nice to meet you," he greeted awkwardly.

Neil looked like he was trying his best not to laugh. "Could you give us some time, Mare? We have a lot of things to talk about."

"Of course," she said without a second thought. She pressed a quick kiss to his cheek before scampering off into the kitchen.

Iancu lowered onto the couch. "An old friend from college?" he queried with an arched brow.

Neil shrugged. "She doesn't know what I am," he returned. He glanced around before settling into the snow-white armchair his wife had been sitting in.

"So, you got married to a human who doesn't know what you are?" Iancu shook his head. "What are you doing?"

"I love her." Those words seemed to justify it all for Neil.

"You can't conceive children with her," Iancu said in a hushed voice. "You know that. Vampires can't conceive children with humans. How are you going to explain that?"

Neil lifted an index finger into the air. "Already got that covered. I told her I'm sterile."

Iancu's eyes widened.

"I love her like I've loved no other woman on the face of this earth," Neil explained, smoothing down his burgundy button-down dress shirt. "I'm happy just being with her. Nothing else matters to me."

"You've been lying to her and you're going to continue lying to her," Iancu hissed.

Marilyn poked her head in the room. "Can I get you anything, um...?"

"Iancu," Iancu reminded her, "and no, I'm fine."

She disappeared again.

Neil smiled wistfully. "Every time I see her, my face lights up," he said slowly without turning to look at his friend. "Whenever she's not in the same room as me, that room feels empty. Whenever I walk in the house and she's not home, I know it *immediately.*

"And no, it's not because I can't sense her heartbeat. It's not because of my superhuman senses. It has nothing to do with our abilities. It's because I feel like half of my soul is missing."

Iancu didn't bother to mention that they *had* no souls.

"I know that this could backfire. I know that what I'm doing is wrong in a sense because of the lying, but I seriously can't imagine living without her." Neil hesitated, as if considering his next words. Then he added, "I feel sorry for anyone who doesn't have someone that they can love as much as I love Marilyn."

"I'm not here to judge you for your actions," Iancu said. "I'm here because of what we talked about."

Looking relieved that the topic had been changed, Neil eagerly braced his elbows on his knees and leaned forward. "Aryk has decided to move forward with his plans. He wants our population doubled by the end of the year."

"How do you know all of this?"

"I'm his accountant," Neil answered. "I'm privy to all sorts of shit."

"How could you work for him? He's a maniac. He's...disturbed. He's-"

"Been there for me more than you have in the past ten years," Neil interjected smoothly. He ran a hand over his short, cropped hair.

Iancu drew back and pursed his lips shut.

"I don't mean to give you a guilt trip. But back when we were friends, you were the person I came to when I was having problems. I was always asking you for advice.

"My transformation was the most painful thing I've ever had to withstand, but you helped me through it all. You left without giving me a heads-up. I didn't know *what* happened to you. You could have been dead for all I knew. Not only that, but when I *did* get news of you, it was from someone else telling me that you'd gone into hiding. That you'd turned your back on your own people."

"My back has always been turned on 'my people,'" Iancu said. "You knew that when you met me."

"What I *didn't* know was how easily you turn that same back on your friends."

Iancu stood up. "I refuse to argue about this."

Neil took a deep breath. "Not all of us agree with what Aryk is trying to accomplish, and as a result, certain task forces have been formed to sabotage his plans."

"That's great."

"My cousin is the head of one of the task forces. I've been calling him all day, but he hasn't gotten back to me."

Neil's cousin, Paul, was an ex-Marine. He'd been turned while he was stationed overseas in the Philippines. Most Marines leave home a boy and return a man. Paul left home a human being and returned a monster.

Iancu had met him and talked to him on more than one occasion. Despite the evil nature that Paul constantly had to battle, he seemed to be a good man.

"I'm trying to get in touch with each task force, because we don't want to jump our guns," Neil went on. "Aryk is powerful and I don't have to tell you that he has Jordana by his side. To come out of this situation as the victors, we are going to have to be organized. If there aren't enough vampires on our side, then we're going to need to find allies."

"We already have one strong ally," Iancu informed him.

Neil's brows shot up. "Really? Who?"

"The slayer."

CHAPTER SIX

Pulse was a club that humans frequented. It was located in Melrose District. The building was nondescript with a flat roof. There was no sign alerting streetwalkers to the name of the establishment and no windows.

Aryk led a pack of vampires through the club's doors, breezing past the massive bouncer with tree trunks for arms. He was dressed in an understated black suit and his bleached blonde hair was slicked back from his round face.

Frenzied humans were bumping and grinding against each other on the dance floor. The women were dressed in tight, whorish clothes and the majority of the men were dressed in dress shirts and slacks. The crowded dance floor drowned in a sea of red lights. The Nine Inch Nails song blasting out of the speakers caused the walls to pulsate and the floor to throb.

"Isn't this place nice and cozy?" Aryk asked the vampire closest to him, shivering in delight. "I do believe that I could make myself at home here."

Flanked by his bodyguards, he continued swaggering through the club until he reached a winding staircase. He ordered two of his accomplices to escort him up the stairs. The other four vampires were to remain at the foot of the stairs and make sure that no one else gained access to the stairway.

With his two bodyguards, he climbed the stairs. A locked door greeted them once they'd scaled the stairs. He pressed a hand against the door and influenced the lock. After hearing the soft telltale click, he shoved the door open.

Before them was a small, cramped office with dented file cabinets, a cracked tile floor, and a rotting wooden desk. Aryk wrinkled his nose in disgust. "Ugh," he muttered, gaining the attention of the short, pudgy man seated behind the desk.

Stewart Gorman jumped out of his chair with an expression of anger on his face. "That door was locked!" he sputtered, waddling around his desk and pointing his finger at them. "You're not supposed to be up here!"

Aryk wordlessly glanced at each of his men. He didn't need to issue orders; the two vampires sprang to action, rushing at the man and seizing him. Aryk proceeded to nose through the file cabinets, peering at documents of interest to him. "You are the owner and manager of this club, correct?"

The man's bulbous eyes widened. He had a greasy, slimy appearance from his worn, tattered shoes to his stained work shirt. He'd lost most of his dark hair. He struggled to get away from the two men holding him down, but that struggle proved to be unsuccessful.

Aryk arched a brow at the man over the document he was reading. "I'm going to need you to sign ownership of this club over to me," he said casually. "I think you have a fine establishment here. With the right contacts, this place could become the *it* place of Los Angeles. Don't you think?"

"You think I'd sign ownership over to you?" the man questioned. "You've got to be fucking bonkers!"

"I have the necessary papers with me," Aryk went on as if the chubby man hadn't spoken. "And we have two lawyers here who can testify to being witnesses. All I need is your John Hancock and the keys."

"You're not getting a damned thing from me!" the overweight, middle-aged man exclaimed.

Aryk placed the documents he'd been reading back in the file cabinet. "I had a feeling you would say something like that." He advanced on the club owner and traced a slender finger down the side of the man's face. Malice radiated from the depths of his amber-colored eyes. A chirping sound came from the cell phone clipped to his hip. He held up a solitary index finger. "I hate to be rude, but hold that thought." He flipped the phone open.

"I've found her," the vampire at the other end of the line informed.

"Are you positive, Nikolai?" Aryk asked.

"I'm positive."

"Good work."

"But..."

Aryk didn't like the sound of that. "But what?"

"Well, we sent out Billy and his crew to lure her out a couple of nights ago, and the plan worked, but...she wasn't fighting alone."

Aryk already knew the next words out of the snitch's mouth. "You've got to be kidding me."

"She and Iancu were working together," Nikolai finished.

"Well...that's not good," Aryk said. The wheels in his head were turning as he thought of ways to work Iancu's involvement to his advantage.

"Should I grab her?"

"No," Aryk said in a distracted voice. He was still thinking. If Iancu was protecting her and watching over her, then that would definitely complicate things. Because of the encounter he'd had with Iancu fifteen years ago, he didn't consider the other vampire a threat. However, he didn't want to take any chances when it came to the slayer. He'd lost her once and didn't want to lose her again.

"Well, what should I do?"

"Don't grab her, not yet," Aryk commanded. "Watch her for a little while. I want to know her routine. I want to know how often she sees Iancu." *And I want to know how the hell he found her before I did.*

"Is that it?"

"Yes, for now." He ended the call and clipped the phone to his belt. A wolfish grin appeared on his face. So not only was the slayer living up to her title and slaughtering vampires...but Iancu was fighting alongside her. *He's back to doing what he does best,* Aryk thought to himself. *Being a pain in my ass.* He turned his attention back to the club owner, who was openly staring at him. "I'm going to level with you, because frankly I'd like to get on with my evening.

"You're going to sign the ownership of this club over to me. I typically like my business transactions to run smoothly. If you don't give me any problems, then I won't kill you. If you *do* give me problems, any problems whatsoever, then I will break your neck and feast on your blood. I mean, it's your call really." With those words, he raised his hand into the air and snapped his fingers.

One of the vampires tossed a thick document onto the club owner's desk. The crisp sheets of paper were bound by a shiny black binder clip.

Stewart didn't know what was happening or why it was happening; at the mention that his life was in danger though, he was eager to sign the papers and get the deal over with. He accepted the pen given to him and bent at the waist to provide his signature wherever it was needed. He owned more than one dance club and in addition to that, he owned several rental properties. Losing one club wouldn't necessarily be his professional downfall.

Aryk watched the man sign the papers with great enjoyment. The grin on his face turned from wolfish to pleasant. "There you go," he coaxed. "Now was that so hard?"

Stewart shook his head. "Can I clear out my desk and leave now? I'll make sure not to get in your way."

Aryk tapped his jaw in mock-contemplation. "On second thought, I don't know if letting you go free would be a good idea. I mean, let's get hypothetical for a moment here, shall we?

"Hypothetically, I could let you go free, and you could alert certain authorities that you were forced to sign away ownership of your night club. That wouldn't be so good for me, would it?"

The club owner was shaking his head rapidly. "I wouldn't do that," he assured hurriedly. "I swear to God I wouldn't. I'll be on my way and I can *guarantee* you that we won't cross paths again."

Aryk's brows furrowed as he pretended to give the man's proposal some thought. "I don't know..."

"I can sign a contract saying that I won't run to the cops," Stewart sputtered. "I can-I can swear to you on the lives of anyone that I know, *everyone* that I know, that I won't say a word about this."

Aryk grabbed the man's face in his hands and stared into his muddy brown eyes. "Let's be realistic here. You'd tell *someone* about me at some point in your life. I can't say that I would blame you, because this would make for a great story to tell the grandkids.

"I'm going to be honest with you. I'm not going to kill you because I think you'll run and tell the authorities. I couldn't care less. No, no, no...I'm going to kill you because I'm a sick, twisted freak, and killing innocent, defenseless people is what I do to get my rocks off."

The fear in the man's eyes escalated. He was sweating profusely, scanning the room for any means of escape that he could find.

Aryk twisted the man's face, easily snapping his neck. He took a step back and let the body crumple to the floor. With his eyes shining brightly, he brought a hand up to his hair and smoothed it back. "That wasn't even a fun kill," he muttered. "I like them to put up at least a decent fight."

The two henchmen stared down at the dead man with expressions of disgust.

"Aren't you going to feed?" Aryk asked them.

They soundlessly shook their heads in unison.

Aryk straightened the cuffs of his suit jacket sleeves. "I wouldn't feed from him either," he agreed. "I'm trying to cut down on my cholesterol. Feeding from him would be like begging for a heart attack. And why feed from him when there are more than three hundred able, healthy bodies downstairs dancing and drinking their cares away?"

He turned and exited the room, confident that the two vampires would follow him. He descended the stairs and clapped the backs of the four vampires posting guard at the bottom of the staircase. "Now that business is out of the way," he told them all, "we can finally have some fun. Spread out."

The cluster of vampires dispersed into the crowd of dancers, sidled up next to the deejay's booth, and covered all of the exits of the place. The hard rock music that the deejay was playing skipped once, skipped twice, and then stopped playing altogether.

The lights flickered and the dancers stopped dancing.

Aryk glided through the crowd of dancers without being seen, breathing in the musky scent hovering over their skin.

The lights snapped off and chaos ensued. Aryk lifted a hand in the air and influenced all of the exit door locks simultaneously. His eyes glimmered and his fangs lowered.

The club-hoppers pressed at the exits, trying their damnedest to open the doors, but the doors didn't give. They were sealed inside.

Jordana rolled over in bed languidly, stretching her arms above her head. Her eyes fluttered open and she woke up with a start when she realized that Aryk wasn't lying beside her. She could sense that he wasn't in the house at all, nowhere on their estate.

Once upon a time, he had been her pet. She had sired him three hundred and fifty years ago; he had been a boy toy that she'd found herself infatuated with. He'd been beautiful and pure of heart before she drank from him and tainted his remaining blood with her own.

His humanity had left him quickly, and everything he had cared for as a human being lost its meaning to him. The people he'd loved as a human, he no longer had feelings for. The hobbies he'd enjoyed as a human, he no longer enjoyed. He lived solely to please Jordana. Everything she asked him to do, he did. Most of the time, she wouldn't even have to ask him for what she wanted; he could tell by looking in her eyes what she required of him at any given moment.

He'd lived in submission as her servant and had catered to her every whim. Somewhere along the line, though, he changed. Living the life of a submissive no longer pleased him. He yearned to have power, *her* power, and in blind lust, she hadn't seen what was taking place.

Now, *she* had to beg him to please her sexually. She practically had to do a series of cartwheels in front of his face to get the smallest bit of attention from him.

She was the oldest vampire known to their kind, and as such, was thought to be the most powerful. She could kill him with a flick of her wrist. He was inferior to her in every way. Why did she continue to live this way? Why did she continue to allow him to order her around as if she were *his* servant?

She got out of bed and padded out of their large, flamboyantly-decorated master bedroom. In bare feet, she walked down a long hallway towards ceiling-height double doors leading into a large study.

Books that she'd pried from the shelves the previous night were still scattered on top of the bulky oak desk in the center of the study. With a yawn, she seated herself behind the desk and continued her research of the legendary prophecy said to have been predicted by Lord Vlad himself. As she did at least once a night, she recited the words of the prophecy aloud. "The One who brings light shall turn dark, and against her and her maker two militias will stand, one army formed for the sake of good and the other formed for the sake of malevolence...greed. Humans and immortals alike will fall at the hands of the Light Bringer." She mulled over the words in her head before turning to the heavy, dusty book opened before her.

She was attempting to interpret the words of the prophecy. She wanted to know what the words meant. She wanted to find the second half of the prophecy. What exactly were these words predicting? There seemed to be an underlying power to the words, and she felt an undeniable force whenever she recited the first half of the prophecy.

She repeated the words again, over and over, while a portrait of Lord Vlad Dracul looked down upon her from over the fireplace's mantelpiece.

It would be easier for me to interpret these words if the parchment that the prophecy was written on was still intact, she thought as she flipped through the book's thick pages. *The second half of this prophecy is out there somewhere, and it's the key to finding out what the hell all of this means.*

She didn't know why she felt a necessity to decipher the prophecy's meaning as soon as possible. With Aryk taking charge and intending to cast a spotlight upon vampires and their existence, it seemed vital to know what the prophetic words meant.

She closed her eyes. "Lord Vlad, I am in need of your guidance," she prayed.

Worlds away in the depths of an old, sealed tomb, life - or a frightening likeness to life - stirred.

Charlie removed a pot of vegetable soup from the stove and poured the contents of the pot into a large bowl. Normally, she slept from the early afternoon to the early evening, but she'd overslept on this particular Sunday night. A heavy darkness had already blanketed California by the time her eyes cracked open.

She'd hurriedly put a pot of soup on the stove. While the soup warmed to a boil, she suited up.

She grabbed a box of crackers from the cupboard, fumbled around the kitchen drawer for a spoon, and set the bowl of soup on the kitchen table to cool. She flicked on the television and listened to the evening news as she ate.

"...Authorities are baffled as to why so many people gathered in the same dance club would be making calls to 911 on their cell phones," a blonde reporter was saying. "But once again for the people just joining us, there is a great deal of commotion in Club Pulse, located in Melrose District. I've been informed that officers haven't been able to gain access inside of the club. All of the doors are locked and at least two hundred people are trapped inside."

She turned off the television, poured the remaining soup into a large thermos, grabbed her keys off of the main room's coffee table, and fled out of the door.

By the time she made her way to Club Pulse, police cars were surrounding the area. LAPD officers spoke to each other on two-way radios and combed their way around the building, looking for a way inside its confines.

Careful not to be seen by them, she crept into an alley and worked her way towards the rear of the building. Just as she neared the metal door, she was yanked backwards and a hand clapped over her mouth. She kicked her legs until Iancu steadied her and wheeled her around to face him.

When he was sure that she wouldn't scream, he uncovered her mouth.

"What the hell did you do that for?" she demanded.

"You shouldn't be here."

"I'm the slayer," she said in a level voice. "I'm the one person who *should* be here."

He looked at some point over her head, then lowered his eyes to meet hers.

"I'm going to go in whether you want me to or not," she told him, reading the cautionary look in his eyes.

He nodded his head as if he'd figured as much. "Then come with me. I have a way in."

She followed him to the back door, warily glancing over her shoulder. She couldn't shake the feeling that she was being watched.

After manipulating the locks, he grabbed the door handle and opened the door. Ignoring the pointed look she gave him, he walked through the door and yanked her in with him.

The place was shrouded in darkness, but they could hear screams for help in the distance. Iancu tilted his head back and sniffed the air. The scent of blood was strong. He couldn't stop his mouth from watering.

His eyes only took a moment to adjust to the darkness. They were in what looked like the backstage area of the club. The power had been cut; no music was playing and the only light in the place was coming from the Exit signs above the doors. The only sounds in the place were loud shrieks of fear and agony. His hand reflexively shot to the hilt of his sword which was concealed by the large overcoat he wore. He sniffed the air again, but this time with purpose. "There are at least five of them," he whispered over his shoulder at her.

She'd fought off five vampires before. "A piece of cake," she mumbled as she followed him.

He reached a door that probably led to the main area. Before opening the door, he turned to face her. "Our best bet will be blending in with the crowd as much as possible," he told her. "Chances are that the vampires are standing guard at different posts, instead of being grouped together. We need to sneak up on each one and kill him quietly, without alerting the others. Can you do that?"

"I can do that," she affirmed.

"Are you comfortable with us splitting up?"

"I've been working on my own for more than ten years," she reminded him.

"All right, then." He pulled open the door, which had been unlocked, and stepped through it.

Most of the surviving dance club patrons were huddled in the middle of the dance floor, some of them holding on to each other for dear life. The floor was littered with bloodied bodies. The bodies on the floor appeared to be dead, but Iancu knew better than that. The bodies on the floor weren't corpses. They were vampires in the making. In a day or two, the transformation would completely take over their forms and they would become what he most detested...they would become what he *was*: a vampire.

Not if I have anything to do with it, he thought, casting a look over his shoulder. Charlie had already left him. His eyes scanned over the many heads of hair in the club; he found her walking in a stooped crouch, towards the club's lounge area where one of the vampires was posted.

When she reached him, there was a tense moment as Iancu watched. The vampire posting guard glanced down with a frown on his face. A moment later, he went down.

Good for you, Iancu thought to himself, focusing his attention elsewhere. He sensed a vampire of a considerable amount of power nearby. He narrowed his eyes, turning around in a small circle as he surveyed his environment.

Aryk was standing near the deejay's booth with a sickening expression of glee on his face. A woman with dark purple hair stood at his side with an impressive-looking weapon cradled in her arms. Her mouth was set in a grim line and there was a fierce look in her pale green eyes.

Iancu dropped to the floor to avoid being seen. *Take care of Aryk last,* he thought to himself.

There's a vampire headed in your direction, behind you.

He froze at the sound of Charlie's voice in his head. She'd done the exact same thing fifteen years ago. *Thanks,* he directed at her. He drew his sword and shoved it into the chest of the jeering vampire standing above him.

The vampire dropped to his knees, sputtering in shock. He looked down at the sword protruding from his chest.

As effective as a stake, the wood from the flat of Iancu's sword infected the wound that the sword's blade had carved into the vampire's flesh. The infected blood, as black as coal, seeped from the wound and bled through the vampire's expensive clothes.

Even though he had missed the vampire's heart, Iancu twisted the sword to the left, then to the right, and pulled the sword out of the vampire's chest. To ensure that the vampire wouldn't heal, he raised the sword over his head and brought it back down with precise aim. The vampire's head plummeted to the floor and rolled a couple of inches, then stilled.

I've dropped two, Charlie communicated to him telepathically.

He'd killed one. That left approximately two more of them. The frightened crowd of dancers was huddled in the middle of the dance floor, too preoccupied with their panic to notice him.

A dark-haired vampire had his arms wrapped around a bone-thin, dishwater blonde with two gigantic basketball-sized boobs attached to her chest. He was leering at her and feeling her up.

Iancu tapped him on the shoulder with the point of his sword. Just as the vampire turned to see who would have the balls to touch him, his head was separated from his body.

The blonde scampered away with tears and cheap eyeliner streaming down her cheeks.

"Everybody hold it!" a strong, authoritative voice shouted.

Our cover is blown, Iancu thought, pressing his back flat against the closest wall and crouching down to the floor.

"Everybody stand still and shut the hell up!"

Across the room from Iancu, Charlie traveled on her hands and knees. For the first night in all of her nights of hunting, she'd left her cloak in the car. She wasn't worried about concealing her weapons; she'd known that she would have to be able to move, and quickly, to survive tonight's hunt. She'd worn her black tank top, her tight black pants, and her boots, but she didn't have a cloak to hide her identity. She also didn't have a cloak to house the stake points she kept inside of the pockets. She had one wooden dagger in the knife sheath wrapped around her thigh, two guns in the shoulder holster, and two guns holstered at her back; that was it.

At the commanding man's voice, she froze where she was squatting. She'd heard that voice before.

Still standing near the deejay's booth, Aryk clapped his hands together high in the air. "Why, I do believe we have some visitors," he announced. "Come out, come out, wherever you are."

Charlie dared a peek at the man speaking. Her eyes widened and she dropped out of sight. It couldn't be the same vampire. Her eyes were fooling her. It had to be wishful thinking.

Her breathing quickened and she closed her eyes, trying to block out the memories.

"What do you want with the girl?"

"This girl right here is very special."

"Let the girl go."

"I can't. She's the slayer."

An image of her deceased brother danced before her eyes. She didn't know for sure that Aryk was the one who'd taken a drink from her older brother, but he had been in the house. It could very well have been him. That was motive enough for her to kill him. And slowly.

That night on Standing Rock Reservation, she'd made the mistake of missing her target. She hadn't known then that the most efficient way of killing a vampire was staking him or her in the heart...but she knew that now. This time, she wouldn't miss.

She blinked her eyes and found herself staring at a stylish pair of dress shoes. Her eyes traveled up a pair of long legs. She found herself staring into the face of Aryk: evil incarnate.

He grinned down at her. "And would you be the slayer?" he asked her jovially.

She stared up at him defiantly. "I'm your worst nightmare."

He chuckled and before she even had the chance to blink, he seized her by the arm.

She looked as disoriented as she felt. "How did you-"

"Where is your friend, hmm?" Aryk interrupted silkily. "I know he's here. I've been watching you."

That would explain why she'd had the feeling of being watched for the past couple of days.

"Iancu!" he yelled without warning, barking at the top of his lungs. "I've got your pretty little girlfriend! I know you're here, so show yourself to me!"

She fought against him, trying to pull herself out of his grasp.

"I know you're not cloaking yourself from me!" Aryk continued. "You don't use your powers! So show yourself to me!"

Her eyes widened. *Iancu never uses his powers in battle?*

"Jade! Simon! Rafael! David!" Aryk glanced around the club. "Where are my men? Where is Jade?" He closed his eyes for a few seconds and then opened them. He pulled her against him, searching her eyes.

She didn't attempt to avoid meeting his gaze. "Dead. All of them." She didn't know whether or not the statement was one hundred percent accurate, but she wanted to see him squirm.

Instead of squirming, he slapped her across the face. The slap was hard enough to draw blood on the inside of her mouth. "You stupid bitch," he muttered. He drew back his fist, intending to punch her.

A hand out of nowhere grabbed his fist and crushed it. Aryk sobered at the sound of his fingers breaking. His fist was released and he was shoved to the floor. "Iancu, I knew you would be joining us," he said dazedly as he rolled onto his back.

Iancu stood above him with his sword drawn. Aryk disappeared from sight, but Iancu anticipated the move and whirled around.

He turned around a millisecond too late. Aryk had a gun in his hands and didn't hesitate in pulling the trigger. Iancu flew backwards and landed several feet away, near the dance floor.

A couple of the women on the dance floor screamed, inching away from the fallen warrior.

Charlie extracted the two guns placed at her back and fired relentlessly. Aryk went down with a shocked expression on his face. As he dipped his fingers in his own blood, she ran over to Iancu. "Are you all right?"

There was a blank look in his eyes. She gave each of his cheeks a light pat and glanced behind her to make sure that Aryk was still on the floor. The woman with hair the color of violets had him sprawled across her lap. She was attempting to revive him, every once in awhile sending daggers Charlie's way.

Charlie examined Iancu's wound; the bullet was lodged in his upper arm. It had to be a silver bullet. A silver bullet was the only kind of bullet that could bring a vampire down this way. Vampires were highly allergic to silver.

Iancu's eyelids drooped down, but his eyes moved restlessly beneath his lids. The sounds of screaming and whimpering faded away, and the sound of Charlie's voice muted. His breathing became labored. He struggled to sit up and found he couldn't. He opened his mouth, struggled to get something out, but failed. Is this what dying felt like?

"What are you going to do? Are you going to cut me with your little butter knife, there? What...you haven't heard of guns? Guns? Guns?

"You have no choice. There's nothing you can do to stop me. You don't use your powers and all you have for a weapon is that dinky little sword...You don't use your powers...You don't use your powers..."

Iancu's eyes snapped opened and he jerked to life. Both of his hands shot into the air, facing outward. A strange energy ebbed from them. The lights in the club flashed on. The locks on all of the doors made a clicking sound, all of them disengaging at the same time.

The people grouped together on the dance floor stumbled over bodies in their mad rush to head towards the doors. Aryk was still stretched out across the foreign-looking woman's lap, staring up at the ceiling.

It was the perfect opportunity to finish him off, if only Iancu could get to his feet. Charlie was on her knees beside him.

"What is it?" she asked him.

"Aryk...we have to finish him off."

"In here!" a male voice called, and a flood of police officers swarmed the club.

Iancu shook his head. "No."

Charlie helped him to his feet. "We have to get out of here."

"We have to finish him off," he maintained in a forceful voice. "We can't just leave him here. They're going to take him to a hospital where they'll remove the bullets. If they do that, he'll heal. We can't let that happen."

"I know," she told him. "Believe me, I know, but the cops are here."

"Look at this mess," one of the uniformed officers muttered.

With a great deal of effort, Iancu clutched Charlie's hand and managed to cloak the both of them, making them invisible to the naked human eye. He allowed his fellow fighter to escort him out of the dance club the way they'd come in.

The night air was warm and breezy as she half-dragged and half-carried him to her car. She assisted him into the passenger seat.

She followed the directions that he gave her, and in less than a half an hour, they were both seated on his living room couch. "I don't know much about removing bullets," she warned him as she took a closer look at the wound. "I would probably know more if I'd had more time with my grandfather. He was a healer."

He was barely conscious, so she couldn't be sure that he could actually hear her. Without his long black trench coat, boots, and sword, he appeared a lot more vulnerable. If she were someone with less than honorable intentions, she could easily stake him here and now and end his life.

His head lolled to the side; his eyes were narrowed into slits. He was whispering something very low, but she'd given up on interpreting what he was trying to say.

She needed to extract the bullet from his arm, but she didn't know her way around his apartment. She settled on using a short knife with a tapered blade that she found in one of the kitchen drawers.

She filled a clear glass bowl with cold water after discovering clean washcloths in the hallway closet. She returned to the living room with the glass bowl and washcloth in hand. Sweat graced his forehead and the roots of his long hair were dampened with perspiration. His body started to shake uncontrollably. She dipped a corner of the wash cloth into the cold water, and proceeded to wipe his forehead.

The tremors ceased and his body relaxed. She sighed and set to work on removing the bullet that was lodged in his arm. Dark blood started to seep from the wound so she used the washcloth to clean the area around it.

She wasn't getting very far by working around the material of his shirt, so she had to remove it. His chest and abdomen glistened with a fine sheen of sweat. She spotted a rather large birthmark on the inside of his right wrist. Upon close inspection, the birthmark looked to be in the shape of a dragon.

Dropping his wrist, she returned to dislodging the bullet from his upper arm. She toiled into the wee hours of the morning, until she struck gold. She successfully removed the bullet from his arm and dropped it into the bowl of now lukewarm water.

After cleaning the wound again, she ripped the shirt he'd been wearing to shreds with her bare hands and used the remnants of one of the sleeves to wrap around his arm. It wouldn't take long for the wound to heal.

She stood from the couch and paced around the living room, surprised to see sunrays shining through the balcony doors. She closed the heavy, black drapes to discourage the sunlight from entering the apartment.

Both of them could very well have been killed last night. Aryk wasn't just any run-of-the mill vampire. He was powerful. He'd moved too fast for her to track. She wasn't used to dealing with vampires as powerful as he was. Most of the vampires that she came across were relatively young and lacked proper training with their supernatural abilities.

Seeing Iancu look so weak and vulnerable frightened her. After he rescued her fifteen years ago, he became her idol. He had embodied the perfect warrior to her. And now, here he was, stretched out on the couch completely unconscious, with his hair draping over one armrest and his bare feet hanging over the other.

She watched him sleep, unable to sleep herself. Hours later, he came awake with a start, jerkily reaching for his sword and realizing that it wasn't sheathed at his hip. One of his hands crossed over his chest and assessed his wounded arm. The wound was closed and healing rapidly.

With narrowed eyes, he took in his surroundings. He was in his apartment. But how? The last thing he could remember was fighting Aryk. His eyes landed on the woman nestled in the oversized armchair.

He wiped at his mouth. He was incredibly hungry; it had been more than a day since he'd last fed. With a groan of effort, he pulled himself into a standing position and ambled into the kitchen. The shelves in his refrigerator were lined with blood packs. Years ago he'd had to steal blood packs from blood banks, but now cloned blood packs were being sold on the street for ten dollars a pop.

He grabbed one of the packs and emptied it into a large white glass with the Lakers logo on it. He nursed the drink while standing in the kitchen. From where he stood, he could look into the living room and watch Charlie's peaceful slumber.

Lying in that chair was the woman who'd most likely saved his life. If the bullet had stayed lodged in his arm for much longer, he would have died. He was certain of that. Once in a vampire's system for an extended period of time, silver bullets turned into liquid and poisoned the system. Vampires' bodies had the ability to neutralize a small amount of silver. One bullet wasn't typically enough to kill a vampire, but because Iancu had hesitated in neutralizing the silver, his health declined considerably until he was unable to heal himself. He didn't know how close he'd come to dying, but Charlie probably did.

In the living room, she stirred in her sleep. He wasn't used to having a woman in his apartment. The only people he was used to dealing with these days were businessmen and businesswomen. His social skills had completely deteriorated due to his self-isolation.

He finished nursing his drink, tossed the cup in the sink, and exited the kitchen. Instead of joining her in the living room, he entered his bedroom. An assortment of guitars and swords lined the walls of his bedroom, resting on sleek, hand-painted stands. One guitar stand was empty, and that was because he'd furiously slammed that guitar into the living room wall.

The swords that he passed by were ones he had forged himself. He hadn't forged a sword in more than ten years. Once in awhile he would have the urge to make a new one.

Despite his attempt to dive into the business world and live a businessman's life, he was a craftsman at heart and ached to work with his hands. Playing the guitar eased some of that angst, but not all of it.

He plucked a neon green guitar from one of the stands. Then, he plopped onto his bed and stretched his legs out. He hugged the large instrument to his bare chest and teased the strings with his fingers.

He leaned his head back against the wall and closed his eyes as he strummed, only opening his eyes when he couldn't think of any other songs to play.

Charlie leaned against the doorjamb with her hands folded across her chest. "Nice," she commented.

Feeling a bit violated, he set the guitar on the bed beside him. "Thank you for what you did." He gestured to the wound dressing she'd tied around his upper arm.

"No problem."

"You didn't have to stay the night with me."

"I wasn't sure whether or not you'd make it through the night," she explained, crossing the threshold and entering the room. "It got pretty bad."

"You should probably get back to your cabin," he told her shortly.

One of her brows rose at the suggestion. "I can't. Aryk told me that he's been watching me. He probably knows where I live."

"Is there anywhere you can stay until you're sure that they are no longer keeping tabs on your cabin?"

She shrugged her shoulders. "I was kind of thinking that you have an extra bedroom..."

She'd nosed around his apartment? He shook his head before she could finish the sentence. "That's not possible."

"You have plenty of room here," she argued.

"I can pay to keep you in a hotel," he offered, standing from the bed.

She followed him out of the room. "Are you serious? You'd rather pay money for a hotel than let me stay here with you?"

"Women don't stay here," he told her firmly. "*Men* don't stay here. *No one* stays here, but me."

"If it weren't for *me*, you would be dead."

"I probably would be," he agreed, "and I thank you for keeping me amongst the world of the living, but you can't stay here."

She planted her hands on her hips and pouted. "What is it you're afraid of?"

He laughed outright. "Afraid of?"

"There's got to be *some* reason why you're so determined to keep me from staying here."

He rolled his eyes. "I don't have to explain myself or my actions to you. I've told you how it is. You've just got to accept it."

"Fine." She sat on the couch, still pouting. "I don't want to stay here anyway."

He didn't respond.

She looked around the room. "Do any of the rooms in this place have a television?"

He gestured down the hall. "The room all the way at the end of the hallway."

There was no way in the world that he was going to let her stay here with him. She would get in the way. She would bother him and get on his nerves. She had the tendency to get on his nerves easily. He couldn't imagine co-existing with her in the same cramped space.

An image of her curled up into a little ball on his living room armchair sprang into his head. She'd looked like a bronze-skinned angel during her slumber, with her dark hair draped over her face. Her beauty was ethereal, and it was perhaps the real reason why he felt so irritable whenever he was around her.

Don't be stupid, he thought.

"Iancu!"

He ran out of the living room and down the hall, stopping just short of the doorway. For some reason, he'd expected to see Aryk holding her by her hair, but she was sitting in front of the television and pointing at the screen.

107

His heart had leapt into his throat at the thought of danger finding her. He steadied his nerves and tried to focus on what the news reporter was saying.

"Last night's massacre rocked the Melrose District last night, and this morning victims from the senseless bloodbath are recuperating in numerous hospitals across the city.

"Witnesses described the event as being like the scene from a horror movie, as five or six suited men stormed the club and physically assaulted many of the patrons within. They have reported that the attackers were biting their victims.

"There is no word yet from the coroner's office confirming that report. As of this morning, no suspects have been apprehended by the LAPD. Bill, back to you."

Charlie looked up at Iancu. "What was he doing there? Is he *trying* to shout to the world that vampires exist?"

He stroked his jaw. "That's exactly what he's doing."

She frowned. "What are you talking about?"

"I've gotten word from a reliable source that he's planning to increase the population of vampires across the country and eventually, the world," he informed her. "I believe that last night was the first phase of his plan."

"Are you serious?" She brought a hand up to her mouth. "That is why you wanted to stay and kill him."

"What?"

"After you were injured, when I told you that we had to get out of there, you said that we had to stay and kill him," she said. "The cops had come in and if they'd found us, they probably would have held us for questioning. If they'd held us for questioning, I'm not sure you would have survived the night, so I got you out of there."

"I can't believe I failed. I can't believe I let him get the best of me like that."

"He didn't get the best of you," she told him, turning off television and facing him. "He did say something that I wondered about, though. He said that you don't use your abilities when you're fighting. What was he talking about?"

"You should take everything he says with a grain of salt." His face remained expressionless, but a battle was going on behind his eyes.

She watched him closely. "You have superhuman abilities and you don't use them when you're fighting?"

Without a word, he turned on his heel and left her sitting in the room alone. She jumped to her feet and trailed after him.

"Is that it?"

"You never shut up, do you?" he growled.

"Iancu is that it?" she repeated, unaffected by his gruff words. "You hate what you are so much, that you won't use your abilities to your advantage?"

"I'm not going to talk about this," he said in a gravelly tone that left no room for argument.

She closed her mouth, but her mind was racing. How old was he? How powerful was he? If he had wanted to, could he have killed Aryk with the powers that he possessed? "You don't have to talk about it," she said softly, "but I'll just say this: I'm a slayer. I'm human. Every night I'm in the line of fire, and every night could be the night that my life is taken from me.

"*You* aren't human. You're a vampire. You've had a lot of time to deal with that, and still you haven't accepted it. You could have died last night, and only when you were nearly dead did you even think to use your powers to let all of those people free. Only when you were nearly dead did you think to attempt to heal *yourself*." She shook her head slowly in disbelief. "I agree with you. I'd be better off in a hotel than I would be staying here with you."

He didn't stop her from leaving. He doubted that he *could* stop her from leaving. Her leaving was probably for the best. She shouldn't hang around with the likes of him. He was a vampire. He was a monster. Whether it happened tomorrow or whether it happened next week, it was inevitable that he would fail her somehow.

He returned to his windowless bedroom and lulled himself to sleep with the help of his guitar.

Aryk sat in bed typing industriously on a sleek Sony Vaio laptop computer. He didn't acknowledge Jordana's presence when she sashayed into the room wearing nothing but provocative lingerie. Her abundance of breasts was all but spilling out over the top of the crimson silk fabric.

She crawled onto the bed beside him and started to massage his back.

He briefly glanced at her and rolled his eyes. "You know I don't like that, baby. Come on, what are you doing?" He turned his focus back to the computer.

She pressed her lips to his bare shoulder and started licking her way down his arm, nipping his skin with her teeth here and there.

He leaned away from her, continuing to type. When she persisted, he groaned in exaggerated frustration. "Can't you see that I'm working?" he demanded. "What do you want?"

She frowned at him. "I want you to pay some fucking attention to me once in awhile. Is that so much to ask?"

"Do you know what I'm on the verge of right now?" he asked her. "Soon, I'm going to have the world in my pocket. Anything we want, we'll have. Total and complete world domination isn't going to mail itself to us first class on a silver platter, baby. It takes work."

Disappointment was etched into the lines of her face. "Is there anything that I can do to help you?" she asked him.

He ran a hand through his hair as he stared at the laptop computer screen. It took a moment for him to realize that she'd spoken. He blinked his eyes and gave her a sidelong glance. "It would really help me if you found a way to convince the other clan leaders that my way is the right way."

She snorted dismissively. "You heard what they said in the meeting, Aryk. They're not interested in sacrificing all that we've accomplished so that we can wage war and declare ourselves superior to humans."

"They're not interested because they're too busy fussing and fighting to keep the old traditions," he said, setting the computer on top of the nightstand and turning to face her. "The concept of tradition is fine and dandy, but one of these days we're going to have to progress and evolve. New generations of vampires are being created, and those new generations aren't going to be satisfied with having to lurk around in the dark, hiding their true identities."

"You've given this speech to me before," she said with a shrug of her shoulders.

"If my followers decided to rebel against the elders, do you really think that they would have a chance?"

"If you encouraged them to rise up against the elders, you would be encouraging them to rebel against power," she responded wisely. "In encouraging them to rebel against power, you would one day have to face their wrath once they turn on you."

He crossed his arms over his chest. "It surprises me that you aren't on board with my plans. You're one of the most ruthless vampires known to our kind, and yet you jump on the bandwagon with the rest of the old cooks."

She tossed the bed sheets aside and stood from the bed. "In truth, I'm torn. I agree with the fact that we shouldn't have to hide what we are to humans. After all, you're correct when you say that we are superior to them. However, they outnumber us right now."

He began to speak, but she interrupted him.

"I know that you wish to increase our numbers, but that would threaten our existence also. The new generations of vampires that you speak of are becoming more and more difficult to control."

He knew that there was truth to her words. With a plan this groundbreaking, though, there were sure to be sacrifices. He was willing to *make* those sacrifices.

She tousled his hair as if he were an adolescent child and gave his shoulder a pat. "What you need to do is get those ridiculous notions out of your head and please me."

He smiled at her patronizingly and, returning the gesture, gave her head a reassuring pat. "When you convince the other clan leaders to join my side, then and *only* then will I give it to you the way you like it." Without another word, he returned the laptop computer to his lap and continued typing.

She sat with her back against the headboard. Three hundred years ago, he'd been her slave. He used to be her pet. Those days were long gone and she couldn't pinpoint the exact moment when the tables had turned.

When he was done with whatever he'd been doing on the computer, he gave her a long, measuring look. "I nearly got skewered last night by your former boyfriend Iancu," he said at last.

Her eyes widened. "I was wondering where those wounds came from."

He looked down at his chest. Multiple silver bullet wounds were scattered all over his torso. "I almost died thanks to him and his little girlfriend," he muttered, fingering one of the wounds delicately.

"His little girlfriend?" she repeated, plucking a piece of lint from the bodice of her lingerie.

"He's teamed up with the slayer," Aryk said, wrinkling his nose in disgust. "Someone needs to put the dear boy out of his misery."

"He's teamed up with the slayer?"

He glanced around. "Do I hear an echo in here?"

She bit back the first reply that came to mind and plastered a sickly sweet smile on her face. "I'm sorry, I'm just soaking it all in."

"Soak it up faster," he retorted as he set the computer aside. He threw his legs over the side of the bed and stood on his feet. "I'm so stressed out. I can't believe I let him get to me like this."

Without saying a word, she watched him saunter into the master bathroom.

"I can't wait to get my hands on that bitch," he rambled on, speaking mostly to himself. "And I hope that Iancu's *dead*."

Jordana's hands flew up to her mouth. "What did you do to him?"

She didn't have to see him to know that he had a triumphant, wolfish grin on his face. "I put a silver bullet in him."

She wrapped her arms around herself and chewed the inside of her bottom lip. "I doubt one bullet killed him."

"He wouldn't use his powers until I put that bullet in him," he called out from the bathroom. "He wouldn't even use them to heal himself."

That sure sounded like Iancu. He'd always been too indignant for his own good. He'd also been too passionate for his own good. Her cheeks flushed as she remembered all of the hot, sweaty nights she'd spent with him. He'd been loving and attentive. He'd never gotten power-hungry the way Aryk had. Just remembering some of what they'd shared together aroused her. She crossed her legs tightly and cleared her throat.

In the bathroom, Aryk stood shirtless before a full-length mirror, even though he couldn't see his reflection in it. Tentative fingers danced across the wounds caused by the slayer's silver bullets. The marred flesh was still sensitive to the touch. He felt a dull, throbbing pain down the stretch of his abdomen, but also an exhilarating, unexpected wave of pleasure. He couldn't wait to get his hands on the slayer. With his fingers still caressing tender scar tissue, he closed his eyes and pictured bending the slayer over and showing her who was boss.

Without feeling the least bit guilty, Neil slinked away from the master bedroom door. He had come on business and had wanted to bring several financial obligations to his client's attention, but after having eavesdropped on the conversation between Jordana and her beau and after having tapped into Aryk's unguarded thoughts, Neil didn't dare knock on the door.

He had to alert Iancu of Aryk's intentions. He had to warn his friend that Aryk would go after the slayer.

Iancu had barely opened his apartment door when Neil breezed past him, appearing to be extremely upset. "We have a problem," he said, running a trembling hand through his hair.

"That much is apparent." Iancu closed the door and turned to face his friend with his eyebrows furrowed. He followed the shorter man into the living room and slipped his hands into the pockets of his navy blue pajama pants.

Neil looked to be dressed for work. He wore a pair of crisp, dark slacks, an orange button-down dress shirt, and recently-shined black shoes. "I'm glad to see that you bounced back from last night," Neil observed with a gesture of his right hand. "It couldn't have been too much fun having to recover from a silver bullet."

A single eyebrow lifted in askance. "How did you hear about that?"

"I was eavesdropping on Aryk earlier. He was telling Jordana about it."

Iancu nodded his head. "And you found that urgent enough to run here and tell me?"

"No, not that." Neil took a deep breath and paced the length of the living room before finally turning to face Iancu. "Aryk is planning to go after the slayer."

"Is that so?"

"We have to get to her," Neil went on. "We have to tell her about his plans. We have to keep her in a safe location, somewhere that Aryk can't get to her."

"She's a big girl. She can protect herself."

Neil's mouth dropped open in disbelief.

Iancu lovingly ran his fingers across the flat of one of the decorative swords hanging on the living room wall. "She's a big girl. She recently told me as much. I've seen her in action. I'm inclined to believe her."

An expression of shock contorted Neil's facial features. "Are you serious?"

Iancu gave a curt nod. "She's the slayer. She is supposed to know how to take care of herself and the rest of the human population. She shouldn't have to rely on the assistance of others in order to perform the duty that she's been assigned."

"You're going to sacrifice her to the wolves because you guys had an argument?" Neil shook his head. "Iancu, that's-"

"She doesn't need me."

Neil folded his arms across his chest and was silent for a couple of moments. "She's a human being. One of the most powerful vampires in existence is practically declaring war against her, and you're going to let her fend for herself? You've got to be fucking kidding me.

"I know she's the slayer. I know that she's strong. I know this, Iancu, but even the strongest slayer wouldn't have a chance against Aryk. He was sired by Jordana and has her at his side. I shouldn't have to tell you that. You should *know* that."

Iancu *did* know that. He knew that if a battle between Charlie and Aryk ensued, there was no question as to whom the victor would be. Neil was right; if Aryk was vowing to kill her, she didn't have a chance on her own.

Neil stood in silence, waiting for a response from his friend.

Iancu rolled his eyes and sighed. "I'll check up on her," he said finally, giving in. "I'm not going to be her personal bodyguard, though. She can't depend on me; she's the slayer. She needs to be self-sufficient."

"Yeah, yeah, totally," Neil agreed, relieved that his friend had come to his senses. "On another note, though, we should meet up sometime soon. We have to come up with a strategy to prevent Aryk from going ballistic and corrupting every human in sight."

Chase didn't know why he was still in Los Angeles. He rarely stayed in the same location for more than a couple of days. He was always on the move.

He found himself smitten by Jade, though. After the meeting that had been held at Jordana's mansion, he'd made his move on Jade and told her that they should hang out some time.

He hadn't gone out on a date in a long time. He usually took his women to bed and then discarded them like yesterday's newspaper. He found that it was different with Jade, though. She wasn't the typical girl that he found himself taking to his bed.

She was very opinionated, always sounding off about something that she didn't like. When he made a move on her, she'd given him a hard look that had stopped him in his tracks. He was certain that he wasn't going to get anywhere with her, physically, until the end of the date when he dropped her off at the gates of Jordana's estate.

Jade had turned to him, gave him a long, hard look, and leaned forward to kiss him. Her kisses were hot and fiery. There was nothing tame or innocent about them. Underneath the dyed hair, thick eyeliner, and tattoos, she was a passionate, vulnerable girl.

The next night, he took her out again. She could never stay out long. She was the head of security and that meant she had to be on the grounds between certain hours. He respected that and made sure that she was back at the house by the time she had to be there.

As he was getting ready for what would have been their fourth date, the door to the hotel suite swung open. She stood in the doorway wearing a slinky black dress and stiletto heels. It was the first time he'd ever seen her in anything other than jeans or dress slacks. She'd released her dark purple hair from its severe ponytail. It cascaded down her back and around her shoulders in soft waves. She'd traded out her bold makeup style for something softer and more subtle. Her lips were lush and pink and her dark green eyes were wide and inviting.

He stood near the closet, where he'd been trying to decide what to wear. Speechless, he watched as she approached him with her eyes lowered. He wasn't used to seeing her this way. He was used to seeing her dressed like a tough tomboy. As he watched her now, he could see that she was truly all woman.

She came to him. "I couldn't wait," was all she said.

It was all she had to say. He took her in his arms and she pressed her cheek to his bare chest. His shaggy blonde hair was damp from the shower and he smelled like aftershave. When she stood on tiptoe to kiss him, a wave hit both of them. He didn't hesitate in getting the tight, black dress off of her. He let her keep the shoes on. He liked those. Everything else came off.

She sat on the bed and worked at taking his pants off. They didn't exchange any more words. The only sounds that were audible were their pants and moans. Their lovemaking was surprisingly gentle. He was usually a lot rougher, but for some reason he wanted it to be different with her. He could sense that she was extremely nervous and he didn't want to hurt her in any way.

After their coupling, he held her and pressed kisses to the top of her head. She lifted her head to peer at the clock on the nightstand. "Shit," she cursed under her breath and moved out of his embrace as she sat up. "I have to get back."

"Already?" he croaked, glancing over his shoulder at the clock.

She smiled and shrugged. "It's all in a night's work." She hunted around the room for her clothes and quickly took leave of the hotel room.

He put a pillow over his face and groaned.

The sound of clapping hands bounced off of the walls of the hotel suite. He removed the pillow from his face and rose up on his elbows.

Aryk pushed himself from the doorjamb he'd been leaning on and entered the room. "Congratulations on that lay," he greeted. "You have succeeded where I failed."

Chase frowned and ran a hand through his hair. "What are you doing here?"

Aryk had been intent on discussing business with Chase. Chase would be an important ally to have. He was extremely influential in the vampire community. However, watching Chase and Jade make love to each other had left a sour taste in Aryk's mouth. Aryk no longer wanted to talk business with Chase. He wanted Chase dead.

Instead of answering the sleepy-eyed vampire's question, Aryk withdrew a gun from the holster at his hip at lightning speed and sent a shower of silver bullets through Chase's skull.

Neil didn't stay at Iancu's apartment for long. He said what he had to say and took his leave. He thought about his wife on the drive home. She'd been acting kind of strange lately, asking him whether or not certain outfits made her look fat. His ex-girlfriends had asked that question of him before, so he wasn't unfamiliar with the question itself. Marilyn had never asked him that question before, though, not once while they were dating.

Of course, he would respond that no, the outfit that she was wearing didn't make her look fat. She would ponder over his reply and then nod to herself with a sullen expression on her face.

He didn't know what was going on with her and whenever he asked her, she closed up and became guarded. He was aware that she was going through some type of emotional stress, but he couldn't pinpoint the stress's source.

It could be the fact that we don't see each other as often as we would like to, he thought as he drove. *I sleep during the day and she sleeps during the night. That could be causing more stress on our relationship than I anticipated.*

If that were the issue though, she would have said something. She would have talked to him about it

He shook out of his thoughts as he pulled his pearl white Chrysler sedan into the driveway of his home. Whatever was the cause of the tension between the two of them, he would find out and he would fix it. He hadn't married Marilyn to increase the amount of stress in her life; he had married her so that he could contribute in making her happy for the rest of her days.

She wasn't waiting for him in the living room the way she usually was. He remembered Aryk's ill intentions toward the slayer and a chilling thought occurred to him. Aryk could have been aware that his accountant had been standing outside of his bedroom door eavesdropping on him. He could have stopped by Neil's house, paid his wife a visit, and kidnapped her. It was possible. When it came to Aryk, *anything* was.

Panic etched into the lines of Neil's face. His worry was preventing him from accurately sensing whether or not there was another presence in the house. Usually, he was able to tell right away whether or not his wife was nearby, but his thoughts were jumbled and confused. He was so fearful that he couldn't think straight. He dropped his stylish leather briefcase at the foot of the stairs and took the steps two at a time. "Mare!" he called fretfully. "Marilyn? Baby? Answer me!"

There was no answer. His house was as silent as a tomb and equally as disturbing.

He burst through their bedroom door, on the verge of tears. If anything had happened to his wife, he didn't know what he would do. The door to the master bathroom door was closed. He wrapped his hand around the doorknob and turned the knob. It wouldn't budge.

There was a shred of hope. His wife might be all right. There might be nothing to fear. He rapped his knuckles on the door. "Marilyn? Honey?" He pressed his ear to the door. Still, he heard nothing.

His heightened senses kicked in. He was able to detect a light sniffling sound. He inhaled deeply and caught the faintest whiff of her scent. She was in the bathroom. She was alive and breathing. Why wasn't she answering him?

"I know you're in there, baby. What's wrong? If anything's wrong, you can tell me."

"Go away, Neil," she called out to him.

"I'm not going anywhere," he said stubbornly. "I want to help you."

"You can't," she whimpered, just as stubborn. "No one can."

"Tell me what's wrong. Better yet, come out here so we can talk about it. I'm tired of talking to you through this door. I want to see you. I have to see that you're okay."

"I just need some time," she said, her voice growing fainter.

He stood back from the door. He didn't know what to do. A loving husband would give his wife a few moments to collect herself if she requested it, but he didn't want to give Marilyn those few moments. He didn't know what was wrong with her. There was no telling what she could do in those few minutes. He had no idea what he should do. "It's not anything I did, is it?" he pressed, in order to keep her talking.

She chuckled, more to herself than to anyone else and answered, "No, it was nothing you did. It's more along the lines of something I did."

He took another step back from the door. What did she mean by that? He knew what he thought she meant, but he couldn't be right. His Marilyn wouldn't ever think of...much less act on...

"You're quiet," she said in a small voice.

"I'm just thinking," he said slowly.

"Thinking about what?"

"Thinking about what you could be talking about," he said, his voice growing just as quiet.

She started to cry then.

He felt like crying too, but he held in his tears. A mental image flashed into his mind, an image of his wife sitting on the bathroom floor holding a razor to her wrists. He squeezed his eyes closed, trying to block out the image. "Baby, open the door so we can talk about this."

"I don't want you to be mad at me," she said in a shaky voice.

"I'm not mad at you. I just want you to be okay. I don't like hearing you like this."

"You're not mad at me now, but you will be," she promised.

"Don't think about what I will or won't be. Just unlock the door."

The silence was thick with expectation, but a moment later the door lock clicked. He turned the doorknob and opened the bathroom door. Just as he'd pictured, his wife was sitting on the bathroom floor. She wasn't holding a razor to her wrists, though. There wasn't a razor anywhere in sight.

Surrounding his wife on the bathroom floor, though, was an assortment of different pregnancy tests. They came in many different colors, sizes, and brand names, but they were all displaying the same results. His wife…was pregnant.

And since vampires and humans couldn't produce children, he could only come to one conclusion: he wasn't the father of the child that his wife was carrying.

CHAPTER NINE

Iancu ducked his head beneath a steady stream of burning hot water. His saturated hair was heavy with moisture. Tense muscles relaxed under the gentle coax of the steaming hot liquid. Soap bubbles graced his forearms, collarbone, and other areas that he hadn't yet rinsed off.

There had been a large number of vampires out that night. They'd been terrorizing humans. It had been an extremely fulfilling night of hunting. He'd slain eighteen vampires. By the time he returned to his apartment, the sun was lazily stretching its rays and preparing to rise.

He couldn't pinpoint the exact moment that he realized he was no longer alone in the bathroom, but his body went rigid beneath the steady stream of water. He continued to lather soap all over himself, but he was attempting to peer through the moisture coating the glass doors of the shower stall. Whoever was in the bathroom with him was invisible; he noticed this at once. He didn't have to see her to know who she was, though. There was no mistaking her presence. She was the oldest known vampire and undoubtedly the most powerful.

He cut off the water. Water droplets beaded off of his skin and dropped onto the shower stall floor. His hair hung over his shoulder, as heavy as a soaking wet beach towel.

He slid the shower stall door open, assessing his surroundings.

A throaty chuckle sounded from somewhere in front of him and she probed into the very corners of his mind. *You know I'm here.*

He grabbed the folded towel perched on the edge of the sink without replying.

I know that you *know that I'm here. Ignoring me is pointless.*

Cloaking yourself from me is pointless, he returned as he proceeded to dry himself off with the towel.

She materialized before him like some kind of mirage, stuffed into a lavender dress that clung to every curve she possessed. Waves of red hair tumbled down her back and over her shoulders. She was quite a vision to see, remarkably beautiful. She wasn't naïve about her beauty, though. She knew exactly how beautiful she was and she used it to her benefit every chance that she got.

She slithered towards him languidly, tapping her cheek with the long, manicured tip of a blood red nail. "Iancu," she breathed, wrapping her lips around his name as if it were a lollipop. "It has been ages since I've seen you last."

"If I never see you again, it'll be too soon," he muttered, wrapping the towel around his waist. "How did you find me?"

"I sired you. You couldn't hide from me if you tried. We're linked for all eternity."

He tried not to cringe and failed. As an afterthought, he mentally put a barricade up so that she couldn't read his mind.

She smiled as if she knew what he was doing. "Oh, Iancu," she said endearingly. "What went wrong with us?"

"What went *right* with us?"

"It wasn't all bad with us," she said, inching closer to him.

He took a step back from her. "It was worse."

She stuck out her bottom lip petulantly, attempting to appear cute and child-like. She was as far from "cute" and "child-like" as a woman could possibly get. There was nothing innocent about her. She was cold and manipulative. "It hurts me when you say that."

"Hurt? You?" Looking doubtful, he strode past her and out of the bathroom.

"I saw what was done to Aryk." She followed him down the short hallway and into the living room

"How *is* Aryk doing?" he asked after a short laugh.

"Are you jealous of him?" she questioned.

"Why would I be?"

"Because he has me and you don't."

He nearly choked with laughter. "Aryk can have you."

The smile was wiped from her face. Her eyes narrowed into slits. "I'm glad to see that you're doing well and haven't lost your sense of humor."

"I'm sure you are," he muttered sarcastically. "Why are you here?"

"You've grown mighty cynical since I've seen you last."

"You've managed to dodge the question," he told her. "And might I add that you did so quite skillfully."

She recognized the words she'd spoken to him during their first conversation. "You have an amazing memory."

"No, my memory is quite faulty, actually," he told her. "I just have amazingly detailed nightmares."

A muscle in her jaw twitched and her nostrils flared. "I hear that you're teamed up with the slayer."

"Word travels fast." He leaned against the wall near the balcony doors.

"What made you team up with *her*?"

A smile touched his lips at the envious tone that strained her voice. "What is your purpose? Why are you here?"

"Certain events will be taking place over the next few months and certain people will take certain sides. I wanted to know where your loyalties lie, and I didn't want to trust the rumors flying around. I wanted to hear it straight from the horse's mouth."

"You just told me a whole lot of nothing," he said, turning his back to her and peering through the balcony doors. A brilliant crescent moon hung suspended in the sky, flanked by wispy, gray clouds. The moon was slowly retreating, making way for its bright orange counterpart. He smiled wistfully. For a moment, he forgot that Jordana was standing behind him.

"You already know what's going on," she told him. She made it a statement, not a question.

"How do you know what I know?"

"Like I said, I saw what you and the slayer did to Aryk."

"Aryk deserved every silver bullet that hit him."

She didn't quite disagree with that statement, but she didn't dare voice that opinion out loud. "And you also put up a mental block. The only reason you would have to block me from your thoughts is to keep me from finding out something."

"You're right. Wanting to keep my private thoughts *private* has nothing to do with it." He drew the sliding doors open and stepped out onto the balcony, welcoming the light breeze.

"I don't know why you have to be so difficult."

"And I don't know why *you*, possibly the most powerful vampire in the world, would be Aryk's lapdog."

She flinched as if he'd burned her.

"Don't look at me like that," he sneered over his shoulder at her. "You know it and I know it. You've lost control of your little pet. You used to run him and now *he* runs *you*."

Her upper lip curled maliciously. "Take that back," she ordered him.

"You have no power over me."

"That is where you're wrong," she told him while her violet eyes spit fire.

"Whether or not I take it back, you know it's true." He turned to face her. "You want to know where my loyalty lies. You can be assured that my loyalty doesn't lie with you. You took my life five centuries ago, and I'll see to it that I return the favor."

She closed the distance between them. The expression on her face was stony. Her eyes were devoid of any emotion. She was statuesque, standing at 5'10" with a curvaceous figure. Much like a statue, she looked cold to the touch. "You have the freedom of choosing sides, Iancu...but if you choose the wrong side, there is no telling what will happen to you."

"If I take your side, I *know* what will happen to me." He would turn into a monster, an even more dangerous one than he was now.

"Aryk is very powerful. He nearly killed you. If you side against him, then last night will seem like a walk in the park compared to what he will do to you."

He nodded his head, folding his arms across his chest. "This is your sales pitch?"

She dared to reach out and touch his bare upper arm.

He didn't flinch or cringe. He stared at her, not trusting her enough to take his eyes off of her. He was aware of the attempts she was making at probing his mind. There were walls set in place, sturdy walls that she couldn't penetrate-even at her age.

They stood that way for several minutes, staring at each other and trying to read the other's intentions. Finally, sensing that he wasn't going to come around anytime soon, she backed away from him. "You're making a very grave mistake," she warned him.

"We'll see about that." He could see that he was getting under her skin. Her well-practiced look of composure was beginning to falter. He suppressed a grin and said, "I'm sure you can find your way out."

She was fuming. "You act as if the gift I've given you is a curse," she shouted at him. "Eternal life. Intensified senses. Supernatural abilities.

"If you are truly to fight against Aryk and myself, then you can't afford any weaknesses. Your own self-hate and hate of our people are your most substantial weaknesses. You are messing with the wrong people. I am the one that made you. I can most certainly break you."

He met her gaze head-on and made no reaction to the blazing force of power lying within it. With the power of her eyes, she could make any human being want to grant her every wish. She could make that human her slave for the rest of his or her life. He, however, was not human. He was nearly as old as she was and possessed a great amount of power himself. That was evident by the way he was able to meet her gaze without blinking. Flames of his own power lay within his eyes, and they crackled to life.

She drew back, her lips curling into a sneer. "You will regret this night."

Frosty blue eyes illuminated. "I will not regret this night more than I regret ever having met you," he said in a level voice.

She nodded her head as if she'd expected him to say as much. She stroked her chin thoughtfully and said, "I wonder how your slayer friend is doing this morning."

"What is that supposed to mean?"

A slender, red eyebrow arched. "I have your attention now, don't I?" she asked and with those words, she turned on her heel and disappeared through the sliding glass doors.

He glanced at the watch on his wrist. It was nearly six-thirty in the morning. *She's bluffing,* he thought. *She's not really going to cause harm to Charlie, not during morning hours when the sun is minutes from relentlessly blazing across the sky.* The hair at the nape of his neck twitched.

He stepped through the balcony doors and ran a hand through his damp hair. *And you aren't going to run off to the slayer's rescue.* He paced back and forth in the living room. If Jordana seriously intended to harm the slayer, she would not have alerted him. She was baiting him. She was trying to *get* to him, the same way he'd gotten to her.

He walked towards his bedroom, where he threw on some clothes and retrieved one of his favorite swords. Even if he didn't think that Jordana was serious about her threat, he had to check it out. There was the smallest chance that she *was* serious and he didn't want to take that chance.

He pushed his arms through the sleeves of his trench coat after attaching a sheathed sword to his waist.

Her heartbeat was racing and her pulse throbbed at her temples. She burst through the wooded trail behind her cabin, pumping her arms and bringing her knees up nearly to her chest. She sprinted as if she were running for her life.

The sounds of the forest muted and all she could hear was her own pulse pounding in her ears and her controlled breathing. Her ponytail flopped against the back of her neck. Beads of sweat graced her forehead.

Who did Iancu think he was, talking to her the way he had? Acting all funny when she told him that she needed a place to stay? If it weren't for her, he would be *dead*. And how did he show her his gratitude?

She continued to run, ducking her head beneath wayward tree branches. Walls of green leaves stood on either side of the well-worn path. A bulbous sun shined down on the forest, only some of its rays filtering through the branches of the many trees lining the trail. She slowed her steps, never bringing herself to a complete halt. She turned on her heel and darted in the opposite direction, running in the direction of her cabin.

Hunting had not gone well the previous night. It had felt odd not having Iancu fighting alongside her. She needed to avoid that line of thinking, she knew, because she was the slayer. She didn't need anyone fighting beside her in battle. She could fight her own battles and come out victorious. Sure, she'd nearly gotten filleted by a couple of super-vamps, but that happened to even the best slayers once in awhile.

Over the sounds of her ragged breathing and her thumping pulse, she heard a twig snapping. She slowed her pace and glanced over her shoulder, peering with narrow eyes. She had the inkling that someone was following her, but she didn't see anyone in plain view. *They could be cloaking themselves,* she thought. *That would make them invisible to the human eye.*

When her cabin came into view, an overwhelming sense of relief hit her. She broke into a leisurely jog shortly before slowing to a walking pace.

As soon as she set foot inside the cabin, she knew that something was wrong. She immediately proceeded to inspect the place, trying her best to appear inconspicuous. She found nothing that was blatantly out of the ordinary, but her senses were still on alert.

She grabbed two of her guns from their respective cases and set them on top of her bed. While standing near the bed, she tugged her tank top up and over her head. She also tugged down the shorts she'd been running in and pulled off her tennis shoes and socks.

After undressing, she padded into the bathroom with both of her guns in tow. Then, she grabbed a washcloth and a large towel from the towel rack and kicked the bathroom door shut with the heel of her foot. She didn't lock the door. Doing so would suggest that she *was* aware someone else was in the cabin with her, and she didn't want to give off that impression.

She set the large towel on the closed toilet lid and stepped into the shower stall. Inside the shower there was a wide, tiled ledge mounted on the wall. This is where she placed her guns.

She stood on tiptoe and adjusted the shower head so that the water flow was directed away from the guns lying on the ledge. She turned the showerhead on and tilted her head back as a stream of warm water rained down on her.

She could sense one other presence, then two of them, shifting within the cabin. There was more than one of them here. *Shit,* she thought, arching a glance over her shoulder even though the glass design on the shower stall door was difficult to see through.

She braced both of her hands on the wall, just below the showerhead, and closed her eyes. *Focus,* she thought. Her eyes danced behind closed eyelids. *You need to know where they are. Just focus.*

She'd spent a lot of time with her grandfather before he was murdered and plucked apart. He had taught her many things about being a medicine man. There were two abilities that slayers possessed. They had the power to heal far more rapidly than the typical human-which basically meant that they could take a beating better than the average person. Slayers also aged slower than most humans did. As a slayer, she had two special abilities that helped in the fight against supernatural creatures. As the granddaughter of a medicine man, however, she possessed a myriad of skills. She could read energies. She could tell the difference between a vampire's energy and a demon's energy. She had knowledge about spells and incantations.

At the moment, she was reading the energy level in her cabin. Images flashed behind her eyes. She could clearly picture what the main room looked like. Near the fireplace, there was a nondescript blur. The blur flickered and moved, stealthily heading in the direction of the bathroom. The image of the blur disappeared from view and another scene took its place. Another blur, similar to the first, was crouching near her bed in the bedroom.

Goosebumps prickled along her forearms at the thought of someone violating her personal space. The hot water streaming down her back wasn't enough to warm her.

One of them was now on the other side of the bathroom door. She could feel their power sliding through the crack beneath the door, could feel that power snaking towards her, beckoning to her.

She turned off the showerhead and wiped the water from her eyes. Her hands crept behind her back, where each retrieved a gun from the ledge mounted on the shower stall wall.

She slid open the shower stall door with water droplets gliding down her torso and limbs. Her wet hair clung to her shoulder blades and shoulders. She stood in front of the bathroom door with both guns raised and cocked.

The doorknob turned slowly and the door started to creak open. It was an effort for her to control her breathing, but she somehow managed to keep it from getting too erratic. The door opened to reveal a dark-haired vampire with pockmarks on his face.

He leered at her; he had probably never seen a naked woman holding two guns before. He drank in the sight of her with his mouth agape, temporarily unable to think or move.

BloodLust: The Beginning

She didn't hesitate. She pulled the triggers of both guns simultaneously. The kick from each gun knocked her wrists back, but otherwise she remained immobile.

The vampire flew backwards, twisting in the air and landing on his stomach. He stayed down. He wasn't quite fifty years old and didn't have the strength or power to heal as quickly as, say, a vampire with several hundred years on him. Such as Aryk...

Who emerged in the hallway with a sick, twisted grin on his face. He glanced down at his fallen partner with mock-sympathy. "The poor guy never had a chance," he said, clucking his tongue. "Not against the slayer." He lifted his gaze to meet hers.

The guns were still raised. Her pulse beat loudly in her ears. Memories rushed at her, images of her parents, brother, and grandfather. Her parents' bodies lying so still in their blood-soaked bed and her brother's corpse coming to life as a vampire and being decapitated by Iancu's sword. Tears started at the corners of her eyes and she couldn't stop them from falling.

Aryk tilted his head to the side and gracefully stepped over the dying vampire's body. The smile never left his face. Seeing tears rolling down her cheeks was a turn-on for him. He enjoyed seeing her in pain and wanted to see her in a great deal of pain before the day was over. He approached her slowly and looked her over from head to toe. "You are truly a remarkable specimen. You're so strong and beautiful. You're a hard-core warrior and yet you're vulnerable. I've dreamt of this moment."

She made the mistake of looking into his eyes; her feet may as well have been planted to the floor. She couldn't move. She was paralyzed, unable to utilize her guns and unable to run. Anger flared in her hazel eyes.

The anger in her eyes only excited him more. He withdrew the guns from each of her hands and carefully set them down on the floor. He reached out and touched her hair. His hand traveled from the top of her head, to her neck, where it lingered. From her neck, his hand moved down to her shoulder and found the slope of her right breast. Again, his hand hesitated. Her heartbeat drummed beneath his fingers. His gaze held her eyes captive. The eerie smile dissolved from his face as his hand continued to roam all over her body.

His free arm snaked behind her back and pressed her body into his. He smoothed her hair back, off of her neck. Her pulse caused the skin at her neck to jump consistently. He could easily grab her neck in his hands and twist it, ending her fragile, insignificant life. It would be so easy. He would never have to worry about her terminating the lives of his people again. He wouldn't have to worry about how powerful she and Iancu were when they worked together.

His excitement was growing more and more evident as he pressed his pelvis against her body. He lowered his head with his eyes still holding hers captive. He touched his lips to hers and savored the taste of her, the smell of her.

Her brows drew together and she tried with all of her might to pull away from him. He was too old, too powerful. She was a prisoner in her own body.

He sucked her bottom lip into his mouth and nibbled on it. His incisors weren't lowered, but they were still incredibly sharp. They grazed over her lip as he nibbled it, several times coming close to nicking her. He released her bottom lip and his kiss deepened. He was a greedy kisser, and it seemed that he was trying to inhale her very soul from the depths of her body. One of his hands rested in her hair. As the kiss intensified, that hand twisted and turned, wrapping her hair around it. Without warning, he yanked her head back and stared at her.

Desire, disgust, and loathing mingled in his heated gaze. "You're resisting me," he said, frowning. "But I know what will make you stop resisting me."

After releasing her hair, he stepped away from her. He closed his eyes and brought both hands up to his face. His cheekbones strained beneath his cheeks as his face contorted. He ran his hands up over his changing face to smooth back his hair, starting at his hairline. As he did, his bleached blonde hair darkened, from root to tip. His hair grew longer right before her eyes. Jet-black waves tumbled down his back. When he dropped his hands from his face and hair, he stood before her looking like a completely different man. The line of his jaw was more pronounced and his eyes had gone from the color of pure amber to a sparkling ocean blue. His lips were fuller and his brows were thicker.

He stripped his button-down shirt from his body. His skin rippled. Muscles transformed and his bones stretched and cracked. The waistband of his dark slacks protested, straining against his widening waistline.

He stood before her with an enticing muscular chest, a newly etched dragon-shaped birthmark on the inside of his right wrist, and the face and hair of Iancu. He had the power to shapeshift. He abruptly broke the paralyzing hold that he had on her.

She stumbled forward at the unexpected release and landed on her hands and knees. She stared down at the floor, not wanting to look up.

He moved forward and knelt to the floor. He slid two fingers beneath her chin and raised her face so that she was looking up at him. "Don't be afraid of me," he said. Even his voice had changed.

Her chin quaked in his hand, but she allowed him to help her to her feet. Her eyes were wide and disbelieving. Never before had she witnessed a vampire shapeshift before her eyes.

Unable to stop herself, she lifted a hand and allowed it to travel over the contours of his face. After that night at Club Pulse, she had done the same thing to the real Iancu. The hills and plains of his face that she had felt that night were the same hills and plains that she was smoothing her hand over now. It was the same face, the same body.

He stared down at her, allowing her to touch him freely. His chest heaved up and down as if he were as exhilarated as she was. When he could no longer take the teasing effect her touch had on him, he caught her wrist in his hand and twisted her around so that her back was pressed to his chest. He lowered his chin and rested it on her shoulder. His hands moved from her upper arms to her breasts, wandering down to her stomach.

She leaned back into him. From where they stood, she could see her reflection clearly in the bathroom mirror above the sink. There was no one standing behind her reflection. She could see certain body parts being pulled and squeezed, but she couldn't see who was doing the pulling and squeezing.

He continued to tease her and touch her, stopping only when she closed her eyes and murmured, "Iancu."

He hesitated with his hand hovering over the apex of her thighs. He had Iancu's face, hair, body, and voice. He didn't know why it was so unnerving to be called by his name, but it was. He didn't want her to be calling out Iancu's name. He wanted her to call out *his* name. *But,* he thought as he gathered her into his arms, *I will take what I can get.*

He turned with her cradled in his arms and faced the perpetual thorn in his ass.

The original, authentic Iancu stood before him, assessing the situation at hand and seemingly unaffected by seeing another man wearing his face.

Charlie's arms were thrown around Aryk's neck, and she was nuzzling her cheek against his.

Iancu's eyes were radiant.

In response, Aryk's eyes, formerly the same shade of blue as Iancu's, glowed an iridescent amber color. He opened his mouth to reveal his lowering incisors.

Charlie turned her head and saw the real Iancu. Her eyes widened, and she looked from one Iancu to the other. She struggled her way out of Aryk's hold, touching her feet to the floor.

Iancu's eyes flicked over to her. He met her gaze. Her blood wasn't tainted. Aryk hadn't claimed her as his pet, not yet. He was surprised at how relieved he was about this discovery. His hand swept back one of the lapels to his trench coat. He gripped the hilt of his sword as his eyes flicked back to Aryk.

"Leave it to you to interrupt an intense moment between the slayer and myself," Aryk said, speaking in his own voice.

Iancu didn't say anything. He didn't trust himself to speak; he was still trying to find out what the hell had been going on before he'd arrived.

"You really do have the worst timing."

"Take off my face," Iancu said softly, removing the sword from its sheath and holding it before him. "Don't make me tell you more than once."

Aryk raised a hand and ran it over the smoothness of his face, his twisted smile returning. "I'm not so sure that I want to discard your face so quickly. I think I'm beginning to like having your face. It sure had an effect on the slayer."

Charlie pressed her back against the hallway wall, avoiding the heated gaze that Iancu sent her way.

"If you don't take my face off now, I will take it off for you," he threatened Aryk, advancing on him with his sword raised.

While the two vampires squared off, Charlie crouched to the floor and retrieved her two guns.

Iancu stood with his legs spread wide, holding his sword as if he were holding a baseball bat.

Aryk took a running start towards him. He abruptly dropped to the floor and slid between Iancu's legs. As Iancu took the time to turn around, Aryk rolled over his dying partner's body and removed the sword from the sheath at his waist. He leapt to his feet and faced Iancu. "You're not the only one who knows how to fight with a sword, Iancu." He bent his fingers, beckoning his adversary over to him.

Iancu stepped over the fallen vampire's withering body and extended his sword. He jabbed the tip of the blade at Aryk, knowing full well that Aryk would block this move. When Aryk *did* block the move, he quickly brought the sword down and slashed at his opponent's waist.

The blade struck Aryk's flesh and his skin burned where the wood of Iancu's sword touched it. He jumped back, his eyes wide. He lunged forward with the sword, catching Iancu in the upper arm. Blood lined the blade of the sword and

Aryk brought the blade of the sword up to his mouth. He slid the flat of the sword across his tongue, lapping up Iancu's blood.

Swords clashed, moves were blocked, and at certain points, steel met flesh. Iancu fought his carbon copy with a determined ferocity. He was fighting the vampire who was intent on increasing the vampire population. He was fighting the vampire who entertained perverted fantasies about the slayer. He couldn't lose. He couldn't let Aryk set foot off of this property. He had to kill him. He had to rid the world of him.

Aryk hadn't been bluffing when he said that he could wield a sword, though. He lunged forward when on the attack and leaned back when on the defense, moving adeptly, seemingly without much effort. He was just as determined as Iancu was. The slayer had reacted just as he thought she would when he'd taken form as Iancu. She had a thing for him. Once he got rid of the real Iancu, he could have the slayer to himself and do whatever he willed with her. As long as Iancu was alive, though, he would always be a pain in the ass, intruding on his affairs and attempting to shoot down his plans.

Iancu dropped to his knees and whirled around, slashing his sword through the air. The sword's blade caught Aryk in the leg.

Aryk shouted a plethora of profanity, staggering backwards. He backed out of the hallway and into the main room of the cabin. How could he have let Iancu make that strike? How could he have not sensed Iancu's intentions and blocked the blow? As blood saturated his slacks, he fell back against the couch in the great room and leaned his head back, astonished at how much pain the wound was causing him.

Iancu didn't hesitate; he advanced on his opponent holding his sword in the air. Aryk leaned heavily against the couch with his dead partner's sword lowered. Iancu brought his sword downward at an angle, aiming for Aryk's neck.

Aryk brought his sword up and fended Iancu off. With the last bit of energy he had, he raised his foot and pressed it against Iancu's rib cage. His kick sent Iancu flying back and landing against the wall.

Charlie, still a bit dazed and disoriented, emerged from the hallway with both guns cocked. Her eyes were cold and her movements were mechanical as she pulled the triggers on both firearms.

Silver bullets rained down on Aryk and he didn't have the energy to fight back. His body lurched and jerked as the silver bullets hit him. She didn't stop shooting until both guns were empty of bullets. Even then, her fingers kept closing over the triggers.

Iancu picked himself up from the floor and went to stand at her back. He rested his hands on both of her shoulders, trying to calm her down. "He's down," he said, lowering her arms. "It's all right. He's down."

She turned and buried her face in his chest.

He awkwardly held his arms around her naked body, not quite knowing what to say. "It's all right," he repeated.

She wiped at her eyes, shaking her head back and forth. "I thought he was...I didn't know...I wouldn't have-"

"You don't have to explain anything to me," he said.

"I just wanted you to know why-"

"I would rather not know," he said honestly.

She nodded her head solemnly. "Is it over now? He should be dead now, right?"

He stared over her shoulder with a telltale look in his eyes.

She turned around and a gasp escaped her lips.

Aryk was no longer lying on the couch. He had vanished, and that meant that it wasn't over at all...because he was still alive.

Jordana was sitting up in bed, conducting research on Lord Vlad when the door burst open and Iancu appeared, leaning heavily against the doorjamb. She slammed the book shut and leapt off of the bed, her eyes wary and alert. "What are you doing here?" she demanded.

He didn't answer. He collapsed to his knees, still holding onto the doorjamb.

Was this a ruse? Why had he come here? Where had all of his wounds come from? Had he had another encounter with Aryk? She remained standing near the bed, riddled with uncertainty. "Have you changed your mind? Have you decided that your loyalty *does* lie with me after all?"

He raised his head and looked up at her, his familiar blue eyes communicating something to her. She didn't know what he was trying to tell her.

"Are you unable to talk?" she demanded.

"H-help," he managed to croak out before falling forward and landing on his stomach.

She stared at him for several moments before taking action. She briskly strode into the bathroom and snatched a washcloth from the towel rack. She flipped the faucet lever up and held the cloth beneath the flow of cold water. Then with the towel in hand, she exited the bathroom and knelt down to the floor. Suppressing the urge to lovingly stroke his long, dark hair, she rolled him onto his back.

His shirt had already been ripped from his body. She unbuttoned and unzipped his slacks and tugged them down his legs. In addition to the deep gash that was above his right hip, there was a deep wound in his left leg.

Fantasizing about how he would express his gratitude to her when he came to consciousness, she worked at cleaning his wounds. He was becoming weaker by the moment; she could feel his power seeping from his body. As his power slipped from his grasp, his hair paled. His facial structure changed before her eyes. His body grew leaner and more compact.

Her lips set into a grim line. It wasn't Iancu who was lying unconscious on her bedroom floor. He hadn't changed his mind about whose side he was on. It was Aryk who was lying on her floor, incapacitated and vulnerable. She grabbed him and slung him over her shoulder as if he were nothing but a sack of potatoes. She carelessly tossed him onto the bed, feeling a great amount of disappointment. She should have known that it had been Aryk all along. She should have sensed that something wasn't right. How could she have been fooled so easily?

Because I wanted it to be Iancu so badly, she thought.

She shamelessly probed Aryk's weak mind to find out what events had transpired earlier that night. She saw him stalking around the slayer's cabin and salivating over the slayer's nude body. She saw him touching the slayer intimately, witnessed him transforming into Iancu and continuing the seduction.

Her eyes shined an unnatural violet color and rage made the muscles in her body as taut as violin strings. She didn't stop searching his mind, though. She watched as her beau swept the slayer up into his arms, intent on making love to her and possibly marking her, and watched as Iancu interrupted his plans. A wry smile curled her lips as she watched the battle that followed. She clapped her hands giddily when she saw the slayer shooting silver bullets into Aryk.

She considered letting him die then and there. It was what he deserved for betraying her. She was infatuated with him, but not infatuated enough to let him walk all over her this way. He had crossed the line when he set one hand on the slayer. He had had the perfect opportunity to capture her, and he had wasted it.

Her eyes continued to shine with an alluring radiance. "The slayer will die," she said aloud, looking down on Aryk's mutilated body. "And I will be the one who takes her life from her."

CHAPTER TEN

Even before Iancu opened the door to his apartment, he sensed that someone was within it, violating his space. He glanced over his shoulder at Charlie wordlessly before testing the doorknob. The door was locked, as he'd left it.

He influenced the locks and opened the door. Nothing looked to be disturbed, but there was a crumpled figure lying on his couch. His hand flew to the hilt of his sword, but a closer look revealed that it was Neil who was lying on the couch.

Charlie, standing at Iancu's back, wrapped her arms around herself. "Do you know him?"

"He's an old friend of mine." Iancu bent at the waist and nudged his friend in the arm.

Neil shifted and finally came awake with a start. He bolted upward into a sitting position. It took a moment for his eyes to focus. He wiped the sleep from them and turned his gaze onto his friend. "Iancu," he mumbled, running a hand through his unruly hair. "I'm so glad you're here."

"So am I," Iancu said, "but what are you doing here?"

"Marilyn," Neil whispered, almost to himself. "My beautiful, sweet Marilyn." His voice became choked with sobs and he shielded his eyes from view as crimson tears welled up in them.

Iancu's brows furrowed with worry. He vaguely remembered that Marilyn was the name of Neil's wife. "What happened to Marilyn?" he pressed.

Neil shook his head this way and that. "She cheated. She cheated on me. How could-how could she?"

Iancu drew back and rose to his full height. "I'm sorry to hear that," he told his friend. He had thought that harm may have come to Marilyn, but the only harm that had been caused was to Neil's ego and pride.

"She was my soulmate," Neil went on. "I would never have thought she would do something like this. It's *so* unlike her."

"Are you sure that she cheated on you?" Iancu asked him.

"She's pregnant," the other vampire spat.

Iancu's eyes widened. Neil was right. There was no question about it; his wife was cheating on him. He sat on the couch next to his friend and braced his elbows on his knees. "Maybe this is for the best. You're a vampire. She's a human. She would find out what you are eventually."

"How could you say that?" Neil demanded, and proceeded to mock Iancu. "'Maybe it's for the best?' She *cheated* on me and she's pregnant with some prick's kid. I love her more than I love *myself*. This isn't for the best. This is the worst thing that could possibly happen to me."

Iancu shrugged his shoulders.

Neil noticed Charlie for the first time. "Who are you?"

"I'm Charlie," she said in a soft voice.

Neil frowned and arched a look at Iancu. "I thought that you weren't into the dating scene."

"We're *not* dating," both Iancu and Charlie insisted at the same time. They looked at each other and then avoided each other's gaze.

Neil witnessed this and cracked a smile. "All right, all right, I'm sorry to imply that you two were dating, geez. But if you aren't one of his conquests, then who are you?"

"She's the slayer," Iancu explained shortly.

"The one you were telling me about?"

"Yes."

Neil looked at Charlie with new eyes. "You two look like you've been through hell tonight."

"That isn't too far off the mark," Iancu muttered. He didn't waste time in bringing Neil up to speed on what had occurred that night. After Neil had come by and warned him about Aryk's intentions toward the slayer, Jordana paid him a visit and made propositions. Once those propositions had been declined, she'd proceeded to make threats. Iancu had gone to the slayer's cabin to make sure that she was all right. By the time he'd gotten there, though, Aryk had her in his clutches. "He had shapeshifted into me," Iancu said with a disgusted expression on his face.

Neil's eyes turned round with shock. "Are you serious?"

"It was strange. He was trying to seduce her."

The other vampire nodded without saying a word. He had witnessed the chemistry between Iancu and Charlie when they'd denied dating each other. Sparks were definitely flying. Chances were that Aryk had noticed this also and had decided to use it to his advantage.

"We fought for a bit and Charlie put some silver bullets into him."

"Did he survive that?"

"Unfortunately, he *did* survive," Iancu replied, mentally kicking himself in the ass for allowing Aryk to set foot outside the cabin.

"That's too bad," Neil said.

"There's still a chance that he didn't survive," Charlie told them. "He left the cabin, but he still may have died before getting the chance to heal."

Neil shook his head curtly. "If he made his way back home, Jordana would have seen to it that he didn't die."

"Chances are that he's alive," Iancu said, "and if he is, then he'll be coming for you again."

Goosebumps prickled along her forearms at the thought of ever seeing Aryk again.

"If there's anything that I know about Aryk, it is that he is persistent, if not obsessive. He'll be coming for you again. We could easily set him up for a major fall." Iancu's eyes were still locked on hers and they were asking something impossible of her.

"You want me to go back to the cabin," she realized.

"He will come looking for you there. And when he does, we'll be ready for him this time."

She shook her head slowly. "I'm not going back there."

"We'll get him this time," he promised, "and you won't ever have to worry about him again."

"I said that I'm not going back there. I can't believe that you'd *let* me go back there. He could have killed us both!"

He didn't react to her tone of voice. He sat on the couch, staring up at her with an unreadable expression on his face. "We'll devise a plan," he said slowly and quietly. "The way we will set it up, he won't be able to lay a hand on you. I won't be in the cabin with you because he would sense me, but I will be nearby. And Neil will be nearby. We will have you covered. No harm would come to you."

She was still shaking her head in refusal. "I want to stay here," she said, her bottom lip trembling. "With you."

Neil coughed loudly and stood up from the couch. "I think I have to piss," he said awkwardly, "so I'm going to go and do that." He disappeared down the hallway.

"Don't say that," Iancu said in a low voice.

"Don't say what? It's true. I want to stay here with you." She sat on the couch next to him. "We work well together. I feel safe when I'm around you. I don't want to stay in that cabin alone.

"I know I'm the big, bad slayer, but I've never fought the likes of Aryk before. Quite honestly, he scares the shit out of me. The last thing that I want to do is return to my cabin without adequate training. I'd be a sitting duck."

He nearly jumped out of his skin when she closed her hand over his. He snatched his hand from beneath hers and stood up from the couch. His mind was racing. He couldn't allow her to stay here with him. She would get in the way. She would be nosey and she'd probably snoop through his things. Not to mention the sexual tension that seemed to sizzle whenever they were in the same room together. Letting her stay here would be a mistake. "It's not a good idea for you to stay here."

"It's not a good idea for me to stay *there*, at the cabin," she countered. "We can come up with another plan to get rid of Aryk."

He'd met several slayers before her. Most of the slayers that he had met had been emotionally detached. They had been lifeless and clinical. They hadn't needed anyone or been as vulnerable as Charlie seemed to be. She was supposed to know how to take care of herself. She shouldn't be dependent on anyone, *least* of all him. Still, it was difficult saying no to those beautiful hazel eyes and that supple, caramel-colored skin. Something within him stirred and he quickly put it back to rest. "You can stay here for a couple of days," he said finally. "That's it."

She smiled triumphantly. "A couple of days will be fine."

Neil volunteered to sleep on the couch, surrendering the guest room to Charlie. Iancu lay in bed on his back, staring up at the ceiling. He could sense Neil's presence, pacing around the living room fretting over the domestic situation he had going on with his wife. He could sense Charlie's presence through his bedroom wall. She was undressing and climbing into bed beneath the sheets. He fought to keep a nude image of her out of his mind, but it was a fight that he lost.

He remembered the way she had looked naked. Her body had been lean and toned, glistening with sweat or oil, he couldn't tell which. Her hair had been soaking wet; she'd probably just gotten out of the shower when Aryk had attacked.

Still trying his damnedest to wipe the image of a naked Charlie from his mind, he rolled over and prayed for a restful slumber.

He approached her bed tentatively, hesitantly. He was probably wondering whether or not he should be in her room, looming over her bed.

She was perched on the edge of the bed waiting for him. Her feet were planted firmly on the floor and she leaned back on braced elbows. She wore nothing but a lacey white camisole and matching panties.

He only paused for another moment before leaning down and capturing her in his arms. He kissed her deeply and scraped his nails along her arms as he pressed her backwards.

He snatched her panties off of her in a quick, one-handed motion. The sound of ripping fabric engulfed the dark guest room. He didn't say anything, never said a word. His movements were quiet as his body meshed with hers. His pelvis ground into hers and they rocked together.

He grabbed both of her wrists and held them above her head as his body enveloped hers. Her body came alive with flaming desire. Her skin burned where he touched her.

His eyes started glowing, but they weren't their usual sparkling pools of blue. They were gleaming bright yellow. Before her eyes, the dark hair fell from his head and in its place were bleached blonde spikes. He transformed as she watched in horror. It wasn't Iancu mounted on top of her; it was Aryk.

She came awake screaming her head off and fighting her sheets, floundering in a bed too large to be her own. Panic seized her and she clamored around the nightstand for a lamp. Her hand found one and quickly switched it on. With her heart in her throat, she glanced around the room she'd been sleeping in. It was sterile, with minimal furniture and adornments.

The bed garments were black and the curtains were solid black. An armoire that housed a big-screen television faced the bed and beside the armoire there was an empty closet. There was no artwork gracing the walls, no knick-knacks atop the armoire. There was no desk or dresser in the room, just a lone armchair awkwardly placed in the corner of the room near the window.

The door was kicked open and Iancu stood filling the doorway with his sword raised. He was shirtless and panting. His eyes roamed around the room, seeking out an attacker of some sort.

She looked small and defenseless in the king-sized bed, grabbing the sheets to her chest.

He entered the room cautiously, still looking around. "Are you all right?" he demanded.

She nodded her head, afraid to tell him that the only attacker had been in her nightmare. "I just had a bad dream," she said softly.

He lowered the sword but his eyes still managed to shoot daggers at her. "I thought..." He let the sentence trail off.

She knew what he'd thought. "I'm fine," she assured him.

He turned to leave, but she called out to him. He halted with one hand grasping the doorjamb.

"Don't leave, not now," she whispered.

"You need to get some rest."

"Can I come and sleep with you?"

A muscle in his jaw twitched. "I don't sleep with anyone, ever."

"Then can you stay in here and sleep in that chair over there?" Her voice was quivering and she was struggling to control it. "If you leave, I won't be able to sleep."

He shot a glance over to the uncomfortable-looking wicker chair. She hadn't been staying with him for more than half a day and already she was causing him grief. He sighed and turned back into the room, heading over to the chair and seating himself in it.

She settled back against the pillows, but she didn't turn off the lamp on the nightstand.

He watched her for a few moments before asking, "What happened in your nightmare?"

"It was basically a recap of Aryk's attack," she lied, clutching the sheets up to her shoulders.

"You don't have to worry about him while you're here."

"I know," she told him. "I wish I could tell that to the part of my brain that controls the nightmares."

He gestured towards the lamp. "Turn off the light and get some rest."

She reached over and flipped the switch on the lamp. Then she sank lower into the bed and rested her head on the bulky pillows. "Why do you hate yourself so much?"

"This isn't a question and answer session. I'm here so you can get some rest. That's it."

"You don't have to be so guarded all the time," she muttered after stifling a yawn.

He was quiet for a few moments. Then he said, "There was a girl that I loved. She was betrothed to another, promised to someone else. No matter how badly I wanted her, I couldn't have her.

"I came across a woman who said that she could help me obtain everything that I ever desired. She...turned me into what I am now. She turned me into a monster."

She waited for him to go on; he didn't. "Just because you changed biologically doesn't mean that you changed as a person," she told him.

"But I did. I *did* change as a person. The woman that I loved, Bridgette..."

"Unhand me!" she had cried when she'd found out what kind of monster he was.

"You must let me explain," he said, and his voice lost its usual hard edge as he tumbled into the past.

Charlie frowned and reached over to turn on the lamp. Light flooded the room, but his eyes remained dark. He looked like a defenseless, frightened child.

"I must do nothing," Bridgette had told him.

"I won't let you walk away from me," he said in a threatening voice. "You are why I became this."

"Iancu," Charlie breathed, watching him with concern etched in her face. She stood from the bed and walked over to him.

"I loved you so much," he said. "I wanted to be with you forever."

"I am to marry another," Bridgette had told him.

"You are to marry me and only me." He wrapped his arms around Charlie's waist and pulled her closer to him.

Charlie smoothed his hair back. She could feel him trembling as he pressed his cheek to her stomach. He was the most composed person she'd ever known. He always looked calm, cool, and collected, even in duress. Seeing him this way now shook her up. She didn't know what to do.

She simply stood there with his arms around her, and her arms around him, not moving when she felt his hot, red tears rolling down her abdomen. He was mumbling to himself, but she couldn't hear what he was saying.

"I ki-ki-killed her," she heard him say. "I loved her. I loved her with everything that I was, every fiber of my being. And I ki-I killed her. I'm a monster. An evil, deceitful, monster. And it's all her fault."

"All whose fault?" she asked, even though she was certain that she knew the answer.

"Jordana's."

He'd been sired by Jordana. A chill raced up Charlie's spine. The woman he'd loved had died at his own hands. No wonder he had issues with allowing people to get close to him. She tipped his chin up with her hand and looked down at him. "I'm not Bridgette," she said softly. "I'm Charlie."

His mouth moved, but no sound came out. He was mouthing the words, "I killed her," over and over again.

"It's not your fault," she told him.

"Yes, it was!" he shouted. "Didn't you hear me? Haven't you heard anything I've said?"

Stunned, she stepped back from him.

His arms fell away from her and he wiped at the tears on his cheeks, staring at the wetness on his fingers as if he wasn't accustomed to crying. "I killed the woman I loved once. So *this*" -he gestured to her, then to himself- "this can't happen."

She turned and got back into the bed. After she switched the lamp off, the room was again shrouded in darkness.

"I hate myself for a number of reasons. That is only one of them. I've done a lot of twisted shit in my day, just to get by. I've killed innocent people on more than one occasion. I have turned humans into vampires. I'm not proud of the despicable things that I have done. I've disappointed myself time and time again.

"You asked me once why I don't use my abilities while I'm fighting. Every time that I have used them in the past, it was like looking into a metaphorical mirror and seeing myself for what I truly am: a vampire. I am someone who fed on the blood of the innocent in order to live, in order to survive. I am someone who has murdered the one woman that I could see spending the rest of my life with." He paused and she could have sworn that she heard him sobbing. "It's a difficult reality to face. Once in awhile, I still like to pretend that I'm a human being, that I'm just a normal businessman who works during the day and sleeps at night."

"There is no use in pretending that you're someone you're not," she told him matter-of-factly. "It doesn't change anything."

"I know that," he snapped. "You don't know what it's like."

"Tell me what it is like," she urged, staring up at the ceiling.

He leaned back in the armchair and closed his eyes. "I never knew my parents. I have to drink blood at least once a day to sustain myself. I can't bring myself to drink it from a person, so I buy cloned blood. I can only tolerate sunlight for minutes at a time. I'm lonely...I can't have any friends, because human friends die on me and fellow vampires usually end up betraying me somehow. I can't date women for the same reason. The only exhilaration, the only true pleasure that I feel is when I'm in the process of killing another vampire. I haven't had sex in more than a century."

Her eyes widened at the last confession.

"The only thing that relaxes me is playing my guitar. I can't trust anyone or depend on anyone. I can't even trust myself."

She cleared her throat. "That is one way to look at it," she said, "but another way to look at it is that you protect the lives of thousands of people. Killing one vampire can easily save one hundred human lives. Every kill you make is a huge accomplishment."

He made a dismissive sound at that.

"You got dealt a bad hand. You hate what you are. Okay, I get that. But it's not about the hand you're dealt. It's about how you deal with the hand you were dealt. You turned your back on what you were and you stopped hunting. Recently, though, you started hunting again. You're taking steps towards improving your life and accepting who and what you are."

"I will never accept who and what I am." He paused, as if considering his words. "Ever."

Silence swallowed the room whole. She mulled over his response for several moments before saying, "After that night on the reservation, I thought that you would come back for me. I didn't think that I would be staying in a foster home for the remainder of my adolescence.

"You never did come back for me, but you were still my idol. You were...my hero."

"I should have been able to save all of them. That night should have never happened. I should never have let it happen."

"You weren't the one orchestrating everything," she said. "That night wasn't your fault. You saved a lot of people that night. You were...amazing, really."

"No...*you* were amazing that night."

Her cheeks flushed in the dark. She recalled the sensation she felt once she'd planted the wooden chair leg into Aryk's back. "Too bad I didn't finish the job," she said softly. "He would be dead right now."

"We'll get him."

"You're right," she agreed. "We will. And in the meantime, stop beating yourself up so much. You didn't ask for any of this."

He chuckled, a low rumbling sound that bounced off of the walls of the room. "Thanks, Dr. Phil," he muttered before noisily shifting in the chair and falling into a deep sleep.

CHAPTER ELEVEN

Iancu's eyes fluttered open. He stretched his arms over his head and glanced at the bed Charlie had been sleeping in. The bed was empty and made. He rose out of the chair and left the guest bedroom. He stormed down the hall and into the living room, where Neil was still asleep on the couch.

He stalked over to Neil and shook him awake.

"What the-" Neil rubbed his eyes and stared up at his friend. "What the hell is the matter with you?"

"Have you seen Charlie?"

"Did she leave?"

Iancu made an exasperated sound and planted his hands on his hips. He checked the bathroom and his own bedroom, even though he was sure that she wasn't in the apartment. The only other person's presence that he could sense was Neil's. She was gone.

An hour or so later, there was a knock on the door. Neil answered the door and announced to Iancu that Charlie had returned.

Iancu strode into the living room, eyeing the several pieces of luggage she'd brought back with her.

"I had to get some clothes and some of my weapons," she told him sheepishly.

"You *do* know you're only staying for a couple of days, right?"

"It's not as much as you think," she told him. She gestured to one of the suitcases she'd brought. "There's nothing but stakes, guns, and other equipment in there."

He watched her heft the luggage into the guest room with a shake of his head.

Neil stood at the kitchen counter sipping blood from a coffee mug. The plastic that had been housing the blood lay on the counter. The cell phone clipped to his belt chirped loudly. He plucked it from his waistband and looked at the number that flashed in the phone's LCD display.

He stared at the display until the phone stopped ringing. A moment later, the display alerted him that he had one missed call and one new voice mail.

Iancu arched a glance at him. "Any reason why you didn't answer that call?"

"It was my wife," Neil said. "I have to break out of here."

"The sun hasn't even started to go down yet," Iancu warned.

"I know, but there's something I've got to do."

Neil jingled his car keys in his hand as he left Iancu's apartment. His wife had called him. He wasn't going to be able to avoid her forever. At some time or another, he was going to have to confront her and have a talk with her. That time may as well be now.

By the time he pulled his Chrysler sedan into the driveway of his house, he had an entire dialogue worked out in his mind. He knew everything that he wanted to say to Marilyn.

He hopped out of the car and headed up the walkway leading to his front door. The front door was unlocked. He turned the knob and entered the house. "Mare?" he called.

She came to the top of the stairs. "Neil," she said softly, nearly tripping over herself as she made her way down the stairs. Her golden-blonde hair was pulled up in a haphazard topknot. Curly tendrils framed her face. She ran to him and wrapped her arms around his neck. She'd been crying. Her cheeks were still wet.

Astounded by the greeting that she was giving him and momentarily speechless, he wrapped his arms around her and held her.

"I couldn't stand being away from you last night," she murmured into his neck.

"I was miserable, too," he admitted.

"I called you awhile ago," she told him. "You didn't answer."

He shook his head. "I wasn't ready."

"I understand." She took a couple steps back and clasped her hands together in front of her. "I left a message telling you about the doctor's visit that I had. The doctor took a lot of tests the last time I went in, and she was supposed to give me the results today. She said that the results from the tests that I took were peculiar, and that she wanted to retest me and the baby."

He nodded his head stiffly, not really wanting to hear about the child growing within his wife's womb.

"She told me that I'm eight months pregnant," she revealed, lowering her eyes and staring at the floor.

Neil frowned. "Eight months?"

"I know."

"You went eight months without knowing you were pregnant?"

"It's impossible for me to be eight months pregnant," Marilyn said.

"So you're saying that the test is wrong."

"Yes."

Unable to look at her any longer, he glanced at some point over her shoulder.

"It only happened once," she whispered, tears shimmering in her eyes. "Our schedules were so different and I hardly ever saw you. I was lonely, Neil."

"I don't want to hear this." He sidestepped her and walked up the stairs, taking them two at a time with his hand gliding up the banister.

She followed him up the stairs and into their bedroom, where she remained in the doorway. "It happened once, and that was only a couple of months ago. That was the only time. If I were eight months pregnant, then the baby would have to be yours."

Those words stopped him cold. He turned to face her.

"Wouldn't that be wonderful?" she asked him. "You thought you were sterile, but wouldn't it be wonderful if the baby was yours?"

He swallowed the lump that had formed in his throat and ran a hand over his light brown hair. It was impossible. Humans and vampires could not procreate. Many couples had tried and many vampire doctors had conducted experiments to prove that this fact was nothing more than a myth, but all attempts had failed. With the wheels in his head still turning, he grabbed a suitcase from the closet he shared with Marilyn. He rummaged through drawers and began tossing clothes into the suitcase.

She watched him without saying another word. Tears filled her eyes and ran down her cheeks. "Why are you so sure that you're sterile anyway?" she demanded. "Doctors have been known to misdiagnose their patients. It happens all the time."

"It's a little more complicated than that, Marilyn."

"Why?"

He looked at her for a moment, considering telling her about everything. She would then know why he was so sure that the baby wasn't his. The baby *couldn't* be his. He wasn't a human being and she was. It was as simple as that. He closed the suitcase and looked at her one more time.

"Come to the hospital with me," she urged. "Take a blood test. That will prove that I'm right and that you're the father."

He blinked his eyes rapidly to keep the tears at bay. How he wished he *could* be the father of the child she was carrying. He thought that he would make a great father. He would spend all the time that he could with his child. His eyes grew misty at the thought of having children. He often had dreams of having children with his wife. Even though he knew that it wasn't possible, it had always been a desire of his.

He dragged his suitcase towards the door and glared at his wife. She stepped out of his way and let him pass. She watched him descend the stairs with both of her hands clasped over her mouth in a vain attempt to stifle her sobs.

A countless number of people aimlessly wandered about Jordana's estate. Bella wondered how the Tudhani vampiress managed to keep track of them all as she was led out of the foyer and into an elaborately-furnished sitting room.

Heavy velvet drapes were suspended from thick rods posted over covered windows. The only light that was allowed to shine within the confines of the sitting room was the light that bore down from an ornate, gold chandelier that floated over a hand-woven oriental rug centered in the middle of the room. Strategically placed against the far wall of the room was a beautifully-sculpted throne where Jordana was seated.

Bella could feel the older vampire's eyes on her, but she couldn't see them. The Tudhani clan leader was seated in the one area of the room that the chandelier seemed to have forgotten, for the statuesque redhead was engulfed in shadows.

Bella stood at the entrance of the sitting room awaiting a greeting from Jordana; she didn't receive one. Jade had escorted her to the sitting room but when she cast a glance over her shoulder, the purple-haired spitfire was nowhere to be found.

The tension in the room nearly swallowed Bella whole. Her nerves were rattling and she didn't know why. Her black halter top and knee-length skirt were all of a sudden too constricting.

"You can step forward," Jordana encouraged.

"You summoned me," Bella said, hesitant to take a step forward. "What do you wish to speak about?"

"I wish to talk business with you."

"You wish to talk business with only me? You don't wish to speak with Alexei also?"

A deep chuckle arose from the shadows hovering around Jordana's throne. She poured herself off of the throne and moved out of the shadows. A gold headband tamed her wild, red waves. Her torso was encased in a midriff-baring translucent blouse that should have been laced up the front; it wasn't. Her nipples were visible through the filmy fabric and her breasts threatened to pop out over the top of her blouse. The same filmy fabric wrapped around her pelvic area in the form of bikini briefs.

She approached the darker-skinned Tudhani, quite comfortable in her particular state of undress. "Yes, Alexei," she crooned as she circled around Bella.

Growing impatient, Bella flipped her dark hair over her shoulder. "Why have you summoned me here?"

"I have summoned you here to grant you a favor."

"What kind of favor is that?"

"Sparing your life."

Bella frowned. "Are you joking?"

"I am a lot older than you are. I could break your neck from where I stand without having to lift a finger. You, by contrast, haven't nearly as much power as I do, so you wouldn't be able to protect yourself from my attack." The redhead tapped her jaw as she pretended to contemplate her options. "No, I believe this isn't a joke at all. I believe I'm one hundred percent serious."

"You can't threaten me," Bella exclaimed.

Jordana rushed at her, slamming her into the nearest wall. She clenched the other woman's chin in her hands and hissed into her ear, "Why is that? Because you've gone and turned yourself into Alexei's obedient whore?"

Bella writhed beneath Jordana's force, but to no avail.

"I've taken his bed once or twice," Jordana went on. "I know what kinds of perversions he indulges himself in."

"You're one to talk," Bella spat out, "seeing as Aryk has got you right where he wants you: wrapped around his little finger."

Anger leapt into Jordana's violet eyes. "I want you to listen to me carefully before you go and get yourself killed," she said threateningly. "Alexei trusts you, confides in you, and most importantly, listens to you. If you value your life or whatever it is you have going with Alexei, you will advise him that he should join forces with Aryk."

Bella's brows furrowed. She appeared to be confused. "All of this is because you want him to side with your boyfriend?"

"Don't make this all sound so trite," Jordana snapped. "His vision is quite dynamic, if you really give it thought. I mean, think about it. The Vikara wouldn't have to live in the damp, disgusting sewers. They would be free to live with the rest of us, because they would be accepted. We would all be allowed to exist as we truly are, without fear of being judged or executed. What Aryk is striving for is a better world, really, a better existence for all of us."

"You're crazy," Bella whispered, tugging at the hands that Jordana had clasped tightly around her jaw. "And you're crazy if you think that I'm going to convince Alexei to side with the likes of you."

Jordana's eyes narrowed and a sudden rush of wind dashed about the room, slamming the double doors to the sitting room. Her hair floated in the air above her head. "If you won't agree to help me, I guess I will have to take care of it myself." She shoved the woman hard enough to send her flying across the room. Her hair whipped around her face as the room filled with her immense power.

Bella found that she couldn't pull herself to her feet. Fear shone in her eyes as she struggled to stand. She remained helpless on the floor.

Jordana drew an arm back with fury morphing her features into something cruel and ugly.

Alexei, please hear me, Bella thought. *I love you, Alexei.* Trembling on the floor, she closed her eyes and prayed that she would once again see the love of her life, Alexei. She made this prayer just moments before Jordana clawed out her heart with remarkably strong, sharp talons.

Alexei's eyes cracked open. He rose up on his elbows and cast a worried glance at his bedmate. Dark hair spilled onto the pillow beside him and he could make out Bella's body swathed in bed sheets.

He nudged her anyway, just to be sure.

She made soft sounds in her sleep and was finally stirred awake by his nudging. She rolled over and looked up into his eyes. "What?" she croaked in a sleepy voice. "What is it?"

He shook his head. "Nothing," he whispered. "I guess it was just a bad dream." He lowered his head back onto the pillow. Moments later he sank back into a blissful slumber while his bedmate lay smiling a ghastly, evil smile in the dying light of a setting sun.

CHAPTER TWELVE

Aryk shuddered and blinked out of a hazy stupor. He was bound to the bed by ankle and wrist restraints. A young blonde vampire was leaning over him, practically scrubbing his skin raw. She couldn't have been embraced more than five years ago. He remembered seeing her around the mansion, fraternizing with the other vampires that lived in Jordana's estate.

He attempted to sit up and failed miserably. He dropped back onto his elbows and tilted his head back against the cushion of overstuffed pillows. Every muscle in his body was sore. When he looked down the length of his body, he could see that his flesh was a mess of intertwined scars. It was a wonder that he was still alive. By now, Iancu's wounds had probably completely healed. The sword Aryk had been using was steel, but the sword that Iancu fought with wasn't a sword at all. It was a sword and stake hybrid, made of steel and wood. It was a miracle that Aryk had made it home in time.

"Don't try to sit up again," the blonde girl advised him. "You suffered a major beating. It's going to take you awhile to heal."

He nodded his head dumbly, not even daring to speak. He tried to remember the blonde girl's name. It was Christina or Cynthia...something like that.

After scrubbing him clean, she made as if to inspect one of his wounds. Aryk's hand flew up and circled around her wrist.

"Don't touch them," he rasped.

"That will be enough, Crystal," an authoritative female voice commanded. "You're needed downstairs."

The girl ducked her head and hastily took her leave of the master bedroom.

He slid his eyes towards the room's entrance, where Jordana was standing. "I see that you are feeling a little better than you were yesterday."

"Why am I bound to the bed?" he asked.

She smiled and closed the door at her back. She was wearing a sapphire blue satin dress with a full skirt. Her hair was pulled back in a neat chignon. Sapphire earrings dangled from her earlobes and a matching necklace looped around her neck. Mirth flashed in her violet eyes as she drew closer and closer to the bed. "I didn't want you moving around and causing even more harm to yourself," she told him sweetly, stroking some of his hair back.

He hadn't felt vulnerable in many years, but he was feeling vulnerable now. Needless to say, he wasn't fond of feeling this way. He preferred power over powerlessness. He jokingly tugged at one of his wrist restraints and pasted a sugary grin on his face. "You can let me out of them now. I've been a good boy. I rested well."

"You need much more rest," she said, appraising him with a keen eye. "Your wounds haven't faded yet. You could have died. What happened?"

As if you haven't read my mind already, he thought. *You would have had the perfect opportunity. I would have been too weak to shield my thoughts from you.* The dashing grin didn't leave his face. "Another run-in with your former boy toy," he said nonchalantly with a roll of his eyes. "Need I say more?"

"I'm surprised he was able to cause so much damage to you," she said in a thoughtful voice. "He doesn't use his powers and he doesn't use guns."

"He got lucky," Aryk spat. "Can you let me out of these restraints now?"

She stared at him for several moments. "That can wait. I'm much more interested in hearing what happened between you and Iancu."

"Why?" he demanded. "We fought. He apparently kicked my ass, but like I said, he had a lucky night. The next time I see him, he won't be so fortunate."

"Nothing else happened?" Jordana asked, smoothing the back of her dress down and perching on the edge of the bed. "Nothing worthy of telling me?"

There was no mistaking the tone in her voice. She knew perfectly well what had happened last night. She knew that the slayer was involved, and she most likely knew that Aryk had impersonated Iancu to seduce the slayer. *I'm fucked,* he realized.

She leaned forward so that her face was merely inches away from his. "Yes, you are," she whispered.

His eyes widened. *How was she able to read my thoughts? I was shielding them from her.*

"Do you really think that you could successfully shield your thoughts from me?" she asked him, standing from the bed and turning her back to him. "I am a natural-born vampire. In less than half a century, I will be six hundred years old. I am the most powerful vampire known to the world and you dare to think that you could possibly have the power to block me from knowing your innermost thoughts? You are nothing. You are an inconsequential piece of shit."

He watched as she threw her head back and laughed. He had underestimated her. He stared up at her, not knowing what to say.

She arched a glance at him over her shoulder. "I could kill you right now. Do you understand me?" She whirled around to face him and her eyes were luminous and shining with malevolence. "You're intelligent enough to know that I'm not going to do that. If my intent were to kill you, I would have done it the night you stumbled in here full of bullet holes and sword wounds."

For the first time in a long time, he was frightened. He was frozen where he sat on the bed; he couldn't even move.

"I'm not going to kill you," she repeated in a hushed whisper. "We're going to relive old times. You are going to be my pet. You are going to serve me, you are going to cater to me, and you will be by my side whenever I see fit.

"If you dare slip up or if I ever catch you looking in the slayer's direction again, then I will destroy you. Have I made myself clear?"

He nodded his head emphatically.

"Good." She raised her hand, influenced the locks on his restraints, and released him. "Now that you're clear on that, I can give you an important assignment."

With great effort, he sat upright and threw his legs over the side of the bed. "What is the assignment?"

"I want you to find the slayer," she said, watching his face closely to gauge his reaction. "I want you to bring her back here."

"Why do you want me to bring her here?"

"Because," she said, a wolfish smile appearing on her face, "I'm going to kill her."

Neil wandered the streets of Los Angeles with his hands shoved in the pockets of his dark, neatly pressed slacks. There was an eerie hush over the city, but he didn't notice. He was too busy worrying about his relationship with Marilyn. He had hated leaving her, but he would have been a fool to stay. She claimed to love him, but she couldn't love him. On some level, she had to despise him to stoop as low as betraying him the way that she had.

He had come close to forgiving her for what she'd done. He had come close to taking her back. The new developments in her pregnancy had floored him, though. Eight months pregnant? For eight months, she hadn't known that she was pregnant? That was impossible. Had she thought that he would believe her?

"She's obviously lying to me," he said aloud as he rounded a corner. "She had to have known she was pregnant. She *had* to have."

"And insinuating that I'm the father...what *was* that?" He couldn't be the father; that much, he was sure of.

Humans and vampires couldn't produce children together. Some vampires could leap tall buildings in a single bound. Others could read minds, cloak themselves from being seen by the naked eye, or travel at the speed of light. Yet no vampire had even been *rumored* to conceive a child with a human.

It was doubtful that he and Marilyn would put to rest a myth that had lasted the course of many centuries. He sighed and ducked his head lower so that his chin rested on his collarbone.

He walked past dark storefronts and for the first time, realized how quiet it was. His steps slowed to a stop and he glanced around. There weren't any cars driving past on the street. The streetlights were unusually dim. Alerts were going off in his head.

He looked this way and that, narrowing his eyes and using his intensified hearing senses. A scream sounded loudly in his head. He stumbled back against one of the storefront display windows, winded by how loud and abrupt the scream had been. It only took him a moment to gather his bearings and take off in the direction the scream seemed to be coming from.

He tore down the sidewalk like an Olympic sprinter. He pumped his arms as he ran. He turned a corner and veered into a dark alleyway, where he slowed his steps.

A tall, attractive brunette was being attacked near the end of the alley, near a rusty green dumpster. Neil didn't hesitate. He launched into another sprint and hurled himself at the brunette's attacker.

The brunette woman was thrown aside. The side of her head struck the dumpster before she hit the ground.

The snarling vampire with glowing red eyes turned to face Neil. "You just made a huge mistake."

"No...*you* made one the minute you pulled that girl into this alley," Neil challenged.

The vampire was dressed extravagantly. His hair had been dyed in several different shades of red. He was tall and gangly. By the smell of him, he wasn't much older than Neil was.

I can take him, Neil thought to himself. *Even though I don't have a weapon on me, I can definitely take him.*

The vampire lunged at him. Instead of dodging him, Neil grabbed the lapels to his dark, ankle length coat and lifted him into the air. He threw the vampire across the alley as if he were nothing but a rag doll.

The brunette was still lying on the ground, unconscious. Neil wished that he could get her to the nearest hospital, but that was going to have to wait. He scoured the alley with his eyes, looking for a makeshift weapon that he could use against his opponent.

There were old, wet flyers, food wrappers, and plastic soda bottles. None of those items would do him much good. He sensed that the vampire was rushing at his back, but before he could turn around, he was roughly pushed to the ground.

The vampire placed a foot in the middle of his back and withdrew a gun from the waistband of his stylish dress pants. "As a punishment, I should make you watch me drink from her," the vampire growled.

The cracked pavement was cold and solid against Neil's cheek. An image of his wife flashed behind his closed eyelids.

"You don't have anything to say now?" the vampire demanded. "You came in here trying to be the hero. You were ready for hand-to-hand combat when you interrupted my dinner. And now you have nothing to say? How unfortunate." The redhead clucked his tongue.

A loud thud reverberated throughout the alley. He turned his head to see who had joined them. Seemingly from out of nowhere, a fist drove into his nose and sent him reeling.

Iancu unclenched his fist and glanced at Charlie, who stood beside him. "Neil, get up," he ordered.

Neil rose to his knees and then eventually, his feet once he saw that his opponent was no longer a threat. "I'm so glad to see you guys," he muttered.

"We were just in the neighborhood," Charlie quipped with a smile.

The vampire stood glowering at all three of them. He seemed to be debating whether he should stay and fight them or scamper away while his legs were still attached to his body. Without warning, he leapt into the air and disappeared from sight.

"He got away," Neil said with disdain.

"We'll worry about him later," Iancu said. "Our first priority is getting this woman to a hospital to get her checked out."

The nearest hospital proved to be St. Therese Medical Center. They assisted the barely conscious woman into the emergency room and made a hasty exit. With how battered the woman was, there would be a lot of questions concerning her injuries.

Once they were out of the hospital doors, Neil tilted his head back. A wash of yellow and red lights bathed his face as an ambulance pulled up to the hospital doors. A man dressed in a white uniform shoved the back door of the ambulance open while the ambulance driver jumped out of the driver side door to assist his co-worker. The two of them wheeled out a blonde, female patient that was mumbling a bunch of nonsense.

Neil frowned at the sound of the woman's voice. He turned and his jaw dropped. His wife, Marilyn, was lying on a stretcher with a hand limply dangling over the side. "Mare!" he screamed, and took off towards her.

Iancu and Charlie exchanged confused glances and approached Neil's side. Iancu recognized his friend's wife immediately.

One of the EMTs called out, "Step back, step back, we have to get her into the emergency room!"

"That's my wife," Neil told him. "I have to go in with her."

"All right, all right, but you're going to have to get out of our way so we can wheel her in. She needs immediate attention."

A hazy, dark red film appeared over Neil's eyes and blood tears spilled onto his cheeks. He obediently stepped aside and turned to face his friend. "I'm going to catch up with both of you guys later. I have to go with her."

Iancu nodded with understanding.

Aryk sat at thirty-foot long dining room table sipping crimson liquid from a crystal goblet. Seated to his left was an overexcited vampire with a poor dye job. He listened intently to what the vampire had to say. After the vampire was done gossiping, he threw back what was left of the crimson liquid and crushed the fragile glass with his bare hand.

So, Neil was consorting with the enemy, was he? He was attempting to spoil Aryk's plans of taking over the world, was he?

Aryk shook his head and chuckled. "You have fucked with the wrong vampire," he said with a dangerous glint in his eyes.

Marilyn looked utterly helpless in the hospital bed. There were bags under her eyes; Neil could tell that she hadn't slept well the past couple of nights.

He caressed her hand. "I'm so sorry," he whispered to her. "I should have been there for you. I shouldn't have been so selfish."

She shook her head slightly. "Don't," she said faintly.

"Why didn't you call me?"

"You were mad at me. You walked out."

He shook his head, cursing himself over and over again.

"This isn't your fault, Neil," she told him. "Stop blaming yourself."

"What did they say was wrong? What happened?"

"There is a complication with the pregnancy," she said in a hoarse voice. "I don't know...all I know is that I was bleeding. A lot."

"Bleeding? Is the baby all right?"

"They don't know." Her bottom lip trembled and she rolled her eyes upward towards the ceiling. "You shouldn't be here. They're going to make you leave sooner or later."

"I'm not leaving you," he vowed. "Not this time."

"I'm scared," she whispered to him. "First, there were the weird test results. Then they told me I was eight months pregnant when I couldn't possibly be that far along. Now this. What's happening, Neil?"

His mind was racing. What *was* happening to his wife? How come there were so many complications with her pregnancy? What was going on here?

He swallowed a lump in his throat and moved his hand from hers. His hand roamed to her chest and lowered to her belly, where it hovered. He was aware that she was watching him, and still he closed his eyes and focused all of his energy on the hand that was hovering over her stomach. He palmed her belly. Heat emanated from his hand.

She cried out in pain. The heat was searing her flesh. In a panic, he tried to withdraw his hand and found that he couldn't. *What the hell is going on?* She writhed against him and the baby beneath his hand shifted its position. He could feel it; he could sense its presence. It was there, living and moving within his wife's womb. He probed further; there was more that he wanted to know.

"You're burning me!" Marilyn was screaming.

Two doctors flooded into the room, alarmed that their patient was screaming at the top of her lungs. "What are you doing in here, sir?" one of the doctors demanded.

He was almost there. All he needed was a couple more seconds. He kept his palm on his wife's belly and probed her womb with all of the energy that he possessed.

"Get security in here," one doctor said to the other. Then the doctor turned his attention to Neil. "Sir, you're going to have to come with me."

Blinding white light flashed in the room and without warning, Neil's hand was detached from his wife's protruding belly. He flew backwards and landed on the floor. His eyes were unnaturally bright.

"Whoa, what was that?" the doctor asked as his colleague returned, flanked by a pair security guards.

Marilyn was staring down at her husband with her mouth agape. She didn't have to speak for him to know what she was wondering. She was wondering what had just happened. She was aware that he'd done something, but didn't know the specifics.

Neil remained where he was sitting, too stunned to stand. He didn't know how they had done it and he didn't know why he and his wife were the ones to put an ancient myth to rest...but somehow, they had done it. Somehow, he and his wife had conceived the first half-human and half-vampire child. He was a father.

The security guards escorted him out of the emergency room. He was too dazed to put up a fight. He stood in the hospital corridor leading to the emergency room. He could easily be mistaken for a drugged-up patient of the hospital.

He could barely function. He was walking as if he'd just learned how to do so yesterday. His legs were shaky and he found himself constantly suppressing the urge to cartwheel all the way out of the hospital.

He hailed a cab and climbed into the back seat. He stared out of the window, watching scenery fly by in an indistinctive blur. He was a father. He had conceived a child with his human wife. It was unheard of.

When the cab pulled up to Iancu's apartment complex, Neil paid the fare and hopped out of the car. As the cab pulled away from the curb, he didn't suppress the urge this time. He leapt into the air, did a series of cartwheels, and whooped with laughter. Then, he made his way up to Iancu's apartment. Without giving it a second thought, he influenced the lock on the apartment door and pushed it open.

Iancu greeted him by putting a sword to his throat. When he saw that it was only Neil on the other side of the door, he lowered the heavy weapon. "Knock next time."

"It's good to see you, too," Neil said with a giddy smile on his face.

"What are you grinning about?"

"You wouldn't believe me if I told you," Neil said, shaking his head. He entered the apartment and plopped down on the couch. "Where's Charlie?"

"She's in the guest room," Iancu replied, hooking a finger over his shoulder. "Why?"

"All this time, I've been worried," Neil said under his breath, shaking his head. "All this time, I was wondering how I could take her back, knowing that I would have to raise another man's kid."

"You know that you're talking to yourself, right?" Iancu asked, carefully laying the sword on top of the kitchen counter. "You're starting to worry me."

"What is the one thing that we've been led to believe?" Neil asked suddenly. "The one thing that we're sure of?"

"That vampires who stay out in the sun too long will get a bad case of sunburn," Iancu said with a shrug of his shoulders.

"I'm serious, man," Neil said, bracing his elbows on the tops of his knees.

Iancu thought about it for a moment.

"You're not the brightest crayon in the Crayola box," Neil muttered. "What I'm talking about is the myth that humans and vampires can't conceive children."

"It's not just a myth," Iancu said, opening the refrigerator and pulling out a blood packet. "They've conducted tests. Many couples have tried. It has never been done."

Neil made a steeple with his fingers. "Until now."

Iancu turned and stared at his friend. "She convinced you that the kid is yours?"

Neil shook his head. "She told me, but I didn't believe her. I had to see for myself. And I did. In the emergency room. It was...unreal."

"You can't be serious."

"I wouldn't joke about something like this."

"I know you wouldn't." Iancu dropped the blood packet on the counter and folded his arms across his chest. "This is monumental."

"Isn't it?" It was a wonder that Neil wasn't bouncing off of the walls. "I mean, when you think about it, who was the person who told us that myth?"

"Jordana," Iancu answered slowly.

"And we believed her because most of what she told us was the truth. She was the only source of information that we had. She is the one who told us what was myth and what was truth. If she'd wanted to tell us blatant lies, she could have. We wouldn't have known better."

Iancu was still shaking his head. "You're sure about this?"

"I'm positive. The baby is mine, there's no question about it."

"So you're saying that she lied to us. She's lying to everyone."

"I thought about it on the way here," Neil said. "And I think I know why she told us that humans and vampires can't conceive. She fears a blending of the species."

"That could be true." Iancu shook his head. "But it still doesn't explain the fact that doctors around the world have conducted tests and experiments in order to find a way to cross-breed humans and vampires."

Neil shrugged. "You're right. I don't know how to explain that."

"Regardless of whether or not Jordana lied to us, you have to make sure not to tell anyone about this."

Neil looked incredulous. "Have you gone bonkers? This is a huge medical find!"

"If you tell anyone else about this, then you will be putting your child at risk," Iancu warned. "Your child will become a target. If your enemies don't get to your kid, then scientists and doctors will. They'll want to conduct experiments on your kid, your wife, *and* you, to see why you were the vampire to prove this myth to be false."

Iancu was right. Neil had been so overcome with excitement and joy, he hadn't thought of the downside of producing a half-human and half-vampire baby. He didn't even know if the baby would survive the birthing process.

There were already complications in his wife's pregnancy. What if other complications arose? What if the baby came out looking deformed? What if Iancu was right and his baby *did* become a target? He had to get back to the hospital.

Aryk hated hospitals. The scent of diseased and flawed blood was enough to make him want to gag. He walked the halls of the hospital without inhaling. He had received a phone call informing him that Neil's wife had been admitted into St. Therese Medical Center. His source hadn't known why she had been admitted, but Aryk didn't need to know why she'd been admitted.

He remembered her scent quite well. He found himself standing in front of the emergency room. The double doors of the emergency room banged open. A team of doctors were wheeling Marilyn Gierying out of ER. From their chatter, he could pick up that they were going to be moving her to the maternity ward.

With his interest piqued, he cloaked himself and followed the doctors. *The maternity ward? Now why would Marilyn need to be transferred to the maternity ward?*

Marilyn was wheeled into a room divided by crisp, blue curtains. Sweat graced her forehead and matted her hair. She appeared to be exhausted. "Have you seen my husband?" she asked of one of the doctors. "He was escorted out by security."

The doctor solemnly shook his head. "I'm sorry, but I have not seen him."

"Could you page him?" she asked tiredly. "He said that he wouldn't leave me."

"I'll be sure to page him. Try to relax and get some rest."

Even from where Aryk stood, he could sense the presence of a tainted individual growing within the human woman's womb. She was carrying a half-human and half-vampire child. His eyes glowed yellow and he crouched to the floor, waiting for the doctors to leave the room.

Once they did, he stood and walked over to her hospital bed and beamed a knowing smile down at her. "Hello, Marilyn," he greeted cheerfully, brushing back blonde strands of her hair that had become damp with sweat.

✠

"My wife was moved to the maternity ward?" Neil asked of the attendant seated at the nurse's station. "That's a good thing, right? It means that she's out of harm's way for now?"

The attendant nodded with a pleasant smile on her mocha brown face. She told him which room his wife had been placed in.

He followed her directions and entered his wife's hospital room. The room was empty, so he returned to the nurse's station. "I'm sorry to bother you again," he said, "but you did say room two-seventeen, right? Because that room is empty."

The attendant checked her records again, asked a nurse to cover the desk, and led him to room two-seventeen. She frowned. "Your wife is supposed to be here," she said, walking further into the room and pulling the curtains back. "I'll ask around for you."

There was no need for her to ask around. There was a sinking feeling in the pit of his stomach. His wife wasn't anywhere in this hospital. Someone had her. Someone had taken his sweet Marilyn from her hospital bed. He turned and lurched out of the hospital room, seized by panic.

CHAPTER THIRTEEN

Charlie watched Iancu as he threw back a thermos full of blood. "Does that actually taste good to you?" she asked with her nose wrinkled in disgust.

He drew the back of his hand across his mouth and tossed the thermos into the kitchen sink. "It nourishes me."

She shrugged and continued suiting up, placing her guns at her back. She could feel his eyes on her, but she didn't acknowledge it. The night air was electric.

Iancu gasped with his eyes wide. He stepped back and bumped against the refrigerator.

She looked concerned. "What's wrong with you? Are you all right?"

"I can hear them," he said with a hand pressed over his chest.

"Who can you hear?" She warily approached him and raised a hand to rest on his shoulder.

His eyes searched hers for a moment and something ignited in them. The flame in his eyes died down and he removed her hand from his shoulder. "No one," he answered finally. He turned his back to her.

"You can't keep doing this, you know," she said to his back.

"Finish suiting up so we can hunt," he said, a bit more gruffly than he'd intended.

She didn't budge and he didn't have to turn around to know that. "I'm not moving until you admit that you want me."

He laughed and walked away from her.

She trailed after him. "Are you seriously going to deny what is going on between us?"

"There isn't anything going on between us," he said without turning to face her. "We fight together. We temporarily live together. That's it."

She raised both of her hands and pressed them flat against his shoulder blades. He didn't protest, so she proceeded to massage his back. She worked her way down his back and then snaked her arms around his waist so that she was hugging him to her.

His body stiffened in her arms, but he didn't move out of her embrace. The barriers that he'd carefully constructed were crumbling. He trembled in her arms and leaned against her slightly, savoring the feeling of having her arms around him. "This isn't a good idea."

"What isn't?"

His knees nearly buckled. "This. I'm not good with relationships."

"I never said it had to be a relationship."

He did turn to face her then, surprising her and causing her to step back. "You have no problem with a no-strings attached arrangement?"

"It would be more convenient for me than the alternative," she said with a shrug.

A look of desire shone in his eyes. "Do you think you could handle me?"

The heat blazing in his eyes took her breath away. *Could* she handle him?

A smug smile touched his lips. "I thought so." He strode away from her, but called over his shoulder, "Hurry and suit up so we can get out of here."

At a loss for words, she stood with her feet rooted to the ground several moments before jumping to action.

Just as she was putting on her cloak, the door flew opened and banged against the wall adjacent to it. Neil filled the doorframe. His shirt was ripped, his hair was disheveled, and there was a deadly look in his eyes. "Someone has her," he said, flashing his eyes in Charlie's direction. "Someone has my Marilyn. And you're going to help me save her."

Iancu emerged from his bedroom, tying his hair back in a ponytail. "Neil? What's wrong?"

The angry look disappeared almost immediately. His expression transformed from one of anger to one of sadness. "Someone kidnapped Marilyn," he said, sounding exhausted and worn out.

"Shit," Iancu said. "Whoever took her knows."

"I know."

"We have to get her back as quickly as possible," Iancu added. There was no telling what her captor would do.

"I didn't know where to go, what to do," Neil said pitifully. "I'm not the best fighter. That's your territory. I'm just an accountant."

"It's all right," Charlie offered. "We'll find her."

Red tear tracks marked Neil's cheeks and he wiped at them in vain. "Thanks, Chuck."

"It would take a powerful vampire to know about you and Marilyn," Iancu said thoughtfully.

"And it would take a powerful vampire to sneak her out of a hospital," Charlie added. "Wait a minute...what do you mean it would take a powerful vampire to know about Neil and Marilyn? They're married, aren't they?"

A look passed between Neil and Iancu. Neil shrugged his shoulders. "She might as well know. My wife is pregnant with my child."

Her brows furrowed. "But you're a vampire and she's a human." She brought her hands up to cover her mouth. "That is why she was kidnapped. Oh my God...we have to find her."

"My sentiments exactly," Iancu said. "Do you have any bright ideas, slayer?"

She nodded her head with certainty. "As a matter-of-fact, yes," she answered. "The plan that we had to trap Aryk...we carry that out tonight."

Iancu frowned. "I don't follow."

"We planned for me to return to my cabin to trap Aryk," she said, "but I think we should alter our plans a little bit so that *he* captures *me*."

"I still don't follow," Iancu stated.

"We don't plan to trap and kill Aryk," she outlined for him. "We plan for him to capture me and take me back to the estate he shares with Jordana."

Neil's eyes widened. "You've got to be fucking kidding me. That's a death wish."

Iancu was staring at her. "I'm not going to let you do that. We're not even certain that Aryk is the culprit."

"He's most likely the one who abducted Marilyn," she said, "and you're not the boss of me. Besides, the plan can't fail."

"What if he decides not to take you back to his estate?" Iancu challenged. "What if he decides to just kill you on the spot?"

"Well there is the slightest chance that the plan might fail," she amended, "but it's worth a shot."

"Hold on there, Chuck," Neil said, bringing both of his hands up. "I can't let you sacrifice yourself like that."

"You don't have much choice," she told him, frowning. "Not if you want your wife to get out of this alive."

"I do have a choice," he said slowly. "I can go in there myself and save my wife and my kid."

Iancu and Charlie exchanged a doubtful glance.

"It doesn't matter whether or not you two back me up," Neil continued. "I know I'm not the best fighter. I'm not used to fighting off ten guys at once. That would be Iancu's modus operandi. I'm an accountant. While I'm crunching numbers, he's punching faces. Despite the fact that I'm not a talented fighter though, that's my wife in there. And my kid. I know Jordana's place inside out. I've been working for Jordana and Aryk for years."

Iancu still didn't say anything.

"I know what I'm doing," Neil insisted. "And besides, whatever Aryk was planning before all of this isn't just going to fizzle into thin air. It's a feeding frenzy out there and you two will need to keep the chaos at bay."

"You still shouldn't go in that place by yourself," Iancu told his friend. "I should go in with you."

Neil shook his head stubbornly. He had made up his mind, probably long before he stepped through the apartment door. "I'm sorry man, but this isn't even up for debate. I'm going in and I'm going alone. This is something that I have to do."

Iancu started to say something, but Charlie gingerly touched his shoulder. "We should let him do this," she said softly. "He's right. We're going to be needed on the outside to prevent as many transformations as possible."

Iancu's mouth set in a grim line. His friend was set on saving his family and there was nothing that he could do to change Neil's mind. He gave a curt nod.

"When I'm back on the outside and when Marilyn is safe, I'll be sure to contact you," Neil said before turning and striding out the way he had come in.

"I'm proud of you for letting him go like that," Charlie said.

"I'm not letting him go," he told her. "I'm going to have to cover him."

She scratched her head, looking very confused. "But you just-"

He cut her off. "If he goes in there by himself, he won't come back out. He was too stubborn to take me with him, so I had to let him think that he was on his own."

"Iancu-"

He brought a hand up in front of her face. "There's no convincing me otherwise. He's the best friend I've ever had, and I'm not going to fail him. He was right about one thing: he can't fight worth shit. He needs me to back him up, and that's what I'm going to do."

Charlie stared at him with an expression of awe on her face. "What *we're* going to do," she corrected him.

He held her gaze for a moment before snatching up his sword from the kitchen counter. "Let's go. There is someone that I've been meaning to visit and I figure we can get some hunting in before saving Neil's ass."

Several miles outside of the Los Angeles city limits stood a stark, nondescript building made of stone. The building itself looked aged and slightly dilapidated. Some of the windows were boarded up and the lawn was neglected. There was a sign perched above the building's front entrance that read: Benton Asylum.

"What are we doing here?" Charlie whispered.

"Visiting an old friend," Iancu responded. "Once we're inside the doors, I'm going to have to cloak us. Don't make a sound once we're inside."

He parked in the visitors' parking lot and led her to the front of the building. He clamped his hand around hers and drew one of the double doors open. The door creaked horribly, sending an audible echo pulsating through each hall on the first floor.

She froze behind him at the loud, telltale sound. From where she stood, she could see that there was an abandoned nurse's station of some sort located ahead of them.

Still gripping her hand in his, he cloaked the both of them. They both shuffled over the cracked, scuffed linoleum as fluorescent lights randomly flickered above them.

The pulse in her throat didn't stop jumping until she saw an orderly making her rounds, peeking her head into rooms lining the hall and briefly speaking with whoever was in residence.

The slayer followed Iancu through a door leading to the stairwell. They proceeded up two flights of stairs before opening the door to a main hall and exiting the stairwell. She trailed behind him until he came to a stop at one of the doors.

A small, square window allowed them to see the dark-haired, slender woman that was trapped within. Iancu glanced this way and that, making sure the coast was clear. He manipulated the locks, opened the door, and tugged Charlie into the room with him.

He made sure to keep the both of them cloaked. There was no telling when an orderly would pop his or her head into the room to check up on the patient.

The dark-haired woman lifted her head. She turned her head in one direction and then another, as if she were aware of another presence in the room. "I know that you're there, whoever you are," she said finally. "It won't do any good to hide yourself from me."

While still holding Charlie's hand, he knelt and stroked the woman's wayward hair. "I'm sorry that I have to cloak myself from you, Luna," he apologized, "but I can't allow one of the hospital attendants to see me in here with you."

The woman lifted a hand into the air, her eyes lighting up with recognition. "It's you." Her shoulder came up, then settled back down. "Iancu."

"It's me. Iancu."

Her shoulder jerked a couple more times. She shook her head to and fro. "No, it's not you," she cried out. "I'm imagining this. I'm hallucinating this. The doctor told me so."

"You're not imagining me," he said calmly. He cast a look up at Charlie, who watched the exchange without speaking.

The woman clapped her hands on her head. She grabbed handfuls of her hair and tugged at them. "Voices in my head," she mumbled to herself. She stood from where she'd been sitting on the floor and roamed about the room. "Voices in my head, voices in my head, got to get them out."

"I need you to focus, Luna," Iancu pleaded. "I need you to focus so you can tell me what is going to happen to Neil."

"Neil." She said the name and closed her eyes, wavering on unsteady feet. "Neil, Neil, Neil, the Toltec that is married to the human."

"Yes," he encouraged. "The Toltec that is married to the human."

She stood at the barred window with her arms wrapped around herself. "So much danger," she whispered. "The Toltec is in so much danger, so much danger."

"Why? Why is he in so much danger?"

She shook her head frantically again. "Voices out of my head. Got to get the voices out of my head."

"Luna!" he yelled, impatient. "I need you to tell me about Neil. I need you to tell me whether or not he is going to live. Focus!"

"No, no, no, no!" Luna screamed at the top of her lungs. "No, no, no, no!"

The locks on the door clicked and two orderlies rushed into the room. They tackled her to the narrow bed, holding her arms at her sides in an attempt to subdue her. She continued to scream at the top of her lungs.

Let's go, Iancu communicated to Charlie. *She's not going to tell us anything. She's not going to tell me what I want to know.*

"I will tell you what you want to know!" Luna shouted as the orderlies cautioned that she should calm down. "I will tell you what you want to know!

"The Toltec and his wife...they will *not* live. They will *not* live!"

A nurse ran into the room with a syringe in her hand. The two orderlies kept a steady grip on Luna as the nurse doped her up. The raving woman sobered almost instantly, remaining on the bed staring up at the ceiling.

"They will *not* live," Luna droned on. "They will die. They will both die. And their son will be an instrument used to fulfill the prophecy.

"*The One who brings light*
Shall turn dark
And against her and her maker
Two militias will stand,
One army formed for the sake of good
And the other formed for the sake of malevolence...
Greed.
Humans and immortals alike will fall
At the hands of the Light Bringer.
And a great, powerful evil
Will rise again to claim his throne,
Only to be challenged by a group of protectors
Destined to overpower
The undead lord and his followers.

These protectors, these Children of the Stars
And their two guardians will be all that stand between
The undead lord and the unsuspecting
Innocents that he seeks to bleed dry." Luna slowly shook her head back and forth, barely able to move. The room was growing darker by the moment, but she had to get out her message. "Neil's son will fulfill a part of that prophecy, and so will you, Iancu. It will be your duty to guide the Children of the Stars, the protectors.

"So while Neil and his wife *will* certainly die, you must look at the larger picture. For an evil greater than any that you can fathom now will awaken and you will be the only one who can lead the Children of the Stars to victory."

Too stunned to respond, Iancu followed the orderlies out of the room with Charlie close at his heels. The orderlies stared at Luna through the window, shaking their heads at each other.

"I wonder who she thinks she's talking to," one orderly said thoughtfully.

The other one shrugged. "Who the fuck cares?"

Iancu practically dragged Charlie into the stairwell and down the stairs. He didn't stop moving until they were standing outside in the parking lot. Only then did he release her and turn his back to her. "She just recited the first half and what may be the second half of the prophecy," he murmured under his breath.

Charlie didn't know whether he was talking to her or himself, so she remained quiet.

He turned around to face her. He told her about the prophecy that Jordana had told him about centuries ago. "She's been trying to crack this prophecy ever since I've known her, and I doubt that she's gotten very far with it."

"And that patient in there, Luna, may have just given you the second half of the prophecy," she said slowly.

His expression sobered as he remembered the other part of Luna's prediction. "She also said that Neil and his wife are both going to die. She can't be right about that."

"She was a Kivar," she breathed, realization dawning on her. "The Kivar are known for their psychic ability."

"She can't be right," he repeated. He shook his head, refusing to accept the truth. "We've got to help him. We've got to get in there and save Neil."

CHAPTER FOURTEEN

Hunter Davis had all-American good looks with a crop of golden-blonde hair, baby blue eyes, and an exquisitely toned physique. Because he'd been born with a silver spoon in his mouth, he also had seemingly endless disposable income.

He spent most of his time frolicking on beaches and dancing it up in nightclubs frequented by other socialites and celebrities.

Weeks ago, he'd been told that he should check out Club Pulse. He parked in the club's parking lot and stood out of a car that was more expensive than the average American citizen's house. *This club can't be as hot as everyone's claiming it is,* he thought. *They don't even have valet parking.*

He briskly walked across the parking lot. He headed towards the club's front entrance, where a line of club hopefuls idly chattered with each other.

He breezed past the line of chatterboxes and flashed a thousand-watt smile at the bouncer posted near the front door. "The name's Hunter Davis," Hunter said.

Each of the bouncer's arms was thicker than Hunter's waist. He wore a black t-shirt that was about four sizes too small and dark jeans just as tight. He didn't acknowledge Hunter's introduction. He simply stared at some point beyond Hunter's head and chewed on a thick glob of bubblegum.

Hunter's smile faltered and he cleared his throat. "Excuse me," he said. "I don't think you heard me. My name is Hunter Davis. I'm the son of Glenn Davis, the actor."

The bouncer continued to chew his gum with a blank expression on his face. He was a frightening piece of work, a pile of muscles topped with dark brown hair shaped into a crew cut. There was something unnerving about the man's silence, too.

Hunter raised his hands to his hips, dangerously close to pouting. "I don't know what your deal is, man, but I'm from a very influential family. If I wanted to, I could have this club shut down. I want you to let me through the rope."

The bouncer rolled his eyes downward and looked directly at Hunter, acknowledging him for the first time. "You want me to let you through, huh?"

"That's why I'm here," Hunter said, spreading his arms out and shrugging. "I'm definitely not here for my health."

Something about that comment made the bouncer smile. He sniffed the air and seemed to consider Hunter's request. "I guess I can let you inside." He unhooked the thick, red rope barricading the line of club hopefuls from barging their way into Club Pulse.

Hunter straightened the collar of his five hundred dollar button-down shirt. "That's a little bit better," he said, tilting his nose up now that he was receiving the respect that he felt he deserved.

Unbeknownst to him, the bouncer's eyes shimmered dangerously as the yuppie sauntered through the doors of Club Pulse.

Lights were flashing every which way and dancers were grinding against one another on the dance floor. The bar's countertop had rows of fluorescent lights gleaming beneath its smooth, glass surface. The fluorescent lights cast an eerie glow on the faces of the people seated or standing near the bar. In several dark corners, couples were getting it on.

It was nothing that he hadn't seen before and still he moved as if he were in a trance. There was a vibe in the place that he couldn't describe or give a name to. Several women smiled covertly at him. He sidled up to the bar and signaled the bartender over.

Without asking Hunter what he wanted, the bartender fixed a drink and placed it on the counter.

"Hey, guy," Hunter called to the bartender. "I didn't order a V8." Puzzled, Hunter swirled a finger in the drink and brought his finger up to his lips. The thick liquid in his glass wasn't a vegetable juice drink as he'd originally thought. It was blood.

Before he could question why a glass full of blood had been placed in front of him, a gorgeous brunette claimed the seat next to him and started chatting him up.

He turned on the charm and in minutes, he had her laughing at his corny jokes and affectionately touching him on his arm and knee.

There was a mystery burning in her cat-like green eyes and he desperately wanted to solve it. "Do you want to get out of here?" he asked her suddenly, leaning closely to her so that she could hear him over the Moby song that was playing over the club's speakers.

She shook her head with only a hint of a smile on her lips. "No," she said huskily. "I like it here."

Ouch, he thought to himself. *Brutally denied.*

Her eyes dragged down the length of him and she said, "But maybe we could get a private corner for ourselves so that we can...talk and get to know each other better."

Fighting the urge to grin like an idiot, he nodded his head. In a struggle to keep his cool, he followed her lead to a dark corner. From where they stood, he could still see the dance floor, but no one on the dance floor was looking in their direction.

She brushed back some of his wavy blonde hair and smiled up at him. Then, she stood on her tip toes and gently kissed his lips.

Shocked, he drew his head back and stared at her. "I don't even know your name."

"Lisa," she answered before seizing his mouth with hers once more.

Her kisses were frenzied and demanding. Was it the movie *Species* with the succubus who frantically searched for a man to conceive a child with her? Hunter couldn't remember for sure, but Lisa's kisses reminded him of whatever movie that was. He found himself pulling back, pulling away from her, which was uncharacteristic of him. Wherever he could find a lay, he got a lay. He never turned *down* a lay from a beautiful woman.

For some reason, though, the last thing that he wanted to do was have sex with Lisa. She kissed him as if she were trying to suck the life out of him.

She held on fast to him and wouldn't let him go, escalating his fear. When she finally did let him go, she drew a forearm across her wet lips. "Not bad," she said.

He closed his eyes, swallowed the lump that had been forming in his throat, and opened his eyes. She was no longer standing in front of him. She had disappeared.

His eyes widened and he turned around in a slow circle. *That's it,* he thought. *I'm losing my mind.*

He turned and headed towards the club's entrance doors. As he walked towards them, he noticed that a couple of the dancers on the dance floor stopped dancing to sniff the air. It was like a domino effect; one dancer would stop, smell the air, nudge his/her dance partner, and he or she would, in turn, also sniff the air.

The tension in the room was mounting. Hunter didn't know why; he just wanted to get the hell out of there. He painted an expression of indifference on his face as he made a beeline for the club's entrance doors. Once he reached the doors, he glanced over his shoulder.

Everyone in the entire club, including the deejay, had their eyes pinned on him.

Hunter shoved the doors open and stood facing the beefy bouncer.

The bouncer had his hands planted on his hips. He stared down at Hunter with a smirk on his face. "I thought you wanted *in*," his voice rumbled.

Hunter threw a desperate look over his shoulder. Some of the dancers were making their way toward him. "I did," he said, "but now I want out."

The bouncer shook his head. "It doesn't work that way, little partner."

Little partner? Hunter shook out of his thoughts. "I have to get out of here right now," he said with urgency in his voice.

"What's the rush?" the bouncer asked.

"Something weird is going on," Hunter hissed. "I can't explain it, but whatever it is, it's...*weird*."

The bouncer chuckled and shook his head. "Once you're in, you're *in*," he said, and used one open palm to shove Hunter back within the establishment.

Hunter flew back and landed on his rear end. He didn't have to turn around to know that he had landed at the feet of his predators.

He dared a look at them anyway and regretted it instantly. Their eyes were glowing in a strange manner and their incisors had lengthened. They were staring at him the way a normal person would stare at an expensive restaurant's dessert tray.

Before he could open his mouth to scream, one of them seized him by the throat and lifted him off of the floor. He kicked his feet and tried to pull himself out of the strong dancer's grip, but it was no use.

"Unhand him," a feminine voice commanded.

Abruptly, he was dropped onto the floor. Tears formed at the corners of his eyes. This wasn't happening to him. This *couldn't* be happening to him. He was Hunter Davis, the son of Glenn Davis-the actor.

The crowd of dancers parted and the brunette that had nearly sucked his face off of his skull materialized. She clucked her tongue in mock-sympathy.

"My name is Hunter Davis," Hunter said with his head bowed. "Glenn Davis, the actor, is my father. I'm sure I could get you some money, if that's what you want. Or maybe you'd like a career in the entertainment industry. I could get you that, too. All I'd have to do is ask my dad. That is all I'd have to do. Oh my God, just don't kill me. Please don't kill me."

The brunette knelt so that she was eye level with him. "Oh, honey," she said, stroking his cheek with the back of her left hand. "I'm not going to kill you."

He wiped at his eyes. "You're not?" he asked with a small measure of hope in his voice.

"No, I'm not," she confirmed. "I intend to do quite the opposite. I intend to give you life. I intend to give you everything that you have ever desired."

His brows furrowed. "I don't understand."

Her eyes changed from green to violet and her hair faded from dark brown to fire engine red. Her petite figure widened, spilling an abundance of breasts over the neckline of her revealing, little black dress. "You don't understand," she told him in a voice less throaty than the one she'd used before. "But you will."

Without hesitation, she circled her hands around both of his wrists and tasted of his flesh.

"I'm not used to seeing Los Angeles like this," Charlie murmured as she peered out of the passenger side window.

"Neither am I."

"Whatever Aryk is doing, it is severely affecting the city. How long is it before it affects the rest of the country?"

He shrugged his shoulders. "Who knows?"

She could see that he was bothered, so she stopped talking. *He's worried about Neil,* she thought to herself. *And he has every right to be.* She pursed her lips shut and continued to peer out of the window at the scenery that whizzed by.

He drummed his fingers on the steering wheel as he drove. If Charlie had carried out the plan that she'd wanted to use, she could have easily been kidnapped and taken back to Jordana's mansion. Once there, he would have the means to communicate with her, because for some reason the two of them were telepathically linked. Perhaps he should have let her carry out that plan instead of allowing his concern for her well-being to cloud his judgment. It surely would have been wiser than sending in his friend Neil. Iancu and Neil weren't telepathically linked. In the circumstance that Neil got into hot water with Jordana or Aryk, there was no way for him to contact Iancu.

A barrage of screams sounded in his head. Shaky hands jerked the steering wheel to the right. As a result, the sleek sedan veered off the road and onto the shoulder.

Charlie covered Iancu's hands with her own and helped him to line up the steering so that they wouldn't fly off of the shoulder and into the embankment stretched out beside the road.

He switched his foot from the gas pedal to the brake pedal and brought the car to a stop. The screaming was still a shrieking siren between his temples. He pressed a hand to each side of his head and soon he was screaming himself.

Not knowing what to do, she turned the car off and calmly set a hand on his shoulder.

The screaming grew faint and the sound of raindrops hitting the windshield replaced it. He timidly opened his eyes and leaned his head back against the headrest. He hadn't heard just one scream. He had heard more than one, and simultaneously. All around the city, people were being attacked by vampires. They needed him.

"Buckle in your seatbelt," he ordered the slayer seated beside him as he started the car.

She obeyed his command without question.

Neil entered the mansion without any trouble and purposefully walked down the foyer. His wife was on this property; he could feel it. From where he stood, he could even smell her.

Vampires were in and out different rooms, up and down the hallways, carrying on without paying him any heed. None of them knew that his human wife was carrying a half-human, half-vampire baby. If they had known, they would have pounced on him the moment they set their eyes on him. Instead, some of them nodded a greeting in his direction. A couple of them asked him whether or not he would be assisting them with their business's quarterly taxes at the end of the year. The others ignored him completely.

Relieved that none of them knew what was going on, he followed the scent of his wife. He followed the scent up the winding staircase and towards a large guest bedroom not far from Jordana's and Aryk's master bedroom.

He raised a hand to the doorknob. It turned easily in his hands. He pushed the door open and nearly dropped to his knees at the sight of his wife bound to the bed. He rushed to her side and withdrew the gag from her mouth. She must have been screaming and putting up a fight. Minor scratches laced her arms and legs.

He sat on the edge of the bed and brushed her hair out of her face. "I'm so sorry," he whispered.

Her eyes fluttered open and she stared up at him. Her bottom lip trembled and she turned her head away.

"Mare," he whispered. His voice was choked up with emotion.

Her head whipped around and she stared at him. "You're really here," she said uncertainly, raising a hand to rest against his chest. "I thought I was imagining you again."

He shook his head. "I'm here."

"You have to get me out of here," she whispered. "The people here are crazy. The things I've seen...the things they said..."

"I know."

"We have to get out of here," she said again, tugging at the cuffs encircling her wrists.

"I'm going to get you out of here, I promise," Neil said, trying to get his thoughts together. He hadn't come up with a structured plan on the way here. He'd just been determined to get in, get his wife, and get the hell out.

"Is there a way you can find a key for these handcuffs?" she asked in a tiny voice.

He was positive that he'd never find the keys for the handcuffs, but he *could* influence the lock on the cuffs. Something was nagging at him, but he shook it off. He leaned over his wife and sandwiched the flat of the handcuffs between his palms. He manipulated the locks and moved down to her ankles to do the same.

Once the cuffs were off of her ankles, one of her feet shot up and struck him in the face. Reeling from the blow, he brought his hands up to his nose in shock.

The feminine form of his wife disappeared. Aryk's tall, lanky body took its place. He lay back on the bed with his arms folded behind his head. "That was fun," he said, grinning.

Neil scrambled away from the bed. "Where is Marilyn?"

"She's somewhere safe," Aryk answered cryptically. "I have a better question for you. Why the hell are you consorting with Iancu?"

"That is why you took Mare."

"Yes, that is why I went after your darling 'Mare,' as you call her," Aryk said flippantly, throwing his legs over the side of the bed and standing. "That isn't why I brought her here, though. I had intended on killing her and being done with it."

Neil watched Aryk pace the length of the room.

"It seems that your darling wife is carrying a very special bundle of joy," the blonde vampire went on, stroking his chin thoughtfully. "Naturally, I couldn't kill her. I have to keep her and the child alive to study them both. One of them may carry the secret to immunity from the sun's daunting rays."

"I don't understand," Neil said.

"Don't you?" Aryk returned. "Your child may hold the secrets to all of our flaws. He is half-human and half-vampire. He could possess all of the strengths of being a vampire, but none of the weaknesses. Could you imagine a world with vampires who didn't have to shun the sunlight?"

"You can't possibly think that something like that is possible."

"It's more than possible," Aryk said, gesturing excitedly with his hands. "Enough of that. Your wife and your child are spared, but what should I do with you?"

Neil couldn't stop the fear from showing in his eyes.

Aryk threw his head back and laughed. "I can't quite kill you either. You may also hold valuable information to me. You're a piece of this puzzle, and you may hold the secret as to why you are the first vampire to conceive a child with a human.

"We can talk more about that later. I bet that you're dying to see your wife. I would be delighted to show you where I'm keeping her."

"Why are we parking in front of Pulse?" Charlie asked, turning around in her seat.

"This is our first stop." Iancu turned the engine off and pulled the key out of the ignition.

She got out of the car and followed him, past the huddled line of people waiting to get in the nightclub. The bouncer at the front of the line looked both of them up and down. His eyes anchored on Iancu and he frowned.

"We're at capacity," the beefy bouncer muttered.

"That's just too bad," Iancu returned, tugging aside the lapel to his trench coat so that the hilt of his sword was clearly visible to the bouncer.

The bouncer whistled and chuckled dryly. "The last cat that I let inside this place thought he wanted to get in, too," he said. "It was a different story once he saw what was in there."

"You obviously don't know who I am," Iancu said.

"I know who you are," the bouncer assured, still eyeing the hilt of the sword. "I just don't think it'll make much difference."

Iancu breezed past the bouncer with Charlie close at his heels. "What did he mean by that?" she asked.

"I don't know, but we'll both find out very soon," he replied, pulling open the club's double doors.

The scent of tainted blood was overwhelming. He didn't sense any humans in the place other than Charlie. The club had been taken over by vampires. That was why there were so many people lined up outside of the club waiting to get in. They never *would* get in-not unless they were an eight-course meal for a hungry vampire.

Charlie tugged on his arm. "There are too many of them," she hissed. "We can't take care of all of them by ourselves."

"I never pegged you for being a pessimist," he hissed back, scanning the crowd of club patrons. He noticed a heap on the floor a couple of yards away. The heap was what was left of a human being, 5'10" or 5'11" with wavy blonde hair and a muscled build. There was nothing that Iancu could do to save him. He had already been bitten and nearly drained. His blood had been replaced with tainted blood. Any minute now he would die and after that, the transformation would begin to take place.

"Are you sensing that someone is in danger?" she asked him, eager to leave the place.

He shook his head. "We're too late."

"Then let's go."

"I can't."

"What do you mean you can't?"

The blonde heap lying beside the dance floor started to twitch. Iancu's hand settled beneath the lapel of his coat and came to rest on the handle of his sword. "I have business to tend to here." He looked down at her and saw the worry in her eyes. "If you don't feel comfortable assisting me, you can step outside."

She rolled her eyes. "Just tell me where you want me."

Several colorful suggestions came to mind, but he didn't speak on them. Now wasn't the time for sexual innuendo. "How many guns do you have on you?"

"Two." Tonight she'd opted not to wear the double holster that strapped around her torso. By looking at the quantity of vampires lounging around the dance club, she decided that she could have made a very big mistake by not wearing her shoulder holster. Something told her that she would need more than two guns.

"Both of them are fully loaded?"

"Yes."

"All right. In that case, cover me. Don't forget to watch your back, though."

She nodded and withdrew the guns that she had placed at her back.

He walked away from her, unsheathing his sword and swinging it over his head. He made no introductions or announcements. He had no cute one-liners to say before beheading the two vampires closest to him. He simply separated their heads from their bodies and moved on to the next two vampires.

The club became pandemonium. Charlie stayed near the door, where several of the vampires attempted to flee. She pulled off a couple of rounds with careful aim and the bullets quickly sailed towards their targets. She made sure to keep her back against the wall so that she didn't have to constantly look over her shoulder. Each of her index fingers hugged the trigger of a gun.

Iancu moved adeptly on the dance floor as he decapitated at first one opponent and then another. She couldn't determine whether or not he moved as gracefully as he did because he was a vampire or whether it was a part of his technique. With how effectively he wielded his sword though, there wasn't much need for her to cover him.

A brunette appeared out of thin air, watching Iancu just as Charlie was. She stood beside the Native American slayer with a hand cupping her chin. "Amazing, isn't he?" the brunette asked.

Charlie moved to bring up her gun, but the brunette grabbed both of her hands, crushing them with her own. Shrieking in protest, the slayer was forced to drop her weapons.

The brunette in the little black dress leaned close to her and whispered in her ear, "You think that you have won. You think that Iancu is all yours. You're wrong, though. He's mine. You'll never have him."

Charlie couldn't think of a comeback quickly enough and soon she was relieved of that necessity. The brunette disappeared just as suddenly as she'd appeared. The slayer dropped to the ground, retrieved her guns, and continued squeezing off rounds with the mysterious brunette's words ringing in her ears.

Across the room, Iancu was wreaking havoc with his sword. His face was twisted with fury. The scent of blood was strong and even though it was tainted, it still brought out his fangs.

"Feed on them," a familiar voice whispered into his ear. "You know you want to."

In the midst of a sea of bodies that he had just slain, he dropped to his knees. Even as he fell, some part of him was aware that he had a battle to fight. But he was falling back into his past and there was nothing he could do to stop it.

CHAPTER FIFTEEN

"Feed on them. You know you want to." Jordana circled around him with her eyes focused on his strong, wide back.

They were at a ball and dressed accordingly. She wore a dress the color of fresh lilacs and had her hair stylishly piled on top of her head. He was sporting an expensive suit that she'd bought him. They were watching the party guests whirl each other around on the dance floor. He was here just to experience the celebration, but she was here to pick out her next victim.

That was the difference between him and her. She was always scouting for her next prey, for the next poor sap that she could control. It was sad, really. There were moments when she was truly beautiful and unaware of it. For instance, it had rained a couple nights prior to the ball. She had danced and twirled around in the rain as a ballerina might have. She had appeared so beautiful and innocent in that moment. He knew better than to think that she was actually innocent. She was the cruelest person that he had ever met. However, for the sake of appearances, she had appeared to be extremely pure. Maybe she had intended it that way; he never knew with her.

Now here she was, with her hungry eyes roving over the crowd of party-goers, picking out whom she would feast on later on that night.

He firmly shook his head. "I'm not hungry."

"You aren't hungry yet,*" she told him. "The hunger will attack you later. And when it does, you'll grab the person closest to you. You might as well choose who the person will be."*

He shook his head again, this time without speaking. He didn't want to feed on anyone tonight. He wanted to forget that he was a monster, if only for this night.

Beautiful women waltzed on the ballroom floor, tossing him coquettish glances over the shoulders of their suitors. He moved away from Jordana and approached the woman who'd been flirting with him from afar the entire night. He asked her to dance.

For the few minutes that he danced with her, he felt human. He smiled and whisked her about the floor. He even cracked a few jokes and made her laugh. When the number ended, they stopped dancing and stood awkwardly on the floor.

The woman gave a quick curtsy and thanked him for the dance. She left him and rejoined her friends. Minutes later, she was laughing it up with them and pointing in his direction.

Feeling as if he were the punch line for some joke, he returned to Jordana's side.

She patted his head as if he were a child and said matter-of-factly, "We are not of their world. They are humans. We are not. They'll never understand us but once in awhile, you will come across someone who senses that you are different than they are."

He watched everyone dance and drink in merriment, feeling detached and out of place. People walked past him without acknowledging him. When people looked in his direction, they tended to be looking through him. Maybe Jordana was right.

She caressed his forearm and whispered into his ear, "You know you want to feed on one of them. I don't know why you deny yourself the simplest of pleasures."

"Feeding isn't what makes me happy."

"Then what does?"

"It doesn't matter."

"It matters to me."

It irked him to see the stars dancing in her eyes when she looked at him. Somewhere in her demented mind, she *really believed that she loved him. That disturbed him. He sighed and said, "Being human made me happy. Knowing Bridgette made me happy. Those are two things I'll never get back. I never* will *be happy."*

"Bridgette wasn't your only love, you know. Being the closest thing there is to immortal, we come across many loves."

"I will never love anyone as much as I loved Bridgette."

"Have you ever thought that you and Bridgette just weren't meant to be?" she questioned him.

"No. She was my true love. I know she was." He wrapped his arms around himself and added, "But I didn't deserve her. Maybe that is why she was taken from me."

Jordana rolled her eyes. "She wasn't taken from you. You're the one that killed her."

A muscle in his jaw twitched and his eyes darkened.

She shrugged her shoulders, not looking the least bit apologetic for what she'd said. "It's true. You have no one but yourself to blame for that. You held the hunger at bay for longer than you should have and for that, you have paid the price. The best that you can do now is to make sure that you don't repeat that error in judgment."

He stalked out of the ballroom through tall, elegant patio doors and walked the length of the courtyard, where she later on brought him a peace offering. The woman he'd danced with, the woman that had made fun of him, was slung across Jordana's able shoulders. The tall, svelte vampire dropped the woman at his feet.

He stared down at the woman with furrowed brows. The woman's throat had already been pierced by Jordana's fangs. "I told you I'm not hungry."

"Stop being so stubborn," Jordana said, coming to stand behind him and giving his shoulders a quick massage. "You're hungry and you know it. If you don't feed as often as you should, the bloodlust will drive you mad."

He stared down at the unconscious woman. The truth of the matter was that he was *hungry. In fact, he was starving, but he didn't want to feed from a human. Not tonight.*

Tonight, he wanted to feel normal. He wanted to feel human again, as if he weren't a wolf hiding in sheep's clothing.

"Feed," she whispered in his ear as if she sensed the battle that was going on inside of him. "You're hungry and you know it. Feed."

He turned his back on the sight of the dark-haired woman in the puffy rose-colored dress. Already though, he felt his incisors lengthening. His eyes turned luminous and began to glow a bright cerulean blue. He licked his lips. He was so hungry.

The hunger started as a burning in the pit of his belly; it then quickly spread to the rest of his body. From the tips of his toes to his fingernails to the top of his head, the hunger burned and ignited within him. He felt hot and cold at the same time. The hunger-the bloodlust-was beginning to take control of him.

He turned with his eyes still flashing, with his body still burning. Instead of seeing the woman lying at his feet, he saw her veins and the blood coursing through them. He saw her body's organs beneath thin layers of flesh and tissue.

He lifted his gaze and saw the look of desire in Jordana's eyes. It always turned her on to see him feed; he didn't understand why and he didn't care to. At the moment, all he cared about was nourishment. All he cared about was silencing the hunger and ceasing it from causing the flaming heat and icy coldness flowing throughout his body.

He dropped to his knees in the fresh, green grass and ripped the bodice of the woman's dress.

Jordana was whispering things, dirty things in his ear and urging him to go further. "Don't stop now," she said. "Don't stop now. Feed. Take your fill. You know you want to."

The monster in him reared its ugly head and took over. He took his fill of the woman that he cradled in his arms. He ravaged her in every sense of the word, egged on by an evil, controlling, and devious creature.

He fed on more people that night. He didn't stop at the woman who had laughed at him. He moved on to her friends, *and then on to a couple of strangers he'd never before set his eyes upon.*

The scent of blood was strong, torturously assailing his nostrils. His incisors lowered; it was a reaction that he couldn't control. Hunger ripped through his body and as a result of the pain seizing him, his muscles strained against the flesh of his arms.

He remained hunched over with his palms pressed flat against the floor. His chest heaved with exertion and his expression was twisted with physical anguish.

Images flashed before his eyes. He could still see Jordana's curvaceous body and still hear her silky, venomous voice. *"Feed on them. You know you want to."*

He was held captive by the searing pain that was shooting through his body and enthralled by the memories that assaulted him. He was so entranced, in fact, that he never sensed the vampire that was rushing at his back.

"Iancu!" Charlie screamed, running towards him with her guns blazing.

The brunette in the little black dress knocked Iancu flat on his stomach. She looked around the desolate club in disdain. All of the other vampires in the place had been executed. Some of their bodies were still twitching, but there didn't seem to be any unwounded vampires in the house.

Charlie pulled the triggers of both guns.

The vampire reached out both hands and successfully caught each bullet. She brought the bullets up to her eyes and studied them. "Silver. Typical." She cast the shiny bullets to the floor and narrowed her eyes at Charlie. "Come here," she said in a voice dripping with ill intent.

The slayer's legs moved against her will, drawing her nearer to the vampire.

"Now drop the guns," the brunette ordered.

"No," Charlie protested weakly, even as she felt the guns slipping from her hands. She looked down at Iancu. *You have to help me.*

"He's of no help to you," the brunette said, effortlessly reading the slayer's mind. "I'm afraid you're on your own. It's just you and me."

"Who are you?"

"I'm an old friend of Iancu's," the brunette said, tilting her head to the side. "Who are you?"

"I'm a *new* friend of Iancu's."

The brunette knelt down and wrapped Iancu's ponytail around her hand. She yanked his head up. "Look at her. Aren't you hungry?"

Iancu's eyes were thin slits. He looked out of sorts, as if he didn't know which way were up or down. His lips were moving. He was trying to say something, but couldn't quite get it out.

The brunette nuzzled her cheek against his and then suddenly released his hair. "He never did know his limits. The hunger…it rules you if you don't confront it. He avoids drinking from humans and instead drinks from his meager little blood packs. Nothing compares to the hot blood coursing through a human's veins, not even cloned blood. He avoids drinking from humans because he can't accept what he is. That will be his downfall."

The expression on Charlie's face was one of indifference, but below the surface she was extremely worried for Iancu's health. The blow that the brunette had given him shouldn't have had such an intense effect on him.

The brunette walked around his body and came to stand in front of Charlie. "You don't look like much to me," she said after a frank perusal of the other woman. She circled around the slayer with one hand balanced on her hip. "I've been thinking of how I should kill you."

"So then you know who I am," Charlie said.

"Of course I know who you are. I'm not dense. You're the slayer. An incompetent one at that, but I've seen worse."

Charlie bit her tongue to keep herself from speaking.

"I would have thought that fighting beside Iancu would teach you *something*, but maybe there are some people who just can't be taught."

"That isn't what Aryk was saying a couple of nights ago," Charlie retorted and blew on her nails nonchalantly.

The brunette's eyes widened. The glamour melted away and she appeared as she normally did, with tumbling red hair, creamy pale skin, and violet eyes. "So you know who I am, then."

"Of course," the slayer returned. "I'm not dense. You're Jordana-an obsessive, manipulative witch who can't let go of the past. I think I can help you with that, though. You see...Iancu doesn't want to have anything to do with you."

"Oh?" Jordana flipped her hair over her shoulder. "And I guess the next words out of your mouth will be that Iancu has fallen for *you*?"

"That is a work in progress."

Jordana laughed silkily. "A work in progress? I *sired* him. I made him what he is today. I've known him for centuries. He and I have made love a countless number of times. I know his wants and his desires, his fears and his nightmares. There is no competing with that."

A loud shriek pierced through the club and bounced off of the walls. A blonde man pulled himself into a sitting position. His movements were jerky and robotic. He unsteadily got to his feet and wavered for a moment before gaining his balance. He assessed the bodies and piles of dust scattered throughout the club with wide eyes.

"You're just in time," Jordana said with a bright smile on her face.

Hunter wiped a hand across his bloody mouth. His clothes were ripped; there was hardly any cloth left clinging to his body. There was a deep gash in the side of his neck and another gash on the right side of his abdomen, below his heart. He jerkily walked up to Jordana and leaned heavily against her.

Jordana gave his head a pat and arched a look at the slayer. "Slayer, meet my friend Hunter. Hunter, this is Charlie. She's going to be your first kill."

Hunter looked between the two women.

Jordana threw an arm around his shoulders and whispered into his ear.

He frowned in confusion, but nodded his head when she clapped him on the back. He turned towards Charlie and headed in her direction.

Charlie couldn't move. She couldn't even feel her legs. What had Jordana done to her? Just how powerful *was* she? *Iancu, please wake up. You've got to wake up.*

Hunter tackled her and managed to uproot her feet from the floor in the process. They both landed on the floor, wrestling each other.

Charlie fended him off with one arm while fishing around in one of her coat pockets with the other. She brought out a sharp, smooth stake and felt no remorse as she planted the stake through his chest.

A shocked expression morphed the features of his face. Charlie rolled his body off of her. He wouldn't explode into a cloud of dust as most vampires did. The vampiric transformation wasn't one hundred percent complete. Instead of being reduced to a pile of dust, his body would take longer to decompose.

Jordana didn't look pleased. "I guess I'm going to have to take care of you myself," she said.

"Go ahead," Charlie spat. "I can understand why you would want to kill me. Two men that you love fantasize about me at night. It has to be tough being you. Unwanted. Unloved. Unattractive."

"You bitch," Jordana screamed, flying towards her at a rapid speed. She attacked the slayer with so much force that both of them soared into the air several feet above the floor until Charlie's back hit a wall. She clamped her hands around the slayer's throat and didn't let up.

Charlie frantically searched her coat pockets for another stake. She'd used them all. *This isn't happening,* she thought to herself.

Maniacal glee danced in Jordana's violet eyes.

There has to be something that I can do. There was nothing that she could do. Jordana was way too strong for her. She couldn't breathe. She clawed at Jordana's hands, but she couldn't pry them from her throat.

Jordana's eyes were locked on hers. Looking into the depths of her eyes was like looking into a bottomless pit. Her eyes were empty and devoid of emotion.

Charlie kicked her legs in vain. *Iancu!* Tears streamed down her cheeks as she felt her life slipping out of her grasp.

A gun went off and the grip that Jordana had on Charlie's throat loosened. The gun went off again.

Charlie slid down the wall, wheezing and tenderly rubbing her neck.

Jordana whirled around, unharmed by the bullets but annoyed nonetheless. "Are you seriously going to attempt to fight me?"

Iancu stood approximately four yards away from her. Clasped in his hands was one of Charlie's handguns.

Charlie wanted to shout to him, but she couldn't talk. It hurt to breathe, let alone speak. She remembered that they were telepathically linked. *You can't fight her with guns alone.*

I know that.

You're going to have to use your powers, Iancu.

Jordana lifted one hand in the air. Energy and light ebbed from it, sailing towards Iancu. A strong force knocked him in the chest.

He braced the blow and remained standing, unmoved.

Jordana frowned.

He raised his own hand in the air. The sleeve of his trench coat slid up his arm, revealing the dragon-shaped birthmark on the inside of his wrist.

Charlie watched him with a concerned look on her face.

I can't do it. I can't, he thought, beginning to get cold feet.

Yes, you can, she contradicted. *If you don't, she's going to kill us both.*

He shook his head and dropped his hand, clearly frustrated with himself.

"You haven't changed one bit," Jordana told him with a satisfied smirk twisting her thin lips.

If you don't use your powers, I'm going to attack her myself, Charlie communicated to him telepathically.

She'll obliterate you, he warned her. *Don't do it.*

Charlie struggled to stand on her feet.

Jordana raised both of her hands with both palms facing outward. Sparks danced around her fingers and shot towards Iancu.

Again, he absorbed the attack without being moved from where he stood.

Charlie ran at Jordana's back full force.

Jordana whirled with her arm extended and caught Charlie in the stomach.

"Charlie!" Iancu yelled.

The slayer crumpled to the floor and didn't move.

Jordana hoisted her eyebrows. "She doesn't absorb an attack quite like you."

Energy crackled at Iancu's fingertips and his eyes grew livid. "You shouldn't have done that," he said in a menacing tone.

"You're no match against me, Iancu," she told him. "I am the one who sired you. No amount of training and no amount of caring that you have in that dead heart of yours is going to change that. Your slayer *will* die at my hands. Would you like to stay here and watch?" She turned her back to Iancu and raised her hands.

Wind rushed at Iancu as he soundlessly levitated off of the floor. He raised his arms in the air. Pure energy flowed throughout his body. The feeling of it rejuvenated him. He could feel the energy flowing up his legs, past his stomach, to his chest, and outward along his shoulders and down his arms. The entire building began to tremble beneath the weight of his power.

The bar counter shook, causing a line of empty glasses to make a tinkling melody. Bar stools uprooted from the floor and flew across the room. The rubber band holding his hair snapped. His hair flew around his head in a dark halo.

She sensed his power before turning around to look at him. Her eyes grew round with amazement and shock. He looked like a dark angel, suspended in the air with his hair fluttering around his shoulders. His eyes were orbs of radiant, bright blue and light reflected off of his sharp, lengthened incisors. The hem of his coat flapped around his legs. He brought his arms down and a stream of channeled energy shot down from his hands.

It may as well have been a bolt of lightning that struck Jordana and jolted her from the way she shook and jerked. She struggled to regain control of her own body. She failed to do so. She was held captivated by Iancu's power and there was nothing that she could do about it.

Jordana used her glamour and took on the face of Bridgette.

Iancu grinned devilishly. "That was your second mistake," he growled, unleashing even more force upon her.

Neil nearly fainted when he saw his wife chained to the dungeon wall. "Are you insane?" he demanded. "She could lose the baby." He ran to his wife's side and affectionately stroked her cheek.

"You're probably right," Aryk said, "but she was starting to irritate me. She was kicking and screaming and causing all kinds of commotion. Who would have thought that she'd be such a little fighter, huh?"

Neil pressed his forehead against his wife's. "I'm so sorry," he whispered. "This is my fault."

She shook her head slowly. "It's not your fault."

"Yeah, actually, it is."

Aryk's brows furrowed. He heard Jordana's voice screaming in his head, but he couldn't make out what she was saying. He glanced at his watch. "I'm going to give you two lovebirds some time together," he said. "There are guards posted outside of this door. If you try to escape, they have orders to kill you."

"Would you really kill us?" Neil asked out of curiosity.

"I would definitely kill *you*," Aryk replied honestly. "You're a hell of a lot more expendable than your wife is. However, if I had to kill her, I would. In the event that I do have to kill her, I can just extract the fetus from her womb."

Neil watched Aryk exit the cramped, dirty room with a scowl on his face. Then he turned his attention back to his wife.

"These people are crazy," she whispered, shaking her head.

"You can say that again."

"How do you know these people?"

"He's a client of mine," he responded automatically without even thinking. He sighed and brushed some of Marilyn's hair out of her eyes. "We have to talk, Mare."

She stared at him without saying anything.

He didn't know how much she'd heard from Aryk or how much she'd observed. He turned his back to her, trying to piece a speech together.

"I thought you said we have to talk," she said to his back.

"I'm trying to think of what to say."

"Don't think about what to say," she told him. "Just say what you have to say."

"There are some things that you don't know about me," he began. "Some pretty...wild and crazy things you might not even believe."

"Go on."

"When we first started hitting it off, I told you that I was sterile. I lied to you."

She frowned. "Why would you lie about something like that?"

He nervously smoothed a hand over his hair. "I was under the impression that I couldn't have kids with you."

"What gave you that impression?"

"I'm not...what you think I am, Mare."

"Neil, look at me."

"I can't." He covered his face with his hands. He was close to crying, but he couldn't break down-not now. He had to tell her. He had to get the story out before Aryk came back.

"You're scaring me," she whispered.

"I know, and I don't want to do that." He turned to look at her. "There's no easy way to tell you what I have to tell you, so I'm just going to come out and say it, all right?"

She nodded.

"I'm a vampire."

Her brows drew together. "What?"

"I'm a vampire," he repeated. "A vampire."

"Like...Dracula?"

He shrugged his shoulders. "More or less."

She stared at him for a moment. "Oh honey," she said. "As soon as we get out of here, you need a vacation. No more work for you. You've been working way too hard."

"I wish I *were* delusional."

Silence dominated the dungeon for several minutes. "You're serious," she said slowly. "You think that you're a vampire."

"Do you remember that night at the hospital? And...I mean, look at where we are right now, Mare. Is it so hard to believe, after all that has happened so far?" He gestured around the dark, musty room with his hands as he spoke. "The strange pregnancy test results, what happened when I touched your stomach, and all of this craziness...this isn't a joke. The guy who kidnapped you was dead serious. If he wanted to kill either one of us, it would be done."

"Vampires don't exist, Neil," Marilyn said.

"Says who?" Neil demanded. "Look...I wish I had the time to debate this with you. I really do. The truth of the matter is, though, I *don't*. I don't have the time to argue with you. I don't have the time to prove it to you. We've been married for a couple of years. You're just going to have to trust me, all right?"

Startled by his outburst, she nodded her head and clamped her mouth shut.

"I just wanted to tell you the truth and tell you what was going on because you're going to see some things, *weird* things, and I wanted to prepare you for that. Hell, you might even see me kill a couple of people. I can't afford for you to freak out if you see something like that. I can't afford for you to run away from me if you see something like that. We are up against some pretty brutal forces here, and if I have to run after you and chase you, that could mean the end of both of our lives. Just know that if I'm killing someone, it's because they deserve to be dead." He paced as he talked. Pacing was a habit of his when he was on edge. "Are we on the same page?"

"I think so," she said, sounding quite uncertain.

"For the longest time, it has been believed that vampires and humans couldn't conceive children together. That is why I thought that I couldn't have children with you. It seems, though, that we blew that myth out of the water. Aryk seems to think that our baby holds secrets about the abilities and faults of vampires. If we play by his rules for awhile, then he's going to keep both of us alive."

She shook her head. "This is sounding crazy, Neil."

"I know it is. I wish I didn't have to tell you any of this, but..." He shrugged his shoulders. "I've wanted to tell you for so long."

She stared down at the floor. She couldn't process everything that he was telling her. It was too radical, too crazy. It was impossible, really. Vampires were creatures that she saw in horror movies. They weren't creatures that walked the same streets that she did-at least, not to her knowledge. How could a secret this big still be a secret? She sighed. *Vampires don't exist,* she concluded. *My husband has just lost his mind.*

The electricity in the air still sparked with residue of Iancu's power. He lowered himself to a floor littered with corpses. His hair settled around his shoulders. A hazy, red film blanketed his eyes and blurred his vision. He wiped at the blood tears with each index finger.

He stepped over mutilated bodies and telltale piles of dust and stopped only when he reached Charlie's fallen, hunched form. He couldn't decide whether her decision to attack Jordana had been foolish or a stroke of genius. On some level, she had known that he would have no choice but to use his powers in the event that she was harmed. She'd sacrificed herself in order to free him from his inhibitions and self-hate.

He could have lost her tonight. All it would have taken was a drop of Jordana's negative energy. Jordana could have killed the slayer whenever she'd wanted to. The fact that she had wanted to savor the slayer's death was what prevented her from successfully ending the slayer's life.

His fingers still tingled. He could still feel the power within him simmering beneath the surface of his skin. Before this night, no one had ever defeated Jordana in battle. It was an unprecedented event. He was having trouble believing it, and he had witnessed it.

He noticed that only an empty space on the floor remained where Jordana's fallen body should have been. She'd escaped, but he had expected as much.

He knelt to the floor and brushed aside wayward strands of the slayer's hair. The tips of her eyelashes kissed her cheeks. Her smooth, tanned face was peaceful in her unconscious state, making her appear angelic and pure.

She's anything but an angel, he thought as his eyes traveled down the length of her. He gathered her into his arms and rose to full height, cradling her as he would a child. Then, careful to step over the remains of mutilated vampires, he carried her out of the nightclub.

There was still a line of club-hoppers waiting outside Club Pulse. All of them turned their eyes upon the tall, dark-haired man carrying the unconscious Native American beauty through the double doors of the club.

The bouncer looked Iancu over with a slight nod of the head. "You came out alive," he said, his voice tinged with surprise. "I'm impressed."

"A lot of people tell you not to believe everything that you hear," the dark-haired vampire said. "I'm the exception. Everything you've heard about me is true." He continued down the sidewalk with Charlie in his arms, leaving the beefy bouncer to wonder at his words.

He seated the slayer in the passenger seat of his car, walked around the car, and opened the driver side door. Before lowering into the car, he looked over the top of the roof. Screams sounded in his head, the screams of humans that were being attacked across the entire city of Los Angeles and beyond.

Four blocks away, a woman was being mauled in a dark, damp alley. A mile away, three vampires were attacking a middle-aged man and robbing him of all of his valuables. Iancu didn't have enough time to get to them. Both of the victims would be dead by the time he reached them.

His gaze lowered to the dragon-shaped birthmark on the inside of his right wrist. He ran a thumb over the birthmark and closed his eyes.

No…he didn't have the time to save everyone in the city. He had to head back to his apartment and nurse Charlie back to health. Once she felt better, he was going to train with her. Tonight, the two of them wouldn't be able to storm Jordana's castle as he'd planned. There was no way that they could rush in to Neil's rescue tonight. In order to ambush Jordana, both he and Charlie would have to be at the top of their game. They couldn't afford any weaknesses. It would have to wait until tomorrow. He figured, though, that Neil would live through the night. Jordana would need time to recuperate from the battle that had transpired. *But tomorrow, it has to happen,* he thought as he started the car. Tomorrow, he would have to do what every good friend has to do once in awhile; he would have to save his buddy's ass.

Jordana stormed through the doors of her residence with her hair trailing behind her. She was livid. She was *infuriated*. She'd sired Iancu and he should have never been able to do what he'd done to her. The power that he seemed to possess was unheard of. Something told her that she'd gotten nothing but a taste of what Iancu could do.

She was the oldest vampire known among their kind. She should have nothing to fear in this world, and yet she feared a vampire that she sired. She feared Iancu.

She raged up and down the halls of her estate, shouting orders at everyone in sight.

Seven vampires lounged in the sitting room, smoking and drinking blood out of sparkling wine glasses. They were speaking to each other in low tones, but all of the speaking came to a sudden halt when Jordana entered the room. They all stopped talking at once and took in her battered and bruised appearance.

She stood in the arched entrance of the room with eyes that spit fire. When she spoke though, her tone was measured and calm. "I want security increased around the perimeter of the house."

Jade stood up from where she'd been seated and assured Jordana that she would take care of everything.

"No one else is to enter this house," Jordana continued. "I don't care who it is. I don't care if you think you know the person or if it's someone who stays here. No one is to be allowed within these walls." She turned on her heel and exited the room.

As soon as the ancient vampiress exited the room, the vampires in the sitting room started gabbing again. Jordana was known for being overdramatic. It had always been believed that no one could cause harm to her, because she was the oldest vampire known in their community. However, she'd been marked up pretty badly and looked pretty frightful. Perhaps for once, she wasn't being paranoid. Maybe their leader wasn't as strong as any of them had thought.

Gossip was a pet peeve of Jade's, so when the vampires began brainstorming about what could have their leader so distraught, she dismissed herself from the room. With her hands shoved into the pockets of her jeans, she walked outside of the mansion and proceeded to walk the perimeter of the estate.

Her sister was a Wiccan vampire. She could most likely contact her and have her perform a spell that would keep any unwanted visitors from showing up on the property. As she walked, she made mental notes to herself on certain security measures that she would like to take.

The night air had a calming effect on her nerves. She stopped walking and inhaled deeply. Her mind switched gears. Instead of coming up with security measures, she started to think about Chase. She started to remember the time they'd spent together. She hadn't heard from him since the night that she'd shown up at his hotel. He had most likely skipped town and she didn't feel insulted by that. It was an Arati's nature to bounce from city to city, state to state, and country to country.

A gentle breeze rolled over her bare arms and caressed the hair at the nape of her neck. The moonlight caused the tattoo sleeves on both arms to shimmer. The tattoo that crawled up her left arm was a dragon. Its tail curled around her wrist and his dark green scaly body encompassed the rest of her arm. A snake slithered down her right arm. She had a plethora of tattoos and even more piercings. Pain didn't cause her discomfort. She sought after pain. Pain was her pleasure.

Jordana trudged up the winding staircase and burst through her bedroom door. She'd expected to see Aryk lazily lying in bed, but he was nowhere in the room.

He sauntered into the room moments later to find her standing near the window, peering out into the night. "I went out looking for you," he told her. "I heard your screams in my head. I didn't know where you were."

"I was out," she responded. "I had a bit of a run-in with the slayer."

Aryk nervously ran a hand through his hair. "Did you kill her?"

"No."

Relieved after hearing this news, he approached her and stood at her back. "Are you all right?"

"No, I'm not all right." She turned to face him. Her face, her collarbone, and her arms were all marked with welts. Her hair, which was usually perfectly sculptured, was in disarray. She didn't look like she'd had a run-in with the slayer. She looked like she'd had a run-in with a tornado.

"What happened to you?" he demanded, his voice filled with concern. He took her face in his hands and studied her closely. Never before had he seen her appear to be less than perfect. She didn't have any moles on her body. He'd never seen her with a pimple or a bruise. Her skin had always been flawless, but now it was far from perfect. Every mole, blemish, and welt stood out against her milky complexion. Pale freckles that he'd never seen before spotted her cheeks and the bridge of her nose. "The slayer could not have done this to you. *No one* could have done this to you."

That was what she had thought. "Iancu was protecting the slayer," she said tiredly, walking around him and sitting on the bed.

Aryk couldn't tear his eyes off of her. "Iancu did this to you? But...you sired him."

"I know."

"How could he overpower you?" *More importantly,* he couldn't help but think, *how can I overpower you?*

"He didn't *overpower* me," she snapped. Fire leapt into her eyes at his choice of words. "He got lucky."

"It shouldn't even be possible for him to be this lucky when you're his opponent," he muttered. "I've never seen you like this."

"I was too weak to use the glamour to hide my injuries."

"Why would you hide your injuries?"

"I'm Jordana," she mumbled, gesturing wildly with her right hand and causing the gold bracelets around her wrist to clink together. "I'm supposed to be the most powerful of our kind. If anyone gets wind of the fact that Iancu was able to harm me...my reputation would be shattered. I can't allow that to happen."

He sat beside her on the bed and settled an arm upon her shoulders. "Don't worry about any of this," he said. "We will annihilate Iancu *and* the slayer. There is no way that the two of them can compete with the two of us."

She hated to admit it to herself, but all of a sudden, she wasn't so sure of that. She wasn't so sure that she and Aryk could defeat Iancu even if he was fighting alone. Never before in her life had she felt fear or doubt, but now she was filled with both of those emotions.

Iancu carried an unconscious slayer into his apartment and stretched her across the bed in the guest room. Beads of sweat lined her forehead, causing tendrils of her long, dark hair to cling to her brow. She'd endured an extreme amount of pain. She would heal at a rate faster than most other humans did, but that didn't change the fact that she could have died tonight.

"You act as if the gift I've given you is a curse," Jordana had told him the morning that she'd materialized in his bathroom. *"Eternal life. Intensified senses. Supernatural abilities.*

"If you are truly to fight against Aryk and myself, then you can't afford any weaknesses. Your own self-hate and hate of our people are your most substantial weaknesses. You are messing with the wrong people. I am the one that made you. I can most certainly break you."

A muscle in his jaw twitched. For the first time in centuries, he'd unleashed his powers. After all of that time, he hadn't forgotten how to use them. He hadn't missed a beat. Using his powers had felt natural to him. It had energized him and made him feel oddly refreshed. He'd even managed to defeat Jordana. He'd never heard of a vampire conquering his or her sire in battle. He had done so and not only that, but he had come out of the battle unscathed. She had taunted him about his weaknesses and mercilessly teased him about the fact that he refused to use his abilities. In the end, she sent him so far over the edge that she was forced to retreat with her tail tucked between her legs.

He gave Charlie's hand a pat and turned to leave the room. He disrobed and took a quick shower. The warm water did little to soothe his taut nerves.

After his shower, he exited the bathroom and sauntered into his bedroom. He tied his hair back in a ponytail, threw on a pair of pajama pants, and grabbed one of his heaviest swords from the walk-in closet.

He flipped off the lights in his bedroom and padded out of the room, down the hall, and into the living room. He spread his legs wide and raised the sword, pointing the tip of it to the ceiling. Then, he swung the sword in front of him in a long, measured stroke, watching the corded muscles of his forearms straining against his skin in protest.

He stepped back with the sword in his hands, ducked with the sword in his hands, and jumped with the sword in his hands. All of his movements were slow and deliberate.

Events from his life flashed before his eyes as he wielded the weapon to and fro. He envisioned a young child eagerly watching knights jousting, challenging each other with dull lances. In those days, becoming a warrior had been his one and only dream.

Fast forward seventeen years and he was a blacksmith enjoying his ale on a dark, lonely night when he was sought out by a manipulative seductress.

"Before I walked up to you, I noticed that you looked troubled. I hope I am not delving into private matters, but I was wondering why you looked so melancholy." She had batted her eyelashes at him and tempted him. He had taken the bait.

She had explained later that they had not met by chance. She had seen him several days before that night in the town square. She had followed him to his shop and memorized his daily schedule. She knew that he frequented the tavern in which they'd met.

She'd attempted to mold him into the perfect pet. She was the only vampire that he knew, the only person who could answer the plentiful questions that he had. Naturally, he latched onto her and did her bidding for quite some time, until he realized what a drone he'd become.

By then, it was too late though, he thought now as he crouched to the floor with his sword in hand. *By then, I'd killed hundreds of people. A great amount of damage had already been done. She'd already molded me into the monster that she wanted me to be.*

Watching him feed on helpless, beautiful women aroused Jordana. It was an act that probably still turned her on to this day. At the time, he hadn't understood her dislike for human beings, but now he did.

She was a natural vampire; she'd been born a vampire. She was cruel and heartless because she'd never known what it was like to be a human being. She didn't hate humans. She *envied* them and their humanity. Humanity was something that she would never possess and she was used to getting what she wanted. Never in her life would she be able to rest beneath a sun's rays for hours on end without fearing its effect on her. Never would she be able to enjoy an eight-course meal that consisted of *real* food, instead of nourishment to satisfy the bloodlust.

His face became damp with sweat as scenes danced behind his eyes. He could barely remember the date of his birthday and it was a struggle to remember just how many birthdays he'd had, but he never had trouble remembering the faces of those he'd slain.

Their faces danced before him now, and for a moment he stood frozen in the middle of the living room with his sword dangling at his side. The people that he'd murdered had had families and jobs, hopes and dreams. They'd had routines and relationships, appointments and obligations. All of their existences had been wiped away for the sole purpose of his nourishment.

He hadn't bitten a human being in a quarter of a century, but the sensation was etched into his memory. He would never forget what it felt like, tasted like. He would never forget the saltiness of the flesh or how wonderful it was to have blood exploding in his mouth after the first puncture.

The hand holding the sword began to shake uncontrollably. His blue eyes blazed radiantly as a rush of sensory overload besieged him. He brought the sword up again and swished it through the air, fighting his own inner demons. He wasn't a monster that was so easily satiated by the violation of a human being. He wasn't a monster whose life was controlled by the hunger, the lust for human blood.

His slow, deliberate movements became quick, noiseless slashes into dead air. He whirled and lunged and crouched and jumped, all the while cutting his sword into the air in a blind, erratic frenzy.

He sensed the presence of someone in the room, and that brought his crazed movements to a standstill. Breathing heavily, he faced a sleepy-eyed Charlie, who'd changed into a white tank top and matching shorts. The tight shorts that she wore revealed the dark bruises splotched up and down her legs. The same tint of purple marked her upper arms as well. Already, the bruises were beginning to fade. She had begun to heal.

Still, shadows passed over his eyes at the sight of the harm that had come to her. Even though she was a slayer and it was her duty to battle against evil, he felt that he was the cause of the pain that she'd had to endure.

She remained in the hallway's entrance, leaning against the wall with her arms crossed over her chest. Her eyes lowered from the crazed expression on his face to the sword he held in a white-knuckled grip.

She moved farther into the room, avoiding his steady gaze until she was only inches away from him. Without saying a word, she reached out and took the sword out of his hands.

He watched her create distance between them by taking several steps backward. She held the sword in front of her face with its blade nearly touching her nose. Both hands were wrapped around the sword's hilt. She closed her eyes with the sword before her and when she opened them, she was no longer Charlie the woman. She was Charlie the slayer.

She raised the sword and slashed at the air with impressive execution. She pointed the tip of the sword at Iancu's collarbone with a flirtatious look in her eyes.

She maintained eye contact with him while wielding the large, heavy weapon. He broke eye contact with her and moved around her as she practiced, rubbing his chin in thought as he noted her strengths and weaknesses with the sword.

He came to stand at her back. He reached around her and spread his arms so that they were hovering over her arms. While drinking in the scent of her hair, he guided her movements with his hands. Together, they moved about the living room. He was her shadow, standing at her back holding her in a partial embrace while giving her a tutorial in sword maneuvering.

She unconsciously leaned back into him, her focus momentarily being ripped away from the sword in her hands and centered more on the strong, able vampire standing behind her.

Time seemed to move in slow motion as he moved with her. His breath caressed her neck, sending a domino effect of shivers rolling down her spine. He disengaged from her and dismounted the other sword from over the mantelpiece of the fireplace. Then, he moved to stand in front of her.

He didn't have to open his mouth to speak for her to know his intentions. He wanted to strengthen her swordplay technique by training with her. He extended his sword towards her with a stern expression on his face.

She touched the tip of her sword to the tip of his and brought her sword up. He held back and fought defensively.

"You're holding the sword way too low," he told her as he blocked one of her attacks. "I'm taller than you. You are fighting as if you are against someone your height."

She frowned and angled the sword higher, leaping backwards when he made a jab at her with the point of his sword. At first, their interaction was tame with Iancu working mostly the defense and Charlie on the offensive, but the tables quickly turned. The tall, dark-haired vampire turned up the heat a notch, adeptly blocking her attacks and expertly attacking her back before she could bring up the heavy sword.

She fought with all of her might against him, wanting to land at least one well-timed blow.

"You may desperately want to land a punch or a blow or a kick, but you can't force it," her grandfather had told her once. *"You have to take your time with it. Your muscles will tighten up while you're in battle, because you will be tense with the desire to win. You have to learn how to relax those muscles and relax your mind. Fight aggressively, but patiently. Keep your focus sharp and keep your eyes on your opponent. Sooner or later, your opponent will slip up, and then you are able to execute the punch, blow, or kick that you wish to land."*

Her eyes grew misty at the thought of her grandfather. He had been an elderly man, but he'd had a youthful nature about him. His heart had been kind. He had always looked out for her to the best of his ability, *despite* his disability.

She hadn't spent a lot of time with her older brother, Randy. He'd always had school work to do or friends to hang out with. Yet, whenever he was around the house and she had advice to ask of him, he would listen to her with a sympathetic ear and offer the best advice that he could.

And her mother and father...she would give her life just to be able to hug them both again. Her eyes misted over and tears blinded her vision. The sword in her hand wavered; the grip that she had on the weapon loosened as she lost her focus.

Iancu brought his sword down with cruel efficiency, knocking the weapon out of her hands. He tapped into her thoughts and was greeted with images of her parents, her older brother, and her grandfather. She was remembering the family that she had once had.

He knew what it felt like to be haunted by the past. There was no running away from it; it always found a way to catch up to him. No doubt, the past was catching up to her, too.

She blinked the tears out of her eyes and stared up at him. Blue locked with hazel as he approached her and cupped her cheek in his right hand. Her lashes brushed her cheeks as she closed her eyes.

He kissed the top of her head and held her.

She sniffled and wiped in vain at the tears tracking their way down her cheeks. "We have to suit up," she mumbled into his bare chest. "We have to save Neil from that monster. I can't let Aryk murder another innocent family."

"We aren't going anywhere tonight," he responded.

She frowned. "Are you serious?"

"You're in no kind of shape to go against Jordana and Aryk," he said matter-of-factly. "You're fortunate to have gotten away from Jordana without much more than a couple of bruises."

"What if they're torturing Neil right now?" she demanded. "What if they've killed him already?"

"They won't kill him unless he gives them a reason to," he told her. "They need him."

"*He* needs *us*," she said, pulling back out of his embrace. "You heard what Luna said and you said yourself that he's not a skilled fighter. If he tries anything, they'll destroy him."

"He'll be safe for the night," he maintained, "and so will you."

She planted her hands on her hips.

He chuckled and shook his head. "We will go after Neil at sundown tomorrow."

She still looked doubtful.

"We'll have time to train together and gather up all of the equipment that we're going to need," he continued. "I don't think you realize the intensity of the situation. Jordana could have easily filleted both of us tonight."

"Not you," she said softly.

He pursed his lips shut.

"We defeated her once. We can do it again."

"It's not that simple." He walked over to the fireplace and mounted both swords on the wall where they belonged.

"I was in and out of it there for awhile, but I saw what happened," she said softly. "What you did back there...that was pretty amazing."

"What I did back there was necessary."

"Were you aware of how much power you had?" she asked him. "Were you aware that you could have an effect like that on Jordana?"

"No. I wasn't aware at all."

"Shouldn't it be close to impossible for you to defeat her if she's the one that sired you?"

He shrugged. He didn't have the desire to talk about what had transpired between Jordana and himself. He and Charlie had gotten out alive and they were lucky to have escaped the evil clan leader's clutches.

Knowing that he was reluctant to talk about the power that he possessed, she stopped asking questions. He had been a truly remarkable sight in Club Pulse. He had appeared to be a dark avenger of good, hovering in the air with power sparking from his fingertips. There was no denying how attracted she was to him after that moment.

"I'm going to head to bed," he announced all of a sudden, sensing the sexual tension between them escalating. "You should do the same."

She watched him stride down the hallway, shirtless and formidable. He glanced over his shoulder and gave her a long look before disappearing into his bedroom.

She chewed on the inside of her cheek, following his example and exiting the living room. She entered the guest bedroom and closed the door at her back. After a moment of thought, she lifted her tank top over her head and dragged her shorts down muscled thighs and toned calves.

She flipped the lights off in the guest bedroom before leaving it. Her heart drummed beneath her chest as she tiptoed down the hall to the door of the master bedroom. She stretched out a hand and let it rest on the doorknob, hesitating before turning it. Was she truly ready for what awaited her on the other side of the door?

Before she could make up her mind, the doorknob was turned for her and the door was pulled open. He stood filling the doorframe, looking her up and down. Without speaking a word to her, he turned and was enveloped by the darkness wrapped around the bedroom.

She entered the room and once her eyes adjusted to the darkness, found him sitting on the edge of the bed, staring up at her.

Once she was near enough to him, he hooked her waist in the crook of his right arm and pulled her closer to him. She lowered down onto his lap and smoothed one hand down the side of his face.

He allowed her to caress him. Behind a calm, expressionless face, though, he was fighting past demons. He had never thought that he could have feelings for another woman, not after having loved and lost Bridgette...not after having been manipulated by Jordana. He never thought that he would be fortunate enough to have a second love, but Charlie was quickly forcing her way into his heart. The walls that he'd so carefully constructed were coming crashing down all around him.

Even in the darkness, she could see the battle going on behind his eyes. "No strings," she promised in a whisper as she freed his hair from its constraint.

He nodded his head, running his hands down the curves of her body. "No strings," he repeated.

She buried her hands in his hair and bent to kiss his forehead. *Don't fight it,* she communicated to him telepathically. *Just let it happen.* She lowered her hands from his hair, down the sides of his face, to his bare shoulders, where they rested a moment before traveling down his chest and teasing his navel.

When he felt her hands dancing across his abdomen, he began to shudder. His hands shot down and covered her hands. "I can't do this."

"Yes, you can," she argued, meeting his gaze head-on.

He shook his head.

She wrapped her arms around his neck. "You're fighting it," she said in a hushed whisper. "Stop fighting it."

"I can't," he whispered, sounding helpless. "I can't."

"I'm not Bridgette and you're not the same Iancu that you were those hundreds of years ago. Don't you want me?"

He did want her. He wanted to drink in the taste of her skin and stroke every inch of her lithe, graceful body. He wanted to sink into her and lose himself within her. He wanted to hold her and never let go. Instead of confessing all of this to her, he cupped her chin in his hand and touched his lips to hers. He pulled her against him and pressed kisses to her lips, her cheek, her neck, and her shoulders.

She tilted her head back, releasing a tiny moan and grinding her pelvis into his lap. When he stopped kissing her, she opened her eyes and looked down at him.

His eyes were glowing, pools of blue in a sea of shadows. His fangs lowered. She drew in a breath but didn't pull away from him.

Her mouth hovered over his as she clawed her nails into his back and rode him with reckless abandon. He tugged on her hair and pounded her into oblivion. They rolled over so that he hovered over her, not once disengaging. As he neared the brink of release, his skin grew hot to the touch. He became feverish with passion. He threw his head back and shouted at the ceiling while she writhed beneath him and begged him not to stop.

A burst of heat exploded within her just as she reached her peak. She arched her back and shook her head back and forth as the waves of ecstasy subsided.

He collapsed on top of her, trapping her beneath him. He embraced her and pressed fervent kisses to her temples and brow.

They didn't exchange any words...but then again, they didn't have to.

Sleepy eyes opened into narrow slits as Bella paced the length of the hotel suite's bedroom. Alexei lay that way for awhile, watching her without speaking a word.

She hadn't been herself for quite some time now. They were usually attached at the hip; it took an extreme amount of encouraging on his part to get her to participate in activities that didn't include him. She rarely wished to do so, claiming that she was satisfied spending her nights with him.

However, Los Angeles seemed to have brought out a side of her that he'd never seen in the fifty-plus years that he'd known her. She claimed that her time was being spent shopping and dancing in night clubs, but he had his doubts. He considered following her on one of her nights out, but chances were that she'd catch him in the act. She was always aware of his presence.

Another thing that bothered him was the fact that she wasn't nearly as old as he was and yet the way she moved told tall tales, boasting her to be an age that she most certainly was not.

He continued to watch her even now, noting how catlike her movements were. He squinted his eyes and examined her. It was his Bella...the same, curly dark hair, the same silky smooth dark skin, and the same hourglass figure. She'd poured her dark brown lusciousness into a sheer, lavender nightgown. The nightgown was something that she would never have previously worn. She didn't look her best in lavender. She usually avoided the color at all costs.

He slowly sat up in bed, still watching her but ceasing to conceal the fact that he was watching her.

She whirled, catching and holding his gaze. "Good morning," she greeted soberly.

"Something has been bothering you these past few days," he said carefully in a measured tone.

She started to deny the accusation.

"Don't think me to be dense, Bella," he interrupted. "I've known you more than fifty years now. Give me more credit than that."

She bit back her retort and stood in the center of the room with her arms limp at her sides.

"What is wrong?" he asked her.

"I have been thinking things over the last couple of days," she admitted after a moment, joining him on the bed. She grabbed one of his hands and pulled it up to brush against her cheek. "I have been thinking about the meeting with the clan leaders."

"That farce?" He snorted derisively. "Why would that be bothering you?"

"Because you seem so certain that Aryk's plan would cause more harm than good," she replied, "while I'm not so certain."

He frowned and snatched his hand away from her. "What are you saying?"

"I'm saying that he could be onto something."

"Or he could be *on* something," he suggested, swinging his legs over the side of the bed and standing on his feet. "I can't believe you're giving that idiot's words a second thought."

"How long do we expect to hide in the shadows?" she questioned him. "Maybe it would be better if humans knew that we existed. Maybe they would be accepting of us. They have movies about us, books about us...there are some human beings walking this earth that truly believe *they*, themselves, are vampires. Would it really be so horrible if they knew that we walk the earth alongside them?"

He ran a hand through his hair and looked down at her. "Bella, Aryk isn't suggesting that we hold a press conference to inform the planet's citizens that we exist. He is suggesting that we take the world by storm and force humans into submission."

"Maybe you're right," she said, clasping her hands together and staring down at them in disdain.

"I *know* I'm right," he told her. When she didn't respond, he rolled his eyes heavenwards and knelt on the floor beside the bed. "I have a feeling that the meeting we attended a couple of days ago isn't the end of that topic. We will be discussing that for the rest of our days. Perhaps someone with more common sense will approach us with a similar plan that isn't so dastardly in nature. That would be a much better course for us."

The expression of disappointment didn't leave her face.

He sighed and rose to his full height. He turned and strode into the master bathroom, leaving the door open at his back.

"So you'd never even consider joining sides with Aryk, then?" Bella called to him from the bedroom.

He chuckled and shook his head. "Come on, babe. You know me way better than that." He flipped on the sink's golden water faucet and held his hands beneath the running water.

When he finished washing his hands, he moved to stand near the hot tub. He grabbed a towel from the rack attached to the wall and began to dry off his hands. As he dried his hands, his eyes wandered around the bathroom. His eyes stopped wandering once they fell upon the hot tub. With a furrowed brow, he carelessly tossed the towel back over the rack.

He bent over the side of the tub and picked up what had caught his eye. *This could have been left by a previous occupant,* he thought as he fingered the object. *It's not what you're thinking. It's not what you're thinking.*

For what was draped across his forefinger...what he repeatedly stroked with the thumb of his hand...was a long strand of bright red hair.

Alarm registering on his face, he turned on his heel and dashed out of the bathroom. The bedroom was empty. Upon a search of the hotel suite, he realized that the entire suite was empty. He was alone, holding an indicative strand of hair in his hand.

Neil sat slumped in a corner of the dungeon, as far away from his wife as possible. He wasn't chained to one of the walls; he didn't have to be. He knew that Aryk never made idle threats. If he attempted to leave the dungeon, his guards would have his head on a platter.

He glanced at his wife. At some point, she'd lost consciousness. As far as he knew, she hadn't eaten since she'd been taken captive. He worried for her health and for the health of their child. He worried for their health not only because of the fact that they were in a dark, musty dungeon at the mercy of a cruel, heartless vampire, but also because of the fact that he hadn't fed in hours. He was starving.

He had crawled away from his wife as soon as she'd lost consciousness, because he knew what it was like to be ruled by the blood lust. Soon, he would be suffering more than just hunger pangs and the urges to feed from his wife. Soon, there would be hallucinations and unfounded paranoia. He'd be unable to move without causing himself excruciating pain. He would then grab the person nearest to him and drain them dry. It wouldn't matter to him that the woman he was drinking from was his wife. It wouldn't matter to him that the woman he was drinking from was carrying a child, *his* child, in her womb. When the blood lust ruled you, nothing else mattered. All that mattered was satiating the hunger.

He shivered in the dark corner with his arms wrapped around himself. He had wanted to dash into Jordana's estate like a hero and save his family, but that may have been the dumbest thing that he had ever done in his life.

He should have let Iancu handle this. Of the two of them, Iancu was the warrior, the fighter. Neil didn't know anything about combat. He should have never set foot inside of Jordana's mansion.

Iancu's going to come for us, he thought, *and if he doesn't, I'm going to find a way out of here.*

He glanced at his wife, who quietly slumbered despite the fact that her wrists were nearly rubbed raw by the restraints circled around them. He could clearly see the veins beneath the surface of her skin. He pictured taking her into his arms and sinking his teeth into her flesh. She would taste so divine.

He blinked his eyes rapidly and shook out of his sordid thoughts. He needed to feed...and quickly. There was no telling what he would do if he didn't receive the proper nourishment.

The streets of Los Angeles were being terrorized. New vampires were being created and innocent people were brutally murdered. Blood hit concrete, splattered against glass windows, and was feasted on by nameless, faceless attackers bundled up in dark coats.

Bodies were abandoned on the streets and in dumpsters. There was nothing discreet about the chaos that ensued on this night. Vampires throughout the city took their fill and then some, raping unsuspecting women and infiltrating popular dance clubs housing crowds of more victims for them to pounce on.

Screams filled the night...

And Iancu's nightmares...

Screams sounded in the night and a familiar voice spoke to him. "You are a fool to think that you are deserving of love."

An image of Bridgette appeared. Her face was lovely and flawless until blood seeped from her eyes, her nose, and her mouth.

"You will betray her just as you betrayed Bridgette. You are a fool to think that things will be different this time."

Images of different people flashed behind his eyelids. There was a blonde woman with a bonnet over her hair. She was wearing a yellow sundress. There was a parasol twirling in her hands. He crouched in the shadows, waiting for her chaperone to turn her back before snatching the unassuming woman and putting an end to her young life.

Thousands of people he'd tasted from over the years, and hundreds upon hundreds of them, he'd killed.

"This is your history. This is who you are. It will never change."

"But I have it under control now."

"There is no controlling it. It will sneak up on you when you least expect it, as soon as you let your guard down."

"I won't let it happen."

"You will fail her. She will die because of you."

"I love her."

"You will betray her."

"I love her."

"You will kill her."

"You don't know anything. You can't see the future."

"Can't I? You are my likeness. I was once like you, stubborn and determined to defy anyone who told me otherwise. I quickly learned, though...that what is to be is to be."

Different faces appeared: women, men, and even a couple of children who had been in the wrong place at the wrong time. These were the faces that haunted him every day of his life.

"This is who you are. It will never change."

Iancu bolted upright. His bedroom was windowless, but sunlight filtered in through his bedroom door.

Charlie quietly snored beside him. Her back was turned to him.

He blinked rapidly, attempting to shake the nightmare from his head. *"This is who you are. It will never change. You are a fool to think that you are deserving of love."* He trembled even as he circled his arms around Charlie and held her close to him.

She stirred in her sleep and snuggled against him.

His dream could be right. He could be setting himself up for failure. He had tried to love a woman once and that situation had gone awry. He couldn't go through that again.

Charlie rolled over and her eyes fluttered open. She smiled sleepily and pressed her lips against his collarbone. "Hi," she greeted.

"Hi," he returned.

"You look like you're deep in thought."

His brows drew together and he found that he couldn't look her directly in the eye. "There is much to think about today. We've got an intense hunt ahead of us."

She groaned. "Don't remind me."

He kissed the top of her head and sat up, running a hand through his hair. "I'm starving."

"You wouldn't happen to have normal food anywhere in this place, would you?" she asked, stretching her arms over her head.

He arched a glance at her over his shoulder.

She shrugged. "I was just checking. I packed some food from my cabin, but I'm on my last can of soup."

"There's a restaurant down the street. They're open in the morning." He stood from the bed and pulled on his pajama pants.

She followed him out of the room. Instead of heading into the kitchen like he did, she walked into the guest room. She turned on the television and rummaged through her suitcase for some clothes to throw on.

"...Multiple reports of brutality that occurred last night," a news reporter was saying. "The local police department is baffled. Their offices are reportedly overwhelmed with reports of strange events that took place last night right here in Los Angeles. Fatalities are still being counted, but so far the victim count is beyond two thousand."

Charlie stared at the screen with her mouth agape. She lowered onto the bed, unable to speak as the camera panned around the Melrose District and Venice Beach. Trash filled the streets, store windows were cracked and broken, and bodies that had been haphazardly covered by tarp littered the sidewalks. "Iancu!" she cried when she finally found her voice.

He appeared in the doorway. He was sipping from a maroon coffee mug.

She pointed at the television screen.

He listened as the news reporter repeated her earlier report. The fingers of his free hand curled into fists and his eyes darkened.

"It'll never be over, will it?" she whispered. "Even if we save Neil tonight...it'll never be over."

He didn't answer the question. Instead, he ordered, "Get showered and get dressed. We'll be training all day." He flicked off the television.

Somberly, she gathered some of her clothes and a clean washcloth from the closet in the guest room and carried them into the bathroom, where she started the shower and stood facing her reflection in the mirror. Most of her bruises were fading into non-existence, but a lone bruise on the slope of her cheekbone remained.

Already naked, she brushed her hair back and stepped into the shower with the washcloth balled up in one hand. She tilted her head back and allowed the sprinkling droplets of water to pour down over her collarbone and chest.

The bathroom door eased open. The subtle squeak of the door's hinges alerted her. The steam on the shower stall glass was difficult to peer through. Goosebumps prickled along her skin. It had only been a couple of days ago that she was attacked while in the bathroom of her cabin.

The shower stall door was drawn open and Iancu stood before her. His eyes captured hers as he stepped into the shower stall and secured the door behind him. The stall was large enough to hold two people, maybe even three, but there was only one shower head. He moved to stand beneath it and angled his head back so that his hair was saturated by the cascading liquid.

She didn't know why she felt so insecure, standing in front of him completely nude. After last night, she shouldn't be timid at all. However, most likely *because* of last night, she was exactly that. They'd entered a no-strings attached agreement and they'd committed several acts of fornication in his bedroom. She'd seen him in all of his glory and vice versa.

He wiped the water out of his eyes and peered at her questioningly. "Why are you standing all the way over there?" He extended a hand to her.

She took his hand and in return, he drew her into a tight embrace. They both stood beneath the water, holding onto each other, until she pulled back a little and stared up at him.

He lovingly caressed her face and bent his head to kiss her. Heat mounted between them as their slick, wet bodies pressed together. Their kiss was long, deep, and playful. She would often catch his bottom lip between her teeth and suck on it.

He groaned and deepened the kiss as he pressed her back into the wall of the shower stall. He cupped her rear end in his hands and effortlessly lifted her up. She slid her legs around his lower back and wrapped her arms around his neck. The kiss was never broken as he lifted her up and entered her. He held on fast to her supple lips.

Her tiny moans only encouraged him. He pulled back from the kiss and pressed his lips to her neck. He could feel her pulse jumping just below the line of her jaw. He pressed tiny kisses there and continued along the curve of her neck and into her collarbone.

Water pounded down on his back as he pushed himself farther inside her. The tiny, tender pecks that he had been pressing to her neck and collarbone soon turned hungrier and more demanding. Using the wall at her back to hold her up, he dragged his hands up the length of her body to grab both sides of her face. He lifted his head and returned to the full succulence of her lips.

Their kisses were so deep and intense that she forgot to breathe. She would have to draw back from the kiss once in awhile in order to catch her breath.

Her hands tangled within the confines of his wet hair and explored the hard angles of his finely toned physique. She gasped sharply as he pulled out of her and then rammed back in. Her legs, still locked around his back, were beginning to tremble. She opened her eyes and took in the sight of him.

As if sensing that she was looking at him, he opened his eyes and stared down at her with heat burning in his gaze. If she could trust what was in the depths of his beautiful eyes, he wanted to swallow her whole. He didn't just want to indulge in the wondrousness of her body. He also wanted to take over her soul and her mind.

He didn't break eye contact with her as he once again pulled out of her and then pushed back into her with brute force. A small wail escaped her lips and he brushed her hair back in a caring gesture, as he regained a slow, steady rhythm with her to ease some of the pain that he'd caused.

"Faster," she whispered in his ear before taking his earlobe between her teeth.

He raised both of her arms over her head and pushed farther into her than any other man ever had. His groans transformed into animalistic growls that most humans were incapable of.

Her legs continued to tremble around his waist. The searing hot sensation that she'd felt with him last night returned. His skin became hot to the touch. Even inside her, she felt unnaturally warm-and the temperature was rising.

He cupped the side of her face in one of his hands. "I want to lose myself in you," he murmured before releasing a rumbling growl.

She clung to him as she contracted around him. After the waves of rapture passed, she untangled her legs and lowered them so that she was shakily standing on her own.

Suppressing the urge to laugh, he embraced her and pressed a quick kiss to her temple. She had told him that they could enter into a no-strings attached arrangement, but what she didn't know was that he wanted as many strings attached as possible. He didn't want to be a friend with benefits. He wanted her to be with him and only him. Unbeknownst to her, she'd altered the way he would live his life forever.

"We have to train," she said breathily with her face pressed into his chest.

"You're right," he acknowledged, but he still didn't let her go.

Without pulling out of his embrace, she stepped back enough so that she could look up at him.

He smiled down at her and licked the tip of her nose.

Her nose wrinkled in amusement. She proceeded with her shower, lathering up with a myriad of bubbles. Once in awhile, she would playfully blow a couple of them in his direction.

When they were done with the shower and completely dressed, he told her that they couldn't let their flirting get in the way of their priorities. "We have serious business at hand tonight," he informed her. "We can't get caught up in distractions and we can't distract each other's focus. Do you understand?"

She nodded and agreed wholeheartedly.

In his apartment complex there were several courtyards. Behind many of the courtyards were areas thick with trees and foliage. Iancu chose the courtyard that was completely empty of people and furthest from the apartment complex's parking lot. They'd brought an excessive amount of weapons to practice with, including two of his best swords. She'd toted several of her guns.

He set his weapons down on the grassy knoll at his feet and straightened. "The first weapon we're going to practice with is the sword," he announced. "We practiced a little bit last night, but you need more practice with swords. If we're in battle and your guns are taken from you, the only weapon you may be able to use is the sword. In that instance, you're going to need to know how to use it."

He started by snatching up one of the swords from the ground and holding it in front of him. "Depending on the height of the person you're fighting, this is how you should be holding the sword. You should place your feet about a foot and a half apart and twist your upper torso like this. You can go ahead and grab the other one, if you want."

She was a student who was interested in learning and she was a quick learner. He'd never trained someone else in sword fighting, but the fact that she was a fast learner made the lesson go smoothly, without a hitch.

He first showed her how she should hold the sword when she was on the defense and when she was on the offense. Then, he showed her a couple of tricks that would bring her from the defense *to* the offense. When she seemed like she was retaining the information that he was teaching her, he practiced fighting with her to test her on what she'd learned. In a short hour and a half, she'd greatly improved since last night.

The sun was beaming down on the courtyard. Even though they were training in the shade, Iancu still felt fatigued. Between training sessions, he paused to take a breather, sometimes sitting down on the ground to rest.

"Are you all right?" she asked him worriedly.

He shook his head. "I'm fine."

"Do you need some water?" She paused. "You probably don't drink water."

He cracked a smile at her. "I drink water," he told her. "For a slayer, you lack an incredible amount of knowledge about vampires."

"I've never really befriended them before," she said with a shrug. "To be honest, the longest conversation I've had with one was with Aryk those many years ago. I never pause to talk to them. I just kill them and move on."

"No research?"

"I do what I can when it comes to researching them, but it's hard to know where to go. A lot of the texts contradict each other. I'd just rather go on my instincts."

He nodded his head. "I know what you mean." He glanced at the watch on his wrist and jumped back up to his feet.

"There is supposed to be a council of slayers and their guides," she mused aloud, "but I've never been introduced to my guide."

"I could easily find out how you can contact the Council," he offered.

A wistful look flashed in her eyes. Because her childhood had been cut short, she had missed out on a lot of things. After her family was murdered, it didn't take long for her to lose her identity. She'd never felt a sense of belonging with the foster families she temporarily resided with. "There would be no point in contacting the Council now," she answered finally. "I've been hunting on my own now for a long time."

Despite the response she'd given him, he was intelligent enough to know that a part of her wished to contact the Council...if nothing more, she would like to have some sort of support system. It felt natural for him to hunt alone and live on his own, but he had never considered how loneliness could affect a young woman in her mid-twenties.

"We should train in martial arts," she suggested, eager to change the subject.

He obliged her and wasn't shocked to discover that she was already a skilled martial artist. It was a shame that martial arts would most likely not come into play when battling Jordana. The powerful vampiress moved too quickly for martial arts to be an extreme benefit. However, he did enjoy watching Charlie execute well-landed kicks and punches. From observing her, he would guess that she'd had training in Muay Thai kickboxing, Brazilian jiu jitsu, karate, and Tae Kwon Do. She proved to be a very competent spar partner.

Winded after their sparring match, he collapsed on the ground again, this time stretching out on his back and staring up at the tree branches that were suspended over them.

She didn't dare ask him whether or not he was all right this time. He had maintained that he was, indeed, all right. Being out in the daylight for this long couldn't be good for him, though.

She gave him several minutes to rest. Then, she pulled her guns from the weapons she'd toted out of his apartment.

He arched a brow at her. "You brought those down?"

She nodded. "I can tell from the way you handle them that you...*don't* know how to handle them."

He chuckled and raised himself to a sitting position. "So you're going to show me how to handle guns?"

She shrugged her shoulders. "You have great aim," she said. "You just don't know how to do everything else that comes with gun-handling."

"For example?" he inquired, standing on his feet and brushing off his pants.

"For example," she elaborated, "you aren't so good with drawing."

"I've never been the artsy type," he joked.

She rolled her eyes. "Okay, watch me closely." She strapped both of her holsters on so that two guns nestled at her sides and two guns were placed at her back.

"I definitely don't have a problem with watching you," he murmured.

She laughed and shook her head. "Wasn't it you who said that we shouldn't be flirting or distracting each other from the task at hand?"

He nodded vigorously. "That's right. You're right. You were telling me to watch you."

"Right." She held both of her hands away from her body. In a series of movements that were nearly too quick for him to follow, her hands were behind her back and then in the position they'd been in to begin with. Both of her hands held guns in them.

A solitary brow lifted in surprise. "That was pretty good."

She beamed a smile at him as she returned the guns to their position at her lower back. "I'm going to do it again." She repeated the same move, except this time she withdrew the guns from the shoulder holster.

"You almost do that too quickly for me to track."

"I know. It's a gift. Now I want you to practice."

"I don't think your holsters are going to fit me."

She dismissed what he said with a wave of her hand. "They're adjustable." She assisted him with strapping the holsters on him. "If you feel more comfortable with drawing and using guns, then we can get you your own holsters before heading out to Jordana's estate."

"I've never really been one to use guns," he told her. "I've never liked them for some reason. They don't compare to the sleek sophistication of a sword."

"I prefer guns over swords," she countered as she finished strapping him into the shoulder holster. Even at its loosest adjustment, it was still too tight around his muscular frame. It would do for now, however. "Swords require that you get up close and personal with your opponent. Because of the numbers we're dealing with, I would just rather get the job done efficiently so that I can move on to the next opponent."

"What you say does make sense."

"All right," she said, stepping back from him. "I want to see your fastest draw."

"Can I have a couple of practice tries?" he asked, looking quite uncomfortable in the shoulder holster. "I've never worn one of these things before."

"Sure," she allowed.

The first time, he fumbled with both of the guns. On his second try, he drew both weapons quickly, but nearly dropped one of them. Only his supernaturally quick reflexes prevented the weapon from hitting the ground. He had the grace to appear sheepish. "Sorry about that."

A warm feeling flooded her chest when he apologized to her in that boyish voice. She cleared her throat and folded her arms across her chest. "It's okay. Try again," she encouraged.

With practice, his draws became quicker and less clumsy.

She observed him with a hand supporting her chin. "Now, I want you to incorporate some of your powers into drawing the weapons."

His brows furrowed and he appeared confused. The expression on his face was priceless. "What do you mean?"

"Superhuman speed. I want you to use it."

He was shaking his head before she got the full request out. "No."

She planted her hands on her hips. "When you said that we were going to train, you *were* planning on training with your powers too, right?"

"If I have to end up using them, I'll use them," he told her, "but I'm not going to practice using them. Not here and not now."

"We can't afford any weaknesses, Iancu."

The words too closely resembled the same words that Jordana had used. He fussed with the shoulder holster. "How do I get this thing off?"

"I want you to keep it on," she said firmly. "And I want you to use your powers to assist you with the draw."

He met her gaze. In all fairness, the challenge she was presenting him with was necessary. He needed to know how to harness his powers. He needed to make sure that he could use them at will. He needed to make sure that in the event that he *did* use them, he didn't cause Charlie physical harm in the process. There was a lot that he needed to know about his powers. He didn't know why he was being such a chickenshit about it. He sighed in defeat and stared down at the guns beneath his armpits. "All right," he said.

She was holding her breath and she didn't know why. Perhaps she was holding it because she knew that Iancu was about to take a large step in training with the use of his powers. Or perhaps she was holding it because she'd witnessed the significant amount of power that he possessed once and was thrilled to see him in action again.

He held his hands away from his body and easily plucked the guns from the holster and aimed them at the wooded area that was facing them. He had done so without her being able to track his movement.

Remembering to breathe, she made a circular motion in the air with her right hand. "Do it again."

He replaced the guns in their respective holsters and repeated the action. He stared at his hands as if they didn't belong to him. He seemed to be surprised by his own skill.

She shook her head. "That was amazing," she said finally.

He was still staring at his hands. He stood that way until she approached him and removed the sleek, heavy weapons from his hands. He blinked a couple of times and shook his head.

She assisted him out of the shoulder holster. "Was it as bad as you thought?"

"No," he said. His voice sounded distant.

"There is so much that you're capable of."

He finally lowered his hands to his sides. "I think we could use a break," he muttered. "I'm getting hungry."

They gathered up all of the weapons they'd brought down with them and made their way back to his apartment. When they reached the floor that his apartment was located on, he suddenly reached out and gripped her upper arm in his hand. He held a finger up to his lips and gestured down the hall.

There was a group of men lined outside of his apartment door. From the way they were dressed, they could have been a SWAT team for all Charlie knew. They were dressed in black and they were all armed.

He pulled her around the corner that they had turned and looked her directly in the eyes. *They could be Aryk's men,* he told her telepathically.

Why would they attack you in the daylight? Wouldn't they be weaker?

He would have the surprise factor working for him. He risked another glance around the corner. The men were still standing in front of his apartment door. They appeared to be conversing about something. He used his supersensitive hearing abilities to listen in on their conversation.

"I don't think he's home," one of them was telling the others.

"His energy lingers. If he's no longer here, he didn't leave long ago."

"Should we wait for him?"

"We have to get some plans in order. What are we going to say to him once we see him?"

"My cousin said that he briefed him about us. He should be expecting us."

Iancu racked his brain. The last man who'd spoken had referred to his cousin. He looked around the corner again, attempting to get a good look at all of the men. Neil had told him about a group that his cousin, Paul, had put together. Could the group of men standing in front of his door be a part of the militia that Paul had assembled?

He grabbed Charlie's hand and rounded the corner with her in tow.

The men standing near his apartment door collectively glanced in his direction. Paul broke out from the group of men. He had a large grin on his face. "Iancu," he greeted cheerfully.

"Paul," Iancu returned.

Charlie looked between the two of them and yanked her hand out of Iancu's grip. "Can someone tell me what's going on here?"

CHAPTER EIGHTEEN

Iancu unlocked his apartment door, allowing Paul and his crew inside so that they could all talk. Paul took a seat in the living room armchair, but the rest of his cohorts remained standing.

"The basic rundown of what is going on here," Paul said after introducing himself to Charlie, "is that Aryk is attempting to do some big, bad things in the vampire community. There are a lot of us that don't agree with what he is trying to do, so we have worked together to devise a plan that would stop him from successfully completing his goal."

"And did you guys come up with a plan?" she asked eagerly.

He nodded. "We did."

She waited for him to continue. When he didn't seem intent on continuing, she demanded, "Well, what's the plan?"

He grinned and spread his arms wide open. "We kill him, of course."

Again, she waited for him to continue. She glanced at Iancu, who was attempting to hold in laughter. She turned back to Paul. "That's your plan? Kill him?"

"Basically."

"But you do have structured steps in place in order to carry out that plan, right?" she prodded.

He shrugged noncommittally. "That's where you two come in."

"So...*basically*...you have no plan."

"This situation is very sketchy," Paul explained, leaning forward and bracing his elbows on his knees. "I waited to strategize because there are a lot of people involved with this. I wanted to wait to see how many people we would have in our crew before coming up with some concrete plans.

"The guys here with me now don't represent the amount of people who disagree with what Aryk is trying to do. There are a lot more vampires who dislike what Aryk is doing, but most of them are afraid to step up. They dread what would happen to them in the event that we lose.

"The guys that are here right now are the only ones with the balls to step forward."

Iancu stood near the balcony doors. "The men who came with you should be commended," he said, peering into the face of each member of Paul's crew. "Jordana and Aryk won't be easy to take down. Those who are afraid to step forward have very good reason to be afraid. If we let Jordana *or* Aryk walk away from this battle…if they live through this, then they will hunt each and every one of us down until we're all dead." He turned his head slightly and glanced out of the corner of his eye at Charlie.

Jade roamed about Jordana's estate restlessly. In a good day, she would get about four hours of sleep. She never slept long. She was often in a state of perpetual restlessness. Early in the morning when the rest of the household was preparing for slumber, she'd been deciding on whether or not she should have her sister cast a spell that would keep trespassers off of the property. Her sister had confided in her that she didn't know how well the spell would work.

"This spell was created in order to keep out those with ill intentions," Roslynn had explained. "So if the trespassers that you speak of are intending to perform acts that are evil, then the spell will hold up. But it sounds like me like the people who you're attempting to protect are the ones who are, in essence, evil. So instead of blocking your trespassers out, you may instead be trapping the people that you're trying to protect within the perimeters of the estate."

In the end, Jade decided not to cast the spell. Her sister offered to reconfigure the spell, but Jade was already sour on the idea of using magic to keep out unwanted visitors. She loved hand-to-hand combat and she was extremely experienced with weaponry. Instead of using magic to secure Jordana's property, she would just increase the amount of guards posted outside.

The courtyard behind the estate stretched as far as the eye could see. Statues of Greek gods were mounted on marble pedestals. Clusters of trees blocked out the majority of the sun's rays during morning hours. A small creek threaded throughout the courtyard. It was truly a beautiful area that went ignored by most of the guests that lived in Jordana's mansion. It was the only place on the entire estate that was consistently peaceful.

A breeze caused her dark purple hair to flutter around her face. She tilted her chin up and welcomed the wind as shadows played across her face. An adrenaline rush hit her and she abruptly broke out into a run. There was a tree directly in her path and instead of running around it, she ran *up* it, sprinting up the trunk of the tree. There was a long, thick branch directly in her path. Instead of slowing down, she continued her sprint and changed direction again so that she was running upside down, along the underside of the branch. At the end of the branch, her feet were striking nothing but air. She rounded out into a backflip and landed onto the ground with steady feet. She had a sea of energy to burn.

Someone clapped at her efforts. She whirled around to face Aryk, who was casually leaning against a statue of Venus. Mirth lit up his eyes as he moved slowly and deliberately towards her. "That was very entertaining."

"You're easily amused," she quipped, brushing her hair back from her face. "What are you doing out here?"

"I was looking for you."

She nodded as if she figured as much. "That would be my cue to leave," she muttered.

She made as if to walk past him, but he reached out and grabbed her by the wrist. His eyes lifted to meet her dark, angry eyes.

"I suggest that you remove your hand," she warned through clenched teeth.

His grip only tightened around her wrist. "And I suggest that you listen to me," he said in a low voice. "You've teased and taunted me long enough. I think it's about time for me to collect everything that I want from you." His eyes roved up and down her body as a wicked smile twisted his lips.

She yanked her wrist from his grasp. She didn't find his tactics the least bit comical or amusing. "You have been hitting on me for years and I have let it go," she hissed at him. "I haven't told Jordana about it and I haven't held you accountable for your actions, but that stops here and now. If you *ever* touch me again, and I mean *ever*, I will go to Jordana and tell her everything. She'll cast you out like yesterday's garbage."

His smile only widened at her words. One moment he was standing in front of her with that sick smile on his face and the next, he was standing behind her, holding her wrists above her head in one hand. He ducked his head down and whispered roughly into her ear, "And for years I have allowed you to lead me on with your head games and teasing ways. That stops here." His free arm wound around her waist and pulled her back against him.

In all the years that she'd worked here, he had never used his powers on her. Not once. She'd often patronized him and tormented him, knowing full well that she would never willingly take him to her bed. He'd always seemed like a weak, powerless child to her. She'd never admired or respected him, and that was probably why she teased him the way she did. Even now that he was abusing his power and threatening her with it, she didn't respect him. He seemed even weaker to her now, because he couldn't get what he wanted without forcing someone to give it to him.

His hand slid upwards from her waist, cupping her breasts and skimming over them to tenderly trace her collarbone. From her collarbone, his hand wandered up to stroke her cheek and from there to her thick, beautiful hair. He wrapped her hair around his hand and let her hands fall from where he'd held them captive above her head. Then he yanked hard on her hair and forced her to turn around and face him.

Her eyes weren't sad, frightened, or tear-filled. Even when she was at his mercy, she looked defiant and annoyed. She met his gaze without holding back any of the fury that she was feeling. As young as she was, she still had a strong, powerful presence.

He chuckled and brushed his hand against her cheek again. "Everyone seems to think that I am just some weakling riding on Jordana's coattails," he said thoughtfully. "I don't mind the misconception. Actually, I *welcome* those assumptions, because they have made it possible for me to discreetly operate several projects of mine without gaining much attention." His hand greedily delved beneath the neckline of her black blouse.

Because she'd met his gaze head-on, she was at his mercy. She couldn't struggle or fight against him like she wanted to. All she could do was stand there and take it.

He didn't hesitate in ripping her shirt from her body. Then and there, in plain sight of anyone who set foot outside of the back door of his lover's estate, he had his way with her...and loved every minute of it.

Alexei strode briskly to the doors of Jordana's mansion. He gave three curt knocks on the door and waited for the doors to be opened.

A slight, young-looking thing with dark brown hair and wide set brown eyes opened the door. She looked him up and down briefly before stepping back and allowing him inside.

With his rage pounding in his ears, he asked, "Where is Jordana?"

"I will have her summoned right away," the child told him. "Until she comes to see you, feel free to have a seat in the sitting room." She made her words sound like an offer, as if she were interested in his well-being. Her tone belied the words, however. The words weren't an offer; they were a demand.

He entered the sitting room but his nerves were too restless for him to be able to sit for a long period time. He stood and remained standing until Jordana appeared in the entryway of the sitting room, dressed in a silver corset dress. Her hair coiled around her collarbone like a snake.

He stared at her openly without opening his mouth. He was searching for something in her violet eyes, and she allowed him to conduct his search without interference.

She walked into the room with her hands at her back in an usher-like position above the curve of her rear end. As she passed by him, she looked at him out of the corner of her eye, slyly and coyly.

He watched the way she moved as she glided towards her throne. She moved the way that cats moved, with long, lithe strides. He'd seen someone move like that before. He lifted his gaze from her legs to her devious eyes and he knew. He knew without even asking her.

And he asked her still. "Where is Bella?"

She reached her throne and seated herself upon it. "Bella?" she repeated, having the grace to sound confused. Her casual tone was coupled with a playful smile.

"Don't play dumb with me, Jordana."

"I really don't know what you're talking about."

"Or maybe you're not playing."

She arched a slender brow at him. "You can't expect me to keep tabs on your girlfriend for you. That is a task to be handled by you and you alone."

"You are known for your use of glamour," he said. "And Aryk is known to shapeshift. I know one of you has been posing as Bella. I just don't know which one. By God, if you have done anything to hurt her-"

"By *God*, Alexei?" she shouted. "Are you even listening to yourself anymore?" In the blink of an eye, she was out of her throne and standing before him with one of her hands lifted to rest against his cheek. "No, you're not listening to yourself anymore. You're too consumed by the fear that harm may have come to your stunningly beautiful girlfriend."

He grabbed her wrist. His eyes blazed the color of sparkling emeralds. "I am a fellow clan leader," he said in a steely, deep voice. "You have no right to treat me as if I were one of your subjects. You're playing games with me and I advise you to stop it now...while you still have your life intact."

She didn't struggle against his tight grip. Instead, she looked up into his face with a challenging look in the depths of her violet eyes. "Are you *always* this rough, Alexei?" she taunted, her tongue darting out to lick her lips.

His eyes widened and he released her suddenly, stumbling back.

She smoothed down the skirt of her gown. "Don't look so shocked."

"The conversation about joining sides with Aryk. That wasn't Bella. That was you."

She arched a look at him. She didn't confirm his allegations, but she didn't deny them, either.

Caught on a wave of emotion, he went on. "For the past couple of days, each time I made love to..." He blinked his eyes, struggling to find the words. "I wasn't making love to her. I was making love to you."

"I've never known you to be the monogamous sort, anyway," she allowed with a nonchalant shrug of her shoulders.

"But I was!" he protested. "With Bella, I *was* monogamous. Until..."

"Until me," she finished.

"So you've what-kept Bella prisoner here so that you could impersonate her?" he demanded. "For what purpose? What could you have possibly gained from pretending to be her?"

"You mean *besides* experiencing your reputed prowess in the bedroom for myself?" She circled around him with a long, tapered fingernail tapping her cheek. "I was hoping that you would give more consideration to joining sides with Aryk."

He laughed outright. "You're serious?"

"His ideas are the future," she predicted with certainty. "With or without your support, his vision will come to fruition."

He shook his head, still laughing. "Jordana, I...I don't know what to say. Is this a joke?"

She came to stand before him. "Do I look like I'm joking?"

He had the decency to stop laughing. He looked her over, taking in the grim set to her mouth and the fire flaming in her eyes. "No, you don't look like you're joking," he said finally. "You look like you're crazy."

She broke out into a grin. "It's ironic that you should say that. It's the same thing that your lovely Bella said before I dug my claws into her chest and pulled her heart out."

Fear gripped him and his eyes turned icy. She wasn't serious. She *couldn't* be serious. She was playing games with him, as usual. Bella was probably downstairs being held hostage in the dungeon. He searched her eyes for the longest time, looking for some sort of hint that she was being facetious. "You couldn't have."

"I *could* have, and I very well did."

"You didn't kill her just so you could get to me," he said, his voice growing louder without his intending it. "You didn't kill her just so you could try to convince me to join sides with your lover."

"An error of judgment on my part, I hate to admit," she conceded.

He shook his head. "No," he whispered, almost to himself. Dozens of images entered his head, images of his beloved Bella. The way she looked when she emerged from the shower...her smile...he could hear her laugh ringing in his ears, even now. Fate wouldn't be so cruel as to exterminate the life of someone that he treasured so dearly, even if he was rumored to have lived the life of a womanizing cad and unethical businessman.

He didn't think. He didn't coordinate his movements in his mind before putting them to action. He rushed at Jordana and knocked her to the floor, clawing at her face.

She lay on the floor laughing as he pummeled her. "Are you going to cry?" she shouted at him.

Most likely he would, but not in front of this heartless bitch. He continued to land blows on her until his fists hurt.

"All right, enough," she said as he beat her face in.

He didn't stop.

"I said, enough!" she screamed, shoving him off of her.

He flew across the room and landed flat against the wall near the room's arched entrance. A small crowd had gathered outside of the sitting room. They were peering in the room with shocked looks on their faces.

He wasn't going to be able to defeat Jordana, not here and now. She was older than he was and he was on her turf. No, this certainly wasn't the time to fight her.

He drew a hand across his face. "This isn't over," he declared before spinning on his heel and exiting the house. His driver pulled a sleek, black limousine up to the walkway, but he before he had the chance to open the back door, he heard someone shouting at him.

He turned his head and saw Jade stumbling towards him. The only article of clothing that she wore was a tattered black blouse. Other than that, she was nude. Taken aback, he opened the limousine door, leaned in, and grabbed his suit jacket from the back seat.

He noticed that she wouldn't meet his eyes as he guided her arms through the sleeves of the charcoal suit jacket. He didn't ask her what she'd lived through. The Jade that he knew had a strong, defiant nature. The creature standing before him was beaten and broken. Without speaking, he extended his arm and gestured for her to get into the limousine and leave with him.

He didn't have to extend the offer twice. She climbed into the car, put her face in her hands, and proceeded to cry.

Marilyn's eyes opened into narrow slits. She hacked and coughed, pulling herself into a straighter sitting position. Her hand instinctively flew to her stomach. She glanced around the dungeon with only a hazy memory of what had occurred the night before. She frowned when she saw the huddled form of her husband in the corner. "Neil?" she croaked in a voice that didn't sound like her own.

The damp, stale mustiness of the room couldn't be healthy to breathe in. Had he breathed in too much? Was he simply sleeping? Had he passed out? Had he been tortured? She honestly couldn't remember whether or not he had been awake before she lost consciousness.

She struggled to stand, forgetting the shackles that were around her wrists and ankles. She sighed in defeat. "Neil?" she called again.

He stirred in his sleep, but didn't wake up.

"Neil? Wake up. It's Marilyn."

Tremors started in his arms and curled down the length of his body to his legs. He appeared to be having a seizure.

She couldn't handle watching him in the state he was in. She turned her head away and focused on the layout of the dungeon. There had to be some way out of this room.

"Mare?" came a groan from the other side of the room.

"Neil?"

"I'm so hungry."

"So am I, baby, believe me." She struggled with her restraints even though her wrists were already raw. "We're going to be all right."

She could hear him shuffling, but she could only see his silhouette. She couldn't see him clearly. There were no windows in the room, no lights turned on.

He ambled towards her, crawling on his hands and knees. Several times, he flattened against the floor as if giving up on reaching her.

She frowned down at him in worry. Had they tortured him? Why did he seem to be in pain?

"It's so hot," he mumbled. "So cold."

"Which one are you? Hot or cold?"

"I'm hot...hot and cold." He moved towards her, sliding forward on his belly. "I have to feed." His voice was raspy. He didn't sound like himself and when she was able to finally see him up close, he didn't look like himself either.

Her mouth dropped open and she released a blood-curdling scream.

The dungeon door was thrown open and footsteps pounded down the stairs. A vampire, no doubt one of Aryk's guards, stared down at both of them. "What's going on in here?" the stocky, blonde man demanded.

Neil didn't even have the energy to turn around and peer up at the guard. He focused solely on the beautiful woman in front of him. He could see her veins. He could see the blood coursing through her veins. "Feed," he rasped. "I need to feed."

The guard's brows drew together. "Shit," he muttered and trudged back up the stairs.

"No!" Marilyn yelled. "Don't leave me alone with him!"

Moments later, the guard returned down the steps with Aryk trailing behind him. Aryk appeared to be thoroughly bothered. "What is it?"

Neil had Marilyn by the throat and his fangs were lowered. He was preparing to bite her.

"For shit's sake," Aryk grumbled, and moved forward. He detached Neil from his wife and threw him across the room.

Neil's body shuddered in protest and due to the agony that was taking over him, he passed out.

"Get the guy a couple of blood packs from the fridge," Aryk ordered the guard. He shot a glance over to the pregnant woman, who appeared as if she were a moment away from coming undone. He knelt beside her and kneaded her shoulder with one hand. "He'll be all right after he feeds. He'll be the same loving husband that you married."

Her bottom lip trembled and she refused to look him in the eyes.

With a shrug, he stood and left the dungeon.

Her husband had been preparing to bite her. If Aryk and the guard hadn't returned, he would have pinched the flesh of her neck with his teeth and drank from her. She shuddered and hugged herself. *We have to get out of here,* she thought to herself. *Now more than ever, we have to get away from this godforsaken place.*

CRACRACRACRACRACRACRACRACRACRACRACRACRACRACRACRA
CHAPTER NINETEEN
CRACRACRACRACRACRACRACRACRACRACRACRACRACRACRACRA

"Chances are that they will have some kind of magic in place to keep us off of the property," Iancu was telling everyone seated in his living room. "That is the biggest problem that I can foresee. If they have some sort of magic in place, we will have to find another way in."

"If they have magic in place, I don't know if we will be able to get in," one of the men pointed out. "If magic was cast in order to protect the estate then the only person who can withdraw the magic is the one who cast it in the first place."

"In the event that there is some sort of magic surrounding the estate, I could hunt Aryk down and allow him to capture me," Charlie suggested.

Paul's group of men nodded at the idea, commenting that it sounded brilliant.

Iancu was shaking his head. "No."

She met his gaze with creased brows. "Why not?"

"It's too dangerous," he protested. "I don't want you in there by yourself."

A couple of the men exchanged knowing glances in response to the lover's quarrel.

"If it's the only shot at getting Neil out of there, then we have to take it," she insisted.

Paul's brown eyes flared red for a moment before settling to brown again. "Excuse me...what was that?"

"I thought that was why you were here," she said, looking confused.

"You thought I was here...because what?" Paul leaned farther forward, looking increasingly angry.

Iancu settled a hand onto her shoulder and answered the question for her. "Neil has been captured by Aryk."

"Are you fucking with me?"

"No."

"Neil is there right now? How long has he been there?"

"Since last night."

"He's been there since last night and you didn't go in after him?" Paul demanded, rising from the armchair. A couple of his comrades came to his side, ready for action in the event that it was necessary.

Iancu also stood up. "The slayer and I were in a battle with Jordana and the slayer was injured. We couldn't survive another attack on Jordana with the shape that Charlie was in. So instead, I gave her time to recuperate and I trained with her earlier today so that she would be ready tonight."

Paul's hands were fisted at his sides. He stared into Iancu's eyes, seemingly searching for something. He finally nodded his head. "Okay," he said finally. "So I guess someone should give me the run-down of what happened last night."

Iancu took a deep breath, reclaiming his seat on the sofa. "What I tell you can't leave this room."

"Of course," Paul agreed, glancing at each and every man in his group. Each man gave a slight nod in his direction.

"Neil and Marilyn were able to conceive a child together," Iancu revealed.

Silence draped over the room like a wet blanket. Shock registered on Paul's face and he stammered as he searched for the words that he wanted to say.

"That's impossible," one of Paul's men said finally.

"That is what we all thought," Iancu said, sounding tired. "He was positive that Marilyn was cheating on him and there was this whole domestic drama...It's a long story, but he said that he checked it out for himself. He was sure that the child was his. Before he could celebrate with his wife, Aryk or one of his cronies grabbed her from the hospital."

Paul made a steeple with his fingers, a habit that he seemed to share with his cousin.

"When he found out that Marilyn had been snatched, he lost it-understandably. And we were all hatching a plan to go in and save her. I wanted to go in and get her back, but I most likely would have been attacked on sight. Aryk has some sort of fascination with Charlie, so she volunteered to get captured and locate Marilyn so that she could bring her back to safety. Neil shot down both of these ideas. He wanted to go in after Marilyn himself."

Paul's frown deepened. "I love my cousin to death, but he's horrible in combat."

"Which is what I told him," Iancu said. "He wasn't listening. So I let him think that I was going to let him go on his own. I was planning on backing him up, though. That was until I bumped into Jordana and she attempted to kill Charlie."

"And both you and the slayer managed to get away from Jordana with your lives intact?"

"You should have seen him," Charlie couldn't help but say. "She was a mess when he was done with her. She was forced to retreat."

Some of Paul's frown eased. He even appeared to be impressed. "We may have a shot in hell after all."

"We have more than that," Iancu assured.

"All right, so back to planning," Paul said after clearing his throat. "The slayer volunteered to be captured in the event that there is magic keeping us from getting on the property. I think we should let her."

Iancu reached out and grabbed Charlie's hand. He maintained eye contact with Paul as he said, "If that were to happen, we would have to have some way to get onto the estate so that we could provide assistance. I can't let her go in there without a support system."

"You don't believe that I can do it?" she asked him.

"It has nothing to do with that," he said without meeting her questioning gaze. "I just...it's not a good idea."

"It might not be an ideal situation, but so far it's all we've got," Paul pointed out. "I understand that you two have something going on. Believe me, I understand that. But there are lives in the balance here, including the life of a baby who hasn't even been born yet. We have to think for the greater good."

"I hate that saying," Iancu growled. "There is no 'greater' good. There's just 'good.'"

Knowing better than to further the argument, Paul sat back in his seat and sealed his mouth shut.

Iancu looked down at Charlie and affectionately stroked her cheek. "You would be all right with being captured by Aryk? You wouldn't have a problem with that?"

"Not if it's our only option."

He nodded. Then he glanced up, squeezing her hand tighter in his. "If there is some sort of spell keeping us off of Jordana's property, we send Charlie in."

"Wonderful." Paul leaned forward again. "In the event that there is no spell protecting the property, which is what I'm hoping for, we need to have a plan of action together."

"They'll most likely have a shitload of guards outside of the place," Iancu said thoughtfully. "Everyone who is armed with guns has to make sure to bring spare ammo. There are going to be guards on the outside of the place *and* on the inside. We can't afford to come up short."

"Do you know the layout of the place?"

Iancu shook his head. "I've only been in there a couple of times, and neither experience was good. If I had a telepathic link to Neil, he would be able to give me a mental picture of what is located where, but I'm not linked with him."

"Neither am I," Paul said, "so we're just going to have to wing it by sensing different energies."

"I was planning on heading out there at sundown."

"Just as they're waking up?"

"I don't want Neil in there longer than he has to be."

"Good point. The guys and I are going to head back to headquarters and stock up on weapons and supplies. We'll meet you back here in a couple of hours."

After Paul and his men left the apartment, Iancu and Charlie suited up and continued their training. He grew increasingly frustrated with her whenever she failed to handle the sword properly.

"Stop yelling at me!" she shouted at him.

"I didn't mean to yell!" he yelled back. He turned his back to her and anxiously ran his hands through his hair. He was coming apart at the seams and this was the worst time for that to happen.

She approached his back, but made no move to touch him.

"I don't want Aryk to be anywhere near you," he said almost too low for her to hear. "I don't want you to let him capture you. That doesn't sound like a good plan to me. I think we should come up with another one."

"Everything will work out," she told him even though she had her own doubts.

"There's no guarantee that he'll even take you back to Jordana's estate," he pointed out. "Even if he does take you to her place, the man she's been with for centuries happens to be showing an interest in you. And she already knows that *I'm* interested in you. If she catches wind of you being on her property, she won't hesitate in killing you."

She finally reached out and snaked her arms around his waist. "I know how to handle myself, thanks to your training."

"Don't even joke about that," he muttered. "I can't fit what I've learned over the course of five hundred years into a five-hour tutorial."

"We're able to communicate telepathically," she said. "If I get into trouble, I'll let you know."

"But what if I can't get to you in time?"

She started to speak, but he cut her off.

"No, Charlie. Just...*no*, okay?" He lowered his head and brought his hands up to his face.

He's thinking of Bridgette again, she thought to herself. *He's thinking that he has already lost one love and that he won't be able to take losing me, too.*

He turned to face her then, so quickly that she thought he must have read her mind. He ran his fingers through her hair and traced the lines of her face with a lone index finger. He shook his head. "If it comes to that," he told her in a soft voice. "If it comes to you surrendering yourself to Aryk...you have to be as careful as possible."

"I will be," she said.

"That's not enough for me. I want you to promise me that you won't do anything reckless."

"I can't promise something like that."

"Promise me." He searched her eyes with one hand on either side of her face. "Promise me, Charlie. If you don't, I won't let you do it."

"You need to stop freaking out," she said.

"Promise me that and I will."

Her bottom lip quaked. Tears came to her eyes and she blinked them back. "I promise that I'll try my best not to do anything reckless," she said finally.

He chuckled and said, "No. You have to promise me not to do anything reckless."

"What if it's completely necessary?" she whispered.

"It won't be. Nothing that will take you away from me is necessary. Nothing."

Tears flooded her eyes at his words and she shook her head soundlessly.

"Promise me," he repeated.

"I promise that I won't do anything reckless," she said in a hushed whisper.

He crushed her against him and rested his chin on the top of her head. It hadn't taken her long to worm her way into his life and alter it to her satisfaction. Now that she had, he wasn't going to let her leave his life just as quickly.

She lifted her face and kissed the bottom of his chin. "We have to stop doing this."

"What?"

"Losing our focus."

"I haven't lost my focus," he maintained. "My focus is keeping you safe. It always will be."

She smiled at him and pressed a kiss to his lips. "The focus at *hand* is making sure that Neil, his wife, and his kid are kept safe," she reminded him.

"You're right," he agreed, sobering up. "You're right. I was lost in the moment. All right, umm..."

"Training," she supplied for him.

"Right. Training. All right."

A short knock sounded on the door to his apartment. She excitedly skipped away from him to answer the door. He turned and lifted his sword, waving it right and left. The light from the overhead fixture glinted on the steel of the weapon.

Charlie returned, but she wasn't alone. Two people stood beside her: a tall man with jet-black hair and dangerous, green eyes and a short, purple-haired sprite with a hard glint in her eyes.

Iancu lowered the sword for a moment, thought better of it, and lifted the sword again, this time at the man's throat.

Charlie looked from one man to the other, shrugging when Iancu shot his gaze in her direction. "He said that you two knew each other."

"Fifty years and this is the greeting that I get?" the other man demanded.

"What are you doing here, Alexei?" Iancu demanded, his eyes darting from Alexei to Jade.

"I'm here to help you," the slightly taller man said. "And Jade, here...she's just along for the ride right now."

Iancu's eyes were suspicious. "Help me do what?"

"Defeat Jordana."

"Jade is the head of security at Jordana's estate. What is she doing here?"

Alexei glanced down at Jade and he shrugged his shoulders. "I haven't had the chance to talk to her," he said after a moment. "But I don't think I have anything to worry about as far as she's concerned."

A muscle in Iancu's jaw twitched, but he nodded his head, allowing Alexei's explanation (or lack thereof) for the meantime. "And why would you assist me with bringing down a fellow clan leader?"

"Because she killed the only woman that I've ever loved," the clan leader said in a choked voice.

Iancu sighed and gestured over to the couch. "You'd better start at the beginning," he said.

That is exactly what Alexei did. When he was finished telling his story, he sat back and ran his hands over his face. "Retaliating against her would be going against the coven. I'm supposed to go through the proper channels instead of committing an act of revenge, but at this point I don't care. I don't have the patience to take this to the other clan leaders and by now most of them have returned to govern over their own regions, anyway. I want Jordana dead. And I want to take her severed head back to Chicago with me, so I can mount it over the mantelpiece in my living room."

"You don't want to do that," Iancu assured. "Airport security is airtight these days."

Charlie rolled her eyes and sat on the couch beside Alexei. "I'm sorry about what you've had to go through," she told him earnestly.

The Toltec clan leader offered her a wavering smile. He closed his eyes and the smile grew more and more genuine. "Every time I close my eyes, I see her," he said. "It's wonderful and at the same time, it's torture. I can't stop thinking about her. I miss her and I want her back.

"I hate it when our kind speaks of eternity and being immortal. We're *not* immortal, don't they see that? We are not exempt in the eyes of fate. We are creatures of the night who have somewhat longer life spans than humans." He leaned forward and ducked his head into his hands.

Everything that he said were words that Iancu had spoken before, after having brutally killed the love of his life. Although Alexei's circumstances were different, the outcome was the same. Despite his lack of sympathy for the other man, he did look concerned. "Are you sure that you're up to fighting tonight?" he asked. "In order to fight Jordana, you have to have your wits about you."

"I'm definitely ready," the clan leader said, standing on his feet. "Even if you turn me away, I will still go after her on my own. I just figured that teaming up with you would increase our chances of defeating her."

"I agree with you," Iancu said. "There is a team of guys that is meeting us here. From here, we will be heading out to Jordana's estate."

"I'm up for it. Just tell me what you need me to do," Alexei vowed.

Jade stood near the balcony doors. She'd been quiet the entire time, but now she turned to face them all. "Aryk attacked me," she said. "That is why I left her estate, why I will never go back to work there. I can let you know how to get in and out of her house without being detected. I can tell you where the property's weak points are. I can even help you to get your friend safely off of the property."

They all stared at her with their mouths agape.

She shrugged casually and sauntered towards them. "Aryk has to learn not to fuck with the head of security," she said bitterly. "I'll be happy to teach him."

Paul and his troop arrived later than they were expected. He claimed that it was due to one of his comrade's overactive bladders. "He was asking us to stop at every McDonald's so that he could use their bathroom," Neil's cousin had quipped. "The next McDonald's we go into will have a Wanted poster with his picture on it, warning their employees not to let him in. He's a serial bathroom user."

After the bladder and pee jokes, Paul turned serious. "We've got enough artillery in the Escalade downstairs to blow up a fort." He noticed that there was another vampire in the room, and a clan leader at that. "What are Alexei and Jade doing here?"

Jade offered a lopsided grin. "Long time no see, Paul," she greeted.

"They're here to help us," Iancu informed. "It's a long story. Are we all ready to go?"

Charlie readjusted her shoulder holster and slipped her arms through it. She wouldn't make the same mistake she'd made last night. She wore both holsters, putting two guns at her lower back and a gun on the side of each breast. She'd checked to make sure that all four guns were fully loaded. After securing her guns in their respective holsters, she stored plenty of stakes in her cloak without worrying about the stake points weighing her down.

Iancu observed this as he watched her suit up.

"I figure if I have to take my cloak off to fight, I will," she told him. "And if I leave it there or if it's damaged beyond repair and I get out of this alive, I will have deserved a new one."

He smiled at her line of thinking and continued to suit up himself. "Don't forget extra ammo," he reminded her.

"Got it," she said, patting two of her pockets. "I think I'm ready."

"You're not *quite* ready," he said and disappeared for a moment. When he returned, he had a sword in his hand. It was the lightest sword in his collection and there was a floral pattern painted on the hilt and sheath of the sword. "This is yours to keep. I want you to have it on you tonight."

She accepted the sword and he showed her how to wear the sword's sheath at her hip. "Thank you," she mouthed to him.

He winked at her and announced to Paul that they were ready to leave.

Because of how many people they were moving and the equipment that they were carrying, they had to take two cars. Paul said that he would be riding with Iancu, Charlie, Jade, and Alexei. He told his men to follow their car.

As Iancu started the engine, Paul said, "I was thinking that if we don't have any magic to worry about, our biggest worry will be the fact that the guards posted outside are going to sense us."

"I was thinking about that, too," Iancu said. "I don't know any way around it."

"I wish that I could be of help in that department," Alexei said from the backseat, "but I've already attacked Jordana once today. Chances are that her guards have word not to allow me back onto the property."

"That's all right, Alexei. I can go in first," Charlie offered from where she sat in the passenger seat. "I don't think they'd be able to read me as quickly as they could you four."

Iancu gave her a look out of the corner of his eye, a look that clearly said, *Stop volunteering for shit.*

"I actually think that it's worth a try," Paul said from the back seat.

"We'll see what happens when we get there," Iancu said noncommittally. "We have to make sure there aren't any spells yet."

"There aren't any spells protecting the property and I know where most of the guards will be posted," Jade announced. "They won't be a problem."

They rode the rest of the way in silence. Occasionally, Iancu's hand slipped over the console to grip Charlie's hand. She was truly touched by the fact that he was worried about her well-being. Ever since her family had been brutally murdered, no one had genuinely cared for her, not even her foster parents. At times it had seemed like her foster parents kept her around just for the tax write-off.

"Don't pull up in front of the house," Paul ordered, leaning between the two front seats. "Drive past the house and park in front of one of those other houses."

Iancu didn't bother to tell Paul that he had intended to do that in the first place. You could take the vampire out of the military, but you couldn't take the military out of the vampire, apparently. He cut off the headlights and parked several blocks away from Jordana's estate. The Escalade that had been trailing them did the same.

Charlie hopped out of the car, operating purely on adrenaline. She bounced up and down, trying in vain to work off some of her energy.

Iancu slowly climbed out of the car, a hell of a lot less excited than she was. He peered at her over the top of the car, his eyes penetrating her to the very core. *Remember what you promised me,* his voice said in her head.

She nodded at him and checked her cloak pockets to make sure that she had everything.

Paul's crew climbed out of the sports utility vehicle they'd traveled in and engaged the alarm. The alarm chirped in response.

Charlie arched a glance at them. "Was that necessary?"

One of the guys shrugged. "You never know."

They started to walk towards the estate.

"The front will most likely have the most guards," Jade whispered, hoping that they could all hear her. "We would be better off entering the property from the back."

"Is it bothering anyone else that we don't have a concrete plan still?" Charlie muttered, shoving her hands into her coat pockets.

The sun was fast setting over the horizon. The sky was a combination of pink, purple, orange, and blue hues. It was a shame that Iancu couldn't pause and admire its beauty. He trudged along the sidewalk with his woman at his side, attempting not to visualize her demise behind his eyes. There were many ways that this could go wrong. Life was ironic. He had already lost Bridgette. He wouldn't be surprised if after having finally found the gonads to love again, it was yanked from him a second time.

Sensing his turmoil, Charlie huddled near him as they walked.

Jordana sat at the desk in her library with a pile of books in front of her. She pored over each and every word on each and every page. She didn't know why; many of the books she had often contradicted each other. Some of the books claimed that Lord Vlad's wife had born an heir, and others claimed that when his wife died, she'd still been pregnant with her first child. Yet another volume would insist that Vlad's wife bore two sons.

Research was often frustrating for her. She rarely discovered information that was new to her. The only reason that she persisted with researching Vlad was because she had become thoroughly obsessed with finding out what the prophecy meant. The second half of the prophecy most likely told the outcome of the battle between good and evil, humans and vampires. She had to know what the outcome was. She had to know what would happen to her people.

She lazily flipped through the book in front of her. She saw something of interest and stopped flipping. Trembling fingers flipped back through the pages, looking for what had caught her eye.

She stopped flipping when she reached a full-page portrait of Lord Vlad. Her breath caught in her throat as her hungry eyes took in his long, dark hair and blazing dark eyes. She'd seen many different renditions of Lord Vlad, many of them being painted by persons who had never actually come into contact with the world's most notorious vampire. One of those renditions was perched on the wall of the study she sat it at this very moment. If she could trust the words of the publication, this particular portrait of Vlad had been painted in the mid-1400's before he left his castle to ambush the Turks.

She ran her hand down the middle of the page. The man in the portrait was strikingly familiar. The lines of his face, the shape of his eyes, the strong angle of his nose and the fullness of his lips...

The double doors of the library were shoved open and Aryk breezed into the room and came to stand at her back. When she didn't acknowledge his presence, he bent at the waist to peer over her shoulder. "Is that a portrait of Iancu?"

She shook her head slowly, shaken by the fact that she wasn't the only one to see the resemblance.

He stared even harder at the portrait. "Are you sure?" he asked her. "He looks just like him *and* he has that damned birthmark on the inside of his wrist."

Her violet eyes grew round as she pushed him backwards with one hand and bent over her book. He was right. The scale of the painting wasn't large enough for her to be able to determine the shape of the birthmark on the inside of Lord Vlad's wrist, but she didn't have to see a larger version of the painting to know what the shape of the birthmark was. The birthmark was in the shape of a dragon, a mark that the members of the Order of the Dragon all had on their bodies in some fashion. Lord Vlad's father had been involved in the Order of the Dragon, a knightly order created in order to prevail over the Turks in the Crusades. Consequently, Lord Vlad himself also participated in that battle. In this portrait of Lord Vlad, he had a dragon-shaped birthmark on the inside of his wrist. There was only one other person in the world whom she'd known to possess the very same birthmark in the very same place.

Rubbing the back of his neck, Aryk unsteadily pulled himself to his feet. "I didn't mean to intrude," he muttered. "I'll leave you to your pictures of your ex."

"It's not a painting of Iancu," she said softly, clapping the book shut.

"Whoever it's a painting of, it's your business," he said with a shrug of his shoulders.

She waited until he reached the door. Then she asked him, "Don't you ever wonder how he was able to defeat you without using his powers? Don't you ever wonder how he was able to hurt me?"

He turned to face her. "We know the answers to those questions already. The guy got lucky. Next time, he won't be so fortunate."

"He didn't just get *lucky*, Aryk," she said. "The page that I was looking at didn't have a portrait of Iancu on it. It had a portrait of Lord Vlad on it."

He crossed his arms over his chest as he attempted to connect the dots. After several moments, he gave up on connecting the dots and prodded, "Meaning?"

"*Meaning*," she stressed, "that Iancu is either Lord Vlad's son...or Lord Vlad himself."

CHAPTER TWENTY

"I'm not sensing any magic around the property," Paul whispered. "That means that we'll be going in. To do that, we should split up in pairs."

Iancu and Charlie stood with their fingers intertwined.

Paul gave a wry smile. "I guess I don't even have to ask who you two will be teaming up with."

Alexei announced that he worked better alone. Jade didn't want a partner, either. Paul and his men paired off into teams and claimed areas that they would cover. It was a shame, really, that there were no shapeshifters in their group. A shapeshifter would have really come in handy about now.

Paul's partner was Damen, a six foot tall vampire who was built as solidly as a brick wall. His dark brown skin gleamed in the sun's dying rays and his startling light eyes held a world of danger in them. Several decades ago, one of the women that he was dating turned him into a vampire without his consent. It hadn't taken much convincing for him to join Paul's crew. He detested the thought of someone hatching a plan to deliberately recruit a slew of vampires.

The two men broke apart from the group, keeping their senses alert.

Damen crept alongside Paul with his hand at his hip, ready to spring into action in case they were caught off-guard. His steps were slow and calculating as he read the lay of the grounds, searching for any signs of tainted energy. His light brown eyes jumped from object to object in the expansive courtyard. Suddenly, he stopped moving and gestured for Paul to do the same.

Reading the expression on his comrade's face, Paul halted his movements and cast wary glances around the both of them. He tilted his nose in the air and sniffed. He could smell the scent of tainted blood close by.

Their environment seemed to hold its breath. There were several trees sprinkled about the courtyard and not one branch swayed. The disturbing quiet enveloped the both of them into a tight embrace.

Both men turned in slow, deliberate circles. They were not telepathically linked, but they didn't have to be. Their eyes met. Buried within the silence, there was a mildly significant source of power...not significant enough to be either Aryk or Jordana, but strong enough to be considered a threat. A trail of powerful energy lazily wafted between them.

Paul's eyes gleamed as he worked to track the source of energy. He blinked once, twice, and then closed his eyes, withdrawing his gun from its holster at his hip. Without speaking a word, he whirled around and dropped to his knees, firing off several rounds.

Damen drew one of his guns, running at full speed towards a heavily shadowed area of the courtyard.

A bolt of energy rushed at Paul, nearly knocking him on his rear end. He shakily got to his feet and turned to face a beautiful vampire with curly blonde hair. She looked young; her life as a human being had probably ended when she was around fifteen or sixteen years old. She was wearing a cotton candy pink tank top and black shorts were tight around shapely thighs.

While he appraised her, she took the time to appraise him, but it took her a lot less time. She summed him up as being a yuppie tight-ass. "You're trespassing," she said casually. Her hands were devoid of weapons. Her hands *were* the weapons. She stood facing him without a fear in the world, unnervingly confident.

The grip that he had on his weapon was firm. "I wasn't aware of that," he returned.

"Now that you're aware, it would be in your best interest to leave," she suggested with a corner of her mouth lifted into a wry smile.

"I don't think that I can leave just yet."

"And why is that?"

"There is some unsettled business that I have to take care of here."

She lifted her chin up a notch. "So you would be here on the traitor's behalf?"

"The traitor?"

"Iancu. The one who kills his own kind."

He gave a careless shrug of his shoulders. "You could say he's an acquaintance of mine. It would be more accurate to say that I'm here on my cousin's behalf, though."

One of her brows lifted. "Who is your cousin?"

"Neil."

She nodded, flexing both of her arms. "You are here to rescue him from our clutches, is that right?"

"That would be correct."

"You are going to have to get through me to do that," she informed him, striking a fighter's pose with her right foot positioned about twelve inches behind the left. "Let's get on with it, then."

She was almost too beautiful to kill, but he lifted his gun without hesitation and fired.

Supernaturally fast, she leapt into the air and dodged the bullets flying towards her. Then she rushed at him, nothing but a colorful blur. She tackled him to the ground and fixed her hands around his neck.

Her strength is impressive, I'll give her that, he thought to himself. He lifted his hands and pried her fingers from around his neck. He held both of her wrists together and rose to his feet, bringing her up with him.

Shots sounded off in the distance. He couldn't tell who had squeezed off the shots, whether it had been his partner Damen or someone else. *So much for our stealthy ambush,* he thought as he shoved the girl away from him.

Iancu used his sharp senses in order to detect strong sources of power. Surprisingly enough, there was no sign of powerful beings anywhere near the back door leading into Jordana's estate. The sounds of gunshots reached his ears and his head snapped around.

Charlie met his gaze and held it. Her mouth pursed into a thin, grim line.

He pressed his hand to the back door. Vampires hadn't yet patented locks that couldn't be manipulated. He was certain that there were spells that could be used for this purpose, but he easily influenced the lock so that the doorknob turned loosely in his hand. He glanced over his shoulder at Charlie before pushing the door open.

They were greeted with the sight of a squeaky clean kitchen. The tiles were shiny and the counters had been wiped down so that they sparkled beneath the dim light fixture suspended over the island counter in the center of the room.

He was able to sense that there were approximately thirty vampires within the walls of the large house. There were eleven or twelve of them upstairs, about eight of them on the main floor, and several more below them in a basement or cellar. The vampires that accompanied him on the main floor were his top priority.

In one smooth, silent movement, he unsheathed his sword. The sleek weapon felt heavy and solid in his very capable hands. He inched farther into the kitchen with his woman at his back, blocking out her sweet floral scent and directing his focus on the duty that they had to carry out. He was increasingly aware of her presence. He didn't have to look over his shoulder to know that she had two guns drawn. Her steps were nearly as quiet as his.

Her dark hair was pulled back into a ponytail and a steely look blazed in her hazel eyes. She, too, fought not to zone in on the animal attraction sparking between Iancu and herself. It would take one hundred percent of her focus in order to survive tonight. She couldn't allow distractions to get in her way.

Bits of chatter floated into the kitchen. Iancu halted his steps, holding his sword at his side. One particular voice drew closer and closer to the kitchen. "Don't worry about it, I'll get it," a female vampire said, stumbling drunkenly into the kitchen.

She had barely a moment to form her mouth into the form of a round *O* before her head was detached from her body. Iancu stood over her with his sword raised above his head. His eyes glittered and shined as she turned into a pile of dust on the kitchen floor.

Charlie stepped over the pile of dust without giving it a second thought. She followed her partner through the archway of the kitchen with both of her guns raised to chest level. Adrenaline surged through her as she exited the kitchen. Tonight was the night. Tonight, it would all go down and there would be only one victor: good or evil.

Time seemed to slow as the two of them crept down the short hallway and into the sitting room, where a group of vampires sat drinking blood and gossiping. They stepped into the room with their weapons drawn and for several long moments, they went unnoticed.

It wasn't until Charlie started pulling off shots that screams filled the small room and the vampires were put into defense mode, crouching low to the ground. They cowered in response to the sound of gunfire.

A ballet ensued, with silver blasting from Charlie's guns as Iancu danced about the room beheading vampires and stabbing them with a weapon made of wood and steel.

A vampire faded from Charlie's view and reappeared directly in front of her, catching her by surprise. He knocked one of her guns out of her hand, but she didn't pause before firing off the rounds of the other gun. As her assailant turned to dust, another vampire grabbed her elbows and forced them back. She felt the vampire attempt to pry her gun from her hand. She whirled and simultaneously drew one of the guns from her shoulder holster. The vampire blinked her squinty eyes once, then twice, shocked at the fact that Charlie possessed the ability to draw a gun so quickly when she was merely a human. Bullets were fired into the vampire's skull at point-blank range and blood splattered into her frizzy brown hair.

Black blood stained the carpets and heaps of dust were scattered about the room by the time Iancu and Charlie were done. They stood in the center of the room not even bothering to lower their weapons. It was only a matter of time before troops came in to defend Jordana's manor.

A vampire entered the room. The most startling feature about him was his blood-red eyes. The second most noticeable feature about him was the bad dye job. His hair had been dyed in multiple shades of red. He appeared familiar to Iancu, but Iancu couldn't place his face.

Whoever the guy was, he had to be given points for composure. He took one glance around the room and clucked his tongue in mock-dismay. "Look at what a mess you've made," he said, his voice thick with an unfamiliar accent.

"You're right," Charlie agreed, playing along. "We've been such horrible guests."

"You're about to make it up to me," the redhead told her. With those words, he whirled on his heel, spinning in an elaborate circle. He spun again, slowly enough to catch the gazes of both of his opponents. As he spun around, he began to pick up speed until he was nothing but a blur of motion. He dramatically burst into a cluster of slick-winged bats.

Without thinking, Iancu reached out and grabbed Charlie by the hand. "He's a shapeshifter," he informed her in a whisper. "Probably sired by Aryk."

The bats fluttered about the room, crowding up near the ceiling where they gathered once again to meld into the body of the vampire with striking red hair.

"Is that the magic show that you put on for your victims?" Iancu asked. "I'm older than you and Aryk combined. I know you didn't expect that to amaze me."

The vampire floated down from the ceiling until he came to stand in front of Iancu. "No, I guess that wouldn't amaze you, would it? Not after you came close to defeating Jordana."

Charlie glanced from one vampire to the other. She didn't know why Iancu was wasting words on this punk. They should just kill him and get it over with.

"Nikolai," called an authoritative and urgent feminine voice. "I need you to go out and secure the grounds. I am told that there is a loud commotion around the estate."

Jordana entered the room with her arms folded across her chest. She cast pointed glances at the piles of dust littering her sitting room floor, but she didn't comment on them. Instead, she circled around her former lover and his companion. A red satin dress clung to her every curve as she prowled about the room in silent assessment of the situation.

Iancu's fingers tightened around the hilt of his sword as his eyes followed her. There was something unsettling about her silence.

"You're very brave to trespass upon my property in this way," the ancient vampiress said finally, coming to a halt near the heavy velvet drapes concealing the sitting room's picture window. "You're either very brave or very stupid."

Like a good little lapdog, Aryk emerged from the house after having heard the bursts of gunfire around the property. Jade followed him, making sure to keep a certain distance from him. As powerful as he was, he would be able to sense her if she got too close.

She maintained distance and watched him as he prowled about the property. She was a force to reckon with and she knew that, but she didn't know whether or not she'd be able to take Aryk down by herself. A smart person would find someone to fight alongside her, but her fury and her pride were too insistent. This was a battle that she had to fight alone. He'd attacked her and violated her and he had to pay for that. She was the only one who could claim retribution for those misdeeds.

When she was tired of following him, she gathered up all of her strength and shoved Alexei's jacket from her shoulders. His jacket would only hinder her. She hadn't asked to use any of Paul's or Iancu's or Charlie's weapons. She was skilled at hand-to-hand combat and she was familiar enough with her abilities to wield them effectively.

The moonlight washed over her nude body as she sped towards Aryk. She pushed him to the ground and stood over him, daring him to stand up.

He got to his feet and turned to face her. "Do you think that you have a chance against me?"

"I can't let you get away with what you did," she told him. "You deserve to die for what you did to me. And I aim to give you what you deserve."

He chuckled and grinned at her. "To punish me for taking what I wanted, you're going to fight me naked? What a sweet, delicious punishment."

She realized at that moment that hand-to-hand combat wasn't going to be of much help to her, not against a vampire as powerful as Aryk was. She needed a weapon in order to defeat him. Her power alone couldn't rival his.

His smile stretched wider. "You're right. Your power couldn't possibly compete with mine," he affirmed.

Her eyes widened.

He laughed and shook his head. "You're out of your league," he said and turned his back to her. "If you want to walk away from this with your life intact, I suggest that you *walk away*."

Anger and fury flowed through her. Unleashing a blood-curdling scream, she ran at him and pummeled his back with her fists.

He whirled and smacked her hard in the face. He smacked her so hard that her bottom lip split open. Looking just as angry as she was, he seized her by the wrists. "Is this what you want?" he demanded, forcing her backwards as he advanced on her. "Do you want me to have my way with you again?"

She stared up at him defiantly, so caught up in her anger that she couldn't speak or act. He didn't have to use his powers to paralyze her. Her own vehemence was enough.

He shoved her hard enough to send her tumbling on the ground. While staring down at her, he drew his gun from its holster at his waist. He pointed the gun at her. "There are silver bullets in this gun," he told her coldly. "This is the same gun that I used to kill Chase."

Her eyes widened and she sat up, wiping the blood from her mouth with the back of her hand. "You're lying," she accused.

"You didn't know that I killed him?" Aryk questioned. "Imagine that."

She hadn't known that Chase was dead. She figured that he'd just picked up and left Los Angeles without letting her know that he was leaving. It had never occurred to her that he might have been killed by a jealous prick of a vampire.

Aryk shrugged his shoulders. "I liked you. Over the years, I've tried my damnedest to get you in bed, but you kept denying me. Chase came along and he got you *easily*. He didn't have to work as much as I did. You didn't make him jump through as many hoops as you made me."

"You never *liked* me," she told him. "You just get off on making others weak. You have an ego problem, do you understand that? You're not big, bad, and cruel. You're overcompensating. Some guys who are having a mid-life crisis deal with it by buying a Corvette or a motorcycle. You just handle it a little bit differently. You make others feel weak and if you happen to be in the mood for it, you kill them."

He tapped his cheek with the barrel of the semiautomatic weapon. "My, but I'm going to miss your gift of gab," he said with a sigh. He knelt down to the ground and aimed the gun at her temple. His eyes traveled down her body and he added, "There are other things that I will miss about you as well."

His finger hugged the trigger, but he never got the chance to pull it. A stake whizzed at him, sailing through the air at a mind-boggling speed. It caught him in the chest and penetrated his heart.

He stared down at the stake point with disbelieving eyes. He tried to turn around to see who'd thrown the stake, but before he could set eyes upon his attacker, he was reduced to a pile of black dust.

Alexei walked up to Jade and helped her up. "That guy always got on my nerves," he muttered.

"I have come to relieve Neil of your possession," Iancu informed Jordana. "I will do whatever is necessary to achieve that."

"I don't have Neil in my possession," she said, tilting her nose into the air. "Neil is our accountant."

A smile graced Iancu's lips. "It seems you don't know everything that is going on beneath your own roof."

She frowned and closed her eyes, tallying up the different scents that assailed her nostrils. Her eyes sprang open and she whirled on her heel, taking immediate absence of the room.

Iancu took off after her with Charlie close behind him.

In the hallway, there was a door leading to a cellar or dungeon. Jordana didn't open the door; she merely pressed her palm flat against it and concentrated her power. "Neil is there," she said in wonderment, almost to herself. "And a woman. A *pregnant* woman. Why would they be in my dungeon?"

Realization slapped Iancu in the face. *Jordana really doesn't know,* he thought after making sure that he had mental blocks in place shielding her from reading his mind. *Aryk must have taken Neil and Marilyn captive without telling her.*

Jordana's hand remained pressed flat against the door.

We could kill her right now, Charlie's voice urged inside of his head. *She's vulnerable. Her focus is elsewhere. I could shoot her down right now.*

The silver would do nothing to her, he responded. *She's of old blood. The silver would be nothing more than a slight annoyance, like a buzzing mosquito.*

Decapitate her, then. Your sword is already drawn.

She can react quickly to just about any situation, he told her. *It's not going to be that easy to kill her.*

Jordana's eyes snapped open and she snatched her hand from the door. "It can't be," she whispered. "It's impossible. An abomination." She slowly turned her head so that she was staring directly at Iancu.

Iancu met her gaze without speaking.

A mystical gust of wind swept her red curls back from her face as she lifted both of her hands. The wind danced around her hands and then proceeded to surge toward Iancu and Charlie.

Both the vampire and his slayer were thrown backwards. They landed beneath the archway to the sitting room.

"You can't honestly think that I'm going to let you walk out of here with that freakish thing growing within her womb," Jordana said in a menacing voice, stalking after them.

Charlie recovered her guns and rolled onto her back. She cocked both guns and pulled the trigger on first one and then the other.

Jordana vaporized into thin air and reappeared farther into the sitting room. "I can smell him on you," she seethed. "And I can smell you on him. It won't be long before you have a wretched creature growing within *your* belly. You are insane if you think that I am going to stand by and watch it happen." She stared at Iancu's right wrist and he could hear a subtle intake of her breath.

He glanced down at his wrist, where the dragon birthmark rested.

"I always wondered why you were so powerful. Even in your first few years of being a vampire, you seemed to have a certain instinct about you."

He didn't know what she was talking about, but he wanted her to keep talking. He continued to circle about the room.

"And when you nearly defeated me...I knew that there was something. It's nearly impossible to defeat your own sire. I'm sure there are ways, but your power was effortless.

"I doubt that you're Lord Vlad," she said, talking more to herself than to anyone else. "Vlad should be lying in his tomb. But it's possible that you could be his son. I've done research and it's rumored that his children, two sons, were born shortly before he underwent the transformation."

As Alexei and Jade made their way to the house, they came across Paul in a compromising situation with Crystal, a petite blonde vampire who seemed to be giving him more of a fight than he had bargained for.

Jade traveled at superhuman speed with her arms outstretched. She yanked Crystal off of Paul. The short blonde was kicking and screaming like a child. Jade carelessly tossed her aside and offered a hand to Paul to help him up.

"I'm sure that Iancu has managed to get himself into trouble by now," Alexei remarked. "We'd better get in there and help him."

As the three of them headed towards the back entrance of Jordana's residence, Crystal jerked a dislocated shoulder into place.

CHAPTER TWENTY-ONE

"There is a portrait of him," Jordana continued. "He looks just like you. He has the mark of the dragon, the same birthmark that you have. It sounds crazy and remarkable, but I do believe it to be true. I do believe you to be Lord Vlad's son."

"Tonight isn't about whose son I am," Iancu said, even though the wheels in his mind were turning at the possibility of finding out about his real family. As much as he claimed to not care about his biological family and as much as he told himself that he was all right with not knowing who had brought him into this world, it was all lies. He would like to know who his real family had been, even if they had abandoned him.

"I know that you have questions," Jordana proclaimed. "If you allow me to, I can answer those questions for you."

A trail of energy snaked into the room and smacked her in the chest, sending her against the far wall, near her throne. Alexei swaggered in the room with Paul and Jade at his heels. "Some women just talk way too much," he commented, coming to stand beside Charlie and Iancu.

"Just outside of this room and down the hall is a door to the dungeon," Iancu told Paul in a hushed voice, clapping the shorter man on the shoulder. "Neil and his wife should be there. Take them somewhere safe. If you need to, use my apartment."

Paul nodded and exited the room to rescue his cousin.

Jordana sagged against the wall and clutched her chest, scowling at Alexei. "That was very rude of you."

"I never claimed to be a nice man," Alexei pointed out.

Charlie's arms were beginning to tire from having her guns raised for such a long period of time, but she didn't dare lower her guns.

"You have all banded together to fight against me, have you?" Jordana questioned rhetorically. "Even you, Jade?"

"I saw the look on your face at the meeting we had," Alexei said. "You thought that Aryk's ideas were ridiculous, just like the rest of us did. Why did you humor him? Why did you allow him to lead you around like a dog?"

"Humans are forgiven for behaving foolishly for love," she responded coolly.

"You killed Bella for a cause that you didn't even believe in." He paused and watched a smile carve its way onto her lips. He'd been counting on that smug smile. "You can smile all you want, Jordana, because as of tonight, we're even. You murdered Bella and I've killed your little sidekick."

Her violet eyes started to glow and fire was visible in their icy depths. "You're bluffing." Even as she spoke the words, she was attempting to sense Aryk's presence. She must have found Alexei's words to be true, because her expression turned livid. "I wish that your precious Bella were still alive only so that I could once again yank her heart out."

Alexei moved to rush at her and found that he couldn't. Charlie also found that she was frozen where she stood. Her guns thudded to the floor. Jade was imprisoned in her own body as well. She was paralyzed, just as Charlie and Alexei were.

Jordana levitated into the air. Her hair floated above her head as if she were under water. "You are all going to regret this night. You had better not let me escape this alive, Iancu. I will come after you and take all that you hold dear."

"Challenge accepted." Iancu joined her in the air. He flew at her and shoved her against the nearest wall, holding his hands around her throat.

Never before had she encountered someone who was powerful enough to choke the life from her. The tightness around her throat stunned her. She sputtered and coughed, tugging at his hands in a vain attempt to dislodge them from her throat. It took a lot of effort, but she was finally able to push him off of her.

She glared daggers at him, gingerly touching her throat. A part of her was in awe of his strength and power.

Because of her, you are the monster that you are now. Because of her, you turned into a brutal killer who murdered a woman that you claimed to love. Because of her, you will never be human again. As the thoughts ran through his mind, he sensed her coming at him and held up a solitary hand.

She stopped abruptly and was frozen. She wasn't able to move, much like Alexei, Jade, and Charlie below them. She was held captive by his power.

Because of her you are forced to live the life of a vampire. That is what you are, isn't it? Your life was interrupted by the cruel intentions of a deceitful, manipulative bitch.

His eyes shined and grew luminous. His incisors lengthened as he raised his arms above his head.

She remained frozen with her arms shielding her face as a sudden wind rushed at Iancu from below, whipping his long, dark hair around his face. His eyes glowed, the brightest source of light in the room, and he bellowed as a wave of energy flowed inside of him and out through his fingertips.

A shrill scream escaped out of Jordana's mouth. She jerked about in the air with a wild, crazy look on her face. Because she was unable to keep a steady grip on her own power, Alexei and Charlie were released from her captivity, free to move about as they wished.

Iancu wasn't done. He continued waving his hands about. Furniture was lifted from the floor and the glass in the sitting room window shattered.

Charlie watched him in amazement. For a brief moment, she could have sworn that she saw wings spreading at his back. "My dark angel," she whispered, unable to tear her eyes away from him.

Alexei tugged at her elbow. "We have to get out of here," he cautioned. "Underneath all of that power he has, this place is probably going to cave in."

She didn't want to leave. She didn't want to allow Iancu out of her sight, but she saw the logic in Alexei's words. Shards of shattered glass swirled about the room in a seemingly endless orbit around Iancu and Jordana. She let Alexei and Jade usher her out of the house.

Iancu, unaware that his comrades were leaving, raised his hands into the air again. Thick bolts of electricity crackled between them. Light burned behind his eyes. He continued to harness the power between his hands with his hair swirling around him.

Jordana struggled against Iancu's power and granted herself limited movement. She looked to be consumed by fear and it was the first time that he'd ever seen her look fearful. Even with the images of those he'd killed floating behind his eyes...even with the memories of the people whom he couldn't save...he almost pitied her in that moment. She had the look that a mouse has on his face when he's pitted against a fat bobcat.

She broke free from the hold that he had on her and hurled herself at him. They flew through the air, burst through the sitting room wall, sailed through more air, and exploded through the kitchen wall of her house. Still they wrestled in the air, each of them fighting to have an advantage over the other. The night air rushed at them until they hovered over the creek that ran through the courtyard.

A couple of vampires had already been slain in the creek. Dark red blood and black dust mingled in the water to create a strange, black-red hue of crimson.

They hurtled through the air until they landed at the start of the creek. Then they broke apart and faced each other. She aimed a stream of energy at him. His image flickered in the air and he disappeared. He reappeared behind her and launched energy of his own.

His energy struck her in the chest and she collapsed face-first into the bloody creek. She didn't have the strength to use glamour to cover up the fact that her hair was a soggy, wet mess, weighed down with a mixture of water, blood, and dust. She waded through the water, glaring up at him as he descended into the water.

His hair flowed with the wind as he stood staring at her. He was daring her with his eyes, daring her to try something. He was certain that no matter what she tried, he would know how to counter her attack. He was probably right.

She tried anyway, speeding towards him and knocking him in the water. She held him beneath the water even though vampires couldn't drown. He didn't know what she was thinking and didn't care enough to read her thoughts. He simply spread his arms outward. Energy sparked at his fingertips. The water in the creek slowly started to part, leaving them on the damp ground that had been lying beneath the shallow creek.

"Try to drown me now," he taunted her.

Her eyes were wild and frantic. Panic was setting in. He wondered if she had ever felt panic a day in her life before tonight.

He took off his trench coat. His plain, black t-shirt was askew on his shoulders and there was a slash across the front of it from when a vampire had attempted to stab him. The poor bastard had only gotten his shirt instead.

Walls of red water flanked them. The scene reminded Iancu of that one Bible story he'd been told as a child. Wasn't it Moses who'd parted the sea in order to help his slave brethren escape from the clutches of their slave masters? Not that Iancu would ever compare himself to a Biblical figure. He was by no means a saint or a disciple. He was merely a warrior who fought for the sake of good.

Aryk was dead and that only left this heartless wretch to kill. In a blur of motion that Jordana's watery eyes never saw, he rammed into her and sent her reeling backwards, towards the house. She never made it to the house, though. The extended sword of one of her statues impaled her.

He walked through the aisle provided from the two walls of water and resettled the red waters of the creek as he walked towards the spot where Jordana would soon die. He looked up at her.

She stared down at him. Her eyes were empty of hatred and despise. They were filled to the brim with unshed blood tears. "You've released me," she said softly, earnestly. "You've released me...Iancu the Impaler."

Iancu's apartment was bustling with injured warriors, a malnourished vampire, and his pregnant wife. Paul knelt by the couch that his cousin lay on. The poor guy had starved for almost an entire day. His face was gaunt and his body had already started to shut down. It was a wonder that he hadn't taken a chunk out of Marilyn. A vampire that went a prolonged period of time without feeding was usually ruled by the bloodlust. If they somehow managed to overpower the bloodlust, then their body began to shut down. Coordination, motor functions, muscle control, and eventually brain function would be lost.

Paul brushed some of his unconscious cousin's hair off of his forehead. *My cousin risked being a vegetable for his wife,* he thought.

The door to the apartment opened. Everyone present-and conscious-drew their weapons until they realized that it was just Charlie, Jade, and Alexei.

"Where is Iancu?" Paul demanded.

"He was still fighting Jordana when we left," Jade answered.

Charlie didn't say anything; she just looked worried as hell.

"Why would you guys leave him?" Paul asked. "What if he needs you?"

"He definitely doesn't need me," Alexei said with a chuckle. "He has it all under control."

Paul didn't look convinced. "I hope you're right."

"So do I," Charlie agreed, sounding tired.

"You should really rest," Alexei told her.

"I refuse to rest until Iancu gets here," she stubbornly replied. "I shouldn't have left him. What if Jordana gains an advantage over him?"

Damen approached Paul. "We're not going to camp here all night, are we?"

Paul shook his head. "Probably not. I do need to wait to get word from Iancu, though. I want to make sure that he's all right."

Charlie paced around the apartment for nearly half an hour before the apartment door opened and Iancu appeared. He looked like he had gone to war and lost, but she failed to take in his battered appearance. She ran at him and threw her arms around his neck.

He cringed, but didn't pull away from her. There was a gash beneath his right eye that would most likely heal, an assortment of bruises that were already healing, and a variety of different scars marking his body.

Paul waited for the lovers to pull out of their tight hug before asking, "So, what's the word?"

"Jordana is defeated," the tall vampire announced.

Cheers boomed throughout the apartment. Paul and his men gave each other high-fives. A couple of them hugged each other, and the remainder of them looked sad and sorrowful at the couple of members that they lost in battle.

Iancu hugged Charlie again, whispering sweet nothings in her ear. Then he stood up straight and said, "We're not necessarily out of the woods yet. There's no telling how many of Jordana's and Aryk's followers are out there. I will stay here and make sure that things settle down, but I don't want Marilyn and Neil to stay here. Too many people know about their...condition."

Paul nodded, his eyes narrowing in contemplation. "What do you suggest?"

"I know of a place that Neil and Marilyn most likely won't be found," Iancu said carefully, looking down at Charlie.

She frowned up at him.

"The reservation," he said.

"The res-" She stopped herself. "Why?"

"No one will find them there," he repeated. "They need to be safe and the people there are dependable. They will remember me. They will help us."

She hadn't been back to the reservation since the night that it was ambushed by the gangly group of vampires more than a decade ago.

"Paul will take Neil and Marilyn there," he continued, "and then you and I will follow."

"Now that you've defeated the Tudhani clan leader," Jade said, "you will be pressured to become the new clan leader of the Tudhani."

"I'm not going to think about that until the time comes," Iancu told her. "We need to focus on getting Neil and Marilyn out of here." He couldn't get Luna's words out of his head.

"No, no, no, no! No, no, no, no! The Toltec and his wife...they will not *live. They will* not *live! They will die. They will both die."*

Iancu shook out of his thoughts, overwhelmed with concern for his old friend. "I'm not kidding. I want Neil and Marilyn moved out of here tonight. I don't even want to wait for morning. Do you guys have any problem with that?"

Paul didn't know why Iancu was so insistent on Neil and Neil's wife being moved so soon. After all, their main concerns had been Jordana and Aryk and both of them were now dead. However, if the victorious vampire warrior was concerned, Paul knew not to take it lightly. "There's no problem with that," he answered. "Just write down the address for me and I'll make sure that he gets there."

"And stay with him until Charlie and I come there to join you," Iancu stressed.

"I will," Paul vowed.

"The worst of it all may not be over yet," Iancu explained. "Jordana's death means nothing. Every vampire in the world will have their ear to the ground to hear whether or not Neil's and Marilyn's child has the capability to walk in daylight. If it does, then all hell will break loose. We can't allow any other vampires near them."

"Understood."

Crystal gaped openly at the destruction of the sitting room. A breeze from the ocean rolled in through the broken window. The skin of her arms prickled with goosebumps. She wrapped her arms around herself and stepped over piles of her acquaintances. Like a zombie, she stumbled through the house and out of the back door. She found Jordana impaled on one of the courtyard statues with shards of glass still embedded in her flesh. She looked up at the ancient vampiress with an expression of worry on her face.

Jordana's eyes fluttered open and she reached down towards Crystal. "Iancu...Iancu..." the woman croaked.

Crystal had never seen her in such horrible shape. She floated into the air so that she could gather the Tudhani clan leader in her arms. She carried her into the house and upstairs in the general direction of the master bedroom, which-thankfully-was still intact. "Don't worry, Jordana," the petite woman said. "You're going to heal from this. And you're going to seek vengeance upon whoever did this to you."

Charlie lay sprawled across Iancu's chest, her brow damp with sweat, panting with exertion. She felt his arms close around her and was content. "I didn't want to leave you there," she said, tracing circles around one of his nipples and looking up at him. "Alexei said that the situation was getting too dangerous for us to be around, but I wanted to stay and make sure that you were all right."

"Everything turned out fine," he said, grabbing the hand that was teasing his nipple. He playfully nibbled on her fingers. "We were very lucky tonight."

"We weren't lucky," she said, her eyes growing animated. She sat up and began gesturing wildly with her hands. "I don't even think you know how amazing you were tonight. You were...you were...dreamy."

He arched a sardonic eyebrow at her. "*Dreamy?*"

"You were!" she exclaimed. "It didn't even feel real. It felt like I was watching a movie or something." She paused. "A movie with really great special effects."

He laughed and settled his hands on her hips. "A movie, huh?"

"You were so beautiful up there," she said earnestly.

He rose up on his elbows, his intense blue eyes gleaming in the darkness. "You're beautiful no matter where you are," he whispered, pulling her down to him so that he could kiss her.

She opened her mouth to him and grinded her pelvis into his. She moved her lips off of his and towards his right ear, where she whispered, "Are you up for it?"

He smiled at her and turned his head away from her without responding.

She reached down and grabbed him. "I mean, I know that you're *up* for it. I guess I should be asking how much do you want it?"

Still raised on his elbows, he frowned.

She pushed him down so that his head was resting on the pillow. He struggled to sit back up, but she leaned down and kissed him. She placed herself over him and guided him inside of her.

He grunted and his mind was an empty slate. His hands grabbed her hips. He looked up at her glorious, naked body and wondered how one man could be so fortunate. She went wild on top of him, and he let her. His skin grew hot and burned where it touched her. As waves of ecstasy rolled over the both of them, Charlie's gasps grew louder and louder. She bucked and screamed on top of him.

Wetness dripped onto his abdomen and the smell of copper filled the room.

He turned his head to the side, still moaning. "That was so good," he groaned into the pillow. One of his hands lay on his chest. It traveled lower, to his abdomen where hot, sticky liquid had already started drying. He dabbed his fingers in the liquid and drew his fingers up to his nose. He expected to smell her sweetness, but he smelled something else entirely.

She started slumping and it was only then that he noticed the sharp point of a sword jutting out between her breasts. The way the sword was propped had been the only thing holding her somewhat upright. There was no telling how long the sword had been in her. When he'd thought she'd been screaming and shouting in ecstasy, she had really been screaming out of horror.

He leapt out of bed and flipped on the lights. The light in her hazel eyes was fading and her mouth went slack. Frozen in despair, he moved closer to the bed without taking his eyes off of her.

A voice invaded his innermost thoughts at that moment. *I could have killed you, too, by just driving the sword a bit deeper.* It was Jordana's voice in his head. *I could have killed you, but I didn't. I figured that it would be much more tragic for you to go on living while your pretty little girlfriend dies before your eyes. And in the throes of passion, as it were. How unfortunate.*

Blood seeped from the wound in Charlie's chest and Iancu didn't know what to do.

You very well know what you can do, don't you, Iancu? The way I see it, you have two choices here. You can allow her to die...the way you're doing now. Jordana paused dramatically. *Or, you can sire her. Take some of her blood before it all leaves her body, and replace it with your own.*

He shook his head with blood tears welling in his eyes. "I can't do that," he whispered. "You know I can't do that."

Tsk, tsk, tsk. I guess you're just going to have to watch her die.

Flashes of Bridgette's face illuminated behind his eyes. The image of Bridgette's face mingled with Charlie's. "I can't," he said again. "I can't watch another love die again."

He inched towards the bed with streams of red running down his cheeks. Her blood was staining the sheets and forming in small pools around her. He sat on the edge of the bed and pulled her onto his lap, flinching when her blood touched his skin. He held her to him and swept the hair off of her neck.

You should have never crossed me. You should have never refused to join my side. None of this would have ever happened. But no, you had to make things difficult. You had to go and team up with the slayer against me.

He ducked his head low and pressed his lips to Charlie's throat. Her pulse was slow as her life flickered. It was a lose-lose situation. If he sat idly by while Charlie died, he would never see her again. He would be forced to live his life knowing that not only had he killed one love of his life, but he had caused the death of a second. If he sired Charlie he would be going against what he believed in. He didn't want to create new vampires. He wanted to vanquish the lot of them and send them where they belonged. *But I can't live without her,* he thought to himself with his lips still pressed to her throat. *I love her too much. I'd miss her too much.*

Jordana cackled in his head. *You'd better hurry up and decide, dear. She has a couple more minutes left at the most.*

His incisors lengthened, but he drew his head back. He swept her hair back again and pressed kisses to her forehead. With one hand, he drew her eyelids downward so that she appeared to be sleeping. He lowered his lips to her throat again with blood red tears still falling out of his eyes. He tried to push himself to bite her. He *had* to bite her. He couldn't lose her. Not now, not when everything felt so right.

He pushed himself and pushed harder. Her life was fading. Her pulse was dying. If he was going to do it, then he had to do it now. And yet...he couldn't. He knew he couldn't. It's not what he stood for. He couldn't create another vampire, even if it would benefit him. He just couldn't bring himself to do it.

And so instead of digging his teeth into his lover's flesh, he held her close to his chest and cried until he could no longer cry.

Marilyn went into labor several days later in a small house in the Standing Rock Reservation community. One of the neighborhood's medicine women helped the distraught pregnant woman through labor and gave her a rancid liquid to drink to subside some of the pain.

She pushed and wailed while Neil held onto her hand. The baby slowly eased out, kicking and screaming.

The medicine woman's eyes widened and she squealed.

Alarmed, Neil and Marilyn met each other's gaze. They hadn't known what to expect when their baby was born. Was it disfigured? Did it look different than other babies? "What is it?" both of them demanded, looking worried.

"It's a boy!" the medicine woman cried, swathing the baby in blankets.

Both parents looked relieved and Marilyn sagged back against the bed tiredly.

There was a knock on the door. Neil went to the door and cracked it open. It was his cousin, Paul.

"Iancu's here," he said grimly.

Neil burst into grins. "He is? I have to tend to Marilyn, but I'll be out as soon as I can."

Paul nodded soberly and then returned outside where Iancu leaned against his silver rental car. A somber moon hung suspended in a starless sky. Iancu seemed to be studying the stars when Paul joined his side. "Neil will be out shortly."

"How have they been?"

"Marilyn went into labor some hours ago," Paul answered, rubbing the back of his neck. "So they're probably stressing over whether or not it'll come out with four noses or three toes."

Iancu nodded his head and looked off into the distance. A few houses down, a middle-aged woman urged her children through the front door of their modest residence. She turned her head and caught sight of the two men leaning against the rented Ford Explorer. She seemed to be staring at Iancu in particular. She stared at him for several moments, as if deciding whether or not she should come over.

He beckoned her over.

She shyly approached them with her hands shoved deep into the pockets of her jeans. "Hi," she greeted.

"Hi," he returned.

"I didn't mean to stare," she said hurriedly. "You just look like someone I used to know."

"Really? Who?"

"Just this...just a..." She stopped talking and smiled. "I'm sorry." She turned and started to walk away, but she gave it a second thought and whirled around again. "You look like someone that rescued this community about fifteen years ago."

"I get that a lot," he said.

"It's...uncanny." She took in his trench coat, his black shirt, black pants, and black boots. She caught a glance of his sword's hilt and gasped, her hand coming up to cover her mouth. "You *are* him. You're...the guy from that night..."

Paul watched the exchange with a sparkle of mirth in his eyes.

"You haven't aged a day," she breathed.

"I get that a lot," he said again, this time much more sorrowful than the first time. "I am glad to see that this neighborhood has been doing well. I haven't been here in a long time."

"Yes, we have been doing well," she said excitedly. "Thanks to you, that is."

He shrugged his shoulders. "I just did what I could."

"You're being very modest," she said quietly. "If it hadn't been for you, I probably wouldn't be alive today. My mother told us the story of that night *every* night. She always read us a story before we went to bed and that night, she'd been reading to us when you stormed into our house. She didn't know whether or not she could trust you because she didn't know you from a hole in the wall, but she's very glad that she did trust you. We all are."

A red film covered his eyes and he had to quickly turn his head away in order to keep her from seeing what she shouldn't see. "Thank you for your praise," he said, wiping at his eyes. "I really have to tend to something..."

"I'm sorry," she apologized quickly. "I didn't mean to interrupt. I just...I just wanted to see if it was you, and since it is, I just want to thank you. That's all." She turned and shuffled down the street.

He turned to face the car. "I can't do this."

"Yes, you can," Paul encouraged.

Neil exited the house and jogged down the porch steps to join them. He embraced Iancu. "Long time no see, huh? It's been what-a week, almost?"

"You look like you've been doing well," Iancu observed, still wiping at his eyes.

"Thanks to you and my cousin here," Neil said cheerfully. "And in addition to having my ass saved, Mare just gave birth to a bouncing baby boy."

"Congratulations," Iancu said, nodding.

Neil peered inside of the rental car's windows. "Where is Chuck?"

Paul repeatedly drew a hand in a straight line beneath his neck, gesturing for his cousin to end that line of questioning.

Not understanding, Neil asked again, "Iancu...where's Chuck?"

"She, umm...she didn't make it," Iancu said lamely.

Neil frowned and realization dawned on him, but he needed to hear it aloud. "What do you mean?"

"After you all left, Jordana...Jordana killed her." The tears refused to be held at bay any longer and Iancu collapsed to the ground.

"You've got to be kidding me," Neil whispered.

"I wish I was," Iancu blubbered through the tears. "You don't know just how much I wish I was kidding."

"So Jordana's not dead."

"No, she's not dead."

"Ouch."

"I needed to check up on you and make sure that things were going all right," Iancu said, "but there is something that I have to do. It shouldn't take that long. I'll be back." He opened the driver side door of the rental car and hopped in. He drove through the neighborhood until he found what he was looking for.

He parked the car and turned off the engine. Then, he grabbed a bouquet of flowers from the passenger seat and hopped out of the car. Streaks of dried red blood trailed down his cheeks. He walked over grass that was well-maintained and came to stand before the tombstone of Charlie's grandfather.

He stood there for a long time without moving. Then he said aloud, "I promised you that I would take care of your granddaughter and make sure that she was safe, but I failed you. For that, I apologize.

"If it's any consolation, though, know that I ache for her to be among the living just as much as you would if you were still with us." He stared at the ground as his voice became choked with emotion. "Know that this isn't over. The monster who took the life of your granddaughter will have her life taken from her as well. There, I failed also. I assumed that she was dead when I shouldn't have. I should have stayed and made sure that I'd completed the job. I'm sorry."

He drew his hand across his mouth as the tears started falling again. "I'm sorry," he repeated, setting the flowers on top of the tombstone. He tilted his head back and stared up at the sky. He was jolted out of his misery, because for the briefest of moments he could have sworn that he saw Charlie floating in the sky with a pair of angel wings at her back.

A mingling of male and female voices grew stronger with each passing moment.

"What are you doing here?"

"You shouldn't be here."

"It's not your time."

"You shouldn't be here, why are you here?"

"You have to go back."

"Yes, she must go back. She can't stay here."

"Your work isn't finished."

"Not nearly finished, the prophecy is just beginning to come into fruition."

"And you have to be there when the prophecy is set into motion."

"Yes, you have to be there, for you are one of the guardians."

"You are to guard the Children of the Stars."

"You are to help them overcome the evil that will rise in the coming years."

"They are just children, they need guidance."

"You definitely can't stay here."

"I'm not sure why you are even here. It is way too soon."

"Yes, way too soon. You have to go back."

"You didn't think that this was the end of your life, did you?"

"It's definitely not the end of your life. It's only the beginning, the beginning, the beginning..."

There was a whooshing sensation and the soul entered the body once again. Chemical odors assailed the nostrils and bright, blaring lights blinded the eyes. Someone in the room was whistling to the music playing on a cheap, plastic AM/FM radio.

The table was cold, way too cold. The shivers started to set in. Once they started, they were difficult to get rid of. The table began to tremble as well.

The M.E., who looked a bit too young to be a medical examiner, danced over to the table and stared down at the subject that should have been released yesterday. "Do you have something to say, hmm?" he asked the still figure lying on top of the table. It truly was an exquisite specimen.

The figure didn't respond.

Just to be sure, he said, "Speak once or forever hold your peace."

She bolted into a sitting position, gasping for air and pressing a hand between her two bare breasts where the sword had punctured her. There was a gaping wound there, she could feel it. Her dark hair hung down her back, the complexion that had once paled darkened to its rich, caramel color, and she turned startled hazel eyes on the medical examiner.

"Whoa!" He jumped back, his eyes wide with astonishment.

She stared at her hands and turned them this way and that. She silkily slid down from the table and headed towards the door to the examination room. She opened the door but before stepping foot out into the hallway, she arched a look at the medical examiner over her shoulder. "It's not the end, not yet," she said cryptically. "It's only the beginning."

Original artwork by Beth Gualda
More of her gorgeous artwork can be viewed at the following website: http://beellegee.tripod.com

The back cover was created by Dori Hartley and more of her amazing artwork can be viewed at the following website:
http://artofdorihartley.com

Sneak Peek of

BloodLust:
Resurrection

Excerpt from
BloodLust: Resurrection

Renee Taylor loved her shift hours. She worked late into the night while more than half the nation was sleeping. As the rest of the country sleepily opened their eyes and gained consciousness, she was just getting to bed. No one she knew could understand the passion that she had for her job. The thought of examining dead bodies gave her friends and family the creeps, but she found it to be quite serene work.

She viewed death as a natural process. She had strong Christian beliefs. In her mind, the body lying on her table was just that: a body. By the time she examined a person's body, she felt that the soul had long since left it. She was inspecting nothing more than a shell, an abandoned husk.

She'd known Evan Reeves when he was alive. He'd been a pleasant man to be around. He'd been *young*. Many young bodies ended up on her table as a result of car collisions, drug overdoses, and on rare occasion, suicides. Many people around town were having trouble accepting Evan's death because he'd been young, engaged, and had a promising future. It was a sad situation; Renee wasn't without sympathy for his family, friends, and fiancé. However, she felt that death was a part of life. When it was someone's time to head into the afterlife, it was their time. She never questioned the Lord's motives. If the Lord had a reason for yanking Evan Reeves from this earth, then that was His prerogative. Human beings were His creation, as *was* the earth. He could take whomever He saw fit.

The only question that Renee wanted to ask at the moment was, *Who had mutilated Evan Reeves?* The torn flesh at his neck hung in strings. Just by looking at his neck, she could tell that it hadn't been a knife or sharp weapon that had been taken to the young man's throat. His skin had been ripped off of him, quite literally. If she had to guess, she would say that teeth were the method of attack that had been used on Evan.

On the body, she corrected herself at once. She didn't like to think of the people lying on her examination table as people. She preferred to think of them as bodies. It was impersonal and clinical, which is the way that she wanted to be.

She bent over the body, eyeing what was left of its neck. She'd performed a toxicology test earlier. Despite the fact that Evan had been in a strip bar prior to his death, there wasn't a trace of alcohol in his system. He hadn't been intoxicated. She hadn't found evidence of any mind-altering substances in his body, but she *had* found several odd circumstances that she'd never before witnessed.

There was the severe blood loss; she had been able to tell that at the murder scene. There was also the fact that the body's pallor seemed to change over time. When the body had first been brought in, the skin was extremely pale and had a wrinkled texture. As the minutes dragged on, the coloring of the body started to flush. Two hours after the body had been brought into the examination room, Evan Reeves didn't even look *dead.* He looked to be resting peacefully, as if at any moment he could sit up and start talking to her. It was a ludicrous notion, but she took the time to check for a heartbeat and a pulse anyway.

She shook her head and took her tray of utensils to the sink against the wall facing the door to the room. The reflection in the mirror over the sink mimicked her every action as she carefully cleansed and sterilized her equipment. She hummed "Amazing Grace" as she turned on the faucet, but stopped when a rustling sound reached her ears. She glanced over her shoulder, her eyes seeking out the cause of the noise. She inspected every inch of the room, stopping only when nothing looked to be out of order. She continued to cleanse the equipment that she used in her examinations.

The rustling sounded again; it sounded to be only a few feet behind her. She whirled around, expecting to see someone standing in front of her. There was no one. She ran a hand through her short, black hair. Her hands were shaking and she didn't know why. In all of her years of medical examining, not once had she ever been nervous. She'd never felt a chill over the fact that she was in a room occupied by cadavers. She'd never been afraid to turn her back to them. She felt silly, being afraid, but she *was* afraid. She was scared to death. Goosebumps prickled along her mocha brown arms.

She looked down at the body lying on the examination table. She was tempted to call his name. The fear that the body would answer her squashed that temptation, but she took a few more steps closer to the table. She clasped her hands together to stop them from shaking.

As soon as her eyes lay on the body, something nagged at her. She couldn't put a finger on it, but something wasn't right with what she was seeing. Her eyes traveled down the length of the body. The arms were lifeless at its sides and the toes were pointed toward the ceiling. There was nothing wrong with how the body was positioned. So what *was* wrong?

Her eyes dragged from his toes on upward. Her gaze fell upon the body's torn neck, except...it was no longer torn. A gasp escaped her lips and her eyes widened. Not trusting herself, she walked around the table so that she was standing on the opposite side of the body. There were two long gashes in the side of the neck, but otherwise the neck was intact. It wasn't *right*. The neck hadn't looked that way when she'd started testing on the body. The neck hadn't looked that way five minutes ago, when she'd left the body to wash her utensils.

As she watched, the two long gashes in the neck started fading. The first thought that occurred to her was that at some point in her shift, she must have sat down and nodded off. The second thought that occurred to her was that she had to get out of here, because what was happening before her eyes couldn't be good.

Before she could turn away from the table, the body's hand shot upward and took a hold of her arm. "What the-"

Renee started, her eyes wide with incredulity. Evan's eyes snapped open and she let out a shriek that could have awakened the very dead...so to speak. She tugged at her arm, trying to pull it free, but the grip that he had on her was unshakable.

"Dawn," he rasped in a voice that made her skin crawl.

"Dawn?" Renee repeated confusedly. Because of the anxiety pumping through her, she couldn't even think straight. If she *had* been able to think straight, then she would have known that he was referring to Dawn Atkinson, his fiancé.

"Dawn," he repeated, then released her arm suddenly. With a bit of a struggle, he managed to sit up. His eyes were taking in his surroundings, his nose taking in the chemical scents of the place, no doubt wondering why he was sitting in an examination room. "So...*hungry*." He raised a hand to his right temple and massaged it gently. The incisions that Renee had made on his body were now gone, as if they'd never existed.

Renee inched backward, attempting to calm herself down. Her steps were wobbly and her legs threatened to give way. She was questioning her own sanity, wondering if all of this was really happening. The fear burning its way to the uppermost layer of her skin told her that she was awake, not merely having a twisted nightmare, but it was difficult to trust what she was seeing.

"Hungry," Evan said again, hoisting his gaze in her direction as if she had a solution for his dilemma.

Relieved that Evan's first priority wasn't causing her physical harm, she rubbed her hands together and said, "There's probably some food in the cafeteria. I can go check on that."

He cocked his head to the side, looking at her. He looked at her as if he were looking at a stranger. There was no recognition in his eyes whatsoever. To Renee, he didn't have the mannerisms of a twenty-eight year old man. He had the mannerisms of a dog or some other wild animal. His movements were jerky and his eyes didn't have a human softness to them. They weren't empty; it was more like they had a depth to them that Renee had never seen in another human being. "It's cold," he said suddenly, glancing around the room as if expecting to see his clothes thrown over the back of one of the chairs. "Very cold."

His voice held no emotion in it whatsoever; it was deep and monotonous, and it was giving Renee the heebie-jeebies. She shivered and wrapped her arms around herself. She didn't know what to say to him and she didn't know what to do with herself. She was itching to take his pulse, itching to make sure that his heart *was*, in fact, beating, but too afraid to get any closer to him.

"I'm hungry. And I'm cold." He slid his legs over the edge of the table and slid his feet to the floor, comfortable with his nudity.

"Let me get you some food," she said hurriedly, dashing out of the room. She made sure to close the door behind her. She stood in the hallway and closed her eyes, willing her heartbeat to slow down.

Evan Reeves was dead when he was brought in, she thought to herself as she strode down the short corridor, walking in the direction of the office's cafeteria. *He was dead and his neck was shredded to pieces. How is it he's alive and how did his neck heal?* The skin seemed to have regenerated itself, but humans didn't have the ability to regenerate at the speed in which Evan's skin and tissue cells had.

The thought hadn't occurred to her, but maybe Evan wasn't a monster. Maybe he was a miracle. Maybe he was a great scientific find. *Maybe* he was Nobel Prize-worthy. She smiled to herself as she pushed through the cafeteria doors and flipped on the light switch. She walked down an aisle flanked by long, rectangular tables. She headed to the kitchen area and made a beeline for the refrigerator. Her thoughts danced around the notion that Evan's condition, whatever it was, could be a major medical discovery.

As she returned to the examination room with a small lunch tray filled with food in tow, she hummed to herself.

She was no longer as afraid of Evan as she had been. She balanced the tray on her forearm and opened the door with her free hand.

Evan was standing at the sink, a hand smoothing down his cheek. He heard the door opening and turned around. "My reflection," he said, a hint of sorrow touching his voice. He no longer sounded as emotionless as he had before. Now, he sounded sullen, like a young boy whose dog had died. "My reflection...I can't see it."

Brows furrowed, she stood on tiptoe and glanced in the mirror over his right shoulder. She could see herself in the mirror, but where she should have been able to see his back, she couldn't. It was as if he wasn't even standing there. The lunch tray in her hands crashed to the floor.

He was walking over to her with his head tilted to the side. "My reflection...it's gone. Why can't I see it?"

"I-I-I-" Renee stammered, stumbling backward until she felt the wall flat against her back. "I don't know."

"You have to help me."

"I don't know if I can," she told him honestly, her eyes still on the mirror behind him.

"My reflection is...*gone*," he said. "I'm naked. I'm hungry. I'm cold and yet my skin...feels like it's on fire. You've got to help me." He was still moving closer to her, until he was within arm's reach.

She shook her head. Her heat pounded like a bass drum. Her breathing quickened. She turned her head to the side, looking towards the door. It was a few feet away, but she doubted that she had time to get away from him. All of a sudden, she didn't want a Nobel Prize for any medical discovery. That was the farthest thought from her mind. All she wanted was to get away from him and return to her family safely.

He raised a hand to her brow and let it travel down the side of her face. He closed his eyes for a moment, enjoying her skin's softness and warmth.

Her back was ramrod straight and the muscles in her body tensed as soon as he touched her. His skin was unnaturally cold and his arousal was becoming more and more apparent. She squeezed her eyes shut and winced.

A smile touched his lips. "It's forbidden," he said softly, as if to himself, letting his hand trail down to her neck. It lingered there as he murmured, "It's forbidden, but it feels so good. So warm. So soft. I want you."

Images of her husband and two children flashed into her mind and tears formed at the corners of her eyes. She didn't think that she was going to get to see her children or her spouse ever again. "Please don't do this," she begged, her voice strangled with emotion. "I won't tell anyone that I've seen you."

His smile widened, exposing lengthy incisors. "No, you won't," he said with certainty. His fangs pierced her throat. Blood beaded at the puncture wounds he created. He gave her neck a gentle squeeze and blood poured like the finest red wine.

Starr Sanders was born in Waco, TX. Shortly after she was born, her family moved to the northeastern suburbs of Illinois, where she was raised.

She has always been an avid reader of books with supernatural themes. As a child, she started writing her own stories. The stories were incredibly short at first. As she grew older, though, those stories became longer. Her first full-length novel was penned at the tender age of seventeen.

She has written two novels in addition to *BloodLust: The Beginning*. She has written a romance comedy called *Open Book* (under the pseudonym Skye Sanders), and a young adult horror novel called *Hidden Treasures: Switched* (under the pseudonym Shiloh Sanders).

Her hobbies include: traveling, reading, writing, video games, volleyball, swimming, shopping, and movies.

She also has interests in the fields of: film production, marketing, and education.

Receive the most up to date information on this author by frequently visiting: www.starrsanders.com

www.ingramcontent.com/pod-product-compliance
Lightning Source LLC
Chambersburg PA
CBHW070544260626
47161CB00002B/495